LAND OF THE FAR HORIZON

Voyage of the Exiles
Angel of the Outback
The Emerald Flame
Beyond the Wild Shores

BEYOND THE WILD SHORES

PATRICIA HICKMAN

BETHANY HOUSE PUBLISHERS
MINNEAPOLIS, MINNESOTA 55438

Beyond the Wild Shores
Copyright © 1997
Patricia Hickman

Cover illustration by Patricia Keay

Published by Bethany House Publishers
A Ministry of Bethany Fellowship, Inc.
11300 Hampshire Avenue South
Minneapolis, Minnesota 55438

Printed in the United States of America.

Library of Congress Cataloging-in-Publication Data

Hickman, Patricia.
    Beyond the wild shores / by Patricia Hickman.
        p.   cm. —(Land of the far horizon ; 4)
    ISBN 1–55661–544–2 (pbk.)
    I. Title.
II. Series: Hickman, Patricia. Land of the far horizons ; 4.
PS3558.I2296B49   1997
813'.54—dc21   97–21022
                                                          CIP

To Jessi

Within you lies a treasure that confounds man's
comprehension of true wealth—a meek spirit and a pure
heart. With these qualities in tow, you will fly with ease
above all the rest.

Unfortunately for me, it's almost time for you
to spread your wings.

Mom

PATRICIA HICKMAN is an award-winning novelist and the wife of a pastor. She is the author of numerous fiction novels for both adults and children. Her works have been translated in foreign editions and have been featured selections for The Christian Family Bookclub. She and her husband, Randy, have three children, Joshua, Jessica, and Jared.

CONTENTS

PART THREE
Everlasting to Everlasting

PART ONE

THE LORD THY KEEPER

"The Lord is thy keeper:
the Lord is thy shade
upon thy right hand."

Psalm 121:5

Welcome ye wild plains
Unbroken by the plough, undelv'd by hand
Of patient rustic; where for lowing herds
And for the music of the bleating flocks
Alone is heard the kangaroo's sad note
Deepening in distance. Welcome ye rude climes,
The realm of Nature! For as yet unknown
The crimes and comforts of luxurious life,
Nature benignly gives to all enough,
Denies to all a superfluity...
On these wild shores Repentance' saviour hand
Shall probe my secret soul, shall cleanse my wounds,
And fit the faithful penitent for Heaven.

Robert Southey
Botany Bay Eclogues

1

STORMS OF THE HEART

"Say a prayer for me, Laurie." Bailey Templeton took a final glance into the old gold locket and then tucked it away in her drawstring reticule. The family keepsake had grown so tarnished that she no longer wore it, but she cherished her younger sister's tiny portraiture inside. Leaning against the weathered door to her cabin aboard *The Victoria*, Bailey reprimanded herself for the seasickness she felt. She had taken many voyages and, loving the feel of the open sea, was usually quick to gain her sea legs. She had no reason to believe that this June afternoon of 1807 would be any different. Forcing her thoughts elsewhere, she determined to overcome the nausea by sheer force of will. Her siblings came to mind, accompanied with the relief that they couldn't witness their aspiring, wandering sister now turning ashen in the face of a little turbulence. Laurie, she assured herself, would laugh. But then she found humor in many of her older sister's actions. She pictured her now—perfectly attired for an ocean-side send-off. Bailey had never been one to fuss about what she wore, so Laurie and her mother had labored unceasingly, until Bailey's traveling trunk swelled with a new wardrobe. *Laurie, you and I are so different from each other.* She recalled the way Laurie and her family had first reacted when she told them of her plans to teach in a far-off wilderness colony—a convict colony, no less. Her mother's worried face—the "what on earth are you doing now" kind of face that she always put on when Bailey vented her ambitions—always forced an uncomfortable knot in the pit of her stomach. *Steady, Bailey.* She stiffened her back and inhaled deeply. But instead of clearing her head, the act caused a negative reaction. Her eyes fell upon the turbulent green sea beyond the rail. The swells churned sickeningly, the adverse winds increasing in velocity. Bailey started for the inside of her cabin, but then thinking better of it, she hurled herself toward the rail.

"Needing some assistance, miss?" The boatswain's mate appeared out of nowhere.

Her hand cupped to her mouth, Bailey shook her head. "No— thank you." Feeling irritable and unhappy with herself, she turned away, perspiration beading on her forehead. Recalling the last few weeks of preparation for the journey, she again pictured the face of each family member in Virginia. Once she had affirmed her decision to accept the schoolmistress position in New South Wales, her self-confidence was renewed. Buoyed by the challenge of teaching in the pioneer school, her contagious joy and practical reasoning had finally convinced her family that any attempt to persuade her to do otherwise would only prove futile. But now fear and uncertainty weakened her confidence. *You wouldn't think I'm so brave now, Laurie.* She gripped the rail, steadied her balance, and lifted her face. Then opening her eyes, deep brown with bright flecks of copper, she assured herself that the seasickness, coupled with loneliness for Laurie, would subside as soon as she could immerse herself in the school.

"Miss?"

Bailey hadn't noticed the sailor still at her side. "I'm sorry. Really, I'm fine—"

"Well, hate to tell you, but the storm brewin' off the port bow is nothin' to neglect. Captain Gabriel's ordered all hands on deck. You'd best return to your cabin." He tipped his cap and made fast for the capstan.

No wonder I'm seasick. A coarse wind tore at her long raven hair, coifed at the neck. Instantly, her hair tumbled and blew about her face and shoulders. Indifferent to her tousled locks, Bailey turned her face to port bow and saw the dark clouds roiling out, darkening the azure sky. The storm clouds blocked out the day like an ominous dark blanket, bringing in its wake impending wind and blustering rain. Finding her way across the rocking deck, Bailey moved cautiously through the doorway and made her way safely inside the cabin. She sighed and snapped the latch on the cabin door. Her traveling gown of turquoise blue wool was much too warm for the confines of the cramped cabin, so unbuttoning the finely tailored frock, she slipped out of it and put it away in her tightly packed trunk. She shook her head, wondering how she would ever find use for all the clothing her mother and sister had packed for her. She hoped that in such a roughhewn place as Sydney Cove no one would find her stylish wardrobe pretentious. But she had never mustered the courage to discuss such things with Laurie, afraid she would never understand. Impatiently, she pulled a lace dressing sacque from her belongings and slipped it on, then positioned herself on the rickety bed and braced her back against the wall. Sighing heavily, Bailey closed her eyes. Strangely enough, the nausea had slightly subsided.

After a short rest Bailey got up, deciding to take another look outside. Through the dingy glass of her tiny window, she saw the lamp trimmer running past and turning up the wicks on the ship's whale oil lamps. She forced back the tattered curtain to lighten the shadowy darkness in the cabin and, walking back to the cot, lifted her Bible from a small tabletop. *Maybe reading will ease my mind*, she thought. But as the ship heaved up and down, she blew out an exasperated breath, tossed aside the Bible, and allowed the mattress to enfold her shapely form. Finding a comfortable position, she tried once again to relax, then chuckled quietly to herself as the loosely bolted table tipped one way and then the other, spilling her velvet reticule with all of its contents onto the dark floor. She quickly glanced toward the window. The sky held just enough light to see the tossing and churning sea. It looked as though she had a long, uncomfortable night ahead.

She leaned across the bed and promptly scooped her belongings back into the handbag, pulling the drawstring closed as she settled back against the wall again. Suddenly, her eye fell upon a small folded sheath of paper that lay nearly hidden behind the table leg. Grasping the letter, Bailey scratched away the wax seal and opened it. "A letter from Laurie," she whispered. Her finely arched eyebrows raised inquiringly. "She slipped a note to me . . . such a scoundrel!" In truth, Laurie had been her biggest supporter in regard to her decision to leave home. The youngest in the family, Laurie had always admired Bailey, albeit a bit competitively at times. But much to Bailey's delight, she and her sister had grown closer as they neared adulthood. Laurie took an exceptional interest in knowing every detail about the various young men who had trickled in and out of the Templeton home over the last few years—all of whom were hopeful of courting Bailey. Never taking them seriously, though, Bailey had discouraged most of them, until a merchant's son, Gavin Drummond, had called one day. With her father's blessing, Bailey had attended a church picnic with the handsome young man. But she had her sights set on schooling and felt the need to discourage this prospect as well. However, his kind demeanor and quick wit had charmed her, and soon she had fallen in love with him. Shortly, Gavin had become central to her every waking thought.

With a flutter of anxiety, she recalled the day she had poured out her heart to him. She had told him how much she loved teaching as well as how much she hated cooking. She cherished the look on a child's face when understanding blossomed under her tutelage. It thrilled her no end to take an illiterate farm boy and turn him into an aspiring writer. To see the wonder on a little girl's face when she opened a book and discovered a world completely different from her own gave her great joy. "I can learn to brew a cup of tea later," she had zealously explained to him, "but if I can hand a child the tools to learning and to thinking, why, I could change the face of a nation." She had shared all her dreams and desires with Gavin, and she would not soon forget his apathetic gaze nor the patronizing manner in which he dismissed it all as "wistful childhood fantasies."

Bailey tried to shake the memory from her mind, but failing, she instead focused her eyes on the page before her. She smiled. Laurie's familiar graceful handwriting made her feel as though her sister were sitting right beside her. The letter began:

Dear Bailey, By now, I'm missing you dearly. But I know you're happy. . . .

A smile settled across Bailey's full rosy lips, and she drank in her sister's words.

You always were the adventurous one. Oh, before I neglect to tell you, everyone sends their love—Father, Mother, Harry, Charles, and Quinton. . . .

Bailey nodded as though she acknowledged each smiling

face—her parents and each roguish brother.

But I have some news I dread to share. This matter is in regard to Gavin Drummond.

Laurie had not interfered when she had made the difficult decision to turn down Gavin's marriage proposal. But Bailey had noticed their conversation became strained whenever the subject arose. Sighing inwardly, she reluctantly continued.

When you informed Mr. Drummond that you would not give up your studies to marry him, he was deeply hurt. He confided in me, and I did not know how to counsel him. I shared with him of my respect for you, Bailey. How could I react otherwise? But he was so distraught that I remained with him one afternoon while you journeyed to the university. I did not intend for anything to happen—

Her fingers tightening around the letter, Bailey's eyes flew up. *Oh, Laurie!* She shook her head. *Please—no!* Forcing her eyes back onto the page, she finished Laurie's letter of confession, her emotions in a turmoil.

But I regret to say that I have fallen in love with Gavin. I could not help myself, Bailey. We plan to marry in the spring. You know I could never do the things you want to do with your life. Gavin is all I need, all I will ever need. Please say you do not hate me. I know you will believe this letter to be the coward's way, but I could not bear to look into your face and tell you that which wrenches my soul to say in writing. If you cannot forgive me, I cannot marry him. I would sooner die. Please write soon with your answer. Gavin contends he must know your feelings as well. He will always love you as he would his own sister. Love, Laurie.

"Fool!" The word shot forth from Bailey's lips without restraint. Her face colored fiercely. She did not know who to scorn first—Gavin, Laurie, or herself! She clenched her teeth, angry and hurt. Had not her relationship with both of them always been above reproach? *Honesty, Laurie, no matter how painful, I've always been honest with you.* She tried to remember Laurie's last words at the harbor but could not recall them. True, Laurie *had* appeared nervous, but under the circumstances, nervousness was the order of the day. "Laurie—*why?*" she whispered. A hot tear slipped down her cheek. She whirled around, flung aside the letter, and buried her face against the musty pillow. She felt ashamed and selfish at the growing anger inside her. *You could've had Gavin, Bailey Templeton, but instead you chose this school! It was your decision. No one else's.*

Outside, the wind howled and the storm vented its fury with force upon the ship. But oblivious to the physical maelstrom about her, Bailey battled a private anguish of bitterness and pain.

Bailey heaved her heavy leather bag out onto the deck. *The Victoria* had docked at dawn. It was a cool, crisp morning that refreshed her senses and somehow diminished the pain of the last few days aboard ship. Placing the toe of her cloth shoe against the cumbersome bag, she attempted to shove it across the dampened deck.

"Allow me, miss," a deep voice called out.

Keeping her balance against the cabin wall, she glanced slightly to acknowledge the speaker. "I'll see to it, thank you."

"None o' that, now." The uniformed gentleman strode toward her, his tone suggesting he was no one to be reckoned with. "Boatswain, fetch Faukner! Hop-to and see the lady's bags are taken ashore!"

Sighing, Bailey smiled cordially at the sailor who scrambled to obey the officer's command. "I can carry this one at least." She lifted the lighter bag. "Thank you—Captain, is it?"

"Gabriel, miss. Captain Robert Gabriel." The stout sea captain lifted the cap from his head and ran his fingers though his reddish brown locks.

Bailey nodded politely at the handsome man and glanced up at the sky. "We've a better day now. I mean, the weather is much better today." She straightened her gray fichu, smoothing it around her shoulders and arms.

"I, for one, will be glad to land on solid ground again," Captain Gabriel acknowledged. There were age lines about his eyes and mouth, muting his youth with strength. "I'll be two months in New South Wales, myself, and I must say I'll be a happy landlubber this go-round."

"You've family in this country?"

Gabriel shook his head. "Just some unfinished business to attend to." He glanced beyond Bailey's face and took a halting step forward.

In spite of a slight limp, Bailey noticed that he carried himself with a firm authority. "Hope you enjoy your short stay, sir." With one final nod and a smile, she headed toward the throng of departing passengers. "I'll be making Sydney Cove my permanent home." Surprised by her own words, she weighed them against her motives, being certain that she held no ill will from the world she had left behind. "Good day, to you, Captain." She offered a polite farewell and smoothed the glistening black curls that cascaded from her crown, then she directed the sailor to follow her down to the dock. Jostled about as she forced her way through the crowded harbor, she realized that she hadn't taken a moment to observe the scenery. Aside from the fishy harbor odors, she saw several similarities between this harbor and the Hudson harbors, but the differences outweighed the similarities. The terrain appeared more flat. The buildings, ramshackle affairs, held the cold look of barracks instead of the quaint appearance of the homes and shops that had sprung up in the Williamsburg colonies. And many of the Sydney Cove colonists held a rather down-trodden appearance. A wave of pity swept through her. The colony children running about were a barefoot, ragged lot, with soiled clothing and soot-smudged faces. She feared some to be without parents at all. Stopping to pull a handkerchief from her reticule, Bailey dabbed her face and heaved out a deliberate sigh.

"Are you all right, Miss Templeton?"

"Yes. It's just—well, the children." The sight of them running ragged in the streets touched a nerve in her.

"Watch 'em now, Miss Templeton. A thievin' bunch they is an' not likely to amount to much."

Bailey pondered the mariner's words, disturbed, but tried not to appear defensive. After all, she was in no position to make a judgment on their lives either way. "Would you mind—I'll need a carriage and driver."

"Which way you headed?"

"I'm supposed to find a Lieutenant Frye at the government building. I understand that the British military controls the settlement—true?"

"Yes, they does. An' a worse lot you'll not find nowheres on God's earth."

Biting her lip, Bailey grew impatient. *It seems he has nothing good to say of anyone.* "Pardon me, but what do you know of Sydney Cove. Ever lived here?"

"No. Just the things that we sailors know about places. We hears from one another."

"Ah. But rumors can't always be justified. Let's hope—"

17

"Not likely I'm wrong, miss. No sane person ever plans to stay here. It's just a jail for England's worst, those they've no room for back in London." He eyed her up and down. "You say you plans to stay?"

"I do. Yes. I'll be teaching at the school here." Bailey allowed her eyes to roam the bustling town square. She did not like his implication that she had judged poorly by coming here, but she saw no future in arguing with the man.

The sailor shrugged, his face twisting in an expression of sour resignation. "Well, there's the gov'ment buildin' straight ahead. They'd be the ones to ask for all you'll be needin'." He tipped his cap, his face dubious.

Fighting exasperation, Bailey lifted her pale silk skirt and marched toward the long building as the mariner trailed behind with her trunk and leather case. Stopping when she had reached the wooden porch, she thanked the sailor with a finality in her tone.

"Good luck to you, then." Setting down her belongings, he turned on his heels and was gone.

Glad to be rid of her pessimistic escort, Bailey inquired of a naval private, who, though looking a bit disheveled, appeared to have a friendly face. "Excuse me. I'm looking for Lieutenant Frye. Would you know him?"

Pursing his lips, the private's brows lifted with keen interest, causing a slight bit of uneasiness to rise in Bailey. "I knows of 'im, miss. Would you be 'is missus?" He leaned toward her with ready interest.

Weighing her answer, she opted for honesty. "No. But he is expecting me. I assume this is the government building—correct?"

The private chuckled. "I'll be happy to escort you, miss—"

"Thank you, but don't bother." She whirled on her heels, not wanting to strike up a conversation with this unkempt-looking fellow. Leaving behind her trunk and leather case, she walked briskly, carrying only her reticule and small bag. She found her way just inside the long hallway, stopping to smooth her skirt, a light gray silk with folds of satin and gray silk-covered rosettes draped with tassels. As she had suspected, her attire did draw more eyes than she had deemed prudent for a teacher in the new colony. In the schoolroom she would dress more like the local women, if indeed she found any to emulate.

Several privates brushed past, and purposefully she kept her eyes to the floor. Quickly, she turned and walked in the opposite direction, her deep brown eyes assessing Sydney Cove's busy seat of government. Gathered about in clusters, military officials, mariners, colonists—mostly men—bantered back and forth with talk of England, the high cost of goods, and the weather. Meandering through each group, Bailey kept her face lowered, glancing up only occasionally to peer inside a few open doorways. The stench of rum pervaded the air, but she made no gesture of her displeasure. Instead, her desire to find the lieutenant evoked a sense of purpose in her stride, therefore causing the gawking men to step aside and allow her to pass.

Bailey had drawn her air of authority from her father, Pern Templeton. A merchant who immigrated to America from England, Pern Templeton found before him a future filled with numerous opportunities in the vast, sprawling, unblemished new land. Pooling all his resources as an English chandler, or candlemaker, Pern immigrated to Virginia, rented a small shop in Williamsburg, and began selling dry goods. His business grew, and before long, he had hired two employees and even retained a tailor in the rear of the shop. He had always boasted of his shrewd ploys to draw customers in the early days. Bailey fondly recalled his personal rags-to-riches story: "I would be out on the streets of Williamsburg by dawn, my arms loaded down with stacks of papers. Keeping my eyes fixed on the shop, I'd hasten toward the store, causing someone to ask one day if I thought the building was afire. 'No,' says I. 'Just too much business to attend to.' " Word had soon spread throughout Williamsburg of the successful shopkeeper, and before long customers lined up in front of Templeton's Dry Goods Store to purchase their wares and to taste the free samples of ready-made breads. Bailey had always admired her father's commanding mannerisms and had learned to emulate them. Pern, himself, boasted often about his feisty daughter and her expert ways about the mercantile. "Her head smarts make up for the fact that she can't brew a cup of tea to save her life!" Although he sometimes doted on his lovely daughter, he also reminded her that pride had no place in the Templeton empire. While her brothers had toiled away in the family mercantile as clerks, Bailey had modeled herself after the old man himself, following him around town, mimicking his interaction with other merchants. Such ways would now be beneficial in Sydney Cove, she decided. None would be the wiser of the lump she felt in her throat or the anxiety that fluttered around her stomach. *No one needs to know*, she deduced.

Seeing a group of five naval officers milling about a small office, she poised herself in the doorway. "Pardon me." The cigar smoke in the air pricked at her nostrils, but being accustomed to such male-affiliated nuisances, she merely cleared her throat and gave a confident glance at the most decorated among them.

Arching one thick brow, the officer stepped out from among the others. "Hello. May we—I help you?"

"I'm trying to locate Lieutenant Frye." She pulled a letter from her reticule and handed it to the man. "Samuel Frye."

"Frye's been gone for a month now, or is it two?" The lieutenant turned to glance at the others, who nodded their affirmation but kept their eyes trained on the beautiful young woman.

"Gone?" The words echoed through the chambers of her mind. But maintaining her composure, Bailey reasserted herself. "My name is Bailey Templeton. I'm the new teacher for the Sydney Cove school."

Several officers chuckled before one finally spoke up. "I remember Frye sending papers to England asking for a school*master*. But you sure ain't one o' *those*!"

The men all laughed at this remark, but Bailey refused to react to their petty observations. "Who, then, would be the replacement for Frye, or am I asking the wrong person?"

The laughing subsided and the lieutenant grew more somber. "Sydney Cove is no place for a lady. You'd best pack up your things and head back for England, Miss Templeton."

Sensing the gravity in his tone, Bailey tempered her words but held her ground. "I'm not from England. I'm an American. And I certainly don't plan to return home."

"What's the problem here?"

At once, the officers turned to acknowledge the one who had entered the room. He was a large officer. So large in fact, his muscular frame filled the entire doorway. "Captain Hogan. Just a bit of a mix-up. This young lady says she's the new schoolmistress," the lieutenant said, quickly addressing the situation.

"Oh?" Meeting Bailey's hopeful expression, the captain addressed her with a somber gaze. "I see." His square jaw tensed visibly.

Bailey studied his rugged yet implacable face. He had a powerful presence, and the dark shadow along his jawline gave him an even more virile appearance. But she refused to be intimidated by this bull of a man. "Captain." She nodded affably.

"I regret to say that I've already sent for a new headmaster. A Mr. Bailey Templeton is on his way this month from America."

The light of humor crossed Bailey's face. She shot a knowing glance in the direction of the other officers, who chuckled among themselves. "A *Mr.* Bailey Templeton, you say?" With a confident lift of her chin, she clasped her gloved hands in front of her. She could not help but wonder if her professor friend in England had instigated this mix-up.

Captain Hogan shuffled the stack of papers in his hands, his thoughts obviously elsewhere. "Hmm?" Visibly impatient, he glanced up at her with one brow arched in a question. "I'm sorry." He shook himself as if coming from deep thoughts. "Yes. A Mr. Templeton has been selected. I decided that the problems of the school could be better handled by a man with a firm hand. If, due to our error, you've traveled a long distance for naught, I'll see to it you're compensated for any personal expenses." He nodded toward one of the lesser officers. "Johansen, will you see to it that Miss—"

"Templeton. Miss Bailey Templeton." Bailey smiled smugly and crossed her arms at her waist.

"Of course, Miss Temple—"

Seeing the shock in his eyes, Bailey took a deep breath and strode toward him. "Captain, I am your new headmaster, headmistress, or whatever you wish to call me. I am Bailey Templeton, your new teacher for Sydney Cove."

2

TWO WILLING
SUITORS

Bailey's clothing lay scattered across the front porch of the government building. Her arms akimbo, she anxiously looked all around in hopes of finding the culprit who had raided her trunk. Fortunately, she had tucked all her money inside the reticule. But the gowns and petticoats her sister and her father's tailor had worked so hard to fashion were scattered around the dusty porch like doll clothing. Examining the trunk's iron latch, she saw at once that the lock had been broken. *Who could have done this?* With a heavy sigh, she began the laborious task of collecting all of her belongings and tucking them once again into the trunk.

Not only had her interview with Captain Hogan been a dismal disappointment, but now everything she owned lay coated in dirt. Suddenly a shadow fell across her.

"I ran 'em off for ye, miss."

Bailey looked up to find the unkempt private grinning down at her.

"You saw who did this?"

"It was the street rats—the urchins."

"*Children* did this?"

"Yes. I chased off the whole lot o' them."

"What is your name, Private?" Bailey stood to acknowledge the man, dusting the soil from her gloves.

"Ferris Dade, miss. No need to thank me, though."

"Oh, of course I'm thanking you."

"Want me to have 'em arrested? I saw 'em all—each an' every 'orrid little face, that's wot."

"No." Shaking her head somberly, Bailey bent to close the trunk. "If I'm going to try to help them, the last thing I should do is have them arrested."

"Suit yourself, then. Want me to put that in your wagon?"

Seeing a spark of sincerity in the man's glistening blue eyes, Bailey accepted his offer. "All right. I suppose the military is sending for a wagon." She recalled the naval captain's condescending behavior but subdued her agitation.

"So you're the new teacher?"

Recalling Hogan's stubborn directive, she shrugged. "For now—until a new schoolmaster is found." She saw a wagon and driver round the corner of the government building. "Must be mine, Private Dade." She bent to snap the damaged latch shut. "I'll purchase a new lock later. For now I believe it will stay shut." While Dade loaded the trunk and her other baggage onto the buckboard, she leaned thoughtfully against the rail. Captain Hogan's words had burned in her ears. "I can't allow a female to endeavor to teach those hostile ruffians! You can stay on as our teacher until a new schoolmaster is hired." She wondered why Hogan was such a difficult man. Eloquent of speech, he had the tough exterior of a ruffian himself. What had hardened him so? And why was he so dead set on hiring a man for the teaching position? When her father's friend had contacted them from England about the teaching situation, he had warned that no Englishman wanted the position. Bailey chuckled to herself. *Well, Captain, you may be forced into retaining Bailey Templeton for longer than you think. Perhaps*, she thought, *this will afford me the time I need to prove to you that I'm the right person for the job.* Now the laughter that spilled from her lips was colored with a hint of undeserved triumph.

"All loaded up, Miss Templeton. Where to?" Dade climbed up next to the driver.

She checked the slip of paper that the captain's assistant had handed to her. "Mrs. Roland's Boarding House."

"I know right where it is," Dade answered confidently.

Bailey lowered her face. "You're accompanying me?"

" 'Course. Pretty girl like you can't be runnin' around this rat-infested borough wit'out a proper escort."

"Surely not." Bailey feigned relief. "And after I've dropped off my things, I'd like to take a look at the schoolhouse."

"But it's boarded up. You shouldn't be about until it's been proper fixed up."

"I'll be the judge of that, Dade," Bailey assured. She hated the manner in which everyone addressed her, as though she were too young and naive. In Williamsburg, she had garnered as much respect about town as old Pern Templeton himself.

The noonday sun heated up the dusty road, and Bailey found relief in knowing they were only a half mile from the boarding-house. When the wagon pulled up in front of the clapboard store-front, she quickly alighted. Asking the driver to wait, she and Dade carried the trunks and baggage inside. The front parlor, musty and hot, was sparsely furnished with one settee, a sawbuck table, and some mismatched chairs used for dining. "Hello?" she called out.

After a short wait, a thin-faced woman appeared from the rear. "Yes? Help you?" Her tone suggested she was in no mood to serve anyone. She untied her stained apron and hurriedly tossed it aside.

Bailey observed the woman's impatient bearing and tempered her words accordingly. "Captain Hogan sent me. I'm Miss Bailey Templeton, the new schoolteacher." She stretched a polite smile across her face.

The woman's lips pursed disdainfully. "*You're* the school-teacher? Hogan said he'd be sending a man."

"I know. A bit of a misunderstanding, but I can assure you that I'm Bailey Templeton." Removing her gloves, she took a breath and continued patiently. "You've a room for me, I hope?"

"Well, I"—the woman studied Bailey's face—"I suppose I do. Still an' all, I was expectin' a gentleman. The room's set up with partitions separatin' two other gentlemen boarders. Not proper a'tall. I'll have to prepare another room. It'll take a bit o' time, if you can wait."

"I've other errands, ma'am," Bailey assured her. "I'm happy to wait. But if it wouldn't be a bother, could I leave my trunk and baggage here? It's difficult to keep shuffling it all over town."

Her patience gone sour, the woman heaved a laborious sigh. "I suppose. Leave 'em behind the table over yonder. No one will bother them, I vow. But if they do, I'm not responsible."

"Thank you." Bailey smiled and, in a gesture of warmth, allowed her gaze to linger. The woman's face softened in response. "Dade, you wish to accompany me to the school?"

Tipping his hat, Dade grinned, his eyes sparking with surprise. "As always, Miss Templeton, at your service!"

A few white clouds softened the glare of the sun, making the ride to the schoolhouse more pleasant. "Dade?" Bailey formed a question in her mind.

"Yes, miss?"

"You know Captain Hogan very well?"

"Know of him. He's a good commander. A bit hard-nosed at times but respected among the British troops."

"I don't think he likes me." Bailey chuckled.

"Who? Hogan? How could anyone not like you, Miss Templeton?"

"I don't think I'm at all what he expected."

"Some folks don't adjust to change as well as others. Now, if this was England, why, a woman teacher—that'd be the best way to run a school. But here in Sydney Cove, miss, there's not too many fine ladies like you about. Oh, there's a few, but not many. You gots to watch out fer convicts and such roamin' the countryside. And the emancipists can be a surly lot. You'd best learn to use a pistol."

A gun? She winced at the thought. "I'll keep that in mind, Dade."

"Here we go, now. There's the school'ouse just ahead of us."

Anxiously following Dade's glance, Bailey saw a flurry of activity around a dilapidated building. "That *shack* is a schoolhouse?" Disappointment tinged her words. She studied the edifice. It was a two-room affair held together with Australian mud and a little luck.

Dade flipped his hand in the air, gesturing toward the pitiable building. "Another reason to want a schoolmaster. To oversee the repair needed."

"Repair?" Shaking her head, Bailey interjected, "Dade, the entire building should be knocked down, and a new one built. There's no overseeing to it." Dismounting from the carriage, she secured the drawstring of her purse and made her way through the bramble of weeds and brush. The sound of hammering echoed through the vale. She surveyed the land and was at least pleased with the natural landscape. It was a lovely area, but the school was in shambles. With dismay, she observed the missing planks and broken glass in the box-shaped edifice. At the sound of stamping feet, she turned around.

"We're not quite ready to reopen."

Shielding her eyes from the sun, she gazed up into Captain Hogan's questioning face. "Hello again, Captain. So I see, but I wanted to observe the facility for myself."

Clasping his hands behind his back, he spoke in an all-knowing tone. "I'm afraid this will only be the first of many disappointments you'll find here in Sydney Cove, Miss Templeton."

"None I can't deal with, I'm sure." Her brow furrowed, and her smile faded somewhat when their eyes met.

Hogan persisted. "And you can see at once why we need a man with some carpentry ability."

Drawing a deep ragged breath, Bailey answered evenly. "But after the building is completed, what then of the children? Will they all need to be taught carpentry skills? What of reading and writing?" She struggled to maintain a conciliatory tone. "What then?"

"In this colony, educational skills will serve them rather poorly, I'm afraid."

"Then why bother with a school at all?" she snapped, her eyes flashing with challenge. Waiting for his reaction, she expected to hear words of her dismissal spilling forth. But instead, a faint smile curved his face. He almost seemed to enjoy her struggle to regain her composure. "You've an obvious education, Captain. What if your only option in life had been carpentry?"

His eyes laughed but his jaw remained taut. His countenance took on a more somber air. "Point well taken, Miss Templeton. I concede." Drawing himself up, he placed a thoughtful finger upon his lips. "Of course I don't expect all the pupils to apprentice as carpenters, but you already knew that, didn't you? Miss Templeton, you've no idea of the problems of this colony. The children here are not esteemed in the same manner as are the civilized, well-bred boys and girls of which I'm certain you're accustomed. Most of them have been reared by outlaws, thieves, and the like. Most don't know who their fathers are. Some are orphans."

She studied his eyes, devilishly handsome and sparkling with confidence. "All the more reason to hire me, Captain Hogan, because I happen to care about them." Locking on his gaze, she said,

"But only time will prove whether I'm right or wrong."

He seemed pensive, neither disturbed nor angry. He lowered his face and answered firmly, "I don't think the young wards under your tutelage will respond to *care*. All they've ever known, most of them, is a savage battle of the fittest. And most have lost."

If she expected a yes or no, she had underestimated him. And she was uncomfortable with the fact that he probably had spoken the truth. So she laid aside her undeclared war and decided to address the issue again at another time. "When can I expect to reopen the school? I'll need to get word to the parents. You say some are orphans?"

"Today is Tuesday. You can reopen in a few weeks—it could be as soon as two weeks but no later than four. Labor here is limited in the worst way. In the meantime, you'll need to restock supplies and schoolbooks. We have some items at the government stores, but they are minimal."

Refusing to offer a note of complaint, she said simply, "I'll manage. It is their minds I wish to reach. If all I have is the tool of my own wits, then that is a start, isn't it?"

Crossing his strong forearms across his chest, Hogan evaded her question. "The orphans and the emancipists are quite another matter."

"Is there a way to entice them to come to school?"

"I'll leave that to you. For now, the colonist's children are our concern."

Bailey pondered his words. "I should be leaving now. I need to peruse these government stores of yours." She also felt it would be a good idea to purchase a few personal items while she had the chance.

"Good day, Miss Templeton." Captain Hogan returned to the matter at hand, and Bailey joined Dade on the buckboard.

"To the government stores, Dade," she spoke evenly, never taking her eyes off Captain Hogan.

"Driver, you heard the lady," Dade barked before stepping down to allow Bailey to take her place between them.

Seating herself, Bailey inwardly mused upon the captain's words. As the wagon pulled away, she turned to look once more at the officer whose implacable will determined her fate. For a brief instant, he turned around also and their eyes met. Pressing her lips together, she allowed a faint smile to dimple her face. He returned the polite smile, white teeth flashing from a tanned face. Then, as though orchestrated by unseen hands, they both turned pridefully away to lose themselves in their own concerns.

The boardinghouse room, however tiny it was, looked somewhat inviting to Bailey. Although sparsely furnished, she imagined what it could look like once she had finished with it. *Here's one matter I'll have a little control over*, she thought happily. A small washbasin on a rickety stand stood idly in front of a single window. In one corner of the room sat her stack of baggage and in the other the bed. Not much bigger than the bed she slept on aboard *The Victoria*, the wooden frame held up a straw mattress covered by a single sheet. The bed was unmade and the floor looked as though it hadn't been swept recently. Though weary and drained from the trip, Bailey could not sleep until the room was spotless. Finding a broom in the front parlor, she set about at once cleaning out the cobwebs and rinsing out the soot-covered lamp. Rearranging the furnishings, she pulled out her family portraits and hung them tastefully about the room. A dried nosegay that she and Laurie had made decorated the only nightstand, which was draped with an ecru doily. Soon the room had a warmth to it that spoke of home.

Before retiring, she crept down the creaky hallway. She could hear the male boarders conversing behind thin walls, and coarse laughter drifted from the rooms. The hall was smoky with tobacco odor, and the tang of whiskey draped the air. Lightly, she tapped on the landlady's door. "Mrs. Roland?" She spoke quietly.

"Who is it?" the woman answered gruffly from behind the door. Her harsh retort surprised Bailey, especially since she was the only female boarder. The woman must always answer in such a manner out of caution. "It's me, ma'am. Bailey Templeton. May I use your kitchen? I've my own tea, and I'd like to make a cup before retiring."

"Clean up after you've finished?"

She rolled her eyes but kept a civil tongue. "Of course, Mrs. Roland." Hearing the woman's shoes padding away from the door, Bailey assumed the answer to be yes. "Thank you," she called out boldly.

Finding the embers in the kitchen fireplace still hot, she stoked them up and set the kettle of water to boil. While she waited, she mentally began to pen the inevitable letter she intended to write to Laurie. But she found the words did not come easily, which caused her to think twice about replying at all.

A rap at the front door brought her to her feet. She knew Mrs. Roland had retired for the evening. Perhaps it would be a service to the woman if she answered the door herself. Checking the water that had yet to boil, she strode toward the barred and bolted door. "Who's there?" she asked politely but with a reserve of caution.

"Lieutenant Evans. Calling for Miss Bailey Templeton."

Bailey shook her head. She had met a room full of officers today, but the name escaped her memory. "I'm Bailey Templeton. Do I know you?"

"We met in Captain Hogan's office."

A brief silence ensued, and Bailey detected a bit of awkwardness in the man's voice. She smiled and chuckled quietly to herself. "You say you're *calling* for me?"

"It would make this visit much simpler if you'd kindly unbar the door, Miss Templeton."

Suddenly feeling foolish, Bailey now laughed out her answer. "I'm so sorry, Lieutenant. I'll open the door at once." Admittedly tired, she suddenly felt enlivened at the thought of company. The wooden bar lifted with a slight resistance, and she stepped back to allow in the caller. She recognized his face at once. "I remember you now." She nodded. The lieutenant had been the first to greet her inside Hogan's office. He was a handsome man, rugged of face and build, and she could not help feeling flattered at his swift appearance on her doorstep. "Is there a problem? Something wrong with the school building?" She bit her lip, realizing how foolish her words sounded. *Of course something's wrong with the school building!*

"Oh no, Miss Templeton." He smiled, his voice a smooth, deep timbre. "As I've just said, I've come to call on you personally. My parents are colonists in Parrametta, and when I told them of your arrival, my mother insisted on cooking dinner for you—"

"Lieutenant Evans?"

Bailey heard a deep rumbling voice from outside on the portico. The lieutenant whipped around.

"Captain Hogan?" He saluted and offered an apologetic excuse. "I'll only be a moment, Miss Templeton."

Her eyes narrowed, Bailey peered around the large weathered door. The men conversed quietly, then Hogan glanced up and saw Bailey looking through the doorway.

"Hello, Miss Templeton."

Bailey nodded but did not smile. "Hope there isn't a problem," she said dryly.

"Oh no. Nothing serious." He composed his face. "I saw Evans' horse here, and I'm in need of his services. I believe my mount has picked up a stone in its back left hoof. Evans has a way with horses."

Standing behind the captain, Evans gave a knowing nod, as though forced to humor the superior officer. "I'll be right with you, Miss Templeton."

"Certainly, Lieutenant," she acknowledged. "I'd best check the kettle anyway. Just step inside when you're finished."

Preparing to close the door, Bailey noticed Grant Hogan now turned and approached her. "I'll join you, Miss Templeton. Fill you in on the details of the school." With a sigh, Bailey opened the door once again. She had wearied of the *details*, feeling the school building was without hope and that the military was anything but on her side. Leaving the captain to close the door, she turned and made her way back to the kitchen. The sound of a home-cooked meal had been her best bit of news all day. She rationalized that although she had no intention of involving herself in another relationship for the time being, she would accept the officer's cordial offer. *After all*, she reasoned, *the offer is from Evans' family*. The event would be a family gathering and would give her an opportunity to begin making acquaintances in the colony. The school was actually located between Sydney Cove and Parrametta. The Evans family might introduce her to some of the colonists whose children would attend the school.

"I feel as though I'm talking to myself, Miss Templeton. Where *are* you?" Captain Hogan stopped just inside the kitchen door and leaned against the doorframe.

Not realizing the captain had been addressing her, Bailey whirled around, her cheeks flushing. "I'm sorry. My mind's on the school, as usual." The statement was at least partly true.

"Not to worry. I know you've a lot to address here in the colony. But I thought it would benefit you to know how our last teacher, Mrs. Dreyfuss, came to leave."

"If you think such a thing is important, I'll listen." The thought had not occurred to Bailey. Distraught over the fact that she herself was not wanted, she had not bothered to ask why the last teacher had left her post. Pouring the hot water into a chipped teapot, she found two mismatched cups and offered one to Grant.

"Let's seat ourselves in the parlor. It's more comfortable out there," she suggested with a friendly smile. Finding the captain in an amicable humor, she hoped to finally kindle a bit of goodwill between them.

The captain lifted his boots to step over the uneven threshold and gestured toward a settee. "Shall we?"

Lifting her skirt and petticoats above the splintered entryway, Bailey breezed past and seated herself. "So, this Mrs. Dreyfuss . . . was she a seasoned teacher? By that, I mean experienced?"

He took a sip of the tea she had made and grimaced. "She had taught for twenty years." With an air of distaste, Hogan placed the cup next to him on a table. "But the children, the boys especially, were so disruptive she couldn't hold a single day of class without a fight ensuing."

"I see." Bailey cringed upon hearing his words but knew in her heart she should expect as much. "And what about the boys' parents?"

"Mrs. Dreyfuss toiled endlessly trying to solicit the parents' help, but to no avail. The emancipists here were transported by the British government as a final solution for their overcrowded jail. Some convicts had originally been sentenced to hang, but having their sentences reduced to transportation, they found themselves unwitting slaves in the new colony. Therefore, the emancipists have an inbred hatred for the military, for the British colonists who settle here, and for anyone in an authority position."

Suddenly the futile problems grew a bit more focused in Bailey's mind. "So Mrs. Dreyfuss quit her position?"

"She couldn't leave quickly enough. She accepted a cramped room on a mercantile ship and left for England the next day."

"Poor woman," Bailey answered evenly. She blew across the top of her cup and sipped lightly. "So you believe the answer to the children's control problem will be found in hiring a man?"

"I'm afraid we've no choice. The disruptive children won't be so hasty in undermining a firm man with a thick switch in his hand."

"Are there any well-behaved children at all—any who *want* an education?"

"Yes. That's the reason I've worked so hard to keep this school going, Miss Templeton. There are a dozen children who could grow up to make a difference in the colony. It is for them that we're going to such great lengths to ensure the promise of a school."

"Then for their sake, you must hire *me*, Captain Hogan. Have you taken the time to study my credentials?"

With a heavy sigh, Grant nodded. "It is I who selected your name from all the other submissions."

"You?"

He nodded once more and stroked his chin, his eyes fixed on some distant object.

"But you believed me to be a man."

"I did. I apologize for that error, as I've done now numerous times." His deep voice took on a kind quality.

Without any further hesitation, Bailey smiled faintly. "Forgiven." She gazed up into his face and for the first time realized the burden that rested on his shoulders. "I apologize as well, Captain Hogan. I had no idea the extent of the problems you face." She lowered her tone, feeling guilty at having been so terse with the man. He looked down at her, and she saw a spark of sympathy in his emerald green eyes. His countenance softened, and he, too, seemed to see her in a different light.

"I hope like the dickens you can survive all this, Miss Templeton."

Without knowing why, she laughed softly. Perhaps it was due to the tension that now dissolved between them. "Why, Captain Hogan? Why do you 'hope like the dickens' that I survive?"

"Captain Hogan?" Evans stuck his head inside the door.

"Yes, Evans?"

"I can't find a stone in her left rear hoof. Are you certain—"

"Perhaps it was her right hoof." Hogan cleared his throat. "Will you take another look? Check them all."

Evans' eyes made contact with Bailey's, taking in the scene of the two of them together on the settee. His eyes sparked with what appeared to be frustration. "Yes, sir. Miss Templeton, I do apologize for the delay."

"No bother, Lieutenant." She beamed at him, finding humor in the matter. With a suspicious gleam in her eye, she reasserted her question. "You were saying, Captain, why you wish for me to survive?"

His face and shoulders now relaxed, Hogan rested his elbow behind them on the back of the settee. But as always, he carefully chose his words. Blowing out a breath, he answered, "Because you're so earnestly determined. I want you to find whatever it is that you're so desperately trying to unearth in this dismal land."

"So you're willing to give me a chance?"

"I didn't say that exactly. I will continue my search for a schoolmaster. But you've ample time to prove yourself with these difficult students. And I've an impossible task ahead in finding a new schoolmaster."

His words did not fully please her, but she accepted them gracefully. "Understood, Captain."

"Captain, your horse must have shook the stone loose. Looks clean to me." Lieutenant Evans strode into the parlor and doffed his hat. "Now, as I was saying, Miss Templeton—"

"Evans, Miss Templeton and I have business matters to resolve. Would you be so kind as to water my horse? That should give us ample time to conclude with our plans."

His face now full of suspicion, Evans reluctantly complied. "Sir, yes, sir." He strode dubiously from the parlor, offering a less-than-congenial salute.

"Poor man." Bailey's eyes shone with the light of sympathy. "And how shall we 'conclude with our plans,' as you say?"

"You may approach the emancipists in any way that you wish. But I would appreciate your allowing me one suggestion."

"I'm quite approachable, Captain, in that regard. Please tell me."

"Would you consider holding a town meeting? Invite all the parents to come—both colonists and emancipists alike. You could hold it at the reverend's house—Reverend Whitley's. If you could allay their fears or concerns—"

"What a wonderful idea, Captain. We could invite the ladies to bring their favorite dish—make it more of a social." Surely she could manage a casual social. She thought of her mother's adeptness at organizing large social events. Not accustomed to much of anything in the way of socials, these settlers would surely be appreciative of anything she could pull together. "Captain, you've a spark of genius."

"I have?" He leaned back, picked up the cup of hot tea, and then, as though a remembrance crossed his mind, he quickly set the cup aside. Raising one brow, he added cynically, "Knew it all along."

"I'll get busy right away preparing some sort of invitations."

"I wouldn't expect a welcome response, Miss Templeton. Remember, you aren't inviting England's royal family to tea. These are ex-convicts, and many of the convict men have married prostitutes. Just because they've sired a brood doesn't elect them to the rank and file of parenthood."

"I know, Captain Hogan." Soberly, Bailey acknowledged his comment with a nod. "I'll just have to prepare myself. Yet I see God's hand in all of this."

"God's hand?"

"I believe He brought me here." She studied the skepticism of his gaze. *Perhaps one day you'll agree*, she thought, breathing a prayer that God would make His direction evident.

Hogan smiled. "Let's hope." He stood and offered his hand. "May I escort you back to your room? Mrs. Roland's boarders aren't the most trustworthy lot." He offered his arm in a gentlemanly fashion.

Seeing the warmth of sincerity in Grant Hogan's face, Bailey accepted. "Thank you, Captain. She allowed her hand to rest on his strong arm. "I am exhausted from the trip and have so much unpacking to do yet." Bailey felt a small grain of confidence grow between them. "We were hit by the worst storm . . ." she began her story.

The boardinghouse door creaked open and Evans stepped inside. He saw Captain Grant Hogan and Bailey Templeton disappear around the corridor. They were both smiling and talking quietly to each other, her hand resting primly on his arm. "Hogan, you scoundrel!" he muttered with a twinge of envy, his words muted for fear of insubordination. Whirling on his heels, he stormed out through the front doorway as the lonely veil of night fell upon Sydney Cove. Miss Bailey Templeton would have no need for two willing suitors.

3
"CONQUERING HOGAN"

Bailey walked out into the glorious sunshine of dawn. The prior evening's discussion had brought many problems to light, and she felt much better about Captain Grant Hogan's strong stand on hiring a schoolmaster. *At least I understand his reasoning now.* Before she could bid a kind good-day to Mrs. Roland and close the door, she heard the canter of horses approaching the boardinghouse. She glanced up at the grinning driver. Waving her arm broadly, she called, "Good morning, Private Dade!"

"Heh! I got me a good job now! I'm your escort, that's wot!"

Bailey adjusted her plumed bonnet. "We've quite a day ahead. Hope you're up to it."

"Beats choppin' wood, an' I gets to ride around wif the one all the town's a-jitter about."

"Who? Me?"

"O' course, you. They's all jealous over me gettin' picked." He scratched his leathery face with a sinewy hand.

"Nothing to get all a-jitter over, Dade. I'm just a dowdy ol' spinster from America."

Dade laughed out loud and slapped his knee. "You'll have a

hard time convincin' me o' that one, missy."

When Dade started to step down, she waved him back. "You'll be jumping up and down all day if I allow. Just stay in your seat. I can climb up without you." Gripping the iron arm of the carriage seat, Bailey hoisted her trim frame effortlessly into the seat. "See? Where to first?"

"Down Wontoobie Lane. Plenty of emancipists livin' that way."

"Such odd names you have for places," she remarked as the carriage lurched forward.

Adjusting the brim of his slightly frayed military hat, Dade nodded. "Aborigine names, some of them, at least."

"Onward, then, to Wontoobie!" The brisk breeze of the autumn morning, which in Virginia would be springtime, urged Bailey to pull her wrap more tightly about her shoulders. Resting her head against the padded seat, she listened for a while as Dade prattled on about his expert knowledge regarding emancipists and Sydney Cove. But soon her thoughts drifted, and she thought again of her conversation with Grant Hogan. Although her opinion of him in regard to his intimidating ways had not changed, she had seen him in a different light. And the manner in which he kept sending the lieutenant back to see to his horse had caused her to chuckle all evening. Suddenly a memory flooded her thoughts. "Lieutenant Evans!" she said, sitting straight up.

Startled from his half stupor, Dade yelped. "Wot's 'at, miss? Wot's wrong?"

"I'm so embarrassed! How could I do that to the man, especially after he traveled all the way from Parrametta." She rested her head in her hands and sighed heavily.

"Wot in blazes, miss?"

"Oh, Dade, I've done something terrible. Lieutenant Evans came to call on me last evening. But Captain Hogan needed to see me, and I totally forgot about Evans."

Chuckling gruffly, Dade winked slyly. "He's a corker, that Captain Hogan. Right smooth with the ladies."

"What?"

"He's known for pullin' rank like that all the time with the men under 'im. If'n he sees somethin' he likes, why, there'll be no stoppin' 'is charmin' ways. Ol' Evans didn't 'ave a chance next to Conquerin' Hogan."

Arching one brow cynically, Bailey answered in amused wonder, "But you don't understand, Dade. Captain Hogan merely discussed the problems of the school with me." She glanced forward, self-satisfied. "Nothing more."

"Like I say, he's smooth all right. Did he know the lieutenant came to call on you?"

"I don't know. If he did, I'm sure he forgot about the lieutenant, just as I did." Her cheeks reddened slightly at the annoying thought. "I assure you, the captain has no other interest in me except in matters pertaining to the school's affairs."

"We'll see." Dade chuckled again.

Realizing Private Dade would never allow the matter to rest if she didn't, Bailey made no further response. But as they neared the first settlement of shacks, she couldn't help silently mouthing, "Conquering Hogan"? She had no intention of becoming entangled in another complicated relationship, no matter how intriguing the prospect. She shook the thought from her head.

The shabby structures before her told a story all their own—roughhewn one-room shanties sitting in littered yards, with packs of mangy dogs barking after dirty-faced waifs. Dade must have read her expression, for he said quietly, "We don't have to stop here, Miss Templeton. We could drive on."

"No, Dade. I want to stop here," she assured him, although the flutter in her stomach warned her to do otherwise. "Perhaps, though, you should accompany me."

Rolling his eyes, Dade smiled assuringly. "Goes without sayin', miss."

Pulling up to the first dismal dwelling, Bailey chose to wait and allow Dade to assist her from the carriage. Before she could alight, a pack of children swarmed around them. "Hello," she called out in the most friendly tone she could muster. "Are your parents about?"

"Not likely." A blue-eyed blond boy laughed sarcastically, and others joined him in kind.

"What did we do?" quipped the youngest-looking waif among them, then hid behind the protection of an older sister.

Bailey followed the little boy with her eyes. "You've done nothing. I've come to call on your parents. But I can come at a later time. If you'll only—"

Seeing a movement from the corner of her eye, Bailey turned and saw a red-faced woman headed for the children. In one bony hand she carried a switch, and as she walked, she swung it fiercely.

"Get back in the 'ouse!" she ordered. "The rest o' ye, get back to your own place now!"

Bailey watched with some discomfort when the gang of waifs scattered in three directions. A few of the youngest screamed for effect, while others shook defiant fists at the woman. Seeing the lanky woman turn abruptly and head in her direction, Bailey remained standing in the carriage not sure what to expect. "Hello, ma'am," she called out boldly, which appeared to serve her well, for the woman's fierce countenance softened slightly, and she stopped within a few feet of the carriage.

"State your business," she replied flatly.

"If you and your husband have school-aged children, I've come to call on you."

"I don't have no husband, and if the brats 'as done somethin' wrong, well, then I'll beat 'em if they needs it."

Bailey indicated with a nod that she was ready to step down from the carriage. Taking Dade's steady hand, she continued, her face composed and confident, but feeling a waver of dread. "No, ma'am. No problem at all with your children. But I trust you wish for them to return to school, true?"

"That school's been nothin' but trouble for this colony. That mistress had it in for me younguns, and we don't have no use for it a'tall."

"I've heard your first teacher encountered some problems, but I'm sure she had the best interests of the children at heart. I'm—"

"Posh! She had 'er own interests at heart! Now, I asked you to state your business. If you're 'ere on matters o' that infernal school, then you've no business wif me!"

Seeing the woman turning away, Bailey stepped toward her. "Wait, please!"

"Wot now?" The woman faced her with a scowl.

"I'm sorry. Please, allow me—I'm Bailey Templeton. And your name?" She held out her hand in a gesture of goodwill.

Not accustomed to a woman offering her hand, the woman's countenance held a quizzical gaze. After a moment's hesitation, she finally extended her own hand and cautiously returned Bailey's handshake. "Josephine Anders," she muttered.

"I'm the new schoolteacher." Seeing that Josephine's face had yet to reflect an ounce of trust, Bailey accepted the handshake as a first positive step toward receiving this woman's confidence. "You say you're rearing your children alone?"

"I am at that. Not ashamed o' the fact, neither."

"No. I suppose not." Bailey lightly shook her head, keeping her face sober. "But I'm sure you would like to see your children have a life that's better than you've had. True?"

Her lips pursed in anger, Josephine shot back, "Wot's that supposed to mean?"

"She means, ma'am"—Dade jumped into the conversation—"that all us good citizens o' Sydney Cove, we've 'ad it bad at times. An' we townsmen want our children to have somethin' better—you know, a place in society, a bit o' respect, and a good piece o' beef now an' again."

The woman turned to stare at Bailey. "You mean you're promisin' me all that?"

Exchanging a questioning glance with Dade, she responded honestly, "I can't promise you the outcome, Miss Anders. But if you'll allow me, as your children's teacher, to give them the tools to succeed, they can map out their own future. Their choices in life will be greater if they're educated." She inhaled deeply and prayed that she could somehow connect. "Does that make sense?"

Still skeptical, Josephine shrugged indifferently. "So when's the school set to open?"

"Perhaps in two weeks." Her face beaming, Bailey cautiously reached out to touch the woman's shoulder. "So does that mean your children can come?"

"They's six of 'em, and I don't make no claims to their good behavior." Josephine's face reflected worry.

"I'll deal with their behavior. You just see that they come. Will you do that?"

Without making eye contact, Josephine nodded. Whipping around, she saw several of her brood swinging on a rope swing. "Get yourselves over here!" She motioned with the switch.

Seeing the children's hesitancy, Bailey smiled warmly. "I want to meet all of you. It's all right. Will you come?" She made a slow gesture with her hand, not wanting to intimidate them.

The youngest, a little boy, stepped out from the shade of the tree and glanced back at his siblings for any show of disapproval. Then an older girl followed. Soon they filed toward Bailey like a gaggle of goslings. The oldest glanced up at his mother defensively. Bailey noticed the way he kept a safe distance from her ever present switch. "I ain't done nothin' to 'er! T'wasn't me!"

"Shut up!" Josephine barked crossly. "This is your new school-teacher, Miss—"

"Templeton," Bailey finished her sentence. "Miss Bailey Templeton."

"I thought we didn't have to go to school no more," the oldest girl said contemptuously.

"I ain't goin', Mum!" exclaimed the boy who appeared to have the greatest influence on them all.

"School starts in just a few weeks," Bailey answered firmly. "We shall have a meeting and invite all of the families to come. The meeting is next Friday at a colonist's home. Do you know of the Whitleys? He's an Anglican minister, I understand."

Josephine nodded, her demeanor relaxing. "I know 'im."

"Good. Friday, then, at candlelight?"

"Maybe we'll come." The mother separated two of the boys who had begun to scuffle.

Addressing the children, Bailey spoke out of a hopeful assumption. "Once school commences, I'll expect you there at half past seven in the morning, five days out of the week." Her voice rang with authority, and she offered no alternatives to the reluctant children. "Please don't be late, all right?"

Josephine observed their blank faces, which kindled her ire. "Go on then!" She tightened her hand into a fist, and her unruly brood scattered once again.

Bailey and Dade went from house to house, finding resistance with every family, but also finding that some of the ex-convict mothers eventually conceded to at least try the school once more. Most agreed to attend the meeting at the minister's house. Where Bailey failed in understanding their views, Dade filled her in with his simple understanding of the poorer families.

"I'm exhausted, Dade." She slumped into the carriage for what seemed like the hundredth time. "These parents are the most unfriendly group of people I've ever had to deal with."

"They're mistrustful, Miss Templeton. Most times they sees the government as out to bring their ruination, not to give them something for free. They're all waiting to see what's expected of them in return. It was real smart o' you to have yer meetin' at Reverend Whitley's place and not at the government buildin'. Real smart."

Weighing his words and the words of every person she had met that day, she sighed inwardly. "Do you think they'll come?"

"I think they'll come, miss. Not all, but most of 'em. Some'll wait an' see wot 'appens to the others first."

Bailey appreciated his attempt at encouragement. "I hope so." She fought with the defeat that threatened to taint her faith.

"But once they do come"—the line of his mouth tightened a fraction more—"then that's when you'll be put to the test."

She didn't fail to catch the note of foreboding in his tone. She shook her head. "I don't have to think about that today, at least. Would you mind taking me back to the boardinghouse? I'm tired."

"Sure thing, Miss Templeton. But we've one more house. You might want to stop at this one."

"Why?"

"It's an emancipist family, but they're quite different from the rest."

"How so?"

"You'll see." Dade whipped the team into action. "We're only a few miles from their place."

Bailey prepared herself for the worst. "How many children does this family have?"

"One couple has three. The other has two. They're the grown children of some emancipists, an' they all live together in one house."

"In one house. Poor things. They must be awfully cramped."

Dade laughed and turned the team onto a dirt path. At once, Bailey saw a sight that surprised her.

"This place is beautiful, Dade." She admired the well-kept fence posts, the green pastures. "It looks like a sheep ranch."

"An' that it is, miss. One o' the finest in Parrametta."

The carriage rounded a curve in the road, and a large two-story house came into full view. Seeing the mischievous glint in Dade's eyes, Bailey laughed out loud. "I trust this family is unlike those we met today."

"Quite unlike. This here is the Prentice farm, an' this land is called Rose Hill."

"Rose Hill," Bailey mused. "The name fits." Her eyes followed the rows of shade trees that lined the path to the house. Beneath their thick boughs, neat English gardens welled with color and floral fragrance. "These Prentices, they're a bit more cordial than some of the others?"

"They're good as gold, Miss Templeton. The Prentices 'ave 'ad their blows just like all the rest, but they rose above it all."

Bailey could not wait for Dade to bring the carriage to a halt.

The thought of meeting friendly faces encouraged her more than she had been willing to admit. Almost before it stopped moving, she was preparing to alight. "Let's hurry!"

All but running to keep up with the energetic teacher, Dade called after her, "Expect to receive a grand welcome, miss. They's—"

"Dwight Farrell!" A woman's voice shouted from inside the house. "I don't ask much of you, but you could at least stay close to home for one Sunday! What about church?"

Bailey froze on the front porch. "Dade, are you sure they're expecting us?" The woman's cross tone intimidated her.

"Well, no. I wanted for you to be a surprise."

"*Surprise?* Oh, Dade, I can't believe you didn't at least warn them. Let's leave now before they know we're here."

"Katy Prentice Farrell!" The woman's husband retorted in loud reaction. "You'll not raise your voice to me. I'm still demandin' a bit of respect around this place!"

"I don't understand you. You and the boys stay gone all weekend every weekend. What about their Bible lessons?"

"We go to church! Out in the pastures!"

"That's not church! It's . . . it's not proper!"

"It's more *Godlike* than anything I see in *this* godforsaken land!"

"But Corbin and I . . . well, I feel like a widow sitting in church without you," the woman pleaded.

Her husband retorted, "It's only for one more weekend. I'll be back in church next week. I swear it!"

"Dade!" Bailey, already making her way to the carriage, shot a warning glance. Hearing the approach of a horse and rider, she glanced up, her countenance etched with embarrassment.

"Hello!" The rider, a handsome young man, pulled up abruptly in front of Bailey. He had a muscular frame, a generous smile, and his hair—various degrees of blond—was swept back into a stylish queue. Dismounting in one graceful motion, he stopped to dust the day's toil from his trousers and boots. As tall as Bailey was, she noticed immediately that he towered over her. Pulling off his hat respectfully, he introduced himself. "I'm Caleb Prentice."

"I'm sorry, Mr. Prentice. But I don't think you all were expecting me." She cast an accusing glower at Dade, who glanced away non-committally.

Caleb reached to offer a generous handshake to Dade. "I believe we've met. Down in Sydney Cove, wasn't it?" Before the private could answer, Caleb stopped at once, hearing the noise from inside the house. He chuckled. "My sister and her husband are having another of their discussions again. Our ranch is expanding, and we've recently acquired more land. The time away from our wives is taking its toll. My wife's none too happy with me, either."

"Your wife?"

"Kelsey. And we have a little daughter, Shannon, and our infant son, Colby."

Relieved at his disarming ways, Bailey beamed. "Congratulations, Mr. Prentice."

"And you are?" His brows arched in an animated fashion, a tight smile stretched across his face.

Bailey blushed. "I'm sorry. I'm Bailey Templeton. I'm the new teacher for your school in Sydney Cove."

Caleb's brows shot up in surprise. "*You* are?"

"I know. You all were expecting a man. But I assure you, I can manage. I grew up with three unruly brothers. I'm sure I can handle these children." She felt as though she were making the statement for the hundredth time.

"*Children?* You may call them that if you like."

Her sense of humor took over, and she laughed her answer. "So I've heard. I've met most of them today. But they are children, although a little misguided."

A low, guttural laugh emanated from Caleb's throat, and his mouth curved into a mock sinister smile. "You're a braver one than I, Miss Templeton." He grasped his chest over his heart with one hand and held the other to his forehead. Looking up with simulated agony, he lamented, "God rest 'er soul. Another victim meets her fate!"

Now they all laughed, and Bailey felt the tenseness drain from her spine. "I'm eager to meet your children here at Rose Hill, Mr. Prentice."

"Well, let's step inside, shall we? If no furniture is flying, then we consider it safe to enter." With a flourish, he led them into the roomy house, making loud his presence. "We've guests! Anyone about?"

Bailey, politely stopping in the entranceway, took a relaxing breath and allowed her eyes to roam the parlor. The high-ceilinged room, tastefully filled with mahogany wood furnishings, held an inviting appeal from the sunny entrance. The bright pillows tossed casually about added a homelike touch to the richly colored tap-estries. And her senses were enlivened by the tantalizing aroma of baking bread, which mixed interestingly with the generous bou-quets of fresh flowers placed informally about the room.

"Dwight? Katy?" Caleb called out once more.

Seeing movement from the corner of her eye, Bailey turned and saw a couple descending a staircase to her left. They both held stoic yet somewhat sheepish expressions.

"Hello," the woman called out, a tight smiled stretched across her lovely face.

Bailey nodded. "Mr. and Mrs. Farrell?"

"Why, yes?" The woman gazed curiously back at her. She was a petite woman, thirtyish with blond hair and striking blue eyes.

Caleb quickly introduced her. "This is Miss Templeton, Sydney Cove's new schoolmistress. You've met Private Dade."

"A pleasure to meet you, Miss Templeton." Dwight Farrell of-fered his greeting in reply. Affectionately, he roughly patted Caleb's back, sending dust into the air.

Katy Farrell added, "We were upstairs—just discussing our children."

"So they heard." Caleb crossed his arms smugly. "It would serve you well to fasten shut your window before engaging in such dis-cussions."

"Oh, Dwight—" Katy blushed, her eyes cast first to her husband and then to the floor. Her shoulders drawn up in an embarrassed manner, she clasped her nervous hands in front of her.

Seeing her discomfort, Bailey quickly responded, "Not to worry. You made me feel at home."

Exchanging amused glances with one another, the Farrells looked back at Caleb and then at Bailey. At once, they all burst into contagious laughter.

"I feel so foolish!" Katy laughed out loud. "You must think us awful!"

"No, not really. Just normal," Bailey assured, still laughing her-self.

"I believe I'm going to like Miss Templeton." Katy cast a know-ing glance at her brother. She joined Bailey and took her arm in a friendly manner. "Join us for tea?"

"Please"—Bailey shook her head and insisted—"don't go to any bother on my account."

"No bother. It's teatime. We've fresh crumpets, too." Katy continued leading her toward a padded chair. "You sit here, and I'll go for my mother. Mrs. Prentice would love to meet you."

"All right, then." Bailey smiled with her reply.

"But you men?" Katy's brow arched cynically.

"Yes, love?" Dwight pulled his dusty hat from his head.

"You go and wash up first."

Bailey glanced at the two handsome English ranchers, their forceful presence suddenly reduced to that of mischievous boys. Their eyes betrayed their annoyance, but at the same time revealed their undying affection for this willful yet charming woman.

"We know when we are not wanted." Dwight nodded at his brother-in-law, his gestures animated. "Miss Templeton." He tipped his hat and placed it soundly on his head. "Dade, you may join the exiled men if you like." Followed by the grateful private, Dwight and Caleb turned and stalked out of the room, gazing obliquely at Katy.

As she took her place on the sofa, Bailey heard the sound of pounding boots on the front porch.

"My sons, Jared and Donovan," Katy interjected. She walked toward the entrance to greet them. The door flew open, and in bounded two tan-faced boys. "Miss Templeton, I want you to meet our sons, Jared and Donovan." She pointed to each in kind. "Meet Miss Templeton."

"Hello," the oldest called out in a friendly manner while the other tipped his hat, the mirror image of his mother.

Bailey smiled broadly. "So nice to meet you both." She studied their faces. The oldest, Donovan, had his father's eyes and dark hair, while Jared had Katy's blue eyes and blond hair. "Your ages?"

"Ten," Jared answered flatly, preoccupied with the aroma of baking bread.

"I'm twelve, Miss Templeton," Donovan answered politely. "You're new to Sydney Cove?"

While Bailey nodded Katy interjected, "Boys, meet your new teacher."

"Teacher?" Jared made a face.

"What a relief." Donovan countered his brother's unpleasant reaction. "Not so old like the last one."

Bailey laughed at both reactions. "Thank you, I think."

"I want you both to march right through the kitchen and wash up out back with your father and uncle." Katy assumed a motherly mien. "If you'll behave, you may join us for tea." As the brothers thundered from the room, she called after them, "Please ask Grandmama to join us in the parlor." Her voice intensified and her face reflected a question. "I hope they heard me."

"You've handsome sons, but Dade mentioned a third child." Bailey glanced up at the maid who entered wearing a printed apron.

"Yes, Corbin is our youngest. She's our only daughter—for now. She's napping, but when she awakens, I'll have her brought down."

"How old is Corbin?"

"She's only three. Not old enough for school." Katy turned to acknowledge the Cockney maid. "We've a guest, Helen. Would you be ready with our tea?"

Wiping her brow with a handkerchief, the maid curtsied. "Tea's all ready, mistress Katy. But your boys won't stay out of the bread."

With a sigh, Katy shook her head and smiled at Bailey. "How shall we rear gentlemen in this wilderness?"

"You can't. No more than my parents could turn my brothers into refined young men in the American colonies."

"Well, at least the boys made an impression on you. You're as well-bred as any English lady."

Now it was Bailey who blushed. "I wish that were true, Mrs. Farrell, but I'm afraid all of the Templetons are cursed with a small degree of the savage in them. It's a survival instinct, I believe. Especially with my being reared in a houseful of boys."

"So my little Corbin is without hope of gentility?"

"I'm afraid so." Bailey laughed and enjoyed the easy manner in which Katy Farrell joined in her levity.

"If you don't mind my asking, when shall our school open once again? I've been schooling the boys, but Donovan is quite adept in his mathematics, and I'm afraid my skills are in reading and writing. I would so appreciate him being exposed to higher computations."

"I'm hopeful that we will open the school in two weeks. Captain Hogan is the government's overseer in the matter." Her face poised, she coated her words with diplomacy. "He indicated that it could take longer to open the school."

"Ah yes." Katy beamed her approval. "The good Captain Hogan."

The maid bustled into the room, her arms laden with a tray of tea and pastries. Following close on her heels were Dwight, Caleb,

Dade, and an older woman whom Bailey assumed to be the boys' grandmother. She was an attractive woman, probably in her late forties or early fifties. Dressed smartly in the English fashion for receiving guests, her eyes sparkled as she beheld Bailey for the first time.

"Hello, ma'am," Bailey acknowledged her at once.

"So you're Miss Templeton?" The woman eagerly walked to greet her. "Please, call me Amelia."
She bowed at the waist and extended both hands to Bailey.

Bailey felt an instant liking for Amelia. She prepared to stand, but Amelia would not allow it.

"Please, stay right there. Helen, our guest is ready for tea."

The maid set about to serve each one, while the men stood around the parlor discussing trade issues.

"Caleb?" Katy addressed her brother.

"Yes?"

"Miss Templeton informs me that Captain Grant Hogan is overseeing the progress of the new school."

"Grant? Ah, now I understand." He grinned ruefully at Dwight.

"Good ol' Conquering Hogan." Dwight chuckled and winked at Dade.

Her brow knit in a frown, Bailey drew herself up. "It seems there's much I need to learn about the captain."

"Ignore them, Miss Templeton." Katy glowered at her husband and brother. "Captain Hogan's quite efficient at his job. He wants what's best for the colony, I can assure you of that fact. And that horrible nickname is completely ill-founded."

Keeping her eyes on Katy, Bailey pressed her lips together and tried to disregard the men's snickering reactions. "So you say that Donovan is a studious child?"

"Donovan is adept at anything you hand him. He'll be governor one day, if I know Donovan. Jared loves the outdoors, hunting, ranching. Place him in a schoolroom, and he'll sit staring through the window wishing he were out riding the pastures. He sits on an English saddle like a nobleman. He's a smart one as well, but it takes some doing to capture his interest."

"I'll do it." Bailey smiled. "And Donovan shall be challenged as well. Mathematics is my strong point, and I encourage gifted students to aspire to higher education."

"You must have been educated in England?"

"Yes, in my earlier years. That's how I came to know about this position. One of my former professors kept in touch with me, and he wrote, telling me of your search for the right teacher. He felt that I was made for the challenge."

"I feel you are also," Amelia added. "Such a delight to know our boys will be taught by such a gifted young woman. I hope you use the Bible. Are you a Christian woman?"

Bailey smiled at Amelia's outspoken yet delightful manner. "Yes. I'm a Christian. How could I teach without God's Word? It's basic to learning, I believe."

"Mercy sakes! If America brings up such godly teachers, then a great country it shall be!" Amelia's somber gaze brought them all to a moment of reflection.

"Well, of course, Mum," Katy said matter-of-factly. "How could a teacher *teach* without the Bible? Why, the students would all turn into ruffians and outlaws."

"Wouldn't that be a change here in Sydney Cove?" Caleb mused sarcastically.

They all chuckled at the irony except Amelia, who vowed, "You bring those emancipist children in and teach them God's ways, Miss Templeton, and you watch the face of this colony change."

A childish giggle trickled down from the staircase, and all eyes glanced up. A pretty young woman stood bundling a curly locked little girl in her arms. "Company, I see." The child's face lit up at the roomful of people.

"She's awake!" Amelia set down her cup at once. "My granddaughter." She beamed proudly.

Bailey winked at Katy. "I could've guessed. This little one must be Corbin."

Katy nodded and poured herself another cup of tea. "And my sister-in-law, Kelsey."

Bailey enjoyed the visit with this family, and she puzzled that any of them could have started out as ex-convicts. She wondered but could not bring herself to ask.

Making short her polite farewells, she and Dade headed back for the boardinghouse. She thanked the Lord for the peace that welled inside of her. In spite of the trying day, God had given her spirit a new feeling of encouragement—*just before the sunset*. She felt almost as though she had been with her own family. Even Dwight's and Caleb's harmless bantering had reminded her so much of her brothers. But she found their references to Captain Grant Hogan even more disconcerting than Dade's comment. She had expected as much from Dade, but the Prentices and the Farrells seemed to be respectable folk. Steering clear of the man to whom she answered could pose a problem. Avoiding Captain Grant Hogan would be like avoiding her next meal. Katy appeared to be the only one to have faith in him. But if Katy were wrong and the others right in their assumptions, Bailey would most assuredly need to guard her heart. *Who are you Captain? Are you Conquering Hogan?*

4
UNEXPECTED
PICNIC

Bailey lifted her skirt to take the final step into the one-room schoolhouse. During the last two weeks, she had made several jaunts to the old building. With each visit, she had found gradual improvement in the school. Even an old rusted bell had been polished as best as it could be and hoisted on a pole outside the door. Glancing about the room, she felt satisfaction well inside of her. The dirt floors had been covered with simple punchcon and then swept clean. The walls, covered with wainscot, now smelled of fresh whitewash. It gave the old room a new, finished look. The desks had been repaired, including her own, and lined up in neat rows facing the writing board. To keep out the sun's torrid heat, some colonists' wives had made checkered curtains for each small window. Now the waiting was over. *Today's the day, Bailey. All eyes will be upon you.* She recalled the meeting at the minister's home. His lovely wife had taken special care to see that each family, no matter their place in the colony, was treated with the highest respect. In spite of a few suspicious glances, she had found a degree of acceptance from most of those present.

She thought of Grant Hogan's skeptical gaze the day prior.

Overseeing a group of convict laborers, he had made certain that every desk, every wall, every part of the room had fallen under his careful inspection. But she, too, had been making her own observations, scrutinizing every remark he cast her way. If Hogan had any intention of adding her to his list of conquests, she had yet to detect a spark of manipulation on his part. He had maintained a completely professional mien between them. For some strange reason, that fact bothered her, albeit she could not determine why. Though she noticed that he was handsome and quite intelligent, she stayed on her guard the moment he appeared.

Hogan had proved a wealth of information, explaining to her the short history of the colony. The colonists, for the most part, had been arrested in England for crimes ranging from stealing a pound of bacon to more serious offenses such as embezzlement. With some facing hanging, they were relieved to have their sentence reduced to transportation. Most were poor and probably just stealing to survive. But a few notable political figures had colored the colony's history. New South Wales' only artist, Thomas Watling, had been transported for forging guinea notes on the Bank of Scotland. Bailey had seen one of the landscape artist's paintings hanging in the government building. Shaking herself from her thoughts, she turned her attention to the sounds of laughter coming from outside.

Making a final inspection to be certain that each desk held the same stack of well-worn books, Bailey tugged at her skirt, gave her coifed hair a final pat, and headed for the entrance. She saw immediately that the once empty school yard was now alive with activity. Skimming the grounds, she recognized most of the children. A few of the girls glanced up and squealed, "Miss Templeton!"

Encouraged by their reaction to her, Bailey strode confidently to the bell and gave it a resounding clang. At once a pack of ruddy-faced boys turned and stormed toward her, leading the others in the race. Realizing her need to act quickly, Bailey straightened her back and held up her hand in an authoritative gesture. "Please stop now!" She tightened her jaw and fixed her eyes on the largest of the boys, Cole Dobbins. "I said, *stop!*" she ordered unflinchingly.

The boys gathered around the steps below her and snickered. Dobbins stood staring contemptuously at her, his arms akimbo. Then running his fingers through his unkempt hair, he looked Bailey up and down, narrowing his eyes critically.

"Mr. Dobbins," she said firmly, "I want you to be an example to the others. You're the oldest, and therefore you've the greatest responsibility to walk a straighter line for the others to follow." She arched one fine eyebrow for emphasis. "You understand?"

Drinking in the eyes of all his amused chums, Dobbins whipped around and lifted a menacing knife in front of himself. "No, lady. I don't understand!"

<hr />

"Private Dade, I'm disappointed you didn't escort our new teacher to her class this morning. She was probably out before sunup. You realize the danger imposed upon an unescorted woman in this settlement?"

"O' course, sir." Dade tapped his heels against his horse's flanks to catch up with Captain Hogan's mount. "But you don't know wot you're askin'. This Miss Templeton ain't like one o' these British ladies. She's a bit headstrong—well, not just a bit—a lot more headstrong than most men I know, sir. She wouldn't let me escort her. I told her it was an order from the gov'ment office, and she said she weren't no officer, that's wot!"

"Why wouldn't she allow you to escort her?"

"She said it was her place to see that she made it safely to the schoolhouse every single day, an' if she didn't start now, she'd just have to start later. So there's no time like the present, an' all that. She made it all sound so right an' proper, why, before I know'd it, she had me convinced, sir." Dade bit his lip, a confused gaze darkening his face. "How you goin' to convince her otherwise, Captain Hogan? How you goin' to make Miss Templeton do wot you want?"

A confident gleam shone from Grant's eyes. "Dade, she's an employee of the government office. We hired her, so she must answer to us or risk dismissal. I'll have to speak to her myself, I see."

"You're a stronger man than me, Captain." Dade shook his head. "I'll admit as much!"

The dawn had lifted the bright orange sun just slightly above a whispering mist of haze. The thin vapor slowly dissipated, drawing back the veils of early morning. As if on cue, the sun winked over the schoolhouse roof in brilliant fingers of light. Hogan and Dade slowed their horses and gazed admirably toward the morning spectacle.

Closing his eyes, Hogan allowed the sun to warm his face and take the chill from his bones. Then returning his thoughts to the task before him, he brought his whip to flank and galloped toward the school, with Dade riding fast behind him.

The school yard quiet, they slowed their horses, hoping to enter unannounced.

"You think she's not goin' to make it, sir?" Dade asked quietly.

"I don't *wish* for her to fail, Dade, if that's what you're suggesting. I just know these emancipist children are impossible to control. That's why I've written England once more to tell them of our problem. If they find a male replacement, I'll have no choice except to replace Miss Templeton."

Pressing his mouth into a frown, Dade shrugged. "It'd be a pity, sir."

Stopping at the closed doorway, Hogan and Dade could hear children's voices drifting out through the open windows. Engaged in a corporate recitation, Miss Templeton appeared to have succeeded in bringing at least some semblance of order. Quietly turning the latch, Grant pushed open the door, but to his great consternation, the old hinges squeaked loudly. He cringed, then sighed when all heads turned to face him.

Surprised, Bailey's eyes fell upon him, and at once she poised herself for the interruption. "Captain Hogan!" she acknowledged with as much respect as she could muster on so short a notice. "Class, please greet our guest."

Most of the settlers' children, respectful of authority, complied with a quiet salutation to the officer. But the emancipists' children hated the military, and one by one they turned their backs in disgust and returned their attention to their teacher.

His face full of apology, Grant shook his head. "I'm sorry for interrupting, Miss Templeton."

"No need to apologize. Is there something we can do for you?" Maintaining control partly by her posture and partly by her attentive expression, Bailey leaned inquisitively toward him.

"No. It's simply that . . ." he hesitated. "I . . . I'll return during your mealtime."

"That would be a good time to return. Mrs. Johnson sent a basket of home-cooked food for me, and I'll never be able eat it all."

Grant's face reddened. "I wasn't inviting myself to dinner. I need to discuss—"

Some of the girls giggled, and one spoke out loud. "You come to call on our Miss Templeton?"

Now the entire classroom filled with sounds of laughter.

Displeasure marking her gaze, Bailey clapped her hands together. "Quiet, please. Captain Hogan is my employer, and he's seen to it that all of you have a proper school. From time to time, I suppose"—Bailey offered him a questioning glance—"the captain will drop in to see that we're all safe and sound." She allowed her eyes to remain fixed on him. "Is that correct, Captain Hogan?"

Hogan nodded mechanically. "Yes . . ." He paused, struggling to find the words. "I'm here to see that *all of you*"—he now pointed his eyes at her—"are safe and sound."

"Thank you." She didn't seem to notice his well-aimed comment. "Let's offer a kind farewell to Captain Hogan." Bailey planted a smile across her face. "You'll be returning at the dinner hour?" She lowered her face in a question.

"No. I mean, yes. That is, I feel we should discuss a few minor problems, but—" Grant heaved a heavy sigh—"but, yes, of course. If Mrs. Johnson has already provided the feast, I suppose we should honor her by eating it," he said resignedly.

"Very well." Bailey smiled woodenly. "We'll see you at half past eleven, then?"

Grant bowed slightly. "Half past eleven, it is." He turned and walked from the schoolroom to face a quite amused Private Dade. "Oh, shut up!" he muttered under his breath.

The small pocket watch on Bailey's desk ticked away toward the dinner hour more quickly than she wished, and Grant Hogan's surprise visit had left her more anxious than she wanted to admit. The morning had started off as a near disaster. It had been with great difficulty that she had step by step dragged the children through her planned morning ritual. Eventually, they had complied, but she realized that great changes in her methods would be forthcoming immediately. Three of the orphaned children she had found in the borough had shown up, if only to satisfy their curiosity. But her first admitted failure had been in dealing with the Dobbins boy. She recalled the cold horror she felt when he pulled his knife on her. In the few short months of teaching in one of London's worst rookeries, she had never had a student pull a knife on her. Desperately fighting the urge to run away herself, she had composed herself and made the only decision she knew to make. She had ordered him to go back home. A relief had washed through her when Cole shrugged indifferently and trudged away. But a new respect had settled across the faces of the students. If she had to sacrifice one boy's education for the good of the group, she knew instinctively that she would have to face the fact that she had no choice in the matter. *Perhaps later, Cole, I can give you another chance.* She hoped so.

"Miss Templeton?" A settler's daughter, Margaret, raised her hand.

"Yes, Margaret?"

"It's time to eat now. I'm hungry." Some of the others stirred restlessly, their gazes hopeful.

"Oh." Bailey glanced down at her watch. "So it is." She stood and glanced through one of the open windows. *Perhaps he won't show up.* "Donovan Farrell, would you lead us in a thankful blessing for our meal?"

The handsome boy stood and smiled. "Happy to oblige, Miss Templeton." His face full of quiet reverence, he bowed his head. "Thank you, Lord, for this your bounty. Please bless Miss Templeton and help Cole Dobbins to repent of his evil ways."

A ripple of mirth stirred throughout the room. Bailey pressed her lips together to stifle a smile.

"In the name of our Lord and Savior, Jesus Christ, Amen. Let's eat!" He grabbed the bundle from under his desk.

"Wait!" Bailey, quick to be the first to the doorway, called them once again to order. "Line up quietly. Girls first."

The boys groaned, and unaccustomed to respect for their gender, the girls looked at one another in wide-eyed wonder. One by one they stood, joined hands with best friends, and lined up at the door.

Bailey waited for the last student to leave the room. "Hungry, Donovan?" She smiled at her top pupil.

"Yes, Miss Templeton. And I want you to know, I'm glad you've come!"

"Thank you." She brightened upon hearing his compliment. "Now, if our Captain Hogan can see fit to allow me to stay."

Donovan laughed. "He's not such a bad sort, Miss Templeton. Really, he's not."

She rolled her eyes to show her good humor. But she was amazed at how the Farrells had such an affection for the man. After all, they were emancipists, and he was with the military. It was certainly one recipe that failed to mix, at least to her way of thinking.

Assured that all the students had assembled quietly beneath the shade of the spreading wattles surrounding the school yard, Bailey spread a cloth out on a mound of soft grass. Eagerly peeking inside the enormous basket of goodies, she beheld a sight that made her mouth water. She had prepared a small luncheon for herself of bread and cheese with a piece of fruit, but the aroma of apple pie and baked ham tantalized her senses. "Oh, dear Mrs. Johnson, we'll have to become the best of friends," she said aloud, laughing.

"Am I too late?" a voice called from behind.

Bailey stiffened upon hearing Grant Hogan's deep voice. "Why, no." She turned to face him and then pulled her skirts to one side to make room for the man. "Just in time, as a matter of fact."

"I feel I should apologize again for my intrusion upon your class." He dropped to one knee and aided her in spreading out the tablecloth she had found inside the basket.

Bailey shrugged and busied herself with placing the contents out upon the cloth. "You've every right to look in on me, Captain." She kept her eyes to task, not wanting to convey a shred of the slight resentment she privately harbored.

"I hope I didn't give that impression, Miss Templeton. I'm not the type to check up on our employees."

Noticing he tempered his words more so than ever, she felt her guard rising. "You said you needed to discuss some problems?" She sat back on her heels and awaited his answer. If she controlled the conversation, she had nothing to worry about.

"Yes, well . . ." He blew out a breath and pulled off his hat. "You certainly are quick and to the point, aren't you?"

"I didn't call this meeting between us, sir. But I feel I should be made aware of any obstacles before they become insurmountable—at the very least."

"Why don't we enjoy some of Mrs. Johnson's baked ham and fried potatoes beforehand?"

Biting her lip apprehensively, Bailey became suddenly mistrustful of his avoidance of the problems. But she could not bring herself to overplay her hand. Deciding to join him in the meal, she wondered if she could recover her appetite on such short notice. But the sight and the aroma of the food stirred her senses. "What a thoughtful person, this Mrs. Johnson. She's in-cluded everything—dishes, utensils, even a small bottle of apple cider." She made haste to fill two plates. "We've asked the bless-ing already."

Grant nodded, the light of humor glinting from his eyes. He chuckled quietly to himself.

"Something humorous, Captain?"

He shook his head immediately, as though he thought twice about revealing his thoughts.

"I love a good joke. You can share it—if you dare." She lifted her face imperiously.

"It's . . . well . . . when you've spent time in the classroom, you speak to everyone as though they're your students."

Surprised at his observation, Bailey's brow furrowed. "I do?" She felt her cheeks redden.

"Yes." He laughed his answer. "I feel as though I should sit up straight in my chair and raise my hand before eating."

Glancing obliquely toward the students who conversed quietly around the yard, she lowered her voice. "I'm sorry. I didn't realize. My brothers used to say the same exact thing."

"Did they?" He hungrily began consuming the thick slice of ham in front of him.

"Yes. I told them that *someone* had to put them in their place." She allowed a smile to play around the corners of her mouth.

Taken aback, Hogan stopped chewing long enough to allow her comment to settle into his thoughts. Swallowing first, he re-marked rather diffidently, "I'll have some more of that bread, with your permission, of course."

Bailey enjoyed the quiet bantering between them, but she didn't allow herself to enjoy it too much. It wasn't long before Cap-tain Hogan was sharing a bit of his family history. Immigrants from England, his parents had accepted the government's offer of free land in New South Wales. Already financially secure in his own right, Hogan's father soon launched a successful farm, one of Sydney Cove's first triumphs. It amazed her that such an affluent family would settle in the midst of so much poverty, and she said as much.

"My father knows opportunity when he sees it."

"What about you? Do you see potential in this godforsaken col-ony as well?" She poured them both another glass of cider.

"That's what brought me into the military. A military surgeon here agreed to allow me to study under him if I joined the military for two years."

"So you're not actually a military man born and bred?"

"Hardly." Grant shook his head. "Only by sheer force of will do I remain so. But this colony will be needing more surgeons, and I plan to set up a proper medical practice."

The news made Bailey take a second look at him. "Such a noble profession, Captain." She glanced down at the loaf of bread as she sliced two more pieces. "Almost as noble as teaching."

Wordlessly, Hogan gazed at Bailey.

Her eyes met his, and for the first time she saw something that caused her to rethink her opinion of him. She smiled back at him. "More bread?"

"Of course." He held out his plate.

The rest of the school day passed gratefully without incident. But an older boy stayed after class and stood anxiously waiting next to her desk. She recognized him as being one of the orphaned children. "Yes, let's see . . ." She studied his face. "You're Stephen?" She recalled his story. Abandoned at the harbor at the age of five, he had made his way in the settlement by begging.

Stephen nodded. "Yes, Miss Templeton."

"You need me?"

"I should tell you that the fellow you sent home—"

"Dobbins?"

"Cole, yes, ma'am. He's trouble, that one. I've run with him, and 'e's caused more problems than even our old teacher knew about. There's more, but—"

"Tell me, Stephen," Bailey sighed. "You may as well be out with it."

"He's not one to be run off by anyone. He'll come back later and . . ." Stephen began to stammer and his lids fluttered nervously.

"Stephen?" Bailey grasped his trembling hands.

"Yes, miss."

"I'm not afraid." She smiled faintly.

Soon the worried boy ran to catch up with the others, and Bailey gathered up all her belongings. One of the lads had watered her horse and given it a rest from the harness by tying it beneath a shade tree for the entire day. Before leaving, the horse and wagon had also been made ready. Encouraged by the goodwill of the children, Bailey felt she could return the next day and face anyone and anything if she had to. Even Cole Dobbins.

The late afternoon sky had darkened slightly, and Bailey realized she should hurry to escape a possible rain shower. Placing all her things beneath the bench seat next to Mrs. Johnson's basket, she unwrapped the reins and flicked them confidently.

Hearing the gallop of an approaching horse and rider, she quickly pulled back on the reins. "Whoa!"

"Miss Templeton!"

Bailey recognized the man she had come to call her ever present shadow. "Hello, Private Dade."

"Whew!" He was out of breath. "I thought I'd come too late. Captain Hogan would have me whipped for certain if I fouled up again."

"Fouled up? However could you have fouled up?"

"I was supposed to escort you this mornin'—"

"Dade, that was *my* decision. You've done nothing wrong." Bailey felt her ire rising.

"Just let me ride alongside you, Miss Templeton, so's I can say I done me job. Please, miss?"

She blew out an exasperated breath. "Forevermore, Dade!"

"Thank you, miss. It'll save me a world o' problems farther down the road."

Once more she surveyed the darkening sky. "We should hurry it up, then. We'll both be soaked soon if we don't."

Dade tipped his cap and elation swept over his face. "Off we go, then." He turned his bay mare at once and led the way. "We can stop halfway at the Farrells' place, if need be."

Almost enjoying the change in weather, Bailey pulled her shawl about her shoulders and gripped the reins firmly as the horse jerked the wagon forward. Recalling the somewhat pleasant luncheon with Captain Hogan made it difficult for her to be angry with him. *Perhaps that is his intent?* She analyzed their conversation and thought of how quickly he worked his way into having lunch with her. Disgruntled and too tired to debate Hogan's motives, Bailey began to plan out her next school day. If these students were to grasp even the fundamentals of learning, she thought with exasperation, then she would have to invent some creative measures to help them along the way.

A streak of lightning, followed by a rumble of thunder, warned of the approaching storm. Her thoughts now consumed with making fast her journey home, Bailey didn't notice the eyes that watched from the dense brush. She breathed a fast prayer for protection from the storm, not realizing a greater threat existed—one that she would never suspect.

5

THE MYSTERIOUS CAPTAIN GABRIEL

Drawing back the thick draperies that covered the room in her window, Bailey sat down to pen a letter to Laurie. She had absorbed herself so fully in the first weeks of school that ignoring the inevitable correspondence to her sister became routine. Seating herself on the only chair in the room, she pulled herself up close to the tiny table and stared blankly at the sheath of paper. After a moment of fidgeting, she reconciled herself to the task and began:

Dear Laurie,

Today is Saturday and I've stayed in a boardinghouse for my first four weeks in Sydney Cove. After much preparation, school has finally begun. Some of the parents, many actually, are quite suspicious of the government—many are former convicts. You can imagine the mistrust they have of their British jailers who are in command of the colony and of the school. It is for this reason that I had a difficult time convincing some of the parents that their children need an education. I have one student in particular who worries me a great deal. His name is Cole Dobbins. Please keep him in your prayers. He's not coming to school now, and I feel his future is doomed if he doesn't turn from the path he's chosen.

Australia's seasons are the exact opposite of those in the colonies. High summer occurs in January. The trees keep their leaves but shed their bark and are filled with squat brown birds that roar with laughter. The wild pocket-bellied beasts called kangaroos that we read about are no myth. I see them all around, although I can't bring myself to eat the meat that is so popular here in Sydney Cove.

But enough about my life here. You must imagine my surprise when I found your letter tucked inside my reticule. I had no idea of your interest in Gavin Drummond. I feel badly that you felt such a thing should be kept a secret from me, Laurie. We're sisters and nothing will ever—

Bailey stopped to compose her thoughts. Writing the letter was more difficult than she realized. She could see Gavin's handsome face as clearly as if he stood in the room with her. She remembered their first time alone at the picnic. Gavin had waded out into a pond to pick a water lily for her. That was when she had realized that Gavin was a special man. *Why, Gavin? Why did you have such an aversion to my teaching?* Recalling their first bitter argument about her going off to England to complete her studies caused her to relive that horrible day over again. Gavin had been so obstinate. He would be taking over his family's business and wanted his wife at his side. He asked her repeatedly why she couldn't be satisfied to stay at home. "Why can't you be content, Bailey?" The question tormented her. And now that she finally had exactly what she wished for, she would have to battle to keep it. Was this teaching position worth all the trouble she must go through? *Why did I come here, Lord? Have I missed your will—again?* But she could not lay out all of her confused emotions for Laurie to see. She wanted Laurie to be happy—not live in fear that her own sister still carried feelings for her husband. Laurie had every right to start her marriage untainted by uncertainties.

Bailey thought of the distance between them now. *Who would've thought that I would miss my own sister's wedding?* Not only was she not disappointed to miss the event, but she felt grateful that she would not be around to watch the happy couple's festivities. *I must convince her that I never truly loved Gavin*, she decided. Lifting the pen once more, she formulated the words in her mind and began to pen the phrases she knew Laurie and Gavin wanted to hear. With eyes moist, she devised the painful words that would ensure a happy future for her sister and a grievous world of eternal silence for herself.

"Miss Templeton? Miss Templeton?"

Bailey stared at the row of pickled vegetables. Lost in a quiet reverie, she shook herself free from her thoughts and turned to face the man who addressed her. "I'm sorry?" she said, putting on a polite smile. How long had she been standing in the government store, staring at the dusty rows of goods?

The sea captain nodded and tweaked his full beard. "Where are we today, miss? Somewhere other than here?"

Laughing quietly, Bailey shrugged. "Definitely not here, Captain Gabriel." Grasping her letter in her gloved hand, she adjusted her bonnet with the other. Then allowing him to grasp her hand in a chivalrous gesture, she returned his genuine smile. "So you're staying in Sydney Cove—for a month, did you say?"

"Actually about six more weeks. I'm awaiting a shipment of goods from England. Then it's out toward the Cape and on up to Rio de Janeiro."

"But your ship isn't actually a merchant ship, correct?"

"No. These goods are for the long journey. I've many passengers waiting to leave. Most will be aboard until we reach England."

Bailey contemplated his words. "I lived in England for a short time. I attended school there."

"You're welcome to come aboard, Miss Templeton, if you find Sydney Cove's not the place for you."

Bailey bit her lip and weighed his offer. If her job as a teacher was still unsecured in six weeks—*perhaps*. She allowed the thought to settle. *But, God, you would need to give me your assurance. . . .* She had to know without a doubt where His hand was guiding her. *If I've missed your voice once, then I don't wish to do so again.*

Gabriel laughed heartily. "Aye, is that wanderlust I see in your eyes, lass?"

She shook her head and answered somberly, "No. Not wanderlust. It's just . . . I'm not sure if I belong here, Captain. Most of all, I'm not certain that I'm wanted here." She hesitated, hating to admit her fear. "I might be asked to leave."

"They'd be losing the best. I can see that right away."

"You're much too kind." Bailey appreciated the man's encouraging words.

Turning to lean against a rack of wooden shelves, Gabriel sighed and stared at the floor.

She read his pained expression and reached out to touch his arm. "Something wrong?"

He rubbed his shoulder and squinted. "No. Fit as a blooming fiddle in most ways, but my arm begins to ache and gives me trouble at times."

"You're not old enough for rheumatism, are you?" She glanced obliquely toward him.

"May have a touch. But this one is an old injury." He waved his hand dismissively. "The story's too long."

"I love stories," she assured him. "What happened?"

"When a lad, I worked on ships as a cabinboy. Grew up on them. One day I fell into the sea."

Intrigued by the tale, Bailey pulled a stool up and sat facing the sea captain. "The fall—it broke your arm?"

"Not at all. Would've made it out all right, but—" He sighed, and his face reflected an inward pain.

"What happened?"

"Sharks appeared. The fleet was headed east and led by our ship, the *Sirius*. Headed for Africa, as best I can remember."

"Well, they pulled you aboard, of course?"

"Left me for dead, they did. Thought I was dead, I'm sure. I felt one of the makos tear into me and closed my eyes so I wouldn't have to see the water turn red with my own blood."

"How horrible!"

"Then something happened that caused some to say I was lucky. I call it a miracle."

Bailey remained mesmerized, her eyes never leaving the eyes of the sea captain.

"A seal appeared out of the blue. A few of the sharks continued to circle me, but I just kept telling myself not to move. Not a finger! It was a sight to see such a large, fat one out and swimming around like that. He was lost, most likely. Then the seal flipped its tail to make its retreat, but the movement alerted the largest beast. The monster dropped its bead on me like a hot potato. Making the first strike on the seal sent the other brutes into a frenzy. While they thrashed about on the poor creature, I made as little movement as possible and slowly swam away. But the *Sirius*, believing me dead, had hoisted sail and caught the wind for Africa. I lay for hours floating faceup. None of the other ships belonging to the fleet passed my way, and I was too weak to signal anyway."

Bailey arched a cynical brow. "Either you're making this up or someone rescued you." She rested her chin on her fists and waited eagerly for the conclusion.

Carefully rolling up one sleeve, the captain showed Bailey the scars above his forearm where the first shark had attacked him. "I was rescued, lass. A fishing boat spotted me. Could've been their fishing that attracted the seal. I don't know for certain. But I had lost so much blood that the captain didn't think I'd make it through the night. But I made it, God help me, I made it. And I stayed on with that captain until I was grown. I owed my life to him. Captain Amos Dawson, they called him."

"That's amazing." Bailey shook her head. "And the fleet's crew—they never knew?"

"I was a cabinboy. What was my worth to them?"

Pressing her lips together, Bailey thought of the emancipist children in the colony. "What is the worth of every child?" she whispered.

"Pardon me?"

"Nothing." She shook her head and slid off the stool. Straightening her skirt, she patted Captain Gabriel's shoulder. "I'm glad the good Lord looked after *this* child. You're a blessing to others, Captain. I'm glad to call you my friend." She straightened her back. "And I agree with you. You're a walking miracle."

"Look! It's Miss Templeton!"

Bailey turned about, surprised to hear her name called out like that. "Why, it's the Farrells." She beamed. Hooking her arm through the captain's, she lifted her face determinedly. "I've some friends for you to meet, Captain."

"I shan't intrude," he answered quietly and took a step back.

"I insist." Bailey's brow furrowed stubbornly and an impish smile dimpled her cheek. She made a friendly gesture for the Farrells to join them. "Hello, Mr. Farrell," she called out.

"Miss Templeton!" Dwight was quick to return her greeting. "Shopping our illustrious government stores, I see." Donovan and Jared, fast on his heels, ran around their father to greet their teacher.

"Illustrious?" She tucked her chin and pursed her lips primly. "I wouldn't say it's as well supplied as our store in Virginia."

"Very diplomatic of you, I'm sure."

They all laughed at the joke as they eyed the poorly stocked shelves.

"Mr. Farrell, I would like to introduce a new friend of mine. Meet Captain Gabriel. He commandeered the ship that brought me from America."

Extending his hand, Dwight offered a warm greeting. "A privilege, sir, I'm sure."

"And to you—Mr. Farrell, is it?"

"Yes. And these are my two sons, Donovan and Jared. I have a daughter, Corbin, at home with her mother. They're preparing a feast for us. Fresh roasted lamb." He stopped as if captured by a thought. "As a matter of fact, Miss Templeton, if you could join us for dinner, we would be so privileged. And you as well, Captain."

"I couldn't." Gabriel shook his head.

"And why not?" Bailey chastened encouragingly. "You're wandering the streets of Sydney Cove for the next six weeks, and then it's off for who knows where. I'll bet you haven't had a home-cooked meal in months."

Pressing his lips together, the captain shrugged in resignation. "Or perhaps years."

"It's settled then!" Dwight exclaimed buoyantly. "A feast at the Farrells. Half past six?"

Bailey nodded. "Agreed. That will give me just enough time to freshen up back in my room. And I daresay the boardinghouse fare leaves much to be desired." Facing Gabriel, she added, "You wouldn't mind escorting me, I hope. I can drive by and pick you up by five o'clock—but where?"

"I'll be here." He smiled broadly and stiffened his shoulders. "Sounds like a merry time. I'll bring the ale!"

Dwight winked at Bailey. "We'll look forward to tonight."

"Hooray! A party!" Jared cheered. "And it's not even Christmas."

"With your chilly June weather it feels like Christmas to me." Bailey shuddered.

Donovan pulled his younger brother's hat down over his eyes. "Good afternoon, Miss Templeton. We shall see you tonight." The Farrells made haste to be finished with their marketing.

Bailey rubbed her hands together. "Just what I've been needing." Her brows lifting inquisitively, she again addressed Captain Gabriel. "I hope this wasn't an imposition." She placed one finger against her lip, and her eyes narrowed. "My father says I can be a bit stubborn at times, although I strongly beg to differ."

Gabriel chuckled. "I'm grateful for the invitation, Miss Templeton. It's a lonely occupation I've chosen. It suits me, of course, but I'm glad to be in such grand company this night."

She was glad to see Gabriel smile. He had been such a serious man aboard ship, and at times forceful. For certain, he carried an air of mystery about him. Although they had made polite talk, she appreciated the bond of friendship that now formed between them. And if it appeared that she could not remain in Sydney Cove, she could always board his ship and make her next stop England. Her former professor had helped her gain this post, and perhaps he could assist with finding a better placement in England. A real position in a *real* school. He would not be surprised to find her returning so quickly and had stated as much.

The thought, however realistic she had intended, struck a sour note inside of her and rang with resounding guilt. Perhaps it was God's way of speaking to her, but she even wrestled with that thought. Hearing God's voice came so easily to some. She wondered if she would ever hear His clear call, and if so, would she reason it away as simply another act of self-will? Hurrying on her way to see that her letter was posted, Bailey made fast her farewells and then headed for the wagon once more. She stepped up into her buckboard and sighed. *I hope you want me here, Lord, I really do.*

The evening meal at Rose Hill and the exceptional hospitality more than satisfied Bailey. Having scarcely been in the colony for a month, she felt in a small way as though the Farrells had adopted her. She observed the children gathered around Gabriel and their fascination with his tales of the sea. Even young Shannon, Caleb and Kelsey's little girl, pushed her way between the others so she could listen. But in spite of the levity, Bailey had noticed that Katy had not entered into the evening's merriment. Instead, Rose Hill's hostess kept busy in the kitchen, even though she had an abundance of kitchen help. Lifting her cup to her lips, Bailey sipped a bit of hot cider and then set her cup and saucer aside. Standing quietly, she walked from the gaiety of the parlor and found her way to the warmth of the kitchen. Peering inside, she saw Katy standing in front of the window looking out over their fields. Her arms folded above her waist, she stared out into the faceless night, her usual serenity darkened by melancholy.

"Mrs. Farrell?" Bailey spoke gently, not wishing to offend the woman.

"Oh, hello, Bailey. I'm sorry." She turned and walked to greet her. "I've been a terrible hostess this evening. Please forgive me?"

"You've been wonderful." Bailey shook her head, her brown eyes fixed on Katy's. "So wonderful, in fact, that we've scarcely seen you."

Katy blew out an exasperated breath. "I should be ashamed."

"No. Don't be. But if there's anything I can do . . ." She waited, not wanting to invade Katy Farrell's quiet solitude. "I'm a woman—if that would help?" She smiled hesitantly, her eyes reflective of the sympathy she felt.

Katy chuckled. "Nothing like that. I'm . . . I'm not sure. I've been so restless of late."

Bailey remembered the argument she had overheard between Katy and Dwight the first day she arrived. "I suppose the ranch keeps Mr. Farrell quite busy?"

Katy lifted her eyes but did not respond right away. Stopping a maid as she went by, Katy quickly lifted a tart from the platter. "One for you?"

Shaking her head, Bailey held her stomach. "I couldn't hold another bite, thank you." Seeing the distant pain in Katy's eyes, she drew closer. "I'm sorry. I shouldn't have followed you back here." She turned to leave, but Katy stopped her.

"Please don't leave." Katy shook her head and took a small bite of the tart. "Come. Join me on the back steps. You've your wrap? We'll talk." She offered a knowing glance. "You're such a discerning young woman," she said, lifting a cloth napkin from a table as she led Bailey outside.

Following her straightaway, Bailey listened while Katy explained how her parents' transportation sentence had brought their family to New South Wales. Caleb had been born aboard ship. Katy, a child at the time, had worked for the fleet's commander, Arthur Phillip. Over the years, Katy's father, George Prentice, had met with many failures in the colony, as had most of the emancipists who had stayed to settle. But eventually his perseverance had won out, and they had acquired Rose Hill.

The two of them seated themselves on the steps, pulling their wraps about their shoulders.

"But your father died?"

Surprised at first, understanding burgeoned in Katy's eyes. "The boys told you."

Nodding, Bailey smiled. "Donovan. I asked the students to write about how they came to live in New South Wales. It really gave me an understanding of the hardships their families have faced."

"What a wonderful way to allow them to express themselves." Wrapping the remainder of the pastry in her napkin, Katy added, "We're so thankful to have you here." She rested her hand upon Bailey's knee. "But I understand it may be short-lived?"

"Yes, but I'm not worried. I believe the Lord is guiding me, and if He wants me to return to England—or to America—I'll go."

"Please don't be so hasty. Grant realizes his decisions affect the entire colony. That burden is misinterpreted at times. Some see only a tough exterior, but I believe he really cares."

"Yes, I see that in him to a small degree." Bailey clasped her hands at her knees. "Though I must admit I have my reservations about the man." Inhaling a draft of fresh air, she lightened her tone. "But I'm supposed to be cheering you up."

"You have. I swear it." Katy did not smile, but her manner appeared more relaxed.

Bailey studied the lovely woman's fine patrician features. She couldn't imagine her or any of the others aboard one of those horrible transports. "So you actually are not an emancipist? But your parents—they were transported?"

Katy nodded, indifferent, as though she had related the story on numerous occasions. "My husband is an emancipist, and so is Caleb's wife, Kelsey."

"So with all of your hardships, I suppose your husband is determined to see you don't relive any of those days."

Katy lifted her eyes to the stars and then back at Bailey. "You're observant, aren't you?" She smiled. "Too observant."

"If society would allow, I'd be a barrister." Bailey followed her gaze into the chilly night sky.

Katy continued quietly. "Dwight is a good man. I love him. But I do wish our farm did not demand so much of his time. I realize that any other woman in the borough would relish my problems." They both sat quietly, listening to their own thoughts and allowing their minds to absorb the silent affinity that had formed between them. "I suppose we should join our party before someone becomes suspicious." Katy shook out the folds of her gown.

"Captain Gabriel"—Bailey bit her bottom lip—"probably believes I've abandoned him."

"And that's quite another matter . . . this Captain Gabriel."

"What about him?" Bailey reached into Katy's napkin and pinched off a piece of the pastry.

"Please don't misunderstand. I appreciate the way he's been so attentive with the children, but he reminds me of someone, that's all." Her voice waned, and she looked away.

"You know him?" Bailey asked.

"No. Not him," Katy assured. "It's his mannerisms . . . and his eyes. I knew someone so like him, but it was long ago. Someone who saved my life aboard the First Fleet."

"He's not from here." Bailey wrapped her arms around her shoulders, feeling the chill through her woolen wrap. "He's worked aboard ships since he was young, or so he tells me. You know how these tales grow more with each telling."

"Interesting." Bailey's words piqued Katy's curiosity. "You say he's worked aboard ships?"

"A cabinboy. He says he fell overboard and was left for dead." Bailey watched as a strange, undefined emotion spread across Katy's face.

"But his name's Gabriel?"

"Yes, Captain Robert Gabriel." Bailey noticed the way in which Katy's brow furrowed. Her voice changed and she was no longer as relaxed. "What is it?"

"*Robert?*"

"What's wrong, Katy?"

"It can't be him. It can't—" Katy maintained her poise, but her voice broke off in midsentence.

Bailey felt awkward seeing the discomfort of Katy's emotions, but she didn't know how she should respond.

"Dear Lord—" Nervously clasping her hands around the napkin, Katy narrowed her eyes.

Pushing herself from the steps, Bailey's eyes widened with concern. "Have I done something wrong in bringing him here?"

"No. I'm wrong about him, I'm certain. It's so silly of me—impossible actually." Katy came to her feet, and they both stood silently for a moment.

"If you feel you know Robert Gabriel, then why not ask him?" Placing her hands gently on each of Katy's shoulders, Bailey kept her tone moderate.

At that moment Katy turned her face purposefully toward the inside of the house. "Walk with me, Bailey. I'm frightened."

Without knowing why, Bailey also felt frightened. She placed her arm around Katy and followed her through the house. When they entered the parlor, Captain Gabriel had launched into another of his stories. Caleb, Dwight, and Katy's mother, Amelia, sat eagerly attentive and smiling at his dramatizations.

"And it was then that I eyed the pirate without a blink!" Folding his arms across his chest, Gabriel crouched low for the children's sake. "And he fainted dead away, and the ship and crew were saved!" Ending on a triumphant note sent the children into cheers and spontaneous applause.

"It has to be—" Katy whispered under her breath.

Bailey smiled at the captain, and he in turn bowed before her and Katy with a flourish.

"Bravo, sir," she said quietly but kept her eyes on Katy.

"Children?" Katy drew their attention.

"Yes, ma'am?" Jared pulled his little sister into his lap.

"I've a story now. I've told you all about a young man who saved my life aboard the transport from England. Do you recall?" She waited for each to nod.

Bailey now watched Robert Gabriel's face.

"Was it you, sir?" Katy stepped toward him. "Did you save the life of a girl named Katy Prentice? Are you the cabinboy from the *Sirius*?"

Bailey recognized the ship's name at once, and her mouth fell open. "Katy?" she gasped.

"If it isn't so, then put my mind to rest so that I may quell such foolishness in my mind."

In disbelief, Dwight shook his head at his wife. "Katy, our guests—"

Slowly turning his cap in his hand, Robert straightened his back, then ran one hand down his full beard. Katy continued, "I saw you first in your little boy's eyes. But when I walked through the door, I knew it was no mistake."

"Oh, dear—"

Bailey stepped away as Katy hastened toward him.

"It is I," he confessed, his eyes cast down and his voice uncharacteristically low. "Sir Robert."

Tears blinding her eyes and choking her voice, Katy said, "I've buried your memory so many times." A trembling smile forced its

71

way onto her lips. "But you've risen from the dead," she said with a note of questioning in her tone. Then she moved quickly to him and threw her arms about his shoulders. "You're alive, Robert!"

Bailey, stunned at the display, watched as the children gathered around them. Instinctively, Robert patted Katy to comfort her.

"It's all right, Lady Katherine. Please don't cry. I can't bear it—" His voice broke off.

Turning to watch the others' faces, Bailey mechanically gathered up a few cups and saucers. "This is all so—amazing!" She stopped when she detected the anxiety on Dwight's countenance. "Dwight!" she whispered, half in apology, half in sympathy.

"I'll take those." He collected the dishes from Bailey's hands. "I wouldn't want to interrupt the reunion. . . ." His voice trailed off in sinking tones. "We've reason to celebrate."

Helplessly, Bailey watched him disappear into the kitchen. She wanted to follow him, but Katy's sobs stirred her to stay. Feeling partly responsible for having brought Robert Gabriel to Rose Hill, she felt mixed emotions wash through her. She walked to Amelia's side and clasped her hands. "What do we do now, Amelia?"

Her face tear-streaked, Amelia gripped Bailey's hands firmly. "Pray, girl, pray!"

6

THE CHURCH SOCIAL

For the next two months, the temperatures warmed and would have been pleasant had it not been for the unbearable odors inside the poorly ventilated old boardinghouse. Bailey took all of her belongings and moved into a one-room house. With a little help from Grant Hogan, she had secured the house and a small plot of ground. It was a wattle-and-daub affair constructed of wood and mud. Its leaky roof during a rainstorm was maddening, and she could not decide whether to keep collecting containers to catch the rainwater or continue the futile effort of trying to patch the roof. She had become adept at climbing a homemade ladder built of small shaven tree trunks and scrambling up onto the roof. With a patching compound she had made herself, she filled as many holes as she could find before the next storm came and revealed new ones. Her family would have laughed at the sight, but she had seen various other ladies of the colony accomplishing far more masculine tasks—one woman hand-plowed her fields while her husband slept off a drunken stupor.

Standing out in front of the almost humorous-looking structure, Bailey eyed it speculatively. With her meager teaching allowance, she could make no improvements. It had taken all the money she could muster just to stock the larder. But she mulled over a thought in her mind. If she raised a little livestock, she could possibly bring in the extra income needed. And if forced to return to England, it would be in her favor to arrive with her finances well intact. *But how?* Getting livestock from the controlling gentry would be quite another matter. England had not begun this colony with a proper monetary system. She was told the silver that Parliament had once sent to stabilize the fragile economy was immediately whisked out due to the imbalance of trade. The currency now sparsely circulated throughout the citizenry filtered in through the foreign sailors who passed in and out of the harbor. Coinage of every kind had become the accepted medium of exchange. Governor Bligh, in his effort to provide a swift cure for the colony's ills, declared the British copper penny worth twopence. The more Bailey heard about this Governor Bligh, the more she questioned his methods.

"Miss Templeton, look!"

Startled, Bailey whirled around. Seeing no one, she quickly glanced down and smiled at the visitor who appeared so suddenly. "Hello, Jared," she said to Katy's young son.

The boy stood beaming, a trace of breakfast at the corners of his mouth. Holding out his arms, which cradled a squirming puppy, he held it up for her to see. "I saw how you liked our sheep dog, Arthur, so Father said it would be all right if I brought you one of our pups. He's just been weaned today." Jared grinned proudly.

Bailey's brows lifted in a sympathetic reaction to his amiable gesture. "How thoughtful." She bit her lip. She could barely feed herself. How would she feed a puppy? "But I'm away all day at the school. I'm afraid your puppy would get terribly lonely. Perhaps you should give it to someone else, don't you think?"

Adamantly, Jared shook his head. "No, ma'am. This pup is just for you. He can come to school with you. *I'll* help keep him company."

Bailey couldn't help but chuckle. "A dog at school? Now, wouldn't that be a—" She stopped, the disappointment in his eyes too much to bear. "Oh, Jared." She sighed. "If I *could* keep him— and I'm not saying that I can—what would I name him?"

"How about *Stubborn*?" A deep, rumbling voice startled her.

Straightening at once, Bailey saw that Grant Hogan had been

74

standing a few feet away all along. "Captain Hogan?" She acknowledged him with some reservation.

Striding toward them both, Grant scooped the puppy out of Jared's arms. "Come here, fella." Stroking the little dog's head, he sighed and gazed wordlessly at Bailey.

"Captain Hogan, it isn't that I'm not appreciative . . ." She hesitated, feeling her words sounded shallow, more like she was offering an excuse. Her eyes met his. A faint light twinkled in the depths of his green eyes. But not one to be taken in by unexpected charm, Bailey kept a polite distance. She did admit to herself that her respect for the captain had grown. His take-charge manner, though annoying to her, indicated he was a man who would stay to his course no matter how adverse the winds of life might buffet him. He was a naval officer now, but soon he would be a surgeon. He knew where he was going and had a plan to keep him there. She felt compelled to search his eyes once more and found in them a light of amusement. He stood holding out the sheep dog pup to her.

"Oh, all right!" She blew out an impatient breath. "Let me hold the little fellow." She succumbed to the man's compelling gaze, wondering if perhaps she had given in to what Dade had called his "spell over women." Nuzzling the fluffy black pup underneath her chin, she smiled at the way the little dog snugged against her. Lifting her face, she found Hogan still looking at her. His eyes, warm and green and flecked like malachite, gazed openly, full of expectation. He appeared to study her now, but for what reason, she was hesitant to determine. "Young Mr. Farrell—" She turned quickly to address the boy. In a moment of weakness, she succumbed to his offer. "I've most certainly been needing a dog all along. I'll accept your generous gift. Thank you."

Jared returned her smile and crossed his arms with supreme satisfaction. He stroked the dog once more and then coaxed it back into his own arms.

"I was wondering how you arrived, young man." She arched one brow, glancing sideways at Grant Hogan. "Now I know."

"I'm taking him fishing," Grant offered nonchalantly. "Dwight's gone out to tend to one of his flocks, so I told Katy I'd take the lad out to wet his line."

Bailey recalled the problems between the Farrells but held her words. "You're quite close to the Prentice family, aren't you?"

"And why wouldn't I be? Aunt Amelia's been like a mother to me."

"*Aunt?*" Slowly inhaling, Bailey clasped her hands together. Sudden realization struck her mind. Was it any wonder that she and Katy Farrell agreed on most matters except those relating to Grant Hogan's handling of the school? "You're Katy's cousin? And Caleb's?"

"You had to find out sooner or later." Nodding slightly, Grant scuffed Jared's jaw affectionately with his knuckles. "They didn't want you to feel as though you had to show favoritism to their sons."

"As if I would." Bailey crossed her arms and lowered her face. Walking in a slow half circle, she gazed across the wilderness landscape. "What would give me cause to show any bias? Because the boys have *you* for an uncle?"

Scratching the top of his head, Grant narrowed his eyes but couldn't suppress the faint trace of humor. "Well, yes, because I— surely you understand?"

Seeing his expression pleading for her relief, she finally smiled and nodded. "All right. But you shouldn't feel you need to keep such details from me. I can manage better than you realize."

"So you've expressed. The colony's respect for you, Miss Templeton, has certainly grown," he finally admitted, his deep, velvet tones laden with respect.

Surprised, she felt a warmth run through her. True, he hadn't spoken the words she had often longed to hear him say—that she had a permanent place in the school. And until now, he certainly had offered little in the way of encouragement. But today it wasn't his assurances that surprised her, but rather his smiling eyes that said more than mere words. However much she had been warned about Grant Hogan, she found herself finding more reason to continue her conversation with him. "Getting back to the matter at hand . . ." She paused. "What should I name him?" Gently, she took the puppy back into her arms.

Not taking his eyes off hers, Grant reached to stroke the dog's soft furry head. His fingers brushing across its back, he lightly ran them across the top of Bailey's hand where she held the pup against herself. Quietly, he answered, "As I suggested earlier— *Stubborn.*"

She swallowed hard, wondering if he had intended to touch her so. Feeling her cheeks redden, she dared not admit even to herself that she had found the least bit of pleasure in it. The last thing she desired was another willful man pulling on her emotions. But his vitality drew her like magnetism. Biting the side of her mouth, she shook her head slightly, then choosing to ignore his pointed observance, she answered him in the same quiet voice. "We couldn't saddle it with such a label. What if we're wrong about it?" Not sure of what she had just said, she studied his face intently.

Grant reached out and stroked the pup again, and once again his hand slid slightly over the top of hers. "You're right," he answered forthrightly. "Making a snap judgment upon first sight is unfair. Isn't it, Miss Templeton?"

Bailey's lashes flew up.

Grant took a step back. "Jared, what would you name this little fellow?"

Bailey kept her gaze on the puppy, hoping her eyes had not betrayed her baffled thoughts.

"He has a noble face. How about a noble name?"

Jared's face grew thoughtful. "Such as Lord Blackie?"

Studying the pup's striking black face, Bailey addressed the little beast with reserved theatrics. "So be it. We dub thee Lord Blackie!"

Grant nodded. "It fits."

"Just feed him scraps from your table. He'll eat anything." Jared held up both hands.

"Why don't you fetch some water for Lord Blackie?" Grant smiled at the young boy. Bailey set the pup onto the ground and watched as it romped after the lad toward the well. Crossing her arms across her bodice, she pursed her lips and looked up at Grant once more. Lifting a cynical brow, she said with slight amusement, "Just what I needed. Another mouth to feed."

"It'll grow to be a fine watchdog. You'll see."

"I should be so lucky to remain here that long. Or have you forgotten, Captain Hogan?"

He shifted uncomfortably from one foot to the other. "Please, could you . . ."

Surprised by his change in demeanor, Bailey arched one brow suspiciously. She had never recalled seeing him so at a loss for words.

Finally, he requested, "I would prefer that you call me Grant." He was the one who now looked away. "Captain Hogan sounds so . . . formal."

A faint smile creasing her cheeks, Bailey held her words. Although enlivened by the friendly gesture, she couldn't help but feel it wise to heed Dade's warnings. Taking a deep breath, she allowed her silence to force a further explanation on his part.

"That is, away from the school and the government building, I'm not one to stand on ceremony."

"But our positions dictate such, Captain Hogan," she answered soberly. Watching his face, she realized she had perhaps chosen the wrong response.

Taken aback, Grant lifted his face but maintained a cool demeanor. "Well, then, Miss Templeton, pardon my lack of protocol." He took a step back. "My mistake."

Now, why did you say that? Bailey had never wanted to recall her words so desperately as she did this moment. But standing toe to toe with this unyielding man seemed to bring out the worst in her. "I . . ." She nervously clasped her hands in front of her. "Well, here comes Jared." She thought she detected a hint of pain in his eyes, but saying anything now might only worsen the situation.

"So I see." Tipping his hat, Grant started for the wagon. "Jared, if we're to catch the early fish schools, we'd best be on our way."

"Did you ask her?" The lad spoke without inhibition.

"Ask me what?" Bailey inquired, curious about the surprise on Hogan's face.

Aiming the boy in the opposite direction, he said flatly, "Nothing. That is, women care nothing for fishing, Jared. Let's be off!"

Smiling woodenly, Bailey acknowledged the boy once more. "Thank you for the . . . puppy, Jared." She took the little dog back into her arms. "Good-bye . . ." She hesitated and then whispered so only she could hear, *"Grant."* The wagon pulled away, and Bailey waved in a friendly manner. But as they drove out of sight, she stamped the ground in frustration.

⬥

Sunday arose with a radiant August sunrise signaling the waning of the Australian winter. Bailey quickly tended to her horse while a kettle of water simmered on the fire. She would still have time for a quick bath and her morning Bible devotions if she hurried. Ashamed to admit it, she had not attended church services since her arrival in Sydney Cove. What with all the hustle and bustle of opening the school, she had scarcely had enough time to prepare her weekly lessons and often had to complete them on Sunday. But eventually working her way into a routine, she started planning out her schedule every Friday before returning home. As her mother had often said, "There's always time for church." Today she looked forward to joining the Farrells and the Prentices at the small church they attended.

Bustling past her small garden plot, she glanced quickly toward the little picket fence she had erected. "What in the wor—" She froze. The small fence posts had each been unearthed and tossed into the garden. What seedling vegetable plants had not been smashed by the fence had been uprooted. Judging by the way the fence posts had been hurled all over the garden, it was not the work of an animal. She stood staring with her arms akimbo for a moment. Then anger ignited inside of her, which was followed immediately by a sense of sadness, not only for her loss but for the one who had done this thing. She glanced all around, hoping to see the culprit fleeing the scene. Walking the perimeter of the plot, she studied the ground. The grassy land showed a few footprints. But she'd had visitors this week who had come to welcome her as the new teacher, and she couldn't recall if anyone had been standing around the garden.

Lord Blackie yipped at her heels, and she turned to shake her head at him. "Some guard dog you turned out to be!" The pup whimpered at her, his tail vibrating like an insect wing. Chuckling, she stooped down to stroke him behind his ears. "Oh, I can't even be mad at you. You're much too cute. Let's go inside for breakfast." She sighed. "I'll clean this up after church."

The ride to the church building served to clear her mind and aid her in meditating upon her morning devotional. Reading from the Psalms, she had found to her surprise that her selected reading had been tailored to her morning. "Fret not thyself because of evildoers, neither be thou envious against workers of iniquity. For they shall soon be cut down like the grass, and wither as the green herb. Trust in the Lord, and do good; so shalt thou dwell in the land, and verily thou shalt be fed. Delight thyself also in the Lord; and he shall give thee the desires of thine heart. Commit thy way unto the Lord; trust also in him; and he shall bring it to pass. And he shall bring forth thy righteousness as the light, and thy judgment as the noonday."

It was not long until she saw other carriages ahead and a few drawing up close behind her. She could tell by the respectable attire of the carriage occupants that their destination was church. *I must be headed the right way.* The little shanty used for the church service bustled with activity. Walking around the grounds, Bailey chatted with some of the women. They were simple people, most ill-educated, she judged, by their poor use of the King's English. But she sensed a tenacity in most of them that she truly admired. Following one of the families up the steps, she was greeted at once by the handsome minister who stood in the doorway, extending his hand to all the new arrivals.

"Hello. Welcome to you!" He smiled, his white teeth flashing from a tanned face.

Bailey loved the minister's enthusiasm. "Hello, Reverend Whitley." She remembered him well from the school meeting held at his home.

"Ah, why, it is our very own new schoolmistress."

"Bailey Templeton," she answered sprightly.

"I remember. Please, Rachel will be so elated to see you again." Turning, he called toward a group of chattering women. "Rachel, dear?"

A red-haired beauty turned her face toward them both. "Yes, love?" She walked toward Reverend Whitley.

"Look who has finally come. Miss Templeton."

Grasping Bailey's hand, Rachel Whitley greeted her warmly, never taking her eyes from her. "Katy's told me so much about you. And my two oldest will be starting your school next year—if I can part with them, that is."

"How many children do you have, Reverend?" Bailey asked with interest. "I've forgotten already."

"Three. Our youngest, Jake, is behind you now."

Bailey twisted around and found a toddler staggering toward her. She reached out to clasp his pudgy hands. "Easy, Jake!" She laughed. Walking him to his mother, she admired his curly red locks. "I see he's blessed with your lovely hair, Mrs. Whitley."

"Poor child." She frowned. "It's a curse, I believe."

"Rachel, don't say such things," the minister chided affectionately. "You'll taint him."

The wooden benches filled up quickly, and Reverend Heath Whitley mounted the rustic podium. "I'll first offer our thanks to God for keeping His hand on us. Then our good Captain Hogan will start our meeting with a song."

In silent amazement, Bailey watched as Grant Hogan entered

from a side door. *And he a known scoundrel!* As quickly as the thought had emerged, she felt a pang of guilt.

Following Reverend Whitley's prayer, Hogan stepped confidently up to the podium. His uniform freshly pressed and his long, dark hair combed neatly into a queue, he struck an impressive pose on the platform. Bailey shifted uneasily in her seat. Growing up in a musically gifted family, she had a natural ear for music. Having seen very little nurturing of such gifts in the colony, she grudgingly prepared to suffer through the worship service.

"The book of Ephesians tells us to not be drunk with wine, but to be filled with the Spirit; speaking to yourselves in psalms and hymns and spiritual songs, singing and making melody in your heart to the Lord. Let us now join together in making a joyful melody by singing, 'Come, We That Love the Lord.'" Grant gestured with both hands, inviting the congregation to stand.

Bailey stood with the others, but she could hardly open her mouth. *He knows the Scriptures?* Her brow furrowed and she glanced sideways at the Farrells, who had seated themselves next to her. Katy smiled up at her cousin and then tapped the boys' shoulders on either side of her to encourage them to join in song. Bailey had already decided that Katy Farrell was blinded by family ties.

Come, we that love the Lord, and let our joys be known;
Join in a song with sweet accord, and thus surround the throne.

Her mouth scarcely moving, Bailey listened intently to the smooth baritone voice that led them in song. Grant Hogan's voice was neither a disappointment nor something to be suffered through as she had feared. But rather, he had a beautiful, commanding voice that rang out in perfect pitch. Bailey, somewhat familiar with the hymn, joined in lifting her high soprano voice along with the others.

Let those refuse to sing who never knew our God;
But children of the heav'nly King may speak their joys abroad.
Then let our songs abound and ev'ry tear be dry;
We're marching thru Emmanuel's ground to fairer worlds on high.

A sense of peace swept through Bailey as she sang. She had not realized what she had been missing over the last few weeks. In a short amount of time, she had allowed her faith to stagnate. She breathed a silent prayer of contrition and then studied Grant Hogan's face. His exuberance was admirable, but she wanted to see something beyond enthusiasm. She had seen many gifted talents parade through the church over the past few years—those who had a natural platform ability and the personality to match. But without fail there were the few who simply used the church as their personal stage to flaunt their abilities. Their desire to serve God and His flock was immaterial. As much as she cringed when a weak singer took the platform, she was equally distressed when an insincere talent commanded the assemblage. Then an odd thought pricked at her emotions. *No matter what the man does, I stand in judgment of him.* She felt shame sweep through her.

Glancing to her right, she saw someone moving swiftly toward her. Curious to see who would arrive so late, she realized with surprise that Lieutenant Evans had come to church. Without so much as a blink, he excused his way around the only couple at the end of Bailey's bench. Removing his hat, he smiled at her and took his place next to her. Lifting her brows, she nodded at the attractive officer, slightly amused at the determination in his face. Captain Grant Hogan could in no way find a task for him now.

Grant finished with the song, led them in another, and then quietly took a seat on one of the front-row benches. Bailey wondered curiously if he had noticed that Evans had joined her.

Reverend Heath Whitley delivered a powerful sermon from the book of Second Peter. Exhorting each of them to be watchful of ambitious men who would tickle their ears with words they desired to hear, he challenged the listeners to be diligent in their own knowledge of the Bible and not to rely on another to feed them their weekly dose of faith. Bailey knew right away that she had found the right church.

"Miss Templeton?" Evans said quietly when the concluding prayer dismissed the congregation.

"Yes? How are you, Lieutenant?" Bailey glanced quickly toward the front bench and then back at Evans. He nodded pleasantly, and she recalled at once the night at the boardinghouse. "Lieutenant, I owe you an apology."

"No apologies needed," he answered in a husky tone, his eyes sparkling with confidence. He stood tall in uniform, a formal contrast against the rustic church interior. "My mother's fixed up a big picnic basket, and I'd be pleased if you would join me here on the grounds for the picnic today."

"There's a picnic today?"

"Reverend Whitley announced it last week."

Glancing once again at the front pew, Bailey saw that Grant had disappeared. "Oh, well, that makes perfect sense. Today's service is the first I've been able to attend."

"She baked up a lot o' her better things. It's a right nice picnic."

Her mind temporarily wandering, Bailey gazed curiously at the man. Then remembering why he stood there smiling at her, she shook herself. "Oh, the picnic. Why—" She hesitated, and the thought struck her, *Was Grant trying to invite me to this picnic himself?* She had unwittingly spoiled his attempt to cultivate their relationship. Resignedly, she answered Evans. "Of course I'll join you. Are your parents here today?"

"They usually come, but they've a cow that's givin' birth this morning. Been up all night with it."

"I see. Your parents are farmers?"

"Yes. They own a large spread of land. I own a large tract myself." He smiled broadly.

Bailey admired his affable manner and his blue eyes that sparkled when he spoke, giving him an almost angelic appeal. She wondered about his faith but knew that as time passed she would come to know more about the young officer.

"Shall we go, then?" He offered his arm. "The picnic's waitin' all done up and out in me wagon."

The day could not have been more perfect, Bailey decided. She and Evans looked around the grounds and spied the Farrells and Prentices spreading their blanket beneath a large flowering myrtle. "Over there." She pointed with her eyes. "There's a good cool shade." She tried to tell herself that she simply enjoyed the company of her newfound friends. But she also chided herself. She knew in her heart of the likelihood that they would be joined by a certain naval officer from their family.

"Bailey Templeton!" Katy waved her toward them. "Join us, please!"

Jared ran and threw his arms around her skirt. "You like the pup, Miss Templeton? Is he bein' a good fellow?"

Bailey nodded. "Yes, but we've much to teach Lord Blackie. Someone tore up my garden and fence last night while the young *lord* slept."

Looking concerned, Katy crossed her arms, her chin lowered. "Did they steal anything?"

"Nothing. That's almost more disturbing, isn't it?" Bailey

spread the lieutenant's blanket next to Katy's while Evans hoisted the basket onto it.

"But you're so new to the settlement. Who would commit such a deliberate act of malice?" Settling her sleepy toddler onto a pillow, Katy gestured for Bailey and Evans to join her. "Dwight?" She called to her husband, who had gathered with a group of men.

When he did not respond, Katy sighed. "I'll tell him later. When he involves himself in one of those political talks, he's impossible to deter."

Bailey could not help but notice the slight hint of contempt in Katy's tone. "So," she said airily, hoping to lighten the conversation, "are your boys enjoying school?"

"As always, Donovan loves school, and Jared would rather go fishing." Katy opened a jar of pickled vegetables but turned her eyes warily toward her husband. "If you can ever interest Jared in reading a book, I'll pay you a month's worth of egg money."

"So where is your indomitable cousin today?" Evans asked Katy while he glanced around the grounds.

"Good question. He sang in church and then disappeared. He's not one for large groups. He may have walked down to the stream not far from here. But he'll smell the food and come begging soon. He always does."

Keeping her tone casual, Bailey asked, "Has he always had such a strong singing voice?"

"Always. His mother said he grew up singing everywhere they went."

"It's unusual to hear such talent so far off the beaten track," Bailey added reflectively.

Katy's mouth curved into an unconscious smile. "Sydney Cove's not running over with great genius, if that's what you mean. But we have a few blessings. The Whitleys are remarkable folks. We're fortunate to have such a gifted minister."

"And wasn't his message poignant?" Bailey directed her eyes toward Evans, curious at his reaction.

"Quite." Evans nodded, his face sober. "I need to study Second Peter again. That's why I respect Reverend Whitley so much. He challenges our hearts."

Her eyes alight with approval, Bailey agreed with him and felt relieved that she was keeping company on this day with a man of faith.

"Oh, look." Katy nodded toward the tract of land behind the

church. "There's my rascal of a cousin now."

Evans laughed. "And, as always, with a lady on his arm."

Bailey, not thinking, whirled around. "Where?" But she didn't have to be shown, for she saw Captain Hogan at once. He had taken a stroll to the stream, all right, but not alone. A lovely young woman walked beside him, laughing quietly at his comments. He carried her basket at his side, and much to Bailey's chagrin, they were making their way toward them. "Well"—she struggled to maintain a calm composure—"we'll enjoy chatting with them as well." Not wanting to show any disapproval, she engaged Katy in further conversation. "Katy, what has happened to our friend Captain Gabriel?" She bit her lip, hoping the subject wasn't a sensitive one.

Her face beaming, Katy smiled. "Wasn't that the most remarkable thing, Bailey? It's as though he was brought here by the hand of God."

"But he's leaving soon, correct?"

"No. He's traded commissions with another captain. Not by his own doing, of course. But the other commander had family in England and desired to leave at once. Robert will be staying for months. We feel so fortunate. It would have been such a shame for him to have *returned from the grave*, so to speak, and then have him taken away from us again. And the children so love him."

Feeling a strange prickling at the nape of her neck, Bailey took a deep breath and held her words. She could see by Katy's enchanted expression that the children were not the only ones enthralled with Captain Robert Gabriel.

"He would've joined us here today, but he had matters to attend to at the harbor." Her eyes once again shot sharp arrows toward her husband, but then turning to look at Bailey, her brittle smile softened. "Just between us, Dwight's having a bit of trouble kindling a friendship with Robert."

"Katy, I can understand such a thing." Bailey's fears finally spilled out into words. "Your husband's not accustomed to sharing you and the children with another."

Katy hesitated, allowing Bailey's words to settle. Then she smiled diplomatically. "Dwight's not being forced to share us. This is simply a new friend who's entered our lives. It's no different than your friendship to us."

"Except that I never saved your life."

Lowering her eyelids, Katy shook her head. "I know what

you're trying to say, Bailey. But you've no need to worry. I would never regard Robert Gabriel with anything more than utmost respect. He's like a brother to me."

Bailey nodded that she understood, but her mind ascertained otherwise. Glancing again toward the distance, one brow arched with surprise. "It appears your cousin has no desire to join us today." She observed that Grant had chosen a different area to set up their picnic.

"More's the better." Evans busied himself with piling up his plate.

Bailey smiled, hoping her eyes concealed the disappointment she felt inside. Turning her attention on Katy's young daughter, Corbin, who now sat up sleepily, she determined to torment herself no more by glancing toward Grant Hogan and his picnic companion.

7
MOONLIGHT
RENDEZVOUS

The nearer the days drew to September, the higher the temperatures rose. Bailey engaged her pupils in decorating the classroom with paper cutouts, dried flowers, and hand-drawn art. She glanced out of the schoolhouse window while the pupils milled about the room in talkative groups discussing their art projects. The greening landscape of late August caused a melancholy to sweep through Bailey. For the first time in months, she felt homesick. Her family would be preparing for snow in a few short months and observing a day of thanks, topped off with a turkey and all the trimmings. Laurie would be involved in her wedding plans. Their mother, Esther, would be engaged in festive party events with all of her friends. If it had not been for Jared's pup, the silence that pervaded Bailey's home would have driven her to distraction.

Clapping her hands together to garner the students' attention, she announced, "Your art projects are looking beautiful. When we complete them all in September, our room will be a showplace. Tomorrow we'll plan our first spring social and invite your parents to come. By then, our schoolhouse will be decorated like a gallery."

Just lacking a little in culture, she thought. She studied the children's skeptical gazes pointed at her and at once read their thoughts. "If I have to, I'll pay a personal visit to each household and invite your folks myself." Her brows lifted with surety. "If you'll all gather your belongings now, we can prepare for dismissal."

The room grew noisy once more, and Bailey collected her own things into a large satchel. She almost dreaded going home. For the last few days she had discovered more and more attempts to destroy everything she owned. She had long stopped hoping for a garden. If it had not been for the kindness of a few of the students' mothers, she wouldn't have fresh produce at all. Everything she attempted to grow had been uprooted, trampled, or poisoned. Fearing for the little dog, she had even followed Jared's advice and brought him with her every day to the schoolhouse, much to the children's delight.

The passenger ship to England had departed a month prior. Bailey, in an attempt to at least garner a little support from Captain Hogan, had met with him just before the ship's departure. But he had offered no hope of security in her teaching position, only his worries that the personal attacks on her property would grow worse. Angry with him, she had departed his office hoping their ways would not cross again for a long time. Unable to reconcile herself with leaving, she had stayed, knowing that her time at the school could be growing short. But her hunger for friendship had led her to accept many invitations to Rose Hill. She was surprised, no relieved, she told herself, to find out that Hogan was never present. She had seldom discussed the man with Katy except on a professional level, so she wondered if it was by his own request that they never attended the same dinner party. Mentioning his name only once, Katy dismissed his absence merely as being due to his growing responsibilities under Surgeon White.

As the last of her students waved farewell, Bailey reflected upon the past few weeks. What remained of her spare time, when not immersed in grading the students' work or visiting the Farrells, had been spent with Lieutenant Evans. She pictured his handsome face, his blue eyes, and the way his blond hair fell casually across his bronzed forehead. In a moment of weakness, she had held hands with him as they walked beside a stream bed at Rose Hill. But although appreciative of Lieutenant Evans' attention, she had found little satisfaction in their time spent together, a fact that greatly puzzled her. He, in his anxiousness to locate a wife, had mentioned on numerous occasions how financially secure he was and of his plans to expand his family's property. But Bailey found his words less appealing than she was sure he had hoped them to be. However hard he worked to impress her, it only served to lessen her interest in the man. She hadn't come here to find a husband. Any urgency on Lieutenant Evans' part to draw her closer to him only resulted in widening the distance between them. Bailey fought with her mind, her emotions, with every part of herself to see all the good in him. He had alleviated, in part, some of the lonely pangs she felt for her friends and family in America. She remembered that her mother had mentioned more than once the futility of encouraging a relationship based on nothing but the drive for companionship. But her physical attraction to him, coupled with her need for friendship, drove her to reconsider seeing him once more. She reasoned within herself that in the short amount of time they had known each other, he truly cared about her. He had close family ties and loved his church. He was a solid man and held to his faith in the midst of unscrupulous men. Tonight she would dine with him at the only inn in town that served hot meals. It was a bit rustic compared to Virginia's fine dining, but she did not care where they met and found herself eager for the evening to unfold.

"Miss Templeton, I'm here to escort you." The private appeared in the school doorway at his usual time.

"Hello, Dade," she said wearily. "I hope we find everything intact this time."

"Captain Hogan's placed a guard on your place, miss. No need to worry now."

The news should have encouraged her, but it only increased her anxiety. *Now he'll see me as a bigger bother than he first imagined. If only I could catch the culprit.* But not wanting to appear unappreciative, she nodded her approval. Dismissing any ill will toward Grant Hogan, she gathered her belongings and tried to fill her mind with thoughts of the evening ahead.

"Governor Bligh, with all due respect, you've not been long in the colony. The emancipists are suspicious people. The young teacher, Bailey Templeton, however much of a mistake it was on the government's part to hire her, has slowly built the respect of the parents. All but a few families are sending their children back to school. I credit the school's success to Miss Templeton's courage and her tenacity in approaching the parents personally. How many teachers have you known who would visit the household of every student? None that I've known."

Bligh watched with growing apathy as the officer paced beside him on the veranda of his home. "Sir, we've resurrected this conversation on numerous occasions, and I grow weary of it. We've sent for a male teacher to replace Miss Templeton, and in the meanwhile, we shall bide our time until such replacement arrives." Reaching into a small tin, he drew out a pinch of tobacco and tucked it into the pocket of his lower lip. Studying the officer's face, he chuckled. "You've a fondness for the woman?"

Grant Hogan whipped around, his face no longer composed. "I've respect for her, Governor. She's the most dedicated educator Sydney Cove and Parrametta have ever known. You've known me long enough to realize that I never allow my personal opinions to interfere with my professional ones."

"Do I?" Bligh inhaled deeply, his extra fold of chin resting on his chest. He turned and walked toward the small table that held a bottle of rum and two small glasses. "Join me, Captain. The hour is late, and I shall soon retire."

Disgruntled with Bligh's casual handling of the matter, Grant shook his head. "It is late, and I've wasted your time here, I see."

"Not wasted, sir. It is always good for leaders to come together and sort out their differences. But we appoint leaders for a single purpose—to make the final decision no matter how unpopular it may be. After much discussion among your military corps leaders, their consensus derived no alternative to the problem except to hire a schoolmaster from England. Although I would never allow the corps to make decisions affecting the colony as a whole, it is on this one point that I must agree."

His patience spent, Grant quietly dismissed himself and departed Bligh's estate. Well aware of the man's history, he knew he could exact no cooperation from him at this point. Surviving a mutiny from a prior commission aboard a ship called *The Bounty*, Bligh had garnered the respect of the British government, while at the same time igniting the suspicions of the military men, especially the army officers. Mounting his stallion in one swift movement, Grant put as much distance between himself and Bligh as he could muster. He couldn't help but notice that Bligh's demeanor had cooled when he had pressed him on the issue of Bailey Templeton. *Why is the governor so dead set on replacing her?* Or was it truly Bligh who undermined his attempts to retain Bailey as teacher?

With the hour approaching early evening, he hastened his ride. He could retrieve his carriage and arrive at the Parkinsons' home before sundown. Their daughter, Emily, had agreed to a quiet meal at the town inn. She had been a lovely girl to get to know, skilled in all manner of handiwork. But by no means would she be considered a person who was well read. Like many women in the colony, she usually kept her conversations confined to domestic matters. She was completely enthralled with his talk of the medical profession, and it flattered him the way she questioned every medical term he used, as if desiring to know each meaning. *Not the least bit at all like that stubborn teacher who has no interest at all in anything except her school!* Exasperated by the thought, he could not help but chide himself for allowing the woman to anger him so. What little heed she had paid him had all been made to secure her position at the school, he was certain.

Not one to supplant the blame for orders falling under his authority, Grant would not divulge Bligh's stubborn directives as any but his own. He was a man who understood his duty as an officer. So for now Bailey Templeton would see him in one light only—as her adversary. *She's repelled by you, Hogan. And rightly so!* He remembered the day that he and his nephew had taken her the puppy. Hopeful that she would be moved by the friendly gesture, he was dismayed to realize that she would accept the gift but reluctantly so. He also recalled how strikingly beautiful she had been that day. Remembering how splendid she appeared standing out in the sunshine, her rose-colored cotton frock billowing in the breeze against her comely frame, he could tell that she had been gardening. Even her dirt-smudged face had not marred her beauty nor dimmed her sparkling brown eyes or her shining black hair. Bailey's stunning face had captivated him. Without thought, he had drawn close to her and, before realizing it, had touched her hand. But to resist would have driven him mad. Her soft skin within inches, he had to touch her—not once, but twice. Seeing the reserve in her eyes, he realized that he had overstepped his boundaries. It was by that one foolish act that he had negated any plans to invite her to the church social. Her chilly reaction had stopped him cold. He recalled looking out over the church lawn and finding her with Evans.

She was not like the other ladies in the settlement—lonely, begging for companionship. Bailey Templeton was confident and in need of no one's help. Or so it seemed. *And so mistrustful*, he thought dismally. He recalled that it was only after much struggle that she had finally consented to allow Private Dade to escort her to and from the school each day. But seeing the repeated attacks on her home worried him. While she blamed an unscrupulous student, he suspected a more dangerous adversary. Fully realizing that he would only be adding to her disapproval of him, he had nevertheless ordered the guard placed on her home this morning. *You're a strong woman, Bailey Templeton. But not as strong as you think.* Seeing the orange moon appear in the day sky, Grant headed his steed toward the Parkinsons' farm, but his thoughts drifted in another direction.

"Lieutenant Evans!" Bailey allowed him to lift her into his carriage. She smiled at his striking appearance. He had donned civilian attire for the evening's dinner. Wearing a dark suit, a white shirt, and a silk cravat, Evans returned her admiring gaze.

"All for you, Miss Templeton," he said smoothly.

Waiting for him to join her in the carriage, Bailey cleared her throat. For some weeks, she had grown weary of the formalities but did not know how to tell him so. "We've been seeing each other socially now for several weeks." She hesitated, not wishing to imply more than she intended. "If you wish, you may call me Bailey. Miss Templeton is so conventional." She smoothed the red tulle and satin dress.

Flicking the horse's reins, Evans straightened his back and looked confidently down at her. "I agree, Bailey." Allowing the horse to saunter toward the inn, he turned to look at her once again, as though he reveled in her striking appearance. "It's time you call me Jonathan."

"I will, Jonathan." She liked his name. It had a pleasing sound to it and, when shortened, had a biblical ring to it. Feeling a renewed camaraderie with the lieutenant, she did not move away when he sat close to her, but rather allowed herself to lean against his sinewy frame. She felt lonelier than usual tonight and needed his companionship. His build reminded her of her younger brother, Harry, who could lift and carry several produce-filled crates at once. Even the largest of bullies knew to steer clear of Harry Templeton.

Enjoying the pleasant carriage ride, Bailey engaged Jonathan Evans in talk about his family, a topic, she soon realized, he never tired of discussing. As he chatted on about his plans to farm, she found herself drifting to thoughts forbidden. So hating the isolation she had first felt when arriving at Sydney Cove, she continued to justify her acceptances of his social calls. But closing her eyes, she wondered what would have happened had she not so coolly received Captain Hogan.

"Bailey?" It appeared he had called out her name more than once.

Shaking herself from her moment of reverie, she quickly said, "I'm listening."

Upon arriving at the inn, Jonathan and Bailey took a stroll upon the wooden walk that surrounded the weathered structure and overlooked a bay near the harbor.

"Once we've decided upon our meal, let's come back out here, Jonathan—if it's all right with you?" Bailey's eyes were wide with anticipation as she awaited his approval.

"My sentiments exactly. It's a lovely evening for a stroll with such a beautiful lady."

"Thank you." She smiled and saw the eager gleam in his face. Without meaning to, she knew she was encouraging Jonathan more than she should. But just for now, she wanted to enjoy herself and enjoy being on the arm of another man besides Gavin Drummond. For the first time in months, she felt free of Gavin. *Let Laurie have him!* She could now say it without contempt for either of them. And Jonathan Evans had helped her in this regard.

The inn, which had a dingy appearance by day, reflected a quaint ambiance at sunset. The room was lit by candles and filled with the fragrance of home-baked pies and smoked meats. "I'm famished," she said, inhaling the appetizing aromas. After being seated at their table, the two of them quickly made their selections and informed their server that they would return shortly.

"After you, m'lady." Evans bowed politely.

Bailey took his arm, and they discovered a rear exit to the dock. Just before walking through the doorway, her eye was caught by a striking couple who entered the inn at the front entrance. But the darkened room made it impossible to identify the couple. Stepping out of doors with Evans, she made haste to find the best view of the moon. "Here, Jonathan!" She leaned against a salt-washed rail. "Let's stand here. There's nothing like the sea at night." She listened as the waves roared onto the sandy shore, the dark water discernible only by the white foam that capped its curling wake. She felt Jonathan's hand slip around her waist and turned her face toward him, poised to deter any romantic overtures on his part. But she saw at once that he only smiled and stood admiring the moon with her. She felt safe with Jonathan. He was dependable and trustworthy. She returned his amiable gaze and allowed her thoughts to drift.

"Lieutenant Evans." A barmaid walked across the dock calling out his name.

Casting a chary gaze his way, Bailey sighed. "You're being summoned."

Evans shrugged and shook his head. "Who would know how to find me here?" The barmaid called out his name once more, and he waved to catch her attention. "Here, miss. I'm Lieutenant Evans."

"Message for you, sir." The barmaid quickly handed him a scrawled note, turned on her heels, and disappeared into the inn.

Folding her arms at her waist, Bailey glanced around at the couples embracing under the moon's spell. It appeared that the magic of the evening had woven its way into every heart but hers. As much as she enjoyed the moment, she would not allow her emotions to be taken in by sheer scenery. She glanced up at Evans in anticipation. Seeing a disgruntled scowl appear on his face, she pursed her lips together, her brows raising inquiringly. "Something wrong, Jonathan?"

"Problem at the government building. A private's gone out and blown his pay on rum, I'm certain. He's causing a disruption in the square."

"But why send for you?"

"I work in the government building. And," he added sheepishly, "it was no secret who I had plans to dine with this evening."

"You divulged our plans?"

"Never again, Bailey." He held up one hand in oath.

His apologetic gaze caused her to laugh quietly. "I'll wait for you here, then?"

"I'll not be long. I swear it." Turning to leave, he stopped as if captured by a thought. Then whirling around he bent and placed a tender kiss upon Bailey's cheek. Eyeing her, he spoke with firm determination. "Wait for me." Placing one last kiss upon her forehead, he turned and was gone.

The longer she stood staring at the darkness, the more she was apt to laugh. Jonathan Evans was a curious man. The harder he tried to know her, the more fate stood in his way. Bailey strolled a little farther down the walk until the planks ran out and nothing stretched in front of her but the sandy shoreline. Remembering their dinner plans inside, she decided to return to the inn. But her ponderous thoughts caused her to slow her steps, and she found herself staring down, her hands clasped in front of her against the wine-colored satin of her basque-waisted gown.

"I can see the wheels turning now. Bailey Templeton tries to save the world."

A short gasp escaping her lips, Bailey turned her eyes upon the dark figure who stood a few feet away in the shadows. "Who's there?" she demanded to know.

"The devil."

"Don't play tricks with me. I . . . I'm not alone!" Bailey glanced around but saw that all the couples had returned to the inn.

A deep chuckle resonated from the man's throat, and he stepped out into the moonlight. "I'm sorry, Miss Templeton. I had no intention of frightening you."

"Captain Hogan!" Her pulse racing, Bailey took a step forward, indignant. "What are you doing out here?"

"I was wondering the same about you. My companion met a few of her friends from England. They're all out in front of the inn having a gay time." Clasping his hands vigorously, he added, "I stepped away for a brief stroll."

Remembering Katy's comments about her unpredictable cousin, Bailey responded knowingly, "Ah, you're not one for crowds."

His eyes narrowed suspiciously at her comment, and he offered, "It was the moon that beckoned me. This bay is lovely at night."

Glancing around, Bailey agreed politely. "So it is." Rubbing her hands together from the chill that had descended with the night, she blew out a sigh and prepared to dismiss herself. "Well, I—"

"Shame to waste such an evening. Miss Emily Parkinson can

talk for hours, and your Lieutenant Evans, well, he's indisposed at the government building."

"How did you know that?" Bailey lowered her face, her gaze suspicious.

"I saw Evans on the way out." Grant shrugged indifferently.

"You're certain that you had nothing to do with—" Realizing how her words sounded, Bailey stopped short of declaring her suspicions.

"You think that I had Evans called away?" His voice took on an edge. "For what purpose?"

Glad for the darkness, Bailey felt her cheeks redden. "No purpose." She turned away and walked toward the railing. She stood for what seemed like an eternity, listening to the roaring wake, hearing no further response from Hogan. Feeling foolish, she realized that the captain most likely had left her standing alone. *You did it again.* She whipped around. Intense astonishment touched her moonlit face.

"Bailey," Grant said her name gently, as though to speak more loudly would shatter the moment. He had drawn near to her but only stood gazing at her, his eyes as full as the moon itself. "Whatever I've done to make you hate me, I—" Now it was he who stopped.

He stood so near, she was certain she could hear his heart beating. Bailey looked up at this giant of a man, more surprised than she was fearful. "I don't understand, Captain Hogan. What is it that you want from me?"

"I want . . ." He drew closer, scanned her critically, then beamed his ardent approval.

Bailey saw that his eyes bore into her with tacit expectation. She told herself to back away. Grant Hogan was not like Evans. She didn't feel *safe* with him as she had with Jonathan. Not because he was a threat but because she didn't trust herself! "Captain Hogan. We should go inside. We've obligations—"

"*Obligations?*" Grant held his face a few inches from her own. "I'm weary of obligations, Bailey. Aren't you?"

As before, Bailey looked admiringly at his comely features. He was even more stunning up close. "What about your Miss Emily Parkinson?" Her voice was shakier than she had intended.

"Emily is a fine young woman, and I've much respect for her. But I've offered no obligation to her, and she's offered none to me. I'm not the only man she sees."

"No?"

"What of your Lieutenant Evans? Is your courtship established?"

Bailey knew she should dismiss herself from his presence, but she could not tear herself away. A slender, delicate thread had formed between them, and she felt energized by it. Something in his manner calmed her fears and caused her to trust him. "Jonathan and I are merely good friends. But he is my escort tonight, and I shall respect him as such." She looked away, feeling foolish.

"And I shall respect Emily as well. But what of tomorrow?" He stepped closer, passing through the invisible wall between them that Bailey had so carefully constructed.

"What of it?" Bailey felt her pulse racing.

"What of it?" Without further restraint, Grant clasped her hands. "It's simply this—I can't bear another day without you in it, Bailey Templeton."

Her brows knitted together, and her voice wavered. "You can't mean what you say."

"Every word." He stepped closer to her, and their clasped hands rested against his broad chest.

"You're toying with me, aren't you?" she asked, her voice barely above a whisper. But she made the comment out of a lack of a better thing to say. "You know they call you 'Conquering Hogan,' don't you?" She saw the fire of his gaze and wondered if she could resist him.

"If I could, I would tear that nonsense from your thoughts." He smiled and spoke gently. "Will you consent to allowing me one moment to revel in your beauty?"

Glancing around, Bailey felt her head swimming. "Now?"

"Come with me, Bailey." His voice velvet-edged, he took her hand. Before she could raise a note of protest, he led her down the walk to the sand, and without knowing why, she followed him. Bailey's thoughts swirled through her like a storm. Common sense told her to run back into Jonathan's arms, to safety, to the place where there was no danger of her being hurt. *Run away, Bailey!* Her mind tried to seize control, but her heart had taken command. Running with Captain Hogan behind a stand of trees, Bailey felt him pull her close.

"I want to kiss you, Bailey Templeton." Grant pressed his cheek against hers, and then drew back his face. "May I?"

"I . . ." she stammered, her heart pounding against her chest.

"I think," she whispered, "that if you have to ask, you shouldn't do it." The ocean breeze caused her coifed hair to tumble about her shoulders, and she felt like a sixteen-year-old again. Responding to the protective strength of his embrace as he pulled her close, Bailey gave in to her awakening feelings for him and lifted her face to meet his. As his lips pressed against hers, she lifted her arms to wrap around his muscular frame. All reasoning washed away with the tide, and she allowed him to kiss her again and again. Like a thief, Grant Hogan had forced his way into her world and unlocked the heart and soul of Bailey Templeton.

Fully intent upon sleeping late on Saturday morning, Bailey instead lay gazing through the window that illuminated her bed with the soft pink light of dawn. Cradling her pillow, she wondered if the previous night on the beach had merely been a wonderful dream. However much she had fought her feelings, she had succumbed to them and taken a precarious chance with Grant Hogan. Evans had been gone for the space of only half an hour, long enough for her to make a decision she had yet to regret. She chuckled at the remembrance, a furtive satisfaction creeping into her senses. With heart still pounding, she had reluctantly joined Jonathan Evans while Grant returned to Emily's table—a promise that she and Grant had made to each other. Forced to watch Grant from a distance across the room, she had been seized with restlessness, and all the while she was finishing her dinner with Evans, her thoughts were full of Grant. Then, during the drive back home, she had politely informed Jonathan that she could no longer see him, knowing that Grant Hogan would be calling at her door this night. Her conscience pricked slightly by guilty feelings, she consoled herself by admitting that she had never entertained serious feelings for Evans. Jonathan, albeit expressing his disappointment, had assured her that their friendship remained safely intact. Having previously divulged her fears to Grant, she soon realized that her misconceptions about him were unfounded.

She could not wait to share the news with Katy. And she especially could not wait to write to Laurie and tell her about the handsome young Australian surgeon who had captured her attention. She knew her parents would voice their concern. After all, her world was only recently rising from the ashes of one failed relationship. Common sense warned her that to plunge heedlessly into another emotional attachment would only increase the likelihood for further pain. But she had never known a man like Grant Hogan. He was godly and self-assured. He would have no qualms about allowing her to teach and would most likely even encourage her in her pursuits. *I've so much yet to learn about you, Grant.* Would he want to visit her family in America? Would they live in Australia? At this point, she did not care. All she longed for was to know all she could about Grant Hogan. The very thought of him caused her heart to race. If she dressed and went into town, perhaps she would accidentally cross his path. After all, it was her regular marketing day. The prospect encouraged her.

Shortly after, Bailey had hitched up her horse and headed for the town square. It would only be a forty-five-minute ride into town. She would take care of her marketing early and then leisurely drive by the government offices. Realizing that Lieutenant Evans might misunderstand a formal visit, she weighed the alternatives. But driven by the thought of catching a glimpse of Grant, she tossed aside all caution.

The market square was already busy with townsfolk. The peddlers pushed their wagons through the clay-packed streets, calling out the wares they sold. Hurriedly, Bailey chose a few items for the week: two loaves of bread, a fresh fish, some eggs, and butter. Loading all into a crate in the rear of her wagon, she took a deep but anxious breath and decided to take a walk past the government building.

A few privates milled about, but seeing the door locked fast, Bailey felt foolish at having ventured out for such a purpose. "The government building's closed today, Private?" she asked one of the men, hoping he did not detect the flush upon her cheeks.

Tipping his cap over his eyes, the private yawned and stretched out his legs in front of him. "Yes, ma'am. All locked up until Monday."

"Thank you." She turned around to return to the wagon. Embarrassed at her own folly, she chided herself for the whole ridiculous plan. Grant, most likely, was out at the penal colony tending to the sick convicts. Katy had mentioned his Saturday medical rounds on more than one occasion. Glad that no one knew of her unsuccessful plan, she reconciled herself to returning to her house and preparing for their evening together. She had never pursued a man in such a way and certainly would not begin such a brazen practice now.

Before returning to the wagon, she strolled toward the bay to catch sight of the ships docking and departing from the bottle-shaped harbor. She had often imagined herself on one of the departing vessels. Now she did not care if she never left Sydney Cove. She had just stepped aside to allow a group of sailors to pass when her ear caught the sound of a crying woman. Distressed at the pitiful sound, she made her way through the throngs milling about the harbor. At once, she saw a blond-haired young woman seated on a wooden bench and weeping. A man stood over her, offering consolation. Her heart rent at the sight, and she said a quiet prayer asking God's wisdom. Then without a moment's hesitation, she approached the couple. "Hello." She spoke quietly so as not to offend the young woman.

Turning up her face, Emily Parkinson gazed forlornly up at Bailey, her eyes red and moist from her tears. "Oh, it's you, Miss Templeton."

"Emily?" She wondered if Grant had been insensitive in breaking off their relationship. They had known each other such a short space of time, surely she was not attached to him already? Holding her hand to her chest, Bailey stepped closer and saw that Jonathan Evans was the man who stood comforting her. "Jonathan, tell me, what is wrong?"

"Oh, Bailey. I didn't expect to see you here." He stepped away from Emily, removing his hand from her shoulder.

"It's quite all right." Bailey tried to read his expression, wondering if he found any irritation in her presence. After all, she had only last night ended their short-lived courtship. "Is there something I can do to help?"

"I'm afraid not, Miss Templeton." Emily dabbed at her nose with a handkerchief. "You see, the man who's been courting me—" Her words broke off in midsentence and she fell into another round of sobs.

"Are you speaking of Grant, Captain Grant Hogan?" Now worried for her own reasons, Bailey felt an uneasiness seeping into the pit of her stomach. *Grant, what have you done?* But Emily did not appear to be aiming her anger in Bailey's direction.

"Yes." Emily nodded. "You see, we had planned to meet again on this night, but he—"she took a deep, broken breath—"he's been called away. The Royal Navy is sending him to Hobart. The penal colony there is in desperate need of a surgeon." Her petite frame shook as she continued to weep. "I fear for his life. It's a wicked place."

Surely he would not concoct such a horrible story on her account. *Hobart?* She knew of the settlement. It was located on the island of Van Diemen's Land. Gangs of convicts roamed the bush country without restraint. Bailey felt small bits of her heart ripped out with each word spoken by Emily. Undoubtedly Grant had known all this the night before. *Bailey, you've been played the fool.* Not wanting either of them to see the pain of her gaze, she composed her thoughts. "When will he—Captain Hogan—return?"

"He offered no hope of return. Isn't that right, Lieutenant Evans?"

Her fists clenched at her sides, Bailey muttered under her breath, "Scoundrel!"

Evans patted Emily's shoulders once more. "I knew I should have warned you, Miss Parkinson. Captain Hogan's reputation as a rogue is well renowned in Sydney Cove."

Shame swept through Bailey. Not only had she deceived Jonathan Evans, she had deceived herself. *Grant Hogan is every bit the rogue that everyone said he was.* Feeling tears beginning to surface, Bailey offered a swift condolence to Emily Parkinson and then turned to go to her wagon. "Good-bye, Jonathan," she said, not daring to look at him.

Accusing thoughts whirled in her mind. *You, of all people, Bailey, should have known!* She thought of the manner in which she had tossed aside a perfectly sound relationship with Jonathan Evans. She could never rekindle his interest after last night. *But why should I want to?* she thought defiantly. She'd had a singleness of purpose in coming to Sydney Cove—to put behind the heartaches of love and to embrace a colony of people who desperately needed her. With Grant Hogan out of the way, perhaps she could still achieve her purpose in New South Wales. Shedding a tear, she climbed into her wagon and headed back for her house, the isolation of it all a bittersweet respite.

PART TWO

OUT OF THE IRON FURNACE

"But the Lord hath taken you, and brought you forth
out of the iron furnace ... to be unto him a people of
inheritance, as ye are this day."

Deuteronomy 4:20

8

BAILEY'S
REVOLT

A fragile shriek arose from Bailey. She couldn't think or breathe. Aware only that something loomed over her bed, she struggled to awaken. Tumbling from the small wood-framed bed, she jumped to her feet and visually searched the room. She staggered to the foot of the bed, braced herself against a chair, and inhaled a tremulous breath. *It was only a bad dream. Just a nightmare.* Her dog, Blackie, nervously sensing her alarm, rolled onto his haunches. "I'm all right," she whispered assuringly. She made her way in the dark to the small washstand and splashed what little water was in the bowl onto her clammy skin. She was exhausted, not having slept an entire night in weeks. "Please, Lord! Allow me rest!" she prayed aloud. In a groggy stupor, she slumped back to the bed and collapsed.

Since Grant's departure almost one month ago, the attacks on her home had increased. The door had been ripped from its hinges, the front windows had been broken out, and her personal belongings in the bureau had been ransacked. Now instead of wishing the captain gone, she began to suspect that he had been her protector all along. To prove herself to Major George

Johnston, the new officer in charge of the school's affairs, she had labored harder than ever to win the hearts of Sydney's emancipist parents. Dade, visiting her only a time or two more, had been reassigned, and she had not seen him since. It had all been so confusing to her. Before seeing her for the last time, Dade had offered her what little information he was able to glean from the gossips around the government building. Hogan had been called out late—the last night she saw him, she recalled privately—and received orders from the governor to leave the next morning for Hobart on Van Diemen's Land island, where his medical expertise was urgently needed. He had departed without a farewell to anyone. Even Emily Parkinson had been given the news after the fact. Bailey, too uneasy to admit her unexpected rendezvous with Grant the night before, could not bring herself to ask more questions about his whereabouts. To do so might raise a few eyebrows. According to Dade, the idle talk around the town square had centered around Emily Parkinson, the abandoned young woman whom Captain Hogan had courted. Glad to be free of any ties to him, Bailey hoped and prayed that no one had seen them together on the beach. That kind of story would only further serve to complicate matters. Before becoming the focus of gossip, she would rather pack up and head home. Let Emily be the spurned lover. She seemed to revel in such nonsense.

So Bailey kept the matter to herself and struggled inwardly to keep her thoughts from straying. In her private world of silent misery, she worked all day and slept little at night. Now wide awake once again before dawn, she faced the torments in her mind alone. She had walked away from one set of problems in America only to exchange them for worse ones here. In spite of her family's love, she had been determined to prove she could make it on her own. If they realized the peril she now braved, they would try to intervene. She had no choice but to confront the consequences of her own decisions. *More than ever, Lord, I've got to lean on you. There is no one else who can help.*

Turning up the lantern next to her window, she found that she had slept until the hour of three in the morning. She had gone to bed by eight o'clock, so it was the most sleep she had enjoyed in weeks. Deciding to make some tea, she slowly meandered around the tiny room before setting the still full kettle to heat. She found some crumpets stored haphazardly next to a stack of mismatched saucers. Organizing her pantry was a task to which she had never given precedence. As long as she could find things, why bother with such a nuisance? Only Laurie would give importance to such things.

Restoking the wood in the fireplace, she settled herself in a rocker and bit off a corner of a crumpet. Her eyes softened their gaze, and she rested her head against the rocker. She scolded herself for her thoughts. She hated thinking of Captain Hogan in any manner other than that of a scoundrel. *A very dashing scoundrel, no less.* She swallowed the stale crumpet. *With intelligent green eyes.* But a part of her wanted to remember him the way he was their last evening together. It was one of those stolen moments that if she had to live over, she would have to deny herself such a thing. He had only complicated her world. But happen it did, and his image now lived in her mind to appear without invitation. Bailey soon had her cup of tea in hand and her Bible in her lap. Relaxing, she glanced around the meagerly furnished house and watched as Blackie curled up once again on a rug close to the front door, his chestnut eyes succumbing to sleep.

Tilting back her head, she basked in the heat of the fireplace. Its glow reflected against her skin, adding warmth to the chilled room. For a moment, she longed for her world in Sydney Cove to be returned to its former peaceful state. True, Grant had not offered her the security she sought, but it appeared that perhaps he had looked out for her. Of that fact she was not entirely certain, but she could not help wondering if her perception of him had really been true, or if she had seen only the well-polished veneer of a complicated man. *Perhaps I'll never know.* She remembered him the way he was the day that he and Jared had brought her Blackie. A smile played around the corners of her mouth as she reflected. Grant had appeared as guileless as the lad, the two of them standing before her and holding out their gift of a puppy. She also remembered her cool reception. *I did behave—well, he said it—stubbornly that day.* Again seeing the disappointment in his eyes when she had spurned his offer to call him by his given name, she felt a sense of guilt and remorse sweep through her. *But none of it excuses your making a fool of me, dear Captain Hogan.* She held the rim of the cup to her lips and slowly drew in the hot brew. She could not help but wonder if his advances toward her had indeed been a sort of revenge. After all, he was not a man accustomed to denial.

Blowing across the top of her cup, Bailey felt her thoughts

drawn deeper into remembrances of him. She recalled the first Sunday she saw him lead the little congregation in worship. She had never before perceived him in such a light. He exuded a joy and a buoyancy uncharacteristic of most men in his position. Observing him from week to week on the church's platform, Bailey could find little fault in him, however hard she tried. His face had radiated a genuine peace, and she momentarily believed that perhaps it was because he had been sincere in his actions and not self-seeking as she had first suspected. But now it became evident that her first suspicions were correct. A grain of contempt presented itself on her face as she mentally returned to the night on the beach. He had appeared out of nowhere, it seemed. It could be, she realized, that he had seen her leaving the inn. He could have followed her, or else she was entirely wrong and providence allowed their paths to cross. A part of her wanted to believe that he had not manipulated Evans' departure. The other part of her did not care.

She remembered everything he wore that night. She recalled the burgundy vest with gold trim, the dark slacks and coat, remembering even the black silk cravat. But it was not his handsome appearance that drew her. It had been something she detected when she looked into his eyes. Something that stirred her soul. Something beyond the moon's magic and the roar of the night sea. Although physically drawn to him, she sensed something deeper between the two of them. But she would never know if something unseen battled to connect their lives or if it were all manipulative tricks. She would never again feel the strength of his arms holding her close to him. And she had only known that pleasure once. Grant Hogan had walked away without a good-bye and, like a thief, had purloined a part of her heart when she was most vulnerable. *God help you, Captain Hogan. God help us both.*

The sky outside her recently repaired window began to lighten to a dusky September gray. Bailey finished her tea and decided to dress for the school day ahead. She would be meeting with the government officer once more, and she wanted to appear as confident and unshaken by her circumstances as possible. It would be her last attempt, she decided, to secure her place as schoolteacher. Weary of the conflicts, the attacks, and, most of all, her silent pain in regard to the elusive captain, she stood in the threshold of defeat. For the children's sake and even for the sake of their obdurate parents, she was determined to stand against this corrupt system. But not to the extent that she would stand in the way of her Creator's guidance. To do so, she realized, would most assuredly drag her into defeat. If the government officer forced her resignation, Bailey would have no choice but to gather up her belongings and depart from Sydney Cove—for good. *I'm in your hands, heavenly Father. Not my will. Only yours.*

Hobart, Van Diemen's Land

Standing outside his surgeon's hut, Grant Hogan surveyed the straggle of temporary dwellings erected in the British settlement. Placed at the mouth of the Derwent River's western banks, Hobart was both wildly beautiful and menacingly dangerous. Grant had taken several treks on horseback up the wild shores of the Derwent, but never alone. He had learned to stay away from the shores that had become a bloody killing ground for greedy sealers. Towering over Hobart, the snow-capped bastion of Mount Wellington had offered refuge to numerous convict gangs who had fled the transportation system to opt for a life in the Aborigines' wilderness.

Dismally, Grant looked at his hands, gingerly bending his throbbing fingers. Chapped raw from the wind and the endless nights spent patching up the infirm convicts and mariners, his fingers ached and swelled. He had neither the proper instruments nor the medical staff to handle the swelling ranks of the Hobart settlement. Fatigue had settled in the pockets of his mind like a nagging woman.

"It's a useless cause." Officer Duddy Wilkes walked up to join Grant, pulling a ragged coat about himself to guard against the wind. Grant made no immediate reply but nodded in agreement. He did not feel talkative.

"Collins wouldn't be here, you know, if it weren't for 'is debts. He had to take the appointment or lose everything." The officer's lip turned out smugly. He referred to Hobart's reluctant leader, the lieutenant-governor, David Collins.

Grant had known Collins in Sydney Cove. "The lieutenant-governor's in more need here than he was in England, Duddy," Grant mused. "David Collins will rue the day he ever accepted this absurd commission."

"Why is England so protective of this place?"

"It's the fisheries. American whalers have already invaded Storm Bay. England wants to protect its interests."

"Why are you here, Hogan?" Duddy eyed him with a wary gaze, his brows lifting up and down.

"They needed a surgeon."

Duddy spat on the ground and cursed. "No, why are you *truly* here?" His mouth curled up at one side.

"Crossed Bligh, or it could be another."

"I knew it!" He slapped his knee and laughed. "The minute you stepped foot off that boat, I says to meself, now, that's a gentlemen wots crossed the wrong man."

Grant studied his face skeptically. "How would you know?"

"Man like you they could use in high places, unless you foul up your politics. Like ol' David Collins. Gets 'isself in debt"—he smacked his hands together— "an' they got 'im. They owns him, that's wot!"

Duddy was beginning to annoy Grant. He sighed and glanced in another direction, hoping the man would disappear.

"Why'd you do it?"

"What?" Grant muttered.

"Wot was the purpose—you know—was it for love or money?"

"Neither."

"You're a 'orrible liar, y'are, Hogan."

"I really must take my leave, if you'll excuse me." Grant tipped his hat and walked away, leaving the man to shout after him.

"I hope it was for a lot o' money! Hobart's the *last* place they sends officers, if you catch me meanin'!"

"Captain Hogan!" A mariner rushed up to meet Grant.

"Something wrong?"

"It's an officer. He was attacked by a gang of convicts. Tried to go after 'em in the bush, but they shot 'im."

"He's alive?"

The man nodded. "Down by the stream. Can you come now?"

Grant ran for his bag and his mount and was quick to be upon the mariner. "Join me. This will be faster!"

The mariner steadied his foot in the stirrup. "Me name's Spence." Giving the sailor a hand up, Grant headed toward the stream while the mariner shouted out directions. Spying the wounded man slumped atop a rock bed, Grant allowed the mariner to dismount and then followed close behind. Checking the victim's pulse, he felt a relief sweep through him. "You acted well, sir. He's still alive!" Grant saw at once that the wound was above the man's heart, lodged in his chest cavity. Quickly, he applied pressure to the wound with as many cloths as he had in the bag. "I don't want to move him just yet, but I'll need more cloths. Ride back and fetch them and bring back a stretcher from my hut."

"Aye, sir!"

Grant appreciated the mariner's prompt response. So many of the sailors at Hobart were beset with lethargy. Trying to focus on the needs of the sickly and the wounded had been a chore he alone had shouldered. Lieutenant-governor Collins, harassed with his own worries, had offered little in the way of support. No officer, no mariner, no settler, and certainly no convict looked upon Van Diemen's Land as a permanent abode. Grant couldn't help but allow his mind to return to the orderly life he had carved out on the New South Wales mainland. Sydney Cove, with all the problems faced by a wilderness colony, now seemed a refuge, a small oasis compared to Hobart. With each passing laborious day, he longed to return to Sydney Cove and to the young woman who stirred his thoughts like no other he had ever met.

Within the hour, he had removed the musket ball from the man's chest and had him transported back to his hut. Sitting by the officer's bedside until the sun began to meld into the horizon, Grant felt encouraged when he observed his patient stir. "Corporal?" Lifting the cloth from the man's head, he moistened it once more and placed it across his brow. "Corporal Haines?" he spoke quietly.

Haines' eyes fluttered open and he glanced around the room, his head not moving. "Wh-where?"

"Don't move, Corporal," Grant warned. "You've been shot. I've removed the metal from your chest, but we've got to keep your fever down."

"I remember," Haines whispered. "It . . . it was that—he stole me foulin' piece!"

"Now, Haines," Grant said sternly, "you can tell us later. I want you well first."

A lieutenant entered the hut, his face grave. "The convicts have disappeared. They're armed now. We'll have to warn the settlers.

111

They could be anywhere—could pick us off like flies."

"Sorry, sir," Haines moaned. "They slipped up on me. Hit me on the head."

The lieutenant's brow furrowed worriedly. "Vicious lot, all o' them! But they'll run out of ammunition soon. If nothin' else, the Aborigines will skin their worthless hides. Don't worry, Haines. You did your best."

"Lieutenant, if you would be so kind. Have one of the ladies in the settlement bring me some hot broth. If I could get some liquid down the man, it would help, I believe." Grant checked the man's pulse once again. Standing to see the lieutenant to the door, he pondered the victim's condition. The pulse rate seemed stronger, but the fever annoyed him. If he didn't get rid of the fever, he could lose him. Pacing back and forth in the hut, he clasped his hands behind his back. He had lost numerous patients to sickness. But this particular one worried him more. Haines had a family back in Sydney Cove. During his fever, he had muttered a girl's name—Delores. He wondered if a young lady waited for his return. *Hold on, Haines! Don't give up!* Glancing through an opening in the hut, Grant saw that the lieutenant had gone for the broth. Walking to the oak chair next to a table where he often studied, Grant knelt. Placing his elbows atop the seat, he pressed his forehead against his fists and closed his eyes. "Dear Lord," he whispered. "I beg you to spare this man's life. Haines is no more deserving of your attention than I. But he is your child. Please take the fever from him. Touch his wound, sweet Savior. Heal him, I pray." Grant did not move for several minutes. His eyes tightly closed, he finally added an addendum to his prayer. "I'm not sure why you sent me here, Lord. At first I blamed the devil, then you. But I trust that whatever any man intended for evil, you will turn to good. And if it be your will, please allow me to return to Sydney Cove. Keep Bailey safe from the blackguard who is intent upon running her out. Watch out for all of Sydney's children. Watch out for *your* children." Grant felt no response from heaven, but he knew that God heard his feeble requests. The one thing that had improved during his trying times at Hobart had been his faith.

He walked to Haines' bedside. The man appeared to sleep peacefully. Grant saw the curtains flutter against the opening and walked to close it up for the day. Following on the skirts of the wind, the fragrance of wild flowers wafted into the room. Stopping for a moment, Grant felt stirred by the remembrance of Bailey's hair. As it tumbled around her shoulders that night on the beach, he recalled her shining locks had the distinct aroma of wild flowers. Reluctant to close up the window, he stood grasping the latch he had fashioned from scrap metal and nails. He could see the wild flowers in the distant field, and in his mind's eye he could see Bailey Templeton smiling up at him as the ocean waves crashed behind them. He had warned himself to keep away from her. Something about the beautiful woman, however confident she appeared, revealed a vulnerable spirit that she herself fought to protect. *If I had left you alone, Bailey, I wouldn't be in such torment.* He pondered his harried departure and wondered if Evans had ever delivered to her the letter he had quickly scrawled before embarking on the ship.

Glancing at Haines, he realized now that although he had been transferred here as a punishment, Hobart's settlers would perish without his help. With one letter to his influential father, he could have had the order reversed, and his return to Sydney Cove would be fast and sure. *Don't hate me, Bailey Templeton. But I cannot return just yet. Wait for me, lovely angel. Wait for this undeserving fool.* He heard Haines groan again and saw he had kicked away his blanket. Grant returned to his side, began the ritual of bathing his brow with cool water, and waited.

"I've no intention of allowing you to harass me in any way!" Bailey paced in front of the door that led to the major's office. "You cannot force me to resign!" She had rehearsed her speech so many times her head ached. She glanced around the hallway, hoping no one had heard her talking to herself. Her arms laden down with books, she found a chair and promptly dumped them onto it. She had been approached by a corporal who was cleaning out an office for an official. His shelves already burgeoning with books, he had donated a stack to Bailey for the school. Hearing a door squeak open behind her, she glanced toward it. Surprised, she saw that Dwight and Katy Farrell emerged from the very official's door who had honored her with the books. "Hello to you both." She composed a smile on her face, although her thoughts were on the officer whom she waited to see.

"Bailey!" Katy, her eyes lit with glad surprise, ran up to greet her at once. "I'm so glad to see you here."

"And I you," Bailey returned the compliment.

"No." Katy looked around, her voice hushed. "I'm *really* glad to see you." She grasped Bailey's hands and pulled her aside. Dwight followed them both, his eyes glancing up and down the hallway warily.

"What's wrong?" Bailey found herself following their probing glances.

"A lot of unscrupulous manipulation, from what I can tell." Katy pulled Bailey closer. "We've just met with someone who tells us that one of the officials is dead set on seeing his brother-in-law employed as Sydney Cove's teacher."

The fact struck Bailey's mind like a hammer. "Who?" Her voice shook uneasily.

"His name is Richard Atkins. He's the colony's judge advocate."

Her hands clasped around Katy's, Bailey pursed her lips. "He's influential?"

"Quite. He's the son of a baronet—a drunkard—but one who knows well how to ply the system."

"His adeptness at currying favor with the higher-ups landed him the judgeship," Dwight added with a sigh. "Atkins is a lunatic. But a dangerous one."

"It all makes sense now." Bailey shrugged wearily. "So I've been fighting a losing battle."

Katy's face was full of strength, and her eyes fiercely lit. "No! Don't say such things. Atkins is not king, but he's caused pressure from England. This goes all the way up to the governor."

Clenching her fingers at her side, Bailey grimaced. "Bligh?"

"He wants no trouble from England. He has a troubled past and is determined to make New South Wales a shining success," Dwight explained.

"But we have our own influences," Katy said glibly. "My cousin's father is retired from the military. Uncle Bartholomew is none too happy about his son being shipped off to Van Diemen's Land. He's made an appointment to see Governor Bligh himself. Dwight is going with him, and I am certain they will leave an *indelible* impression."

"You speak of your cousin, Grant Hogan?" Keeping her tone reserved, Bailey looked away.

"Yes. Grant had plans to be Sydney Cove's next surgeon. Surgeon White will be retiring and heading for England soon. But beyond all that, our family is worried about his well-being. Hobart is a treacherous place."

"So you believe that Grant had no idea about his transfer until—"

"Oh no. He was taken quite by surprise, as was the young lady he courted. Miss Emily Parkinson, I'm certain, is quite grieved." Katy's eyes sparked with an indefinable emotion.

"Katy, I'll bring our carriage round." Dwight tipped his hat at Bailey.

"Good day, Dwight. And thank you for finding out the truth of the matter." Bailey smiled faintly, hoping she sounded appreciative.

Seeing that her husband had disappeared, Katy lowered her voice once again. "Bailey, we can't have this drunken man's unscrupulous brother teaching our children."

"But what can be done?"

"Stay and fight. You've done nothing to be dismissed for. Tell the lieutenant today that you've made no plans to depart, that you've made progress with the school. Tell him anything, but don't abandon us, Bailey. Don't abandon Sydney Cove's next generation. They need you. We all need you." Katy pleaded with her, abandoning all pretense.

Bailey forced her lips to part in a stiff, curved smile. "I've been so weary of the harassment. I didn't believe that anyone cared whether I stayed or left. You've given me new courage, Katy."

"Good! Now, pack up your things this afternoon. Dwight and I would love to have you stay at Rose Hill with us—for your own protection."

Bailey thought of the comforts of the Farrells' home. Freshly cooked meals, servants hustling to meet one's every whim. Rolling hills—*peace*. Drawing herself up, she placed her hands upon her waist. "I can't, Katy. I can't let them drive me away from my home. Somehow, this military junta has to be given a message from us colonists—they're here to serve us, not the other way around."

Katy chuckled. "You're my kind of woman, Bailey Templeton. Stubborn as I am and just as ferocious!"

The two of them laughed as the door to the major's office opened and a private stepped out. "Miss Bailey Templeton?" He glanced questioningly at the two of them.

"I'm Bailey Templeton." Squaring her shoulders, Bailey gave Katy's hand a final squeeze and then winked. Waltzing confidently through the major's door, she planted a smile upon her face and greeted him. "Good afternoon, sir. Thank you for granting me an audience today. We've much to discuss. I'm Sydney Cove's teacher, and I feel it only right to tell you that I've no intention of leaving. Ever!"

9
A HOPELESS BOY

Bailey's time spent inside the small schoolhouse found better days. The students, for the most part, all improved in their studies. Some of them would never be studious adults, she realized. But, like it or not, they had all begun to learn, and the majority could read. She saw at once their interest in money—perhaps because of their lack of it—and so she fashioned some coins from clay and taught them arithmetic.

"So if Elwin buys a side of bacon from you, Stephen, and he pays you sixpence, did he pay you what you asked, or does he owe you more?"

Stephen counted the clay coins that Elwin had just placed inside his palm. "Why, ain't no bloomin' way Elwin Sewell's goin' to pay me anythin'. He's never worked a lick for nothin', and he steals the merchants blind."

"Ain't so!" Elwin's face reddened and his back stiffened.

"Is so!" another colonist's son shouted. "Elwin's father's an emancipist!"

The students all jumped to their feet, the colonist children shouting down the emancipist children.

Bailey sighed inwardly. One by one, she made her rounds, and one by one, the students quickly found their places again behind their desks. Her arms folded at her waist, she tapped an impatient finger against her forearm. "Students, your actions today are shameful." Making eye contact with each one, she stared them into submission. "We are not divided into emancipists and colonists in this classroom. You are all students with a future in this colony."

"Yes, and some of us will spend it here," one boy blurted out, "and others on Norfolk!"

Bailey whipped around. "Frederick, you will write one hundred times, 'I will not interrupt Miss Templeton ever again.'" Composing herself, her face reddened. Bailey had heard of the cruel penal system with its brutal punishment at Norfolk Island. Katy Farrell's own sister-in-law had spent time at Norfolk as a young girl. The thought of it made her shudder. "I suppose if you tell someone enough times that they will never amount to anything in life, they may begin to believe it." She could see at once their sober expressions. "Or those of you who are weary of the prejudices have another choice. You can rise above it. The future of New South Wales lies here in this room and is formulating in each of your minds."

Some of the emancipist children brightened at her words and glanced smugly at one another.

"But it will take much work on the part of everyone. Some of you, before you came here to our school, had no formal education at all. Now you can read. You can make a purchase, and no one can shortchange you. You understand the value of our monetary system. You can add and subtract. No one can ever take these things from you." With a sense of deep conviction, she gazed at them all, hopeful that at least part of what she said would be grasped.

Standing with her back to the rear of the classroom, she did not see the schoolroom door open wide. She did notice that some of the students grew restless and whispered uneasily to one another. Young Mary Spencer caught her eye and pointed to the rear of the room. Bailey turned around. "Hello," she said in a reserved tone. Observing the disheveled man scowling at her, she chose to stand guardedly and await his response. The man removed his hat.

"Blaine Dobbins," he snapped out his name.

"Something we can do for you, Mr. Dobbins?" Sensing more

unrest among the students, Bailey strode toward the man.

"Me boy's Cole Dobbins." Dobbins turned to acknowledge the ruddy youth who ambled reluctantly through the door. "He's been kicked out o' this place, an' I want him back in!"

Bailey felt a chill touch her nerves. "But, Mr. Dobbins, your son—" She stopped. "We should discuss the matter outside, sir." She stepped out into the yard, the gray clouds overhead casting a pall over the landscape. Hoping the man and his boy would follow, she stopped and waited, her face expectant. Soon Dobbins emerged but ordered his son to take a seat inside the classroom.

"Thank you, Mr. Dobbins. I felt your privacy was—"

"I don't mince no words, lady!" Dobbins marched menacingly toward her. "I aims for Cole to get a proper education, an' you or no one else'll stop 'im."

Raising fine arched eyebrows, Bailey lifted her face confidently. "Mr. Dobbins, your son pulled a knife on me the first day of school. He intended to use it, and I acted accordingly."

"Cole don't bother no one lest they bothers him first."

"As your son's teacher, my authority must be respected. How can the other children learn if they feel another student can recklessly threaten their teacher?"

"He ain't got the knife now," Dobbins argued.

Seeing that she was getting nowhere with the man, Bailey clasped her hands in front of her. She dreaded the task ahead of her. "I'm afraid—" The sight of a horse and rider caught her eye. Seeing the flash of the British coat, she felt relief wash through her. Although the lieutenant's appearance from time to time had annoyed her, she felt certain that the military presence might quell Mr. Dobbins' temper. "Mr. Dobbins, I want to see Cole learn as I do all the other children, but I can't allow violent behavior."

The officer approached the two of them. "Good afternoon, Miss Templeton." He tipped his cap. "Is there a problem?"

Bailey saw the defensive glint in Dobbins' eyes. "Nothing we can't solve, Major Johnston." She remembered the day she stood in this officer's office and declared her intention to stay on as teacher. But in spite of her reserve about the major, she felt glad for his unexpected visit.

"Well, allow me to assist." He spoke with a quick, clipped British accent. "Perhaps I can help."

"This woman won't let me boy Cole come 'ere to this school."

"Oh?" Perkins' left brow lifted inquisitively. "Why not, Miss Templeton?"

Not at all pleased with his cool manner, Bailey maintained her composure. "Mr. Dobbins' son, Cole, pulled a knife on me the first day of school. Your predecessor, Captain Hogan, was made aware of the matter."

"Hogan's gone now. So we shall treat the matter as being reopened until we've resolved it to my satisfaction."

Seeing the light of humor in Dobbins' face, Bailey pulled her brows into an affronted frown. "Major, the matter *has* been resolved. You don't understand—"

"No, I'm afraid *you* don't understand, Miss Templeton." Folding his arms across his chest, the officer stared smugly. "You're here to educate the children of this colony without regard to their family history."

Outraged at his implication, Bailey retorted, "I, of all people, would never use such a bias upon which to base my decisions!"

"Whatever your reasons were for expelling this emancipist's child, the boy should be allowed to return."

Not believing what she heard, Bailey held her words and chose to weigh the matter before reacting impetuously.

"Thank you, Major." Dobbins stepped inside the schoolroom. "Cole!" he said gruffly. "You don't pay no 'eed to this woman. You're stayin'!" Turning on his worn heels, he glared threateningly at Bailey. "I'll be watchin' you, Miss Bailey Templeton. Me boy an' me better not have any more trouble from you."

Certain that his shallow threat would evoke a reaction from the major, Bailey glanced obliquely toward Johnston. "Is this what you wanted?" she asked quietly.

"I'm sorry for any trouble you've experienced, Mr. Dobbins." Johnston shook the man's hand. Walking him toward his wagon, he muttered just loudly enough for Bailey to hear. "Please understand that Miss Templeton is an American and somewhat frustrated. She'll learn our ways soon enough."

Drawing back proud shoulders, Bailey felt an anger growing inside of her. *He's purposely attempting to provoke me!* Seeing Dobbins pull away, she stood waiting for Major Johnston to return. As he drew near, she knew that she would have to choose her words carefully but allowed herself a withering stare. "Major, you surprise me."

"See here, Miss Templeton." Johnston ignored her glower. "I

realize that the emancipists are a different breed of people—"

"*Breed?* I do not speak of humans in the same context as animals, sir! With all due respect, I have spent unceasing hours visiting these same emancipist families. I hope my reputation goes before me. I have no such prejudices, only compassion for these oppressed people. But Cole Dobbins is—"

"Is entitled to the same education as the colonist children," Johnston interrupted again.

"His societal status is not in question. It is his violent behavior that concerns me and should concern you as well." Bailey listened as the officer droned on about the colony biases against emancipists. It was as though he heard nothing she said, and she realized that the attacks on her home had been mild compared to this sort of undermining. How could she battle such a thing?

Quietly dismissing herself from his presence, she returned to the classroom to restore the order once again. The confrontation caused a sickening physical response from her senses, and she struggled to maintain a composed demeanor. Glancing back at Cole Dobbins, she saw his self-satisfied smirk. He would be more impossible to deal with now than ever. Biting her lip, she fought the urge to cry and instead tapped her measuring stick against the desktop. She recalled the children's cruel comments in regard to the emancipists. But in spite of Johnston's ludicrous accusations, she knew her own heart and would teach accordingly.

"We've been discussing our treatment of our fellowman." She determined to complete the discussion that she had begun. "We call ourselves Christian because we believe in God, but the Bible tells us that we will know a tree by its fruit. I hope we've all realized that through our actions we show the world the good or bad that's inside of us," She took a ragged breath and hoped her voice did not waver. "And if we purposefully observe one another in our daily practices instead of merely judging this one or that one by their family name, we will learn to see each person for who they are instead of from whence they came." She deliberately made eye contact with Cole. "I pray that you all see in me and in one another good fruit and in that same way will go forth to accomplish some good in this world."

Indifferent, Cole Dobbins leaned back in his seat and began to converse with another boy, ignoring her words in defiance.

Bailey sighed and concluded the lesson. The next few days, she realized, could determine her future in the colony. *I know what*

Johnston really wants. Nothing would please him more than if I would pack up and leave. Seeing the children's faces anticipating her next move, she instructed, "Prepare your books for reading aloud." She smiled upon hearing their groans. She cast a chary gaze once more toward Cole and then back at the others. "I know it's almost time to go home. But let's finish up with reading." He made no attempt to comply but instead rested his face in his hands. Waiting as the others opened their tattered books, she pondered Cole's fate and that of her own. *Against my own will, Lord, you've allowed me to face a boy despised by all as a hopeless cause. Is he hopeless to you?* She lifted her book to prepare for the recitation. *Am I?*

"Katy Farrell! You've got to do something about it!" Katy sat upon the wagon seat along the meandering road. Awaiting the arrival of her two sons from school, she pondered the distance that continued to grow between herself and her husband, Dwight. He had gone again for the remainder of the week to tend to the other land and flocks he had acquired just north of Parrametta. In the beginning, she and her parents had known so much hardship and poverty that she had welcomed Dwight's diligent hand in managing the affairs of Rose Hill. But with the success of Rose Hill no longer being simply a means of support to Dwight, she worried that it had instead become his obsession. She could no longer stand by and watch their marriage deteriorate while the sheep ranch flourished. The myrtle trees around her rocked lazily in the breeze. She allowed the beautiful wildness of the countryside to lull her senses momentarily. She recalled the horrible conditions they had lived in early on. The dangers had lessened only slightly in regard to renegade convict gangs and belligerent Aborigines, but her world in the material sense had greatly improved. She and Dwight were now able to help assist other emancipist families in need. Dwight had donated building materials to Grant to aid in the repairs of the school building. Their youngest child, Corbin, had never known want. In spite of the insidious military junta and corrupt governors, they had overcome their mountainous problems. *But only to trade them for another*, Katy thought woefully. She could hear the plod of horses' canter and the squeak of wagon wheels rounding the dirt road just beyond where she waited. She sat up in the seat and composed a smile. *Can't have the boys seeing me in such a state.*

"Mum!" Jared called out, his face animated.

Katy's brows lifted with surprise. "Bailey?"

Bailey drew her wagon up beside Katy's. "Hello. Mrs. Spencer was in a hurry today to prepare for dinner guests, so I volunteered to drive the boys out to you."

Katy's brow furrowed. "I hope it wasn't a bother."

"Now, you stop it!" Bailey fussed. "You and Dwight do so much for the school, you can at least allow me this one chance to return the favor." She dabbed her neck with a handkerchief. "Everything all right at Rose Hill?"

"Yes. Thank you." Katy smiled. "Hop in, boys." She slid to the side to allow Donovan to take the reins.

"I don't suppose—" Bailey hesitated.

"Allow me one guess." Katy smiled knowingly. "You wish to join us for dinner?"

Bailey blushed. "Katy. Have you ever known me to invite myself to dinner?"

"I believe it's time you started."

"No. Nothing of the sort. I just wanted to inquire about your cousin. I know your family's been concerned about him."

"My cousin? Oh, you mean Grant."

Bailey nodded casually.

"Uncle Bartholomew received a letter from him last week. The conditions at Hobart are far worse than we ever imagined."

Bailey's face clouded with worry. "I . . . I'm sorry to hear that."

"So were we. But Grant refuses to allow his father to interfere. He says that he'll make the necessary arrangements when he feels he can leave. But an epidemic of fever has broken out, and he's the only medical help available. He's so willful about these matters."

Bailey gave a sidelong glance at Katy. "Must run in the family."

Choosing to ignore the comment, Katy lifted her face imperiously. "So are you joining us for dinner, Miss Templeton?"

The boys immediately begged, so Bailey conceded defeat. "All right. If you insist. But allow me to bring something this time. Some fresh cakes."

"Sounds lovely."

"You're certain you've enough for company?" Bailey asked.

"Quite. We are expecting the good Captain Gabriel as well. Come around six o'clock. We should have plenty for all."

"Good." Bailey made her polite farewells, glad for the invitation. "Around six, then," she confirmed. Heading toward home, she told herself that an evening with the Farrells would do her heart good. She had accepted few invitations since Captain Hogan's departure. But recalling her conversation with Katy, something in her good friend's eyes had disturbed her. She hadn't seen Katy in weeks, but she knew her well enough now to know that something troubled her. Perhaps that was why Katy had insisted upon her coming. *She needs someone to talk to.*

Dismissing the events of the school day from her mind, Bailey allowed her thoughts to drift to a sweeter time that now lingered in her senses like a dream—a moonlit evening, a handsome couple running along a sandy shore, then a stolen moment of bliss. The sweet reverie carried her along in its imaginary arms until she reached home. Then the facts of life in Sydney Cove crashed in upon her musings and crowded out the things that would never be to make room for reality. *I need a friend now, too, Katy.*

"Quickly now! Fetch some of that boiling water! We'll need these cells swabbed at once!" Grant shouted to the privates who aided him in the contagion's. "Hanson! Help this patient to his bed," he called to another.

"We're runnin' out o' beds, sir!" The private's hoarse voice brimmed with anxiety.

"Then go for more blankets. Some will have to sleep on the floor." Life had become a bitter battle for Grant. He slept seldom and ate as little as was necessary. With the onslaught of fever that had swept throughout the small military company, the limited medical aids had been stretched beyond their capability. Grant walked from the ward and out into the fresh air. A cloud cover blocked the sun, causing a chill in the air. Leaning against a post, he turned his face downward and sighed inwardly. Beads of moisture clung to his forehead. He raked his fingers through the dank tendrils of hair clinging to his brow. His dedication to the encampment waning, he wanted nothing more than to crawl into his own bed back in Sydney Cove and sleep for weeks. Terrible regrets assailed him. He had not offered a proper farewell to anyone, his duty having become more paramount. Only a little mail had trickled in to him besides that of his parents begging him to allow their intervention with Bligh. He felt himself weakening to the temptation. He wanted to go home. He ached to see friends' faces once more and to enjoy quiet dinner conversation with the Farrells at Rose Hill.

"Captain Hogan! More patients, sir!"

He rubbed his bristly jaw and tried to massage away the languor that settled in the bags under his eyes. "Coming, Private." His words sounded hollow even to himself. He had lost all compassion and now moved numbly through his work like a mindless beast.

"Letters! Letters from New South Wales!" A youth ran toward the main tent. The sailors and soldiers ran from all around the Hobart encampment in a rush to hear news from their loved ones in Sydney Cove.

"I'll run for you, sir." The private bolted for the tent. "You take your rest."

"Thank you." Grant slumped against the post. He had almost fallen sound asleep when the man returned. "Letter for you, Captain Hogan," he heard him say. His eyelids fluttered open. The news enlivened him. Examining the handwriting, he noticed at once the graceful, feminine pen strokes. *She wrote to me.* The thought of Bailey Templeton finally returning his hurriedly scrawled letter offered a moment of intense pleasure. Breaking the wax seal, he flipped open the letter. Disappointedly, he realized the letter to be from Katy. It read:

Dear Grant,

The children and Dwight send their greetings. We're all greatly sorrowed about your unexpected departure. A certain young woman, I'm sure, is especially grieved.

He flashed a brief smile.

Emily sends her best.

A suggestion of annoyance hovered in his eyes. He continued reading the letter but with little interest. Grateful as he was for Katy's letter, he could not help but believe that Bailey Templeton must surely hate him by now.

Bailey meandered her way through Katy's English garden. The moon now high over Rose Hill, she had opted for a walk alone. The house had numerous guests, most being families from neighboring farms. Several of her students were present, and she greeted each family cordially. But with her strength enervated by the emotionally strenuous week just over, she felt a sudden urge to be alone. Amelia and Katy were handling the early arrivals like perfect hostesses, so she decided to slip away unnoticed. She paused beneath a flowering myrtle. The sounds of laughter from inside the house caused her to chuckle quietly as well. Then a mixture of feelings surged through her. Although glad—no, grateful— that she had met the Farrells, she couldn't help being concerned about their marital woes. Dwight possessed an unusual financial aptitude and had proved a fearless crusader in the matters of the colony. In regard to the school, he had been invaluable. Unable to meet with Governor Bligh, he had stormed into Major George Johnston's office and demanded answers. Bailey was certain he had left an unforgettable impression on the corrupt officer. But he was sometimes too quick to forget his duties on the home front, as were many husbands in the brutal settlement. Even though Katy quickly defended Dwight's as yet delayed arrival to the party, Bailey could read the hurt in her friend's eyes. Occasionally, she noticed Katy walking past the front parlor window, peering through the draperies, and then walking away disappointedly. *Dwight Farrell, where are you?* Bailey felt frustration rising inside of her. Katy had become like a sister to her. Helpless to speak, she had gripped Katy's hands, gave a gentle squeeze, and forced a sympathetic smile. A silent thread of understanding had passed between them, but Bailey chastened herself for her lack of proper words. She hoped that Katy somehow felt the strength of her prayers.

Again she heard laughter, only closer. Bailey turned to see a couple walking past the myrtles. They had not noticed her, and she, being glad for the privacy, rested against the trunk until they passed. Deciding she should join the party, she started for the house, but then glanced back to see if she recognized the couple. What she saw shook her sensibilities, for it was Katy who walked along the garden path, but not with Dwight. The shadows kept her from seeing his face, but she could tell by his bulky build that the man was not Katy's husband. Bailey's eyes grew wide, and intense astonishment touched her face. She felt foolish for standing in the pathway gaping awkwardly, but something drew her to go after them. Taking a deep, unsteady breath she followed along silently. Finally, the twosome seated themselves on a wooden settee. Half in dread, Bailey positioned herself behind a large thicket and stole a closer glance at the man. It was indeed who she suspected—Captain Robert Gabriel! They conversed quietly and in friendly tones.

"Thank you, Robert, for rescuing me tonight. Our guests find you delightful, with your many stories."

Robert sat quietly for a moment, his gaze fixed on Katy's face. The moon illumined them both, and the only sound was the hum of the cicadas. Finally he broke the silence. "I'll be leaving soon. I'm glad our paths crossed again."

"Why must you leave so soon?"

Bailey bit her lip, fearing for Katy's vulnerability.

"I've been here several months now, and I must go away now I've a ship to man."

"Don't you like Sydney Cove?"

"I love Sydney Cove—especially her people." He shifted, glanced up and down the pathway, and then continued. "I shall be forever changed from this time forth. But I don't belong here as you do, Lady Katherine."

"I find it strange you should make such a comment. I never believed I would belong here, either. But I've changed over time."

"Yes, you have. But for the better. You're a woman now with a beautiful family." He looked away. "A husband who loves you."

"Robert?"

"Yes?"

Katy hesitated.

Bailey heard the sounds from inside the house grow louder. Someone had opened the rear door to the kitchen. She made her way quickly back down the path. If someone else walked up, she did not want to be found hiding behind the thicket. To have even done so now caused a pang of guilt. She must place her friend in God's hands and trust Katy to use good judgment.

Stepping hurriedly along, she kept her eyes to the path. Without intent, she ran headlong into the approaching person. "Excuse me, please!" she apologized and felt her cheeks redden.

"Bailey?"

Her fingers flew to her mouth. "Dwight!" She stepped back. Still dressed in his work clothing, she could see the weariness around his eyes. Her heart swelled with sympathy for him. She struggled to find the words to speak. "You look exhausted, Dwight. I'll bet you're in no mood for a party."

"No, I don't mind at all. I did have some trouble along the way, though. Bushrangers stole some of our flock, but nothing we can't surmount."

"I'm certain of it, too." She folded her arms casually. "I'll see you soon inside, then?"

"Yes. But first I must find my wife. I owe Katy an apology. I've spoiled her evening, I'm certain."

Katy! Bailey knew she must not show the worry on her face. Dwight Farrell being an intelligent man, she could do nothing to evoke suspicion. Although Katy and Robert had been engaged in mere pleasantry, the growing tension between Dwight and Katy could erupt. "You didn't find Katy inside?" She bit the inside of her lip.

"No. I was told that she'd gone outside for a walk. She isn't with you obviously."

"Obviously not." Paralyzed with indecision, Bailey finally offered, "Why not go and clean up upstairs. I'll find Katy and we'll surprise her with your return." She hesitated, hopeful that he did not detect the guilt in her eyes.

"Thank you. That's a wonderful idea." He started to turn away, but the sound of Katy's voice caused him to whirl around. "What's that? I hear her now. May as well let her know I'm here."

"No!" Bailey gripped his forearm and then saw the surprise of his gaze. "That is, you forgot about the surprise, didn't you?"

"Oh, of course." Dwight glanced down, his eyes casting a curious stare toward the grip she had on his arm. "But it isn't the surprise that concerns you, is it, Bailey?"

Quickly releasing his arm, she answered, "What do you mean?"

"She's with *him*, isn't she? She's with Robert Gabriel."

No longer able to hide her worry, Bailey nodded. "Yes, Dwight. Katy's with Robert."

10

PRAYER OF THE RIGHTEOUS

Bailey filled her basket with wares from the store shelves. Her school day finished, she had opted for a drive into the bustling town square of Sydney Cove. A new shipment of goods had arrived at the harbor, and a buying frenzy had ensued. Indeed happy to see the large pile of onions and fresh potatoes, she gathered all that she could afford and then began to maneuver her way through the throng of women who mobbed the dry goods table. A smartly dressed red-haired woman stood with her back to her. "Pardon me," she said as politely as she could to the woman.

"Of course—" The woman stopped, and then a smile spread across her face. "Hello, Miss Templeton."

"Oh!" Bailey returned the greeting, surprised to see the minister's wife. "Hello to you, Mrs. Whitley. Quite a crowd, eh?"

"Quite." Rachel Whitley glanced around. "I spotted another table in the back. They're unloading more crates onto it," she whispered. Holding her youngest, Jake, close to her, she adjusted his cap. Then she commented with genuine sentiment, "Your dress is lovely."

Not remembering what she had donned that morning, Bailey

glanced down at herself. The dress was made of ecru crepe de Chine, with an overskirt edged in a broad box-pleated trimming of blue silk. Laurie had made it for her as a going-away gift. "Why, thank you." She snugged the matching parasol beneath her arm and followed Rachel through the mob to the rear of the store. Close on Rachel's trail were the other two siblings, Luke and Ariel. Little Ariel, she could see, had learned the ways of the world through her brothers' eyes. She bounded around her mother's green woolen skirts to prove her speed to her older brother. Watching for Rachel's reaction, Bailey found delight in Rachel's adoring gaze. She had never observed a mother so enthralled with her own children.

Selecting some thread and a handful of buttons, Rachel offered, "Why not join me for tea, Miss Templeton? We've not had a proper chance to visit."

"Tea?" She hadn't counted on adding to her social calendar at all this week. "This afternoon?"

"Yes, please. I should become acquainted with the one who will be teaching my children next year." She smiled. "And you should know me as well."

"Thank you. At your home?"

"Yes. It isn't far. You could follow us there."

Considering her own list of chores for the afternoon, she hesitated. "I wouldn't want to impose."

"No imposition at all. And I promise I won't keep you long."

"All right, then." Bailey had cultivated a certain smile lately whenever she knew the task before her was obligatory. But she had so limited her friendships to the Rose Hill women that she chastened herself for her selfishness. "I've a few more things to purchase." Her brows lifted with a surety.

"Splendid! We'll wait for you out front." Rachel Whitley steered her children through the crowd of shoppers and disappeared.

Making short work of her errands, Bailey located the Whitleys' wagon and team. At the helm was a Cockney driver hired by the minister for his wife. He tipped his cap at Bailey. "Follow me, miss. Your wagon close by?"

"Yes. Right around the corner." Bailey awkwardly juggled the packages in her hands and headed toward her wagon. Mounting the buckboard, she followed the Whitleys through the borough. She was surprised to discover that the Whitleys lived within miles of her home. The minister's home was a simple affair, the walk up to the front porch ended swiftly Bailey joined Rachel and the children on the porch and assisted the busy mother in helping them remove their caps. "Such beautiful children, Mrs. Whitley. And little Jake is the spitting image of you."

Rachel laughed out her reply. "Poor child."

Bailey reached out to the toddler and grasped his pudgy hand in her own. "You're a good-looking man, Jake, no matter what your mother says." Unable to resist, she allowed a soft ringlet of red hair to curl around her fingers. A shaft of sun struck his hair, and it gleamed like gold. Tired of Bailey's doting attention, Jake swatted lightly at her fingers, then brushed his hair back and forth in annoyance. His reaction amused her, but she stifled her laugh.

"Teatime!" Rachel opened the door and allowed the children to bound through. "I'm putting them all down for a rest. I'll join you shortly." Rachel removed her own soft blue bonnet.

"Point me toward the kitchen, and I'll start the tea," Bailey offered.

"Dear me, no!" Rachel waved away her response. "How inhospitable I would be!"

"Nonsense!" Bailey insisted. "You British are such lovers of custom. I'll find the kitchen myself." She hurried past Rachel, ignoring her stunned expression.

Quickly rummaging through Rachel's quaint kitchen, Bailey found an amply filled larder. A small jar clearly marked "tea" caught her eye. Within minutes, she had the fire stoked and the kettle simmering. Although earlier she had dismissed the invitation to tea as merely obligatory, she now found herself beginning to relax. The quiet moment to herself had energized her. Taking a seat on a cushioned chair, she leaned back and allowed the sunshine streaming in to bask her face in warmth. For an instant, a wistful expression stole into her countenance. The events of the prior evening at Rose Hill had troubled her, and a cloud of worry followed her throughout the school day. But now she felt she could perhaps see the matter in a more positive light. *The Farrells are a reasonable couple. They're Christian people and know that God can see them around this obstacle.*

"I'd give half a crown to read your thoughts, Miss Templeton."

Bailey sat up, surprised to have her moment of respite interrupted. "Hello, Mrs. Whitley." She quickly composed a reply. "Children all asleep?"

"Asleep or simply pretending to be." Rachel checked the kettle and then busied herself with the teacups and with preparing a plate of biscuits and jam.

"One day I'll know of such joys. But for now it appears God has other plans for me besides homemaking and motherhood."

"Your day will come, I'm certain. Why, any man in the settlement would see your hand as a prize." She set a saucer and steaming cup in front of Bailey and then seated herself across from her.

Pursing her lips, Bailey blew across the cup's rim. Her left brow arched cynically. Rachel's words caught her by surprise. She never knew exactly how to respond to a compliment. "My day will come *if* fate allows me to stay in this wilderness." Reflecting on more realistic facts, she smiled. "And if that certain someone doesn't mind his wife teaching."

"You're so dedicated to the children, Miss Templeton." Rachel slipped her feet out of her cloth slippers and crossed her stockinged feet on the rug. "I know few women with your courage. You'll be an ideal role model for the girls in our settlement." Taking her first sip, she frowned and squinted at the taste.

Bailey felt more relaxed than ever. She liked this minister's wife. She had such an unconventional mien about her. They conversed easily for an hour, mostly about the school. All but forgetting the time, Bailey spied a large clock in the corner. "Goodness! I've papers to grade before tomorrow." She stood at once. "Forgive my abruptness, Mrs. Whitley."

"Not at all." Rachel rose fluidly from her chair. "I've so enjoyed our chat. And—would you mind? I prefer to be called Rachel." Glancing toward the children's room, she stirred uneasily.

Adjusting her own hat, Bailey smiled broadly. "Wonderful! And you'll call me Bailey?"

"As you wish." There was a pensive shimmer in the shadow of Rachel's eyes. Her gaze focused on something distant, then she clasped her hands in front of her and sighed.

Bailey could see the change in her demeanor, for Rachel's face clouded with uneasiness. Suddenly she felt as though she had been insensitive. Perhaps Rachel had not wished to discuss the school after all. "Rachel?" Not having tied her bonnet, she pulled it off. "I've enjoyed our visit today. But did you invite me here for another purpose?"

She bit her lip. "Am I so transparent?"

"Forgive me for not noticing sooner." Bailey laid her bonnet aside. "You wish to tell me something?"

Nodding slightly, Rachel pointed to the chair with her eyes. "Would you mind?"

Bailey seated herself at once. A strange quiet filled the room, but she held her words, giving Rachel ample time to share her thoughts.

"You've befriended one of my dear friends—Katy Farrell."

Bailey nodded, depicting an ease she did not necessarily feel.

"Perhaps you've noticed that a problem exists in the household."

Bailey acknowledged her steadfast gaze. "You know?"

"I've known for some time. I could see the chasm widening between Katy and Dwight. But then the problems would seemingly lessen. I kept praying, hoping."

Bailey felt relieved that her secret fear could now be discussed, at least in part. "I want no part of gossip, you understand."

Rachel's cheeks colored slightly. "That's the furthest thing from my mind. My intentions are also pure. But we cannot pretend the problem doesn't exist. Our friends need our understanding but also our honesty. We must be held accountable one to the other, true?" The animation had drained from Rachel's face. She could no longer hide her secret pain.

A sense of despair enveloped Bailey. She had not intended to become so involved. But now she could not help but feel Katy's sorrow as deeply as did Rachel. And she empathized with Rachel's helpless anxiety at having known about the problem. "I don't know what to do, Rachel."

"Have you shared your fears with Katy?"

A sense of guilt pricked at Bailey's emotions. "No. I thought she would feel that I was interfering. I respect her privacy."

"As do I," Rachel said evenly.

"Has Reverend Whitley spoken with Dwight?"

"Yes. To a small degree. Dwight Farrell can be quite single-minded, however. He feels that his family understands his absences. Building Rose Hill will be, in his mind, a legacy for his children and grandchildren."

"But if the children never see their father—"

"I know, and I agree. But how do we persuade Dwight Farrell otherwise?"

"I suppose if I were a true friend, I would have shared my concerns with Katy already." Bailey sighed. "When it comes to relationships, it seems I always fail."

"Don't say such things," Rachel interjected gently.

"It's true," Bailey chided herself. "In the arena of life, I'm always a mere spectator." She thought of her sister, Laurie, well on her way to marital bliss. And of Emily Parkinson waiting patiently for Grant Hogan to return. Tossing aside those thoughts, she forced herself to address the issue at hand. "If I attempted to speak with Katy or Dwight, what would I say?"

A curious smile played around Rachel's mouth. "We're going to have to pray for God's wisdom for that. When I've been at a total loss for answers, I've often seen His intervention."

"But should I speak to them, Rachel? Either way, I could lose an important friendship." *There*—she had finally spoken her deepest fear of all. "I need my friends, though that is selfish of me, I suppose."

"I can't answer that for you." Rachel stood, walked toward Bailey, then knelt and grasped her hand. "But don't berate yourself. In such cases, all those who love hurting people are subject to taking the blame for their pain upon themselves. That isn't what God intends for us." Closing her eyes, she spoke barely above a whisper. "Dear Lord, we know not what to pray. Katy and Dwight need your help. We're at a loss for words but yearn to help. Help our faith in this matter—faith in you and not in man."

Bailey felt a peace envelope her, and she sensed a stirring from within. She nodded as Rachel prayed aloud but inwardly also made her own confession. *I want to help Katy, Father. You've given her a wonderful family. She needs you now. Give her strength so she won't despair. Give her faith to stand when temptation comes.* Bailey felt her bottom lip quiver slightly, but she held fast to her emotions. *And there is one who never gives a thought about me, yet I can't help but be mindful of him. Please protect Grant Hogan and bring him safely home to his family. Not for my sake. I ask nothing more—just bring him home.*

"What? Macarthur's denied the transfer?" Grant's temper flared, but he maintained control of his words. "Is there an explanation for the denial?" He stood towering over the officer, his arms folded tightly.

"No, Captain. Only that your medical expertise is needed here in Hobart." The officer lifted his face and shoved his spectacles back with his finger. "Desperately needed, Captain." His gaze softened sympathetically.

"I know that," Grant answered quietly. "It was foolish for me to attempt a transfer now. Perhaps in the future." *So it was Macarthur all along!*

The officer nodded hopefully. "We all want our time finished here, sir. Me wife, especially, wants me to return. She's bore our son now, and I've never laid eyes on him."

A twinge of guilt pricked at Grant's emotions. He had no wife or children back at Sydney Cove. Only a perplexed young woman, who by now had no doubt allowed her interests to stray elsewhere. But he no longer bore guilt on behalf of Bailey Templeton. His days of ruing those few moments of bliss alone with her had ended. Regretting no more that he had kissed her or made her a promise that circumstances forced him to break, he now saw his actions in a new light. For he now cherished the memory of her touch, which at times was the only thought keeping him alive. If all Bailey became to him now was a memory, *then so be it!* At least that stolen moment in time offered something tangible between them and not something merely hoped for.

He walked wearily back to his bunk to catch a few minutes of rest before beginning his rounds in the contagion ward. Laying his head atop the tattered mattress, he closed his eyes and allowed his thoughts to drift. Within moments, his mind traveled to a sandy shore where he could beckon, and she would appear. Every time he relived the moment, his heart had turned over in response. His mouth curved into an unconscious smile. But then his face darkened. Her memory faded and he could no longer remember her intense eyes and the warmth of her kiss. The vision clouded and his mind grew restless. *Can I not even now find rest?* Dragging himself to his feet, he trudged from the officers' tent and made his way toward the contagion. *Perhaps I belong in Hobart after all!*

Heading her wagon toward the bend that would lead her home, Bailey contemplated her visit with Rachel. She realized that even after leaving the Whitleys' home, she had remained in an attitude of prayer. In that sense, she felt that she had grown somewhat. Prayer had become her buffer in this unfriendly colony. She also found comfort in realizing that her compassion for mankind had grown while in this harsh land. Caring for someone again brought comfort, even though part of that caring was coupled with worry. She had not realized until now how callused she had grown in America. Perhaps having everything her heart desired had not been a catalyst for growth but instead provided a comfortable place in which to become more detached from those in need. She had arrived in Sydney Cove nursing a wounded heart, yet determined to prove her worth. Now she realized how self-centered she had been. She had wanted it all—a world of her own choosing. Her motives for teaching had not centered around the children but around her own need to prove herself. *God, forgive me.*

Glancing behind her, she beheld the resplendent sunset. The reds and yellows marking the end of the day bled across the sky like burnished gold mingled with blood. *Royalty and sacrifice.* She pondered the spiritual symbolism found in the heavenly gift of color. *You, Lord, forfeited one for the other.* Suddenly, the picture grew more clear to her. She had given up marriage for God's caring will in her life. *These children really do need me, don't they, Father?*

A sudden, explosive sound rocked her world. At first, she felt nothing but stunned shock. Then a fiery pain began to build in her shoulder. She groaned without conscious effort. She felt her heart pounding, heard it echoing in her ears. Breathing rapidly, she glanced down as though in a trance. Trickling down across her silk blouse, a stream of bright red blood sent another wave of shock through her. Her head began to spin. *I've been shot!* Realizing the sniper still lurked nearby, she gripped the reins. *I can't faint, not now! Not yet!* She commanded the horses and snapped the reins, her strength draining. The wagon bolted forward. Another explosion sent a musket ball past her head. The gunman missed his mark. She wanted to go home, yet home may not be safe now. *Why didn't I listen to Katy? I should've moved out to Rose Hill.* She couldn't think or reason. The wagon rattled wildly beneath her, the world turned gray, and the road ahead grew dim. She could see the horses' manes blown straight back yet could feel no wind against herself. The reins were whipped from her hands, and she gripped the seat as tightly as she could. Whispering a prayer, she numbly remembered the ones who loved her and needed her. The pitiful faces of children flashed in front of her eyes, and then all was black.

"Who told John Macarthur to transfer out all of our best offi-cers?" Bligh rolled a pinch of snuff between his fingers, his heavy brows pulled together in an affronted frown.

"Macarthur's corps 'ave run this colony since Grose and Pat-erson gave 'im the run of it—since b'fore you came, Governor." The corporal stood stiffly, holding his cap in his hands.

"Grose and Paterson are not in charge now. I want Macarthur brought in here at once!" he roared. Shoving his large leather chair away from his desk, he stood and marched to the window.

"He's not one to be reckoned with, Governor." The corporal's voice quivered. "With all his land and money, he's the wealthiest man in New South Wales."

"Silence, man!" Bligh paced impatiently. "Macarthur's man-aged to slip out of every noose England has slipped around his neck. Well, he'll not undermine *this* authority. And he'll not slip away from me." He whirled around to face the corporal. "At once, man! Bring me Macarthur—by tomorrow morning! Now go for my driver at once!"

<hr/>

A chill wind swept across Bailey's face, tumbling her hair over her ear. *I'm alive!* she thought feebly. Attempting to move, a bolt of pain shot through her body. Gradually she realized she had fallen from the wagon. But with the horse and wagon nowhere to be seen, Bailey realized how fortunate she had been. If the gun-man had tried to follow, the runaway team would have led him away from where she had fallen. The sky was black, giving no ink-ling of time and no bearing on her location. Reaching up, she tried to feel the wound in her shoulder, but the pain prevented touch. She rolled onto her back, moaning faintly. Sleep finally overtook her, bringing nightmarish bouts of sleeping, then groggy wake-fulness for what seemed like hours. Slowly opening her eyes, she stared at the dark firmament. *Am I dying?* If so, she must have been at the dark portals before arriving in heaven, for she saw no angels nor any heavenly light.

The moonlight reflected on an embankment rising up next to her. Realizing that she had tumbled down into a gully, she hoped she had fallen near the road. But she could not shout, for to do so might alert the gunman. *If I can crawl close to the road, then I can see better.* She willed herself to move, but her limbs would not cooperate. *Get up, Bailey!* This harsh lesson had certainly taught her to never travel alone after dark. *How many times did Grant Hogan try to warn me?* She breathed in short, shallow gasps. After lying still for a moment, she bent her knees and slid her feet up close to her body. Her fingers trembled, but she steadied her hands and pressed them palm down against the cold ground. Mildly surprised, she felt herself sit upright. Relief swept through her. *I can move!* Holding her hand close to her throbbing shoulder, she forced herself to stand. Her knees buckled, and the pain sent spasms throughout her body. But her lips were forced shut so no sound would burst out. Wordlessly, she crawled up the shallow embankment.

A flicker of light in the distance caught her eye, and she could see the road sprawled before her. She froze. The light grew brighter and soon became two lights. Pushing herself painstakingly down into the ditch, she watched cautiously, fear knotting in her stomach. The sound of carriage wheels became distinct, and she knew at once that she must make her presence known. Mustering her strength, she prepared to call out, but only a hoarse cry emanated from her throat. Despair sank into her heart. The carriage drew near, and she knew that if she remained alone outside all night, her chances for survival would be slim. "Help me!" she cried, determination welling inside her. "Please! *Help!*"

The carriage slowed. Bailey dug her fingernails into the sod and dragged herself closer to the road. Panic set her heart to beating because she knew not whom to trust.

"What is it, Mr. Mead?" a voice called from inside the carriage. "Why are we stopping?"

The driver gazed out apprehensively, the two carriage lamps his only light. "Sorry, sir. I thought I 'eard somethin', I did."

"Then you should keep going, Mead," the voice answered blandly.

Forced to take her chances, Bailey inhaled deeply and shrieked, "Down here, sir! I've been wounded!"

"It's a woman, sir! She's hurt!" The driver prepared to dismount.

"Careful, Mead. Could be a convict that's escaped."

"I'm no convict!" Bailey felt the tears surface. Trying to pull herself to her feet, she yanked the tousled bonnet from her head.

"It's not a convict, sir. It's a lady, all right. A right fine lady."

The carriage door opened slowly. "Bring her aboard, Mead. I'll have her tended to when we arrive home."

Bailey thought her heart would burst for joy, but the dizzying pain prevented a response. Staggering toward the carriage light, she suddenly felt two strong arms supporting her, then sensed her limp body being lifted into the carriage. After being placed on a cushioned carriage seat, she heard the door snapped closed and knew distinctly that she was not alone. A crisp British voice, full of authority, ordered the driver to proceed. Shivering, Bailey perceived someone covering her with a blanket. After a few moments of basking in the blanket's soft warmth, she squinted, desirous to know her rescuer. She coughed weakly and tried to speak. "Sir?"

"Lie still, miss. You've been shot. We'll be getting you help soon," he said with quiet emphasis. His deep voice comforted her.

"Who—" Bailey succumbed to her weakness, her eyes closing once more.

"I'm Bligh, miss. Governor William Bligh. Governor of New South Wales."

11
THE
GOVERNOR'S
MANSION

A whale oil lantern flickered dimly beside Bailey. She squinted to make out the details of the lantern and the room, but a veil prevented her eyes from focusing. Rolling onto her back, she grimaced and instinctively reached for her throbbing shoulder. At once she detected a clean white bandage. Confusion filled her mind. She remembered nothing about receiving medical care. Struggling to free herself from the cobwebs of delirium, she closed her eyes tightly and forced herself to concentrate. *Where are you, Bailey? What's happened to you?*

Her clearest recollection came to her in a hostile image—a musket fired, a horse in the brush, everything dark . . . Her eyelids fluttered open, and she heard herself moan.

The soothing touch of a soft, damp cloth against her forehead brought her glance upward. Standing over her, a severe-looking woman bathed her face and felt her pulse.

"Awake now, are we, miss?" The woman glanced at Bailey, her eyes creased at the sides with age. Deliberately, she folded up the cloth and laid it aside.

Bailey weakly inclined her head in a polite gesture of thanks.

"Thank you," she whispered hoarsely. "Thirsty." She ran her fingers slowly down her throat.

The woman made no hesitation but swiftly turned and brought back a glass of water for Bailey. Sliding long fingers between the veils of fabric that hung from the bed's canopy frame, she pushed back the curtains. Bailey realized that in her groggy stupor, she had been trying to see through the bed curtains. The woman lifted Bailey's head, and parting her dry lips, she sipped the cold water. As grateful as she was for the drink, she felt just as relieved to have her head back against the feathered pillow. "My head—" Her fingers tightly gripped the sheets as the room began to whirl and nausea swept over her.

"Easy now, miss." The woman spoke firmly. "You've been on your back a few days now. You're likely to feel a bit woozy."

"Then I must sit up. Will you help me?" Bailey's eyes widened. She hated feeling so helpless. But once again, the woman complied with her wishes and slowly began to prop up more pillows behind her head.

"Let's try it this way first. Later on today you can try to sit up, but I wouldn't try it now, miss." She took a step back and eyed the pillows. "That ought to do. Now, is there anything else you'll be needin'?"

The woman still had not smiled, but Bailey, grateful for the care, forced a faint smile of her own. "You've been so kind." Her cheeks colored slightly. "But could you tell me, please—where am I?"

Lifting her face, the woman allowed herself a guttural chuckle. "Doctor said you might be sayin' such things. You're at the governor's house. Governor William Bligh."

Nodding politely, the aging servant departed from the room. Bailey, left with nothing but the ticking of a large clock, heaved a heavy sigh. Forcing herself to focus her attention on the last few days, she soon began remembering parts of her ordeal. But she could not recollect the man's face who shot her. The sounds of the bustling household caught her ear. She imagined herself up and about soon, but her weary body failed to respond to any motivation. After some time, she did sit up just as the doors to the bedroom flew open. She smiled at the servant girl who entered carrying a serving tray.

"Hot soup for our guest. Tilly said you was awake. You gave us all a fright, that's wot." The girl placed the tray right over Bailey's lap, speaking to her in a familiar tone. "Homemade and straight from Cook's pot just today!"

Bailey smiled genuinely now. The girl's friendly manners encouraged her. "You've all been so kind—and me a stranger to you all."

"Not a stranger to me, Miss Templeton. You is the reason my Alfred kin read and write."

A warmth spread throughout her being. "You're Alfred's mother? Alfred Simons?"

"One and the same mother o' Alfred. I'm Ellen Simons."

"Have we met?" Bailey did not recognize the woman, but she had met so many new parents.

"Not officially, but I've seen you. The driver found your reticule with a letter on the inside addressed to you. That's how we all knew it was you."

"Thank goodness. I never expected to see my reticule again." Bailey continued her questioning, her tone tactful. "What of Alfred's father? Have I met him?"

"No. His papa ain't never been nothin' to the boy. You wouldn't have met him. But *you* give 'im somethin' o' worth, Miss Templeton. I'm indebted to you, as we all are—all o' us emancipists."

"I'm so grateful to hear you say that, Mrs. Simons. What you're saying, well, I don't hear many kind words like yours." Bailey chose her words carefully.

"They's lots o' hard folks in Sydney Cove. You know wot I mean by *hard*?"

Biting her lip, Bailey answered, "Do you mean some of the parents are callused?"

"Yes, and rightly so. Most 'ave seen nothin' but 'ard times and ill treatment from the military. I don't think most emancipists knows 'ow to accept kind treatment. Not unless someone wants somethin' in return. We're a suspicious lot."

"From what I've seen, Mrs. Simons, everything you say is true. The emancipists are treated cruelly. I don't blame them at all for being mistrustful of me."

"You've more than earned my trust. Like I say, Miss Templeton, you gave me own young Alfred a chance to better 'isself. He'll be a better man for it someday."

"You're too kind." Preparing to eat, she interjected, "Pardon me, please." Bailey bowed her head and thanked God for her meal. "Looks wonderful." Spooning the hot soup between her lips, she delighted in the delicious taste and realized how famished she was. "Will I meet Governor Bligh today?"

"It's possible, miss. Governor Bligh works long hours but seldom misses his evenin' meal." She stepped toward the door.

"Good. I want to thank him for saving my life. I'm greatly indebted to the man."

"He's a good man, miss. A bit touchy at times, but decent." Before leaving, the servant girl added, "He'll find out who took the shot at you, too. Bligh don't put up wif no crooks runnin' free."

Stretching a smile across her face, Bailey responded, "What a relief." She was glad to hear that Bligh would take an interest in her plight. And Ellen was a delightful person, but more than anything else, the young woman's comments about her son encouraged Bailey. She had often wondered if any of the emancipist parents appreciated her efforts. Not that she would ever teach based upon how many accolades she would receive. If that had been the case, she would have quit some time ago. She remembered her vow to God just before the shooting incident. Without any doubt now, she knew how badly the families needed her—just as she knew that some desperate men wanted her gone. That God had brought her to Sydney Cove for a purpose was indelibly printed on her heart. She glanced down once again at her wound and weighed the cost of staying. *The Sydney Cove School will go forward no matter how far this colony sinks into ruin.*

"It ain't proper! Miss Templeton, you shouldn't be climbin' down those stairs!" Ellen stood, arms crossed at the foot of the expansive staircase.

"I can't stay in that bed another moment. I want to take my own bath and sit up properly at the dinner table." Bailey, ignoring the girl's reprimands, held fast to the stair rail. The sunset outside her window only served to remind her that time fleeted past. The longer she stayed in bed, the longer the school would remain closed. "How shall I find something to wear, Ellen?"

"I can have someone send for your things, miss, but please crawl back up to your bed. The governor will be angry with me otherwise," Ellen pleaded to no avail.

"I can explain myself to the governor. But I can't present myself in this condition." She held the enormous nightgown out on either side.

"Here now, wots this?" A larger woman appeared beside Ellen. In her arms lay Bailey's frock that she had worn the night of the shooting.

"My dress?" Bailey gazed curiously.

Pursing her lips, the housemaid said, "It was a fright, miss. All dirty and torn from that musket shot. But I've fixed it up. It's all clean now, freshly ironed, and you can't tell it was ever torn. Cleaned up your bonnet, too."

"There you have it, then, Miss Templeton." Ellen smiled brightly. "I'll help you back up to your bed, and in a few days—"

"I'll take the dress now, Ellen." Bailey proceeded to descend the stairwell.

"Miss Templeton, you really shouldn't." Ellen frowned.

"I'll be the judge, Ellen." Holding out her hands, Bailey politely took the dress from the maid. She offered a meek smile. "I will be needing a bit of help drawing the bath water."

"Allow me, Miss Templeton," the maid volunteered. "A nice hot bath with some perfumes. How's that sound?"

"Don't go to any trouble." Bailey arched one definitive brow.

"None at all. About a half hour, I'll come for you in your room."

Bailey turned and began the laborious task of ascending the stairs. Wincing all the way, she felt relieved to lie down again. But she dared not allow the servants to know of her pain.

Within a few moments, a knock at the door brought her to her feet. Before she could cross the room, the door opened. "What's this?" A stylish older gentleman stood staring at her. Replacing a monocle to his right eye, he frowned patronizingly.

"Sir! I'm not dressed!" Bailey scolded the man.

"And I am your doctor and don't give a shilling for how you're dressed! Please return to your bed at once, Miss Templeton!"

Puzzled, Bailey folded her arms across her chest. "You're *my* doctor?"

He bowed politely. "So glad to see you awake, Miss Templeton. You had us worried for a bit. Allow me to introduce myself." He strode quickly to her side and clasped her wrist in his hand. "I'm Surgeon White. I'm a naval officer and physician here in Sydney."

Bailey felt herself being led back to her bed. She hated being treated like a child, but in her weak state she succumbed to his orders. Lifting her feet from the floor, she slid her legs beneath the sheets. "I want to go home, Doctor White. When may I?"

"What's your hurry?" He pulled the sheets around her. Turning his face, he called out, "Mrs. Griggs?"

"I'm the only teacher in Sydney Cove. I must return to school at once."

The door opened again. The first servant woman that Bailey had met walked in. "Doctor White? You called, sir?"

"I'm ordering strict bed rest for our patient. If you must stay in the room with her to accomplish such a thing, then so be it!"

"Yes, sir." Mrs. Griggs curtsied. "Did you hear your doctor, Miss Templeton?"

Breathing out a sigh, Bailey smiled woodenly. "Yes, Mrs. Griggs."

Doctor White looked gravely into her face. "Any idea who did this to you?"

Leaning back on her elbows, she addressed the matter to the best of her weak ability. "There's been quite a dilemma about the school since my arrival."

Peering beneath the bandage, Dr. White addressed Mrs. Griggs. "More ointment—in my bag."

"Captain Hogan thought he was hiring a man, but he wasn't— that is, I'm not a man—"

"You're certain of that?" White asked blandly.

Biting her cheek, Bailey lay back against the pillow. "I'm certain that my refusal to give up my teaching position has made me the target of the attack."

White stopped, narrowing his eyes. "You've informed Bligh of your suspicions?"

"I've not had the privilege of meeting Governor Bligh."

"Allow me, please," called a voice from the doorway.

Bailey, along with Dr. White and Mrs. Griggs, turned abruptly.

"Hello, Governor!" Dr. White greeted Bligh.

"Hello, White. How is our patient?"

"Obstinate. Stubborn. Other than that, she'll be on her feet soon." White applied more ointment to Bailey's wound.

Biting her lip, Bailey offered a polite nod to Bligh. "Governor Bligh. At last we meet." She winced.

"Not under the best of circumstances, I'm afraid." He took off his tricorn hat and walked to the foot of the bed. "You're a lucky young woman."

"Yes, I believe I am." Bailey studied his commanding face. His bulbous nose dominated his meaty features. He was a stocky man of medium height and attired as a naval officer. Judging from his uncompromising air, he was not a man to be trifled with.

Bligh's voice was stern but held a shade of sympathy. "I sent a messenger to the school this morning. School will be dismissed until your return."

"Thank you, Governor." Bailey, elated to hear of his swift decision, felt relief sweep through her. But she was wary of the school's being closed.

"Is there anyone else we should notify?" Bligh asked with an air of cool authority.

Bailey thought of Grant Hogan, which surprised her. "No. If you notified the students, then all of my friends will hear the news. I teach all of their children."

"Anything else?" he added hurriedly, his mind on other matters.

"I have a wagon with two horses that one of your officers provided for me. I lost the team when I fell from the wagon."

"All secured at the Government House. They were brought in yesterday morning by a colonist who found the team grazing in his field," Bligh answered readily.

Her face colored with astonishment. "This is all so unbelievable. You've been extremely kind, Governor. How can I ever repay you?"

"When you're up to it, we've some questions. I heard part of what you were saying to our good doctor here."

"I'm up to it now." Bailey felt a surge of energy. "What I was saying is true. Someone or several people are trying to run me out of Sydney Cove. I have one friend who believes the military junta is behind the scheme, but I can't say for certain." She decided to keep the Farrells' name out of the matter.

"I can't act on your suspicions, Miss Templeton." Bligh's brow furrowed. "We must present facts. Evidence."

"Of course." Bailey organized the thoughts in her head as well as she knew how. "I know that Captain Grant Hogan must have been my protector. When he was abruptly assigned to Hobart, the attacks on my home increased. The man who escorted me to and from the schoolhouse was also reassigned."

"*Captain Hogan*, did you say?" Bligh stiffened.

Bailey noticed his change in demeanor. Guardedly, she answered, "Yes. I thought Captain Hogan wanted me gone as well, but now I think better of it."

"Miss Templeton"—Bligh drew himself up to his full stature—"Captain Hogan spoke on your behalf. He defended your abilities as a teacher." Ruminating thoughtfully, the governor confessed, "I felt, and some of our other leaders decided, that a man would better survive the rigors of this school. But I didn't have Hogan reassigned. And I wouldn't have you shot!" His eyes sparked with an emotion not defined. "You're certain about Hogan's abrupt transfer?"

"It is true, Governor, what she says about Hogan." Dr. White spoke up. "The captain was abruptly assigned to Hobart. He was studying under me to be a surgeon. We desperately needed him, both in the colony and at the penal camp here in Sydney Cove."

Bligh's mood veered sharply to anger. His face red, he spat out a string of dark oaths.

Mrs. Griggs fanned her face, but Bailey sat up. "What's happening, Governor? What is going on?"

His face a glowering mask of rage, Bligh snapped, "*Macarthur!* That's what's happening!" Shoving his hat back onto his head, the furious commander turned on his heels and stormed out of the room.

Stunned by his angry outburst, Bailey glanced first at Dr. White and then at Mrs. Griggs. Not knowing exactly what to say, she finally said quietly, "This Governor Bligh, is it safe to say that he's on our side?"

❖

As much as she wished to comply with Dr. White's orders, Bailey soon convinced Mrs. Griggs that a few moments of sunshine would do her a world of good. She seated herself on an oak settee out on the immaculate lawn and allowed the doting woman to place a blanket across her lap. Basking in the sunny rays of autumn sunshine, she surveyed the beautiful woodland that surrounded the governor's home. Soon a Cockney male servant appeared bearing a tea service on a tray. No longer embarrassed by all the attention, Bailey accepted his gracious offer and selected a hot pastry from his silver platter. "Governor Bligh's household staff is most hospitable," she remarked to Mrs. Griggs.

Pouring herself a cup of tea as well, Mrs. Griggs nodded quietly.

"Well, is it no wonder you're not at the school!"

A familiar voice roused Bailey from her sleepy stupor. "Katy Farrell!" She laughed. "And Rachel!"

The two women stood over her, arms akimbo. Katy winked at Rachel. "I would certainly dally as long as possible if I were in Bailey Templeton's shoes!"

"Wouldn't you?" Rachel chided affectionately.

"Stop it! Both of you, please! This is all so embarrassing." Bailey set her teacup aside. Lifting her feet off the long settee, she turned to face them, her cheeks tinged pink.

Taking a seat on either side of her, the two women laughed giddily.

"You're both so cruel!" Bailey could not help but laugh as well. "And me in my fragile condition." She held her hand to her forehead.

"Now, *you* stop!" Rachel gripped her forearm. "We've been so worried."

"Yes," Katy agreed. "The children all ran home in a panic the next morning when you didn't arrive at school. My two sons caught a ride with a neighbor. They thought you were dead." She lowered her face, her eyes full of mock gravity.

"You can assure them both, I'm not dead." Bailey's brows lifted, her eyes sparked with humor. Sobering, she added, "Although I hate to admit it, I am frightened."

"Don't you worry. Dwight is riding out to the Government House today. He is insisting on a permanent escort for you, just as Grant had ordered." Katy spoke with firm assurance.

"I'm glad to hear of it, because I plan to be back at the school immediately." Bailey folded her arms assertively.

"I feared as much, Bailey." Rachel spoke worriedly. "Perhaps you should wait. Or better yet, hold the school at someone's home for a while. I'm certain that Heath wouldn't mind having our home turned into a school temporarily."

"You say that now, Rachel, but having a houseful of students all day long—you would weary quickly of such a thing. We all would." Bailey offered a sympathetic smile.

"She's right, Rachel," Katy said thoughtfully. "But, Bailey, you must come out to Rose Hill at least for the first few weeks. Dwight and I have to drive in every morning, regardless, to bring Donovan and Jared to school."

"Yes, Bailey," Rachel agreed. "There's your solution. You would never be alone. At least until the gunman is found."

Bailey glanced obliquely at Katy. "You and Dwight certainly don't need to be bothering with me." She stopped short of expressing her true worries about the Farrells.

"Dwight and I will not be bothered. We love you, Bailey. Let us help."

Taking a quick glimpse at Rachel, she saw a spark of hopefulness. Remembering their conversation, she gave a helpless shrug. "All right, Katy. But please be certain that Dwight doesn't mind."

"I shall." Katy smiled confidently.

Bailey and Rachel exchanged discerning glances.

Within a few days, Dr. White offered Bailey the news she had been begging to hear. Meeting him in the parlor of the governor's mansion, she sat fully dressed and her mind full of anticipation.

"You can go home, Miss Templeton. I've informed Governor Bligh, and he's arranged your transportation."

"Thank you, Dr. White." Bailey's spirits spiraled upward and a calm assurance settled in her mind. "I can't thank you enough for all your help."

"Just keep those bandages clean for another week or so. Promise me that?"

"Aye, sir." Bailey saluted. She had grown to like the surgeon, and somehow she couldn't help but believe that he would aid in Grant Hogan's return. But she could not bring herself to ask about Grant. "I need to inform the governor's driver that I will be staying with friends for a while."

"Let Billingsly know." Dr. White referred to Bligh's butler. Placing both hands upon his lap, he said, "I believe you're making a wise choice, Miss Templeton." He closed his bag with a snap. "I've had some concerns about you staying alone after this incident. If you had been robbed, I would've had my doubts about this plot of which you speak. But you were purposefully targeted, or so it seems."

Bailey stood to walk the doctor from the parlor. "I wish none of this were true, but it's all a reality I must face."

"At least a reality you won't have to face alone. Sounds as though you have good friends."

"And faith, Doctor." Bailey's gaze held his. She had never been one to preach but could not deny her source of strength. "This world would spin out of control without it."

His brows lifted with some skepticism, Dr. White commented, "I'm not so sure it isn't at times."

"Rest assured. There is a Pilot on this ship. I could never weather a storm without Him."

"I can sense that in you, Miss Templeton. We could use more people like you in this colony."

Her steps slowed and she pondered his words. "I'm no example, I'm afraid." Her brows lifted with humor and she laughed quietly. "But if people like us can endure the madness, perhaps we can lead the way. It's conceivable that this colony will have a future."

"You've more faith than I can muster, that's for certain, Miss Templeton."

Bailey walked him to the door. Notifying the butler of her plans, she paced her energy and made a slow ascent up the stairway. Collecting her few belongings, she took one last glance in the mirror. Her cheeks had regained their color, but her eyes still had telltale circles. She made a final inspection of her frock. The servant woman who had repaired her dress had completely replaced the lace around the bodice. The high collar and new laced bodice completely hid the bruised and bandaged area around her wound. For that, she was grateful. Knowing how curious schoolchildren are, she wanted nothing to distract from her teaching. Before she could appear downstairs, she heard the sound of a horse and carriage from her open window. Glancing out, she saw that the liveryman made fast to provide her transportation to Rose Hill. Her spirits high, she lifted the reticule from the mahogany dresser and proceeded downstairs. Her brows lifted when she saw the smiling face waiting for her at the foot of the stairs. "Ellen!"

"Hello, Miss Templeton." Standing arms akimbo, Ellen pressed her lips together, her eyes misty. "I'm almost sorry you've recovered so quickly."

Bailey bit her bottom lip, her mouth curving into a sympathetic smile. "Thank you, but I must disagree. Someone has to teach your boy, Alfred."

"I'm so glad it's you." Ellen's mouth trembled, but she straightened her back and held in her emotions. "I'll miss having you about."

"I'll miss you, as well. But I'll have another social at the school. You'll come then?"

Nodding her affirmation, Ellen said, "I'll be at every social you plan, and I'll even help out. I'll be speaking to the other emancipists, too. If we parents don't care about our own, then who will?"

Bailey held out her arms. Ellen returned her affectionate squeeze but then excused herself. "I'd best take me leave, Miss Templeton." She dabbed her eyes. "But first, I heard somethin' I believe would interest you. It's about that 'orrible man, you know, the one wot runs the Rum Corps."

"John Macarthur."

"Yes. Macarthur. He was called in for questionin' by the governor." Ellen spoke in a barely audible tone.

Being certain that they were alone, Bailey drew Ellen close. "And?"

"Macarthur's been arrested." Ellen tried to cover her smile with her hands. "The louse!"

"You know this for certain, Ellen?" Bailey tried to mask her own elation. "Who told you?"

"You know the governor don't allow us to discuss his affairs, Miss Templeton?"

Pursing her lips, Bailey's brows lifted expectantly.

"But I believe it was the driver who first knew of it. Now the entire staff knows."

"I suppose if this is all true, the Farrells will know. I must hurry." Bailey placed a kiss on Ellen's cheek. "Good-bye, Ellen. And thank you!" Bailey hastened through the front doors. She allowed the liveryman to assist her into the carriage and waved a final farewell to Ellen.

Later, certain that she had been carried far from the governor's estate, she leaned her head back and laughed to herself, but quietly so the driver would not imagine her mad. John Macarthur had controlled the colony affairs so long through his Rum Corps, that everyone, including Bailey, thought the man's power to be unconquerable. Yet knowing the scope of his corrupt machine, Bailey wondered if even Governor Bligh could stop the man. Macarthur had men from every walk of life in his back pocket—the rich, the poor, the powerful, the powerless. Both emancipist and colonist had somehow been seduced through his subtle prowess. Closing her eyes, she breathed a quick prayer for the colony. Lifting her face, she realized that only the foolish would proclaim a victory too soon. *No, John Macarthur. You've too much at stake to give up this easily, haven't you?*

She began organizing the next few months of schoolwork in

her mind. She might have to stay with the Farrells for longer than even she had anticipated. She hoped and prayed that her friendship with Katy could withstand the perils that lay ahead. *We've a long summer ahead of us, Katy. I hope you won't grow weary of the burden. I may soon be the most unpopular colonist with whom to associate in Sydney Cove. I hope you won't regret your decision to befriend Bailey Templeton. I need your friendship now more than ever.*

12

CRISIS AT ROSE HILL

The smell of a home-cooked breakfast wafted up to the guest room where Bailey slept. Mornings at Rose Hill came early, but the bustle of the family and the ranch hands provided a pleasant atmosphere for the start of each day. She looked out the window from her bedchamber and saw a mist rising over the hills. As far as the eye could see in any direction, the land belonged to the Farrells and the Prentices. Bailey enjoyed making acquaintance with the rest of the family. The heir to Rose Hill, Katy's younger brother, Caleb, had built a home one mile west of the Farrells' home. He and his wife, Kelsey, often joined the Farrells for breakfast. Caleb and Dwight used this time to plan and delegate the workload for the hands and for themselves. Bailey loved the chatter of all their children and the attentiveness of their grandmother, Amelia.

A short time later, with her arms full of books, Bailey strode briskly into the dining room. She found Amelia seated in a large Windsor chair, bouncing two young children on her lap. "Good morning," she said, placing her books atop a small pedestal table.

"Mornin', Bailey." Amelia had a wonderful low voice with a gentle Cockney accent.

"Would you mind telling me their names again?" Bailey eyed the two tow-headed youngsters. Although cousins, they could have passed for twins.

Kissing one of the girls atop her head, Amelia answered, "Not at all. This one is Corbin—Katy and Dwight's daughter. The other one is Shannon. She belongs to Caleb and Kelsey."

Bailey lifted Corbin into her arms and held her against her breast. "I should know you by your eyes, little Corbin." A broad smile dimpled Bailey's cheeks. "They're just like Katy's." She addressed Amelia once more. "They're almost the same age, true?"

"Almost. Shannon is three months older than Corbin."

Shaking her head, Bailey laughed. "How do you keep it all straight?"

Katy followed a servant into the room, both bearing generous platters of piping hot victuals. "Mum, will you feed Corbin this morning?"

"Yes, love."

She placed her platter on a serving cart. "Thank you. I've so much to do today." Her hands in the air, Katy looked all around the room. "Has anyone seen Donovan this morning?"

Bailey glanced up and down the dining hall. "Now that you mention it, I haven't seen him all morning."

"I don't believe he's come down yet," Amelia commented quietly. She kept her eyes on the children.

Bailey would not have noticed anything unusual about Donovan's tardiness to breakfast had it not been for Katy's look of worry. Pushing herself out of the rocker, she quietly joined Katy at her side. "Something I can do?"

Her face poised, Katy lifted her chin and said tactfully, "Thank you. Would you mind knocking on Donovan's bedchamber door? He'll not have time to finish breakfast if he continues to dawdle."

"Glad to oblige." Bailey, her face somber, made her way quickly from the dining hall, then strode to the stairwell. From the foot of the stairs, she could see Kelsey in the keeping room nursing her newborn infant. Bailey called out to her but kept her voice low so as not to disturb the baby. "Kelsey? Have you seen Donovan?"

Pressing her lips together, Kelsey lifted her face and answered in a crisp Irish brogue, "Probably in his room sulking." Her eyes reflected sympathy for the boy.

Not wishing to pry, Bailey offered her thanks and continued on her way up the stairs. Her feet padding quietly down the carpeted hallway, she made her way past the first few bedchambers until she had come to the room where Donovan and Jared slept. Curling her fingers into a fist, she rapped firmly at the door. Hearing nothing, she rapped once more. "Donovan?" Knowing she did not fully understand the situation, she kept her tone gentle. "It's me, Miss Templeton."

After a moment, Donovan's voice answered almost curtly. "My mother sent you?"

Bailey frowned. "Yes—"

"I'm not hungry, Miss Templeton."

"But you should eat. And Cook's made a large supply of hot bread."

"I don't feel well."

Folding her arms skeptically at her waist, Bailey countered, "May I enter, please?" Waiting momentarily, she had almost decided to go downstairs and leave the matter to Katy. But the door handle slowly turned and the wooden door squeaked open. She could see into the room, but Donovan had not made himself visible. "Hello?" she called out.

"I'm here."

Stepping cautiously into the quaint chamber, Bailey glanced around and saw that he had seated himself upon his bed. Still wearing his nightshirt, he sat cross-legged and stared out his window. "We'll be leaving in a moment for school. Shouldn't you dress yourself?" Standing in the center of the room, she studied his face, puzzled by his brooding disposition. "You shouldn't worry your folks, Donovan. You need to eat." But she knew the problem surely went deeper than his lack of hunger.

"I'm not going to school today, Miss Templeton." He hesitated, then stated awkwardly, "I've a fever."

Bailey bit her lip. "Let me see." She felt his forehead and his arm. "I don't believe you do, Donovan." She seated herself next to him. "But I do believe that someone's made you angry."

He shrugged indifferently.

"It won't help to sulk. If you've a problem, it's best to talk it over with whomever you're angry." She spoke with quiet assurance. "Is it your mother? Are you angry with her?"

His eyes narrowed and his mouth hardened in a sullen frown.

"Katy's a good mother, Donovan. You can talk to her—"

"She's unfair! She and Papa argue, and then she forbids me to go with him to the far pastures!"

The dilemma evident at once, Bailey held her words, not wishing to overstep her boundaries.

"I'm weary of their fighting! I hate it!" He ground his teeth. "I hate *her!*" His voice was cold and exact.

With steady calmness, Bailey placed her hand upon Donovan's shoulder. "You don't mean what you say. You're merely angry. Hate is a strong word."

"I do mean it! My mother uses me to punish Papa. And he does the same to her."

"You're mistaken—"

"Am I?" Vehemently, he interrupted her. "When Mother's friend, Captain Gabriel, came to take Jared and me fishing one Saturday, Papa forbade me to go. He and Mum had just finished with a horrid fight."

Bailey clasped her hands upon her lap and looked away.

His eyes rimmed with tears, Donovan said bitterly, "They don't love each other, and they don't love me!"

Bailey was uncertain as to whether he meant what he said or if he was simply trying to draw a response from her. Unable to quell the lump in her throat, she wrapped her arms around his trembling shoulders. "Such fables, child. You don't believe any of this. You know your parents would die for you." She pulled him around to face her. "You know that, don't you?"

His body tense, Donovan looked squarely in her face and shook his head. "No. I don't."

"*Donovan!*" an exasperated male voice barked from the doorway.

Bailey whirled around. "Dwight, I—"

Speaking evenly, Dwight said, "Thank you, Miss Templeton, for trying to help." His face stoic, he turned his gaze on the boy. "But you've no need to be bothered with our family matters. Donovan! Be dressed in five minutes and downstairs, or I'll come up and dress you meself!"

Momentarily abashed, Bailey stiffened. At once, she felt the contempt between them. Donovan hesitated, his eyes avoiding his father's accusing stare.

"Did you hear me?" Dwight's tone increased with severity.

Nodding stiffly, Donovan whispered, "Yes, sir." The insolence in his voice was ill-concealed.

Bailey stood, smoothed her skirt, and heaved a guarded sigh. "I'll see you shortly, Donovan." Bustling quickly past Dwight in the doorway, she saw the angry intent in his face. In an attempt to ease his embarrassment and hers as well, she said in a hushed tone, "I'm sorry, Dwight." An unwelcome blush crept into her cheeks.

"Not to be concerned, Miss Templeton." Dwight lowered his face assuredly, but his own discomfort evident, he kept his eyes fixed on his son. "I'll have this matter straightened out soon enough."

Bailey heard the door slam behind her. *Don't be too hard on him, Dwight.* She breathed a silent prayer for both of them and then again made her way downstairs. As she had earlier feared, the problems that existed in the Farrell family had slowly crept into her own world. In addition to the problems in the colony, the school, and those created by John Macarthur, she now felt herself being drawn into the personal lives of a family she greatly respected. As much as she had tried to avoid the conflicts, it was becoming increasingly more difficult to escape involvement. She could see the relationship's slow, downward spiral, the erosion of trust, and the increased tension between Katy and Dwight. Now their unresolved problems had started to affect their oldest son. Surely all the family members knew, and yet they all stand silently by, afraid to interfere. *God, what do I do now? Give me the words or teach me to hold my tongue.* Bailey hesitated outside the doorway. Stretching a smile across her face, she entered the dining room, acknowledged each person seated at the long table, and then quietly took her place next to Kelsey. Seeing the expectancy of their gazes, she said, "Donovan is getting dressed. He'll be down shortly." She clasped her hands in front of her. "Have we prayed?"

John Macarthur paced behind bars. Stripped of his British uniform, he had been relegated to the lowest caste in Sydney Cove—that of a convict. A spark of venom gleaming in his hawklike eyes, he proceeded to pace the short length of the cramped cell, turn and gaze out expectantly, then resume his ponderous ritual. A guard stood outside his solitary confinement cell, his back to the door.

"Any sight of my men, Rowley?" Macarthur growled.

Turning nervously to peer in through the small window in the door, the guard shook his head. "No, sir. We'd best not talk, sir. They've someone watchin' me as well."

"Vurry well," Macarthur muttered in a Scottish dialect. "Keep your eye out. They'll not keep me here for long."

Bailey, holding an oilskin overhead, shielded herself from the rain that swept across the lush grazing pastureland of Rose Hill. "Here comes the storm!" she shouted above the thunder to the Farrell boys. But the rain did not dampen her spirits. The school day had commenced on a good note. Edward Simpson, an emancipist's son, had won the school spelling bee. It had been a landmark day for Edward. Bailey, seeing the triumph in his face, had felt the victory as though she had won it herself. But she had also empathized with Donovan Farrell's plight. Donovan nearly always sprinted with ease through the class competitions, ever the prominent scholar. But his gloomy demeanor pervaded his every thought, his every endeavor. When Bailey called upon him in hopes of drawing him into the events of the day, dejection etched his expression and darkened his words.

Rain pelted against the oilskin and against Bailey's face. Lightning streaked the sky, a stark white jagged outline against the ever darkening firmament. "Run, boys!" Bailey called to Donovan and Jared. The vault of heaven flushed out the rains and pummeled the ground with a force. Mud splattered onto their shoes and onto Bailey's skirt and petticoats. Seeing that Jared's oilskin blew out of his hands, she threw her own around him. "Not to worry, Jared. We're almost to the house." She urged him on and ran the rest of the way unprotected.

Amelia stood on the porch frantically waving them on. Allowing the boys to run ahead of her, Bailey sighed resignedly and trudged slowly up the steps. *Why hurry now?*

Lifting her water-soaked skirt to take the last step, she took shelter and then began the task of wringing out the mud-caked fabric.

"Inside, boys," Amelia said with a frown.

Bailey couldn't help but chuckle at Amelia's piteous mien. "We made it, Amelia! We're home!" She laughed as Amelia shook her head and followed the boys into the house.

Bailey turned to witness the torrent of rain upon the land. Sheets of white swept across the earth in an almost militaristic fashion. She could not help admiring the sight. So much of Sydney

Cove was nothing more than a muddy, unkempt squalor, but Rose Hill always received both storm and blue sky with dignity and beauty. She pushed the saturated strands of hair from her face and turned to go inside. Quickly wiping her feet on an old rug placed beside the door, she ran in and nearly collided with Dwight Farrell. "I'm sorry," she said.

Dwight quickly stepped aside. "Hello, Miss Templeton." He had a distracted gaze.

Still feeling somewhat awkward in regard to the morning's conflict, she pressed her lips together and cleared her throat. "I suppose I've been apologizing a great deal of late."

"You've no need to explain," Dwight offered. "If you're referrin' to this mornin's bout with Donovan, Katy explained to me that she had sent you to find the boy. You only reacted in a natural fashion."

Although appreciative of his diplomacy, Bailey nevertheless felt uncomfortable. Choosing her words, she finally said, "I'm not one to pry in others' affairs, Dwight. I just feel horrible about the entire incident."

"I know," he answered quietly. "So do I." He pulled on his own oilskin and hat. A hint of humor glinted from his eyes as he looked her up and down, finding her appearance amusing. "Amelia's drawn you a bath in the kitchen. G'day!" He departed quickly out into the storm.

"But it's raining—" His haste to depart puzzled her. But she turned her thoughts to the matter at hand. *Mind your own business, Bailey.* Lifting the heavy skirt, she draped it across her arm as though it were a train. Somehow, she had to proceed upstairs to retrieve a clean frock and then return downstairs. Passing through the dining hall, she nodded at golden-haired Kelsey, who sat slicing vegetables. Using a needle, Katy's lovely sister-in-law threaded the vegetables on a string and prepared them to dry.

The housemaid, Mary, clasped her hand to her mouth. "Mercy sakes, Miss Templeton!"

"I've spoiled your clean floors, Mary. Forgive me?"

"I'll do more than that. You go an' clean up out in the kitchen. I'll bring you a fresh dress in an instant."

"Thank you." Bailey pinched the wet fabric away from her skin.

"Looks as though you and the boys didn't quite make it home, lassie. Not before the storm, at any rate." Kelsey ran the knife through a small pepper. Giving Bailey a second glance, she commented pleasantly, "Better give your frock to Amelia and let her clean it up for you, aye?"

"Poor Amelia. She does so much already." Bailey glanced at the trail of mud behind her. "Look what I've done now. I can't allow her to clean up after me." Peering into the kitchen, she could see Katy giving young Corbin a bath. Over the roaring fire in the fireplace, Amelia had set a large pot to boiling. She tended it closely, the steam reddening her face. The charming scene would have held a quaintness, but a peculiar melancholy hung in the air. Bailey beheld Katy, whose face was clouded with a sullen pout, and Amelia, who stood silently, her arms crossed. "Hello," Bailey called out to them.

Amelia glanced up first, but her face did not light up with her usual gay smile. "I've drawn you some bath water," she said, her tone low, and she turned to stare again at the pot.

"Yes, Dwight told me. Thank you. I'm so grateful." She held out her drenched skirts, but neither bothered to glance up and notice the humor of the moment. Bailey glimpsed around to be certain of their privacy. "I'll bathe in the rear of the kitchen, if that's satisfactory with you both."

"Go ahead, dear." Amelia took two potholders from a shelf. "Help me with this?"

"Please, allow me." Bailey quickly grasped a thick towel and reached for the other side of the kettle handle.

Katy finally looked up, but her eyes glinted with tears. "Bailey, did you see my husband? Has he—did he leave?"

Bailey gave a tense nod. She and Amelia stepped quickly toward the rear of the kitchen, careful not to slosh out the kettle's simmering contents. "Dwight ran out into the storm." After they filled a washtub with the steaming water, she turned and looked somberly at both women. Reading their faces, she could no longer hold her words. "What is wrong, Katy?"

Protectively, Amelia interjected. "Simply a ranch problem."

Katy countered quickly, "We have a cow down near the stream. It's lodged in the mud."

"I'm sorry." Bailey knew the value of livestock in Sydney Cove. In some cases, a man's livestock was considered more important than some human life. But sensing their disquiet, she awaited a further explanation.

"I asked him to delay his trek into the far pastures—until the weather subsides, at the very least. But he's so stubborn." Contempt shot from Katy's eyes. "Sometimes I believe he chooses the opposing path simply to irritate me."

"Katy—" Amelia's face tensed, her eyes pleading with her daughter. "Bailey is our guest."

"Bailey isn't blind, Mum." Katy turned to face her, her eyes glittering with emotion. "Are you, Bailey?"

Reaching for a bar of homemade soap from the cupboard, Bailey felt her stomach knot. She caught herself glancing uneasily over her shoulder. "No, Katy, I'm not blind. But sometimes it would make things much easier if I were."

"Stop, Katy, please," Amelia implored.

"My apologies to our guest." Stiffening her back, Katy lifted Corbin from the small washtub. Wrapping a towel around the toddler, she lowered her voice. "I've been"—her voice choked, and tears glistened on her pale Patrician features—"a bit emotional most recently." The tears slowly found their way down her cheeks, and a sob escaped her lips. "My apologies," she said once more. Holding Corbin close, she ran from the kitchen.

Mary walked in with a fresh dress for Bailey draped over her arm. "I'll leave this right 'ere for you, miss." She placed the frock over a chair back and departed.

"Thank you." Helplessness overwhelmed Bailey again as it had that morning. She watched Amelia take a few steps to follow Katy and then stop at the doorway. "Should I go after her, Amelia?" she asked, while struggling to maintain a balance on her own emotions.

"Let her go, Bailey." Amelia slowly turned. Her eyes clung to Bailey, imploring her understanding of the matter. "She's hurting. Sometimes pain is a necessary part of the journey." She swallowed hard. "I hope that doesn't sound cruel."

"Not at all." Bailey slipped the rain-soaked dress from her shoulders and allowed it to drop to the floor. "Many times I struggle to offer the right words when conflicts arise, yet all along the wiser choice would be to remain silent. Other times, when I should speak up, I say nothing at all. And you know I'm not the least bit timid." She heard Amelia chuckle and glanced up. "You find me humorous, I see."

"You're wiser than you realize, Bailey." In spite of the flicker of pain in her eyes, a smile radiated from Amelia's face. "It's often more difficult to join a hurting friend in their pain than it is to offer a simple solution."

"Like Job's friends? Or worse yet"—Bailey reflected upon her own past—"to indulge our loved ones in their self-pity."

"See wot I mean, young lady. There's wisdom in your heart, as well."

"I wish I could see myself in such a way." Pouring a jug of cool water into the washtub, Bailey swirled the water with her hands. "It's as though I see both of their dilemmas, but I cannot be the bridge between them." She slid into the tub, and a comforting sigh escaped her lips. "I would be that bridge if I knew how." The warm water enveloped her chilled body, and she sighed, enjoying the pleasure of a hot bath. "But I can't."

"Nor can I." Amelia chuckled. "I'm only a mother. Wot do we mums know?"

They laughed together. Amelia assisted Bailey with her bath and, in spite of her protests, set about to clean the muddy frock. An hour passed and their moment of leisure spent together did Bailey's heart good. She felt a deepening of their friendship in spite of the problems that surrounded them.

While Amelia worked on the muddy raiment, Bailey donned the clean dress and combed out her matted tresses. Before Amelia could react or offer her disapproval, she ran with towels and soap to clean up the muddy entry. "Look, Amelia." She stopped next to a window. "The sky is clearing—just before sunset."

"So it is," Amelia remarked gently.

"I feel better now." Opening a window to allow in the last remaining rays of sunlight, Bailey sensed that her soul had been restored. Hearing footsteps on the stairs, she turned to find Katy running toward her. "Hello." She smiled, but her eyes could not hide her concern.

Breathless, Katy ran past Bailey and then whirled around. "Mum! Bailey! Please, someone!"

"What is it?" Bailey's brows raised inquisitively.

"Forevermore, Katy!" Amelia ran out into the dining hall. "Whatever's the matter?"

"It's Donovan!" Her stunned gaze spoke louder than words. "He's gone!"

13

A FUTILE SEARCH

"Mary, please come to the blackboard."

"Yes, Miss Templeton."

"Show us how to solve this arithmetic problem."

Mary nodded. Bailey's mind wandered. Donovan Farrell had not been found. The first twenty-four hours had launched the family in a frantic all-out effort to locate him. In the days to follow, their fears began to mount, worried that harm had come to him.

During the balance of the school week, Bailey labored to preside over her class with an air of calm and to keep the students focused upon their school tasks. But news of the runaway spread throughout the borough and became the talk of the schoolhouse. Jared had remained home for two days. But this morning, troubled and drained from his parents' frenzied search, he had come at his mother's insistence that he join Bailey for the wagon ride to school.

Bailey's hopes that Donovan had merely hidden out somewhere among the spreading expanses of Rose Hill had so far proven to be nothing more than a hopeful ambition. The tracks of his bay horse had led them to a rushing stream and then disappeared. The boy, unlike the outdoorsman found in his younger brother, had not harbored a love of hunting wild game or other outdoor pursuits. But he had acquired an acute sense of confounding his adversaries and, in this case, his parents. In the past week, Bailey had slept little and began to rely less on her instincts and more on her desperate prayers. *Please, God, keep Donovan safe!*

"I believe we should discuss our concerns for Donovan Farrell," she said aloud to the class but cast a wary eye toward Jared.

A young colonist in the front row shot up her hand, waving it frantically.

Lifting one brow, Bailey asked formally, "Faith? You wish to speak?"

"I've heard that Donovan ran away because he was angry with his parents." Primly, Faith adjusted the pink ribbon that wound around her auburn curls.

Seeing Jared shift uncomfortably, Bailey swiftly answered, "And this is exactly why I wish to discuss the matter. Faith, if several of you begin to spread such news, then others may start to believe you. You've not spoken to young Mr. Farrell yourself; therefore you don't know what has happened to him, either." Clasping her hands against her russet skirt, she leaned comfortably against the weathered desk. "You understand what gossip is, don't you?"

Faith nodded but planted her eyes on Jared. "Maybe *he* should tell us what happened. Then we would all know the truth."

Jared scowled at the pretentious girl, a look of contempt glinting from his eyes.

"But why should he, Faith?" Bailey continued. "You see, if you wish to know something because of your concern, well, that's one thing. But if you only wish to have your curiosity satisfied, that's quite another."

Faith sighed. "Yes, ma'am."

"Jared and his family need our prayers during this time, not our opinions." Bailey allowed her words to sink into their thoughts, hoping to end the cruel torrent of gossip. Unobtrusively, she took long, purposeful steps and made her way to her chair. Settling the students into an interval of quiet study time, she seated herself at her desk and attempted to focus her attention upon grading papers. Sifting through the disheveled stack, she organized two neat piles and then determined who had not completed the assignment. She called out the names of three students whose papers she could not find. She hesitated before calling on the fourth pupil, Cole Dobbins. Remembering the boy's past record, she recalled that Cole had seldom turned in his work and had performed poorly on his daily work in class. Bailey sighed and then gazed toward Cole. "Mr. Dobbins, have you a report for me?" She kept her tone even, although he exasperated her increasingly more every day.

Cole seldom offered any show of emotion but rather stared back at Bailey with a somber air of indifference. "Not doin' a report." He purposed his gaze upon a few of his classmates, a haughty triumph registering on his face.

Without any hesitation, Bailey said quietly, "When school is dismissed, stay afterward, please."

Cole shrugged, cocked back his head, and stared mockingly at the ceiling.

Bailey could not allow him to draw her into a conflict in front of the other pupils. With firm tenacity, she plowed into the remaining plans of her day. Seeing the familiar shadows of midafternoon stretching across the wood floor, she stole a fast glance at her father's pocket watch. She felt it was time to elevate her pupils to the next level of learning. In spite of the few who always complained no matter the assignment, she gave some evening reading and arithmetic drills and dismissed school at the usual time. Before the year was out, she wanted to draw out the more gifted ones to challenge them toward higher education. The next few weeks would determine her list of prospective candidates.

Taking her usual place at the back of the schoolroom, she bid farewell to each pupil. Occasionally, a friendly student would lean toward her with outstretched arms and offer an affectionate hug. She cherished those moments, deeming their value to outweigh the objectionable aspects of teaching.

Jared slowly strapped up his books, waited for the others to leave, then bustled past. "I'll wait for you in the wagon, Miss Templeton."

The fact that he kept his eyes to the floor and all but sprinted from the room alluded to his discomfort in regard to his brother's disappearance. Bailey wanted to speak, to reach out to Jared. She knew of his inward distress, but to further alienate himself from his friends would only add to his misery. Mulling over the matter, she decided to give him more time. *We'll have all the time in the world on our way home.* Crossing her arms, she heaved a heavy sigh and turned her attention upon Cole Dobbins. From the corner of her eye, she saw him rise from his desk. "Please stay where you are." Her voice firm, she also managed a tactful lilt in her tone. "I'll join you." She pulled her skirt aside, her petticoats swishing against the table legs as she made her way between the desks. Seating herself across the aisle in a student desk, she leaned back and intertwined her fingers at the nape of her neck. Waiting until the silence had grown slightly uncomfortable, she spoke barely above a whisper. "I'm trying, Cole." She didn't look across the narrow aisle to read his face but kept her gaze steady and forward. Finally, she heard his heavy leather boots scrape against the floor.

"Wot do you mean—*trying?*" His brusque adolescent voice did not ring out across the room as she had often heard it reverberate across the school yard. But rather, it held an odd tremor, slightly awkward. Bailey had intended to throw the lad a bit off balance. He had hidden behind his false show of confidence for so long, she felt certain that even he had forgotten all about the real Cole Dobbins.

Taking yet more time to answer, she said, "I'm trying to see this schoolroom as you see it." She stared at the desk where she usually sat. She allowed her eyes to follow the straight, rugged lines of the wood floor and to move upward to each empty school desk. Then she raised her eyes to find him looking at her. Without a hint of emotion, she said, "Trying to understand how Cole Dobbins thinks."

Biting the side of his mouth, Cole glanced away, his brow knit stubbornly.

"But I'm not certain that even Cole understands himself." Bailey sat forward and rested her palms on top of the desk. She waited for him to return his gaze to her own. "Do you, Cole?"

His eyes met hers disparagingly. "I understand I ain't bowin' to the likes o' you or any woman."

"Why do you come here, Cole? Does your father make you come?"

"Ask 'im yourself if you wants to know."

"You tell me."

Once again he diverted his gaze and stared straight ahead. His sullen eyes spoke far beyond his words.

"I want to teach you, Cole, but I cannot force you to learn." Bailey waited for an answer, but it became evident that his obstinate mood would prevail. "Tomorrow at this time, I wish to have

166

a visit from your parents. You'll deliver a letter to them?"

He shrugged again, but before Bailey could respond he said flatly, "Me mum's dead. If it's me father you want to see, he ain't one to reckon with."

Somewhere along the way, Bailey felt certain she had been informed of Cole's family situation, but she could not remember how his mother had died. The facts now escaped her. "I'm not afraid, Cole. I want to help you. I'm sure your father would wish to know of your lack of discipline. I'm going to tell him. Now, answer me, Cole, will you deliver the letter?"

A mischievous smile played around the corners of his thin mouth. "I'll give him the letter, lady." Planting his boots hard against the floor, he stood. "I'll be leavin' now."

"Wait one minute, please. I'll only be a moment." Bailey made her way back to her desk and lifted her quill from the inkwell. Quickly scrawling a request to meet with Blaine Dobbins, she folded the paper and handed it to Cole. "Thank you. I'll expect to see Mr. Dobbins directly after school tomorrow."

Without so much as an acknowledgment, Cole lifted the letter from her steady hands and shuffled from the school building. Still within earshot, Cole shouted, his voice tinged with scorn, "You ain't goin' to be likin' your meetin', Miss Templeton!"

Bailey gripped the edge of her desk and waited for Cole Dobbins to disappear from view. *I'm placing my trust in you on this matter, Lord. My complete trust.* She blew out a sigh of frustration.

Nearing Rose Hill, Bailey scarcely noticed the cool shade guarding their way into the homestead. Her mind played anxious scenarios just before her arrival each afternoon, hopeful to see Donovan safe and in the care of his worried parents. But with every passing day she found the Farrells and Prentices plummeting deeper into despair over the lost boy whose life they all cherished. Katy was sick with grief. The worry had taken its toll, and the tension rose heatedly among the family members. Seeing that Jared craned his neck toward the house, Bailey patted his leg. "I wish I could tell you not to worry." Jared's face fell and he slumped against the wagon seat. "I'm sorry for you, Jared, and for your family. But we can't lose hope. The Lord is looking after Donovan. We must believe that."

"Why won't they allow me to go with them, Miss Templeton? I'm the best tracker in the family."

"I'm certain they don't wish to chance losing another son."

Running both hands through his hair, Jared said defensively, "Donovan's never been good at hunting and exploring like me. That's probably why he's lost."

"Your father and your uncle Caleb are good trackers. But if all the men leave, who will take care of the women at Rose Hill?" Bailey held her mouth to one side, her eyes glinting with a hint of amusement. She saw that her comment encouraged Jared.

"That's right," Jared finally agreed. "Someone's got to look after the women." He folded his arms across his proud chest.

Hesitating, Bailey slowed the team and gazed somberly at him. "I'm sorry about the schoolchildren. They don't understand, do they?"

"I suppose not." He shrugged indifferently.

"Once we find Donovan, I'm certain they'll be glad to see him."

"They will, Miss Templeton. Don't you worry. Donovan has lots of friends. They miss him, I'm sure."

Bailey could not help but chuckle. She had hoped to comfort Jared, but now it was he who offered comfort to her. "Let's go home. I'm famished."

The household did not bustle with the usual lighthearted commotion. Even the servants plodded gloomily about, a silent cloud of despondency darkening their gazes in spite of the beauty of the October skies. Bailey did not ask about the search for Donovan, for she knew without query. Seated about the dining table, Amelia conversed quietly with Katy and Kelsey.

"Oh, look," Amelia said, trying to force a cheery smile, but her eyes betrayed her pain. "They're home."

"Jared, Mum's fixed you a pastry," Katy said gently to her youngest son. "And when you go upstairs, please walk softly. Corbin's yet sleeping."

"Join us, Bailey?" Kelsey pulled out a chair. "Tea and crumpets, fresh from the Prentice bakery."

Inhaling deeply, Bailey set her books aside. "I would love to join you all, thank you."

"We're discussing the Rum Corps." Kelsey's words held a portentous ring.

"Does anyone know, then?" Bailey poured herself a cup of tea. "Was Macarthur arrested?"

"Indeed! Bligh's thrown the blackguard behind bars. I hope he stays there, but I 'ave me doubts about it." Amelia shook her head.

"Enough about politics. How was your day at school?" Pulling her golden hair up into a knot, Kelsey turned their attention on Bailey.

"Mostly productive. Jared's first day back—" Bailey stopped, seeing Katy's concerned gaze—"was fine. He's keeping a chin up. We all could learn from him, I suppose." She decided to save the school gossip dilemmas for another time. "How are *you* doing, Katy?"

Katy did not answer right away but instead shrugged. "Dwight and Caleb scouted all of the settlement. Not one person has seen Donovan since his disappearance." Her eyes red from the continuous tears, Katy gazed wistfully through the glass and toward the distant mountain peaks. "He wouldn't have gone into the wilderness alone. I'm sure of it, Bailey." Her bottom lip trembled.

"I agree, Katy, but no possibility can be ruled out." Bailey stirred a lump of sugar into her tea. "Perhaps Donovan didn't run away at all."

"I shudder to think it." Katy rested her forehead against her clasped hands.

"Now, let's all remember that Donovan's a smart lad." Forever the loving grandmother, Amelia stretched out both hands to grasp Bailey's and Katy's hands as well as their attention. "Bailey's accurate about the possibility. It would comfort me to know that this crisis is not the spiteful invention of a mischievous lad. But until we know more, we're doing ourselves more 'arm to carry on so." Her eyes misted, and Bailey patted her hand.

"I know, Mum." Katy's voice faltered. "But I know Donovan's out there, and it may be all my own fault." She tossed down her napkin, pushed away from the table, and numbly marched from the dining hall.

Bailey felt the gnawing pain inside intensify. *Poor Katy. You torture yourself both day and night.*

A rap at the front door caused the women to gaze curiously toward the front landing.

"We've company." Kelsey peered through the window.

Her fingers curled into anxious fists, Katy stopped abruptly and looked back at the others. Being only a few feet from the door, she composed herself and made haste to answer it. "Please, God . . ." Her voice trembled.

Bailey stood. "Katy, if you want to go upstairs, I'll answer the door."

"No, I'll do it." Katy smoothed her violet silk dress and black grosgrain jacket. Adjusting the comb in her chignon, she opened the door, her tear-stained face marked with anxiety.

Bailey observed the softening of her gaze.

"Hello, Robert." She stepped back. "Please, come in."

Robert Gabriel strode haltingly through the doorway. He did not see at once the women from the dining hall. With a sincere nod of his head he spoke quietly. "Dearest Katy, may I extend my heartfelt sympathy for your plight."

"Thank you, Robert." Turning away, she offered a formal announcement. "Ladies, we have a guest."

Amelia smiled first. "Join us, Sir Robert," she offered affectionately.

"I cannot stay, dear madam." He doffed his tricorn hat. "I am here on an urgent matter."

"Please tell us." Katy took his arm and urged him to follow her into the dining hall.

Bailey strode to meet them, followed closely by Amelia and Kelsey. "Something's wrong, Captain?"

"Nothing wrong. But I must away. A friend of mine, William Lawson, is a commissioned explorer in Hobart. If I can persuade him to return to New South Wales, he could lead an exploration crew in search of Donovan."

"Hobart?" The news piqued Amelia's attention.

"Oh, Robert . . ." Katy's lashes shadowed her cheeks. "Please don't misunderstand my questioning you, but I feel we've so little time. You know of the horrible crimes committed sight unseen in the wilderness here. What if Donovan—"

"I'm leaving at once," Gabriel interjected. "But I will not depart for Hobart if you forbid."

"I won't forbid." Katy leaned against her mother and grasped her hand. "But we shall continue the search until you return. It is my hope to tell you upon your return that your trip was for naught."

He broke into an elated smile. "So be it, Lady Katherine."

"And bring back that rascal nephew of mine, Grant Hogan." Amelia's lip quivered and her eyes sparkled with moisture.

"Please do," Bailey blurted without thought. Glancing at their curious gazes, she completed her abrupt statement. "Captain Hogan is dearly missed by his family."

"Indeed!" Amelia's right brow lifted inquisitively. "Indeed, he's missed by all."

14
BAILEY'S
REPLACEMENT

November's Australian spring had ushered in a showy palette of colored trees, ruffled with pink and yellow and violet blooms. The land became perfumed with new life, and the farms spread out their blankets of green and golden fields. The streams had swollen their banks, and the Hawksbury River had overflown, flooding the nearby farms. But Rose Hill had known neither flood nor fire, only the remorse of unmended emotional fences and unacknowledged regret. Bailey kept her hopes high that Donovan Farrell would soon be found and the Farrell household restored to peace. She had enjoyed another productive day of school and had begun to feel satisfied that the junta had greater worries than harassment of a teacher. Arranging a large bouquet of flowers on her desk, she felt a peace well inside of her. A colonist's daughter had bestowed upon her the fragrant hand-picked nosegay. Her sister, Laurie, always domestically gifted, would have most likely arranged the flowers differently. But she arranged the blooms as best as she could, centering her favorite varieties toward the front of the bouquet.

Her thoughts still turned to Laurie from time to time, albeit melancholy. The wedding ceremony would be held in a few short months. She had hoped that as the day neared she would find comfort in the matter. But as a girl, she had always fancied herself the first to marry. And she had always believed that when Laurie married, she would be chosen as her first attendant. Now the event would take place without her. Living in New South Wales, Bailey would observe the day as she would all other holidays—with simple remembrance, without ceremony.

Checking her gold watch once again, Bailey had all but decided that neither Cole nor Blaine Dobbins would grace her with her requested visit. Cole had not come to school at all today, and she wondered if he had bothered to show his father her letter.

She walked impatiently across the schoolroom, her striped reverse panniers bustling behind her. She had bought the pale green dress in England and made some modifications, having learned a few tailoring skills from her mother. She had wondered how long her limited supply of dresses would last in such a place. But with the occasional shipments of dry goods to the government stores, a little lace, and a little luck, she had managed to keep a modest wardrobe.

"Miss Templeton?" a stern voice called from the schoolhouse landing.

Bailey whirled around. "Major Johnston." She tried to mask the surprise in her voice.

"I understand you've requested a meeting here today with Mr. Dobbins and his son, Cole." Johnston's temperament suggested he was no one to be reckoned with. As he walked through the entrance, he was followed closely by Blaine and Cole Dobbins. "I've come to mitigate."

Incensed at the outrage, Bailey tempered her words discreetly but spoke plainly. "Major Johnston, had I known that you were in the habit of frequenting discussions between myself and the pupils' parents, I would have notified you much sooner." She folded her arms across the stylish basque that cinched her waist. She avoided Cole's avenging glare and instead turned resignedly to make her way back to her desk.

Johnston continued to use a strong, defensive tone. "Mr. Dobbins feels, once again, Miss Templeton, that he needs the military's intervention. Would you deny him such a privilege?"

Bailey's lips thinned with irritation. "Mr. Dobbins"—she directed her words to Cole's father—"you know of our concern for

Cole. Why not pay your visit with me first? Then if you find me so *inflexible*, by all means, bring in the Royal Navy." She allowed a hint of irony in her voice.

Dobbins gazed uneasily at the officer, choosing to speak over Bailey's head. "She's given me boy nothin' but grief since he started. But Cole's kept it to himself until now."

"Cole—" Bailey fought more than ever to maintain a conciliatory tone but felt her anger rising. "Is what he's saying true? You told your father these things?"

His face dropping to the floor, Cole's shoulders lifted, and he shoved his hands inside his pockets.

"Keep your comments to the elder Dobbins and myself, Miss Templeton." Johnston gave an almost apologetic nod to Cole Dobbins. "We can't expect a boy to converse as we older folks do, can we?"

Bailey glanced obliquely, detecting the well-controlled exchange of glances between the major and Cole.

"It appears you've already conversed with the boy, sir. And it also appears that your conclusions, your assumptions, and your judgments have already been decided—all without consulting me."

"Now, Miss Templeton, you mustn't hasten to draw your own conclusions. I am fair minded and am here to offer you a chance to speak." A bright mockery invaded his stare.

Bailey could not allow herself to feel threatened. "How generous of you, Major Johnston," she snapped. "And how neatly wrapped you bring the plight of this persecuted boy." A war of emotions raged inside of her, but she could not succumb to the provocation.

"See 'ere!" Dobbins interjected, his ire raised.

"But for now, I want to listen to all you have to say, Mr. Dobbins." She lowered her tone, took her place at her desk, and gazed up expectantly at both men. "I'm here to serve you and your son, not to bicker needlessly."

"Very well." Johnston did not take a seat but instead paced in front of Bailey. "I asked you, Miss Templeton, to allow this emancipist's son to come to our school for one reason—to offer him the same education as all the other children in the colony."

Bailey stared up at Johnston, baffled by his words.

"We understand that this colony has some prejudices against emancipist children—"

"Major—" Her back stiffened, and she could no longer hide her discomfort.

"You vowed you'd listen and it's best you do, Miss Templeton."

A sinking feeling settled in the pit of Bailey's stomach as Johnston continued his tirade. He knew better than anyone of her compassion for the emancipists. Some of her dearest friends were former convicts—Amelia Prentice, Rachel Whitley, and Dwight Farrell, to name a few. The junta's plan to run her out of the colony had failed on numerous occasions. So now the ploy had been reorganized to a more subtle, more polarized approach—*they're going to destroy my reputation, disavow my abilities to teach*.

"And you have been made aware on more than one occasion that Sydney Cove's school cannot offer a suitable arrangement for a proper young lady such as you. Although we do admire your tenacity, it takes a firm hand to keep some of these children in line."

Bailey's mind refused to register the significance of his innuendo. She had determined to make Sydney Cove her home months ago and therefore had made no other arrangements for the future. Upon her arrival, the colony was without a school. She, following what she believed was God's leading, had built it from nothing—from ashes. She had nurtured the relationships with the families and built their trust. She now possessed enduring friendships herself. But most of all, in spite of the worries and conflicts, Sydney Cove had become her home, and she didn't want to leave. She placed her hands upon the desk and stood to her feet. Looking Johnston directly in the face, she squared her shoulders and asked with as much courage as she could muster, "Major Johnston, are you demanding my resignation?"

Johnston's face reflected his surprise at her question. "I did not say anything of the sort." He cast a chary eye toward Dobbins and his son. "Did either of you hear me say such a thing?"

"No." Dobbins shook his head. But Cole cowered behind his father, the severity of their interchange intimidating him into silence.

"I'll ask once more, then," Bailey said deliberately. "Are you, Major Johnston, demanding my resignation?"

"Not demanding, no." Johnston grew more flustered, his control slipping from his grasp.

"Then I have no intention of offering it."

A dark silence settled in their midst, and Bailey gathered her books into the satchel. "Mr. Dobbins, I will continue to teach Cole along with the other students. If you wish for him to succeed in our school, then you must encourage him to complete his tasks. Otherwise, he will continue to fall farther behind, and all's the pity." She looked directly into Cole's deep brown eyes. "He's remarkably intelligent in spite of his inability to see his own faults." Snapping the satchel closed, Bailey drew her belongings under her arm. "I can't imagine why that is so." She walked briskly past them all and waved to Jared, who sat patiently in the wagon. She glanced back only briefly before leaving them all staring dumbfounded after her. "Some matters can never be explained."

"We don't need his help, Katy. I can't imagine why you agreed to such a ludicrous plan." Dwight paced uneasily before his distraught wife while she stitched a pair of his trousers. His face taut, he spoke in generalities, although his attention was aimed at some unnamed fear.

Looking up at her husband, Katy sensed the smoldering emotions coiled beneath a facade of tempered self-control. "I'll do most anything to have Donovan returned, Dwight. Short of selling my own soul!" Katy glanced back down at the ripped seam. "And even that—"

"But why Robert Gabriel? Caleb and I have searched every part of Sydney Cove and Parrametta. We'll find our son soon."

"We don't know anything for certain." Katy set aside her sewing. Dwight had not been himself and neither had she. But she had to make him understand. "Donovan may have fallen into unscrupulous hands. You've heard of the horrid attacks on colonists out in the wild. What if something's happened to him?" Shaking her head, her eyes grew wide with fright. "I'll accept Robert Gabriel's aid or that of anyone else who wants to offer. We've no room for pride, Dwight Farrell!"

"I simply don't understand why I was not included in a decision this important, and you know of my mistrust of the man. He returned to Sydney Cove for one reason."

"Dwight Farrell! Robert Gabriel is an honorable man. He was a childhood friend. He saved my life, and that is all that exists between us!"

"And you don't believe he has feelings for you?"

"Not in the way that you imply. Robert sought me out, that is true. But only to lift from me the guilt I've lived with all these years. I blamed myself for his death, Dwight. Can you not understand that?" Her eyes grew misty, and she turned away from him in miserable disbelief.

"And you've no feelings for him?"

"You sicken me with your words. Is this all we've left of our lives—suspicion and distrust?"

"I sicken you. I'm glad to know that now."

"Stop! Please!"

"Perhaps you should have shared your feelings long ago."

"Dwight!" Katy whirled around, her cheeks glistening with tears. "Can you not see beyond your own blind fears?" She moved toward him. "I love you, Dwight." The sobs spilled freely from her lips. "More than life itself—I love you!"

Dwight stared at Katy, his eyes narrowed somberly. He could not speak or move or say anything to remedy the matter. With trembling hands, he stretched out his arms to her. "Help me, Katy." His voice low and gravelly, he took a few panic-stricken gasps of air. "I . . . I'm losing everything important to me. I feel . . . lost."

Katy fell against her husband's chest and felt his strong arms wrap around her. She closed her eyes as if in prayer. Then she looked up at him, and a strange smile spread across her face. "You've not lost me, Dwight Farrell! You're just a little frightened. That is all."

"God help me!" He held Katy tightly, as though she would disappear if he didn't. And perhaps she might, so he did not let her go for a long while.

The late afternoon sun did not linger, so Bailey and Jared hurried on their way.

"Are you all right, Miss Templeton?"

"Yes."

His hands tiring of holding the reins, Jared caught the leather straps between his knees. Intertwining his fingers, he stretched out his hands, yawned lazily, and then resumed his grip. "Cole Dobbins is a mean fellow, eh?"

"You know my rule, Jared. I don't discuss the other pupils with anyone else."

Jared shrugged. "I know."

"It isn't proper."

"Hmm." He nodded agreeably.

Finally Bailey laughed aloud. "But if I ever did break that rule, I'd have to agree with you at least somewhat." She felt mischievous for having admitted such a thing, but Jared had a way of bringing out the honesty in her.

Jared's eyes widened and he smiled, tight-lipped. "That I do know."

Between bared teeth, Bailey said, "Such a rascal!"

"Me?"

"No, silly boy. Cole Dobbins."

"Miss Templeton?" Jared drew his lips together thoughtfully. "Do you miss your people? Your father and mum?"

Bailey did not answer right away. She pictured them first—Father bustling around the mercantile, and Mother entertaining ladies for tea. "I do miss them. Especially my father, Pern Templeton. He's a hard-working man, a good employer. But most of all, he understands me better than anyone I've ever known."

"What's to understand, Miss Templeton?"

Laughing once more, Bailey untied her bonnet, gray and green with scalloped straw, and pulled it from her head. She feigned an exasperated sigh. "Master Farrell! I'll have you to understand that I am a woman of the most profound complexities. You've a great deal to understand about me!" She lifted her brows in mock cynicism.

"I am sorry, Miss Templeton." The lad cowered slightly, but a playful smile curved his reddened cheeks. "Didn't mean to offend."

"Of course not." Tying the ends of her bonnet ribbons together, Bailey glanced up at the few shops along the road. The meager businesses had sprang up in the wake of a population growth within the colony. "If you will, let's stop at Farraday's Mercantile."

"Yes, ma'am." Jared pulled right on the lines. "You needing some goods?" He adjusted the collar on his lightweight coat to shade his neck from the sun.

"Apple cider. Join me?" She regarded the anticipation in Jared's face. "Thought you'd be pleased. Also, Mr. Farraday said that he would have a sack of letters for the Parrametta colonists today. It will save all of us a long trip to the government stores if I pick them up now."

A group of farmers and their wives had clustered about the front counter, all awaiting news from faraway loved ones. "Let's find the cider first, then we can inquire about the letters." Bailey strode inconspicuously past the waiting throng, followed fast on her heels by Jared. She perused the dry goods as always and found little in the way of selection. Most of the better textiles were found in the government stores. She planted herself in front of a shelf containing some of the cheeses made at home by local farmers' wives. Next to the cheese selections, she spied two large containers marked by hand "apple syder." "Here we are. My goodness, those containers are much too large. Let's see if the Farradays can pour some of this cider into a small container."

"I'll ask for you, Miss Templeton." Jared bolted for the front of the mercantile and made his way through the maze of farmers.

Lifting her reticule to examine the amount of money she carried, Bailey had not at first noticed the two men who conversed in the rear of the shop quite close to where she stood. One wore the uniform of the Royal Navy, and the other spoke in quick, clipped English. "I am employed with my brother for now, but I await with great anticipation the position for which I was hired."

"How fares Richard?"

Bailey sidestepped them both to peruse a table behind them. She did not recognize the Englishman as she did most of the citizenry. He was a short, balding man of medium build. His face etched by age, the man seemed a nervous sort, glancing around suspiciously as he spoke.

"Well as can be expected, Lieutenant Commander." The short Englishman clasped his hands behind himself. "Father's curried many favors to win this judgeship for Richard. He's most relieved to have me here to look after him."

"Oh, I do recall. Your father's a titled man, correct?" The lieutenant commander lifted a tobacco-stained pipe to his lips.

"Baronet." The Englishman gave a smug nod. "It's an inherited title, but one that finds comfortable niches for foolish offspring," he said glibly.

Bailey had heard of a baronet somewhere, but exactly where she was not certain. Some lovely buttons caught her eye. She rolled them about in her hand. *Katy would love these buttons. They look like small pink rosettes.* She had a little extra money left over from her shopping, and with her room and board provided, she could afford a bit of luxury for a close friend.

"Richard will benefit from your counsel, I am most certain."

"And I am most certain that he will not," the Englishman retorted dryly. "A drunkard seldom listens to counsel. No, Richard is more adept at making one believe him to be sincere."

Drunken son of a baronet? Folding her fingers over the buttons, Bailey felt a stab of betrayal piercing her senses. *Johnston?* Katy had warned her months ago about the judge advocate's plan to install his brother in her position. She had known of Johnston's ties to Richard Atkins. But in her heart, she held the belief that the pupils' parents would intervene on her behalf. Most had expressed their appreciation to her, implying that as Sydney Cove's only teacher, she had brought nothing but positive change to the school. And never would she have believed that the junta would stoop to such hostile tactics. *Bailey, you're so naive.* She pieced together the incidents. The events of the day in regard to Cole Dobbins left no doubt about Johnston's intent. If Bligh had unearthed any tangible suspicions about the junta's involvement in the shooting incident, she had not been informed of such. Her suspicions that the marksman had been hired by the Rum Corps had never been proven, but the thought that her replacement might be standing within inches of her sparked an anger that threatened to rage out of control. She felt her senses spinning and her stomach churned. Today's fiasco at the school with the Dobbins boy had all been a ploy to force her into a resignation. *It won't work, Major Johnston!*

"Mr. Atkins, is it?" Clasping her fingers together, she quite casually snugged down her white gloves.

The Englishman turned and acknowledged Bailey. "Were you addressing me, madam?"

"You *are* Mr. Atkins, aren't you? Richard Atkins' brother?" Her eyes traveling up to meet his, she poised herself with the utmost of decorum.

"Yes. I am Orville Atkins, and Richard is my brother." He spoke with a hint of distaste upon mentioning his brother's name.

"So nice to meet you." Bailey extended one gloved hand, and he received her in a gentlemanly fashion. Before he could ask her name, she responded, "I'm certain that Richard is pleased to have you here. Will you be staying long?"

"As a matter of fact, I plan to make Sydney Cove my permanent place of residence."

"How interesting." The struggle to conceal her anger grew, so she said evenly, "Will you be accepting a government post? Richard is a dear in regard to such matters."

Jovially, Orville Atkins strolled quite willingly into Bailey's snare. "I am actually a schoolmaster."

"Splendid!" Bailey detected a hint of censure in her tone, and it smacked of the ire that threatened to spill over inside her. "Sydney Cove is in need of schoolteachers, eh?"

Giving a knowing glance at the lieutenant commander, Atkins chuckled immodestly. "So I've heard."

Her fingers curled tightly around the green woolen fabric of her skirts. She could not reveal the anger that threatened to erupt. "I must be going. If you gentlemen will excuse me—"

"Here's a smaller container." Jared lifted the jar in front of her.

Bailey turned quickly away from the two men. "We must be on our way, Jared." She forced a formal, matronly tone, hoping that Jared would not react. She placed her right hand behind the boy's neck as if to propel him gently forward. If she stayed one moment more, she knew without doubt that she might blurt out some regretful words. She could not lower herself to such a level.

Shrugging at her sudden withdrawal, Atkins called out, "Sorry, I did not ask your name."

Bailey could not bring herself to acknowledge him. But Jared glanced back over his shoulder. Confused about their abrupt exit, he opened his mouth to speak to Miss Templeton. Then beholding the Englishman who stood with arms akimbo staring after them, he replied matter-of-factly, "Name is Jared Farrell, sir."

Atkins smiled at the friendly boy. "Thank you, lad. Good day, Mrs. Farrell."

Bailey paid for their cider, accepted a letter from Mr. Farraday addressed from America, and bustled hurriedly from the mercantile. She could not make any impulsive decisions, she realized. She had sworn that she would never resign. But she could not stand idly by and allow her character to be destroyed while men like Johnston laughed behind her back. If this was God's way of sending her away, she would have much preferred to have gotten the message some other way. She stopped momentarily to compose her thoughts as fear clouded her mind. *Please speak to me, heavenly Father. I don't know which way to turn. I can't hear your voice from where I stand.* She glanced up almost expectant of an answer, but all she heard was the wind whisking through the swaying tree boughs and the distant approach of rain.

PART THREE

EVERLASTING TO EVERLASTING

"But the mercy of the Lord is from everlasting to everlasting upon them that fear him, and his righteousness unto children's children."

Psalm 103:17

15
THE
ABDUCTORS

Three figures wound around a ledge, down an embankment, and hiked across a rocky outcrop, their dusky frames moving phantomlike against the darkening blue of the horizon. One man halted, waving his hand furiously at the last small member who trailed behind them. "You're movin' too slow. Holdin' us back, mind you, and I won't allow it!"

"Give me rest, sir! I can't—" A breathless boy pleaded to lie down. "I can't go on."

"Shut up, boy! I'm weary o' your complaints."

"What did you do with my horse?" the lad demanded to know, his weariness giving rise to agitation and dulling his sense of fear.

"You'll not be needin' it."

"Then I cannot take another step!"

The hulking man loomed over the lad. "I said *move!*"

His eyelids heavy, the boy stood panting, his mouth agape. His thinking was muddled. The hours and the days stood like far-off specters in his mind, and he could no longer distinguish between time and what was tangible. He was almost certain he had been gone from his precious home for weeks. But he longed to know the time again, and if his only possessions had not been stolen from him, he would surely sell them just to know the day of the week and the hour of the day. But his captors had stripped him of all that he owned—the few shillings in his pocket and his horse. At night, he shivered from the cold, and the only warmth he found lay in his memories of home. And now even those things slipped from his groggy mind. The largest man who had first dragged him from his horse had not spoken his name once. And so he would speak his own name from time to time and think of Papa and Mum, his aunt and uncle, his cousins and comrades. *I am Donovan—Donovan Farrell.* His captors, cunning and shrewd, had not so much as mentioned their own names to each other. And so, in his mind, Donovan had referred to them both as monsters. Scarcely dreading the lashing that was sure to come, he stumbled forward and plunged to the hard ground. His first few nights with his captors he had hated the vagabond manner in which he was forced to live. But now the ground felt good to him. He curled up like an infant while the large monster screamed furiously at him.

"Imbecile! Get up! I say, get up, now!"

Donovan heard the man, and although he had a stubborn nature, it was not his unyielding ways that prompted him to defy him. He felt frozen against the rocky ground and wondered if perhaps he was dying. He could no more get up than could the rocks beneath him. The monster's partner, the smaller man, dressed in a shabby blue coat, quieted the irate man. Rolling onto his back, Donovan found a smoother place on which to sleep. He parted his eyelids only slightly to see the early stars that salted the twilight sky. He realized that he shared the same sky with Rose Hill, and the connection encouraged him. *Why haven't you come for me, Papa? I want to go home. I'm here, Papa.* His thoughts trailed off. *Right here . . .*

"Land ho!"

Captain Robert Gabriel offered a grateful wave to the mariner positioned in the look-out. He turned quietly and repeated the news. "Land ho, Captain Hogan." He acknowledged his sea-weary passenger from Hobart.

186

Grant Hogan folded both arms in front of him and leaned leeward against the gunwale. "I've never heard more welcome words, Gabriel." He thought with anticipation of the reunion that lay ahead.

"And I'll never again be so glad to be rid of a passenger," Gabriel retorted, chuckling.

"I'll not be traveling this far or this long from Sydney Cove again, I vow." Hogan studied the land that rose ahead.

"Oh, so you've turned into a landlubber, eh? You believe you'll make Sydney Cove your home?"

The mere mention of the name Sydney Cove caused a wave of bliss to sweep through Hogan's senses. He recalled the Sunday church services, the sound of hymns rising out of the twig-covered roof, the gay picnics, the aroma of home cooking, the hearty laughter of the men, and the prim chatter of the women. Realizing that they were only a few miles from it all seized his mind with anxious thoughts. He had labored hard in Hobart and found a suitable medical replacement. Now he could put their plight behind him, but only to a certain degree. For he had not felt their burden until he had become a part of their lives. Now he left behind a part of himself just as he had done when he had departed Sydney Cove. He likened it to loving two women but for two entirely different reasons. One had stolen his heart and the other became his fulfillment. But his heart outbid his fulfillment and drove him to return to her beckoning shore. Beyond the fond recollections of home lay memories that tormented him privately. In spite of the letter he had written and had left to be hand-delivered to Bailey Templeton, she had never returned his letters. Katy had mentioned Bailey's name only once in her letters but had given no indication that she had asked after him. From all appearances, she had washed her hands of him. *Bailey Templeton, you must loathe me. On first sight of you, I may fall at your feet as a beggar.* He shook the thought from his mind upon realizing that Gabriel now stared dubiously at him. He could not recall Gabriel's words. "Pardon me?"

Robert Gabriel laughed. "I asked if you knew for certain that you wanted to call Sydney Cove your home?"

Grant nodded. "Without a doubt, Captain. I've wandered too far from home on this last journey. I'll not repeat the mistake. What about yourself?"

187

"Once I've dropped off your carcass, I'll be setting sail for England."

"England's your home, I vow."

"The sea is my home. But once there, I've a widow to see. She's still a young thing and has written me since her husband's death now three years nigh."

"My cousin will miss you, I am certain. And her brood as well."

"She's a dear friend, and I desire nothing more but to see her boy brought home. That's why I fetched you and William Lawson. But I'm satisfied now to know that she's well and that she beheld me fit as a fiddle and not eaten by the sharks as she had supposed." He chuckled.

"I commend you for your swift actions, Captain. And we *will* find Donovan for Katy, I pray. And I'll see that Dwight joins us on the journey."

"Katy has found herself a good man who sees well to her. Quite a feat in this colony."

"Yes. They've much to be grateful for." Hogan reflected on Katy and Dwight. Hogan's family had moved to New South Wales when he was but a youth, and he'd had the opportunity to observe both the strengths and the foibles of their marriage. But always within the turbulence, a flame of fierce love burned for each other. Now they faced a giant that threatened to destroy their entire family. "With Donovan missing, I fear the worst for them. Katy must be frantic."

"She's worried herself sick." Gabriel sighed. "She's not accustomed to leaning on anyone, and it kills her soul to do so."

"All will be rectified when Donovan is returned. We'll find him if I have to turn every house in the borough upside down. Then perhaps I can begin to sort out my own life."

"And you'll return to the lass who's caught your eye?"

Hogan turned his face from the sea and stared quizzically after Gabriel. Seeing the amusement that flickered in his eyes, he spoke with some reserve. "Who, pray tell, do you speak of?"

"Why, the schoolmistress, of course."

Casually, he allowed his eyes to wander back out to the white-capped horizon. "I declare, I don't know what you mean."

"Of course you do, Captain Hogan. She's the pretty school-teacher you had your eye set for all along."

"Tell me why you say such things." Ambiguous to Gabriel's

knowledge of the matter, Hogan clasped his hands in front of him. His heart rent tender, his will was too stubborn to admit such a thing. "Tell me, unless you've downed a pannikin of seawater, and then I shall understand your plight." His mouth turned up on one side.

"See here, good Captain Hogan. Your secret is safe with me." He held a finger to his lips. "You're as transparent as leather, and none would be the wiser had I not chanced to take my evening stroll along the shoreline near the tavern. And what did I see but two lovers. Thought you'd stolen away, I'm sure."

"You are mad!" His brows pulled together in an affronted frown, Hogan could not hide the humor he felt in the matter.

"Perhaps, but I'm not blind."

Hogan looked one way and then the other. His first thought— to deny the incident—crumbled beneath the weight of truth. He strode to the mast behind the captain and leaned forward against it. Bowing his head, he closed his eyes and said quietly, "No, dear Captain Gabriel, you're not blind."

Bailey seated herself in the midst of the ladies of Rose Hill as they chatted quietly. In futility, Amelia stubbornly insisted that her young daughter-in-law, Kelsey, be as finely skilled in needlepoint as was she. Demonstrating a stitch, she then handed the work to Kelsey, who laughed at her own clumsy efforts.

"I can't do it, Amelia!" Kelsey winked at Bailey. "You try it, Katy. I'm a fine one to be trying such a thing."

Bailey gazed admirably at the stunning Irish girl. She sat poised in a tufted chair, her trained dress of violet China crepe bustling about her. Her golden hair had been carefully arranged around her face in ringed curls and cascaded down her neck and over her shoulders in soft, shining tresses. In spite of having borne two children, her curvaceous figure had remained striking. Katy, dressed equally as elegant—her shoulders wrapped in a blue and white scarf fichu—sat silent, sullenly facing away from the other two women. Although distressed at the look of despair on Katy's somber countenance, the sight of the women fussing over needle-point caused Bailey to smile.

"Would you wish to try it yourself, Bailey?" Kelsey lifted the needlepoint fabric out to her, a sheepish glimmer lighting her eyes.

Bailey mulled over the offer for a moment. She hated such things but would not admit it to Amelia. She could not bear to disappoint her. "Perhaps I'll try later." Her nose wrinkled and she squinted her eyes. When Amelia turned her face down to examine the needlepoint, Bailey winked mischievously at Kelsey.

"Oh, give it to me, then." A hint of exasperation in her tone, Amelia took the handiwork from Kelsey. "I'll do it meself."

A hint of smile still on her lips, Bailey asked Katy, "Where is your husband today?"

"He hasn't returned yet from the parcel of territory beyond Parrametta. He took two men with him. There was rumor of a boy seen wandering the roadway along that piece of country-side."

"Yes." Kelsey frowned. "But no sight of Donovan's horse. It's all so peculiar." The sunlight flooding through the window crept across her face. "Caleb returned to oversee the flocks as well as seeing to all of Rose Hill's affairs. This is so difficult." She stood to close the drapes.

Hearing the sadness in their voices and seeing how the matter weighed like lead upon them all, Bailey could not bring herself to divulge her own bad news that she had overheard at the mercantile. Instead, she announced, "I want you all to know that in spite of the turmoil in your household, young Jared almost won the school spelling bee yesterday."

"*My* Jared?" Katy spread her fingers across her chest.

Seeing Katy's reaction sent a feeling of relief through Bailey. She thought she had detected a faint smile, although a guarded one, as though to do so might break the spell over the search.

A proud blush spread across Amelia's cheeks. "The little scamp!"

"He didn't say a word." Glancing around the quaint parlor, Katy clasped her hands in her lap. "Did he tell you, Mum?"

"No." Amelia shook her head, a question in her eyes.

"Nor I," Kelsey commented, her curiosity piqued.

"But then, why should he? We're all so preoccupied with finding Donovan—" Katy stared distantly and stopped when her voice broke with emotion.

Bailey could see Katy heaping more guilt upon herself and could bear it no longer. "Katy, please, you must stop blaming yourself for all that's happened recently."

"Yes." Amelia nodded. "Bailey's right. Worry won't bring our dear Donovan back home, Katy." She smoothed out her black bodice and sat forward.

But Bailey could see that worry had also taken its toll upon Amelia. Her face was etched with permanent grief.

"I know that, Mum." Her voice intensifying, Katy's eyes narrowed and she grew defensive. "But it is my fault. I'll never forgive myself if—"

"Jared!" Bailey's eyes widened, and she stretched a smile across her face. "We were just talking about you." She nodded toward the doorway to indicate the lad had entered unannounced.

"Why?" He bit into a piece of fruit.

Her face flush, Katy composed herself, although her eyes still brimmed with bitter tears. "Miss Templeton told us about the spelling bee," she finally responded. "I'm very proud of you, son."

"I didn't win," he said matter-of-factly. "Studied and all that, but still didn't win. Donovan would've won. He always did."

"Donovan will be proud of you when your papa brings him home." Katy ran her slender fingers down his arm. "Just like we are now."

Glad that their attention had turned to more pleasant matters, Bailey quickly responded, "Something has sparked a fire inside of Jared. I wouldn't be surprised if he wins the next bee hands down. I'm sure of it."

The happier subject, in addition to Amelia's needlepoint nonsense, helped to wile away the long Saturday afternoon. After tea, Bailey felt more relaxed than ever with the women. The urge to confess her decision grew paramount in her mind. "Before you take your rest this afternoon, Amelia, I've something weighing on my mind."

The women looked at one another curiously. Amelia asked, "You mean to tell us you've 'ad something to say all day? Mercy, Bailey, you should've told us sooner."

No longer able to withhold the news, Bailey began, "This is a difficult matter to discuss or admit. As you all know, I've had my share of problems at the school."

Nodding her understanding, Amelia commented, "And took it all on like a warrior, I vow."

"I wish that were true, Amelia. How I wish. But I believe that because I refused to leave the school, I've brought on some of the problems here at Rose Hill."

"Absurd!" Kelsey's brow furrowed.

"It isn't true," Katy disagreed strongly.

"Hear me out, please." The pain was greater than Bailey believed it would be, and she looked away from them to regain her composure as best as she could. "Katy, your cousin Grant Hogan tried to warn me about the junta. When all along I thought that he wanted me gone, he was trying to protect me. At least, that is one conclusion I've drawn."

Katy interjected, "Bailey, had I known of your earlier suspicions, I would have told you so myself. My cousin spoke on your behalf on numerous occasions. He even requested an audience with Governor Bligh himself. The outcome I never was certain about because he was transferred the very next day."

"He spoke with Bligh about me?" The words stunned Bailey. Katy nodded her affirmation. "He never told me." She recalled their liaison on the shoreline. He could have informed her then, but he didn't.

"But you seldom spoke with Grant, true?" Katy asked, her eyes kindling a curious light.

"Seldom." Growing quiet, Bailey regained her train of thought. "But after Captain Hogan's departure, my home was ransacked, my garden destroyed. You recall?"

"We know all of those things. That is why we invited you to live here." Sitting forward, Katy's voice held a hint of desperation. "You feel safe here, don't you?"

"I did. But now that Donovan has disappeared, I can't help but suspect more foul play. Somehow, the junta is behind it. I'm sure of it."

"We can't know that, Bailey." Kelsey stood and walked to Bailey's side. "Donovan was upset when he disappeared."

"He was also a level-headed young man." Lifting her hand, Bailey allowed it to rest atop Kelsey's on her shoulder. "And I've discovered another bit of news. My replacement is already living here in Sydney Cove. With great anticipation, he awaits my departure."

"You know for certain, dear?" Amelia laid aside her needlepoint.

"I do, Amelia. His name is Atkins, and he is the judge advocate's brother."

"They're all beasts!" Katy stood, her fists clenched at her sides.

"And the fact that I won't resign must certainly be placing more pressure on Major Johnston."

"So you believe Macarthur's Rum Corps took Donovan because we've come to your aid?" Katy's chest heaved, anxiety evident.

"They're retaliating against anyone who stands in their way. Their leader's been jailed and revenge is the order of the day." Bailey drew her arms against herself, still finding it difficult to look squarely at Katy. "But if I resign—"

"No! We won't let you do that." Katy moved swiftly toward Bailey, her skirts bustling behind her.

"No, we will not!" Agreeing, Amelia joined the coterie around Bailey.

Bailey felt Amelia slip an arm around her waist. She treasured their show of support. Not since she had left home had she received such love and encouragement. Wrapping her arm around Amelia's shoulders, she gazed first at her and then at the other two women. "You've been so supportive of me. Imagine— an American attempting to run a school in the Australian wilds. If I had given it much more thought, the likelihood of my accepting such a challenge would be small. But I did and I'm glad of it. But if staying means to risk the lives of those I dearly love, then perhaps I'm wrong in my stand, however noble we believe it to be."

"But Sydney Cove is your home now." Kelsey offered her own argument. "We fought the junta before you came, and we shall continue to fight it until England sees fit to dissolve its power.

"The last few months have been extremely emotional. Don't make your decision now. Please?" Katy pleaded, her face full of desperation. "If you give in to Atkins, then our children's education will be placed in the hands of corruption."

"I've considered all you're saying, Katy. But the fact remains that the Rum Corps will stop at nothing to control this colony. And until England recognizes this fact, one American teacher is easy prey, along with all those who befriend her. I've made you all the target of their destructive whims."

"Dwight must hear all you're saying, Bailey." Katy grew insistent. "If the Rum Corps has anything to do with our son's disappearance, then we could be searching in all the wrong places. And what if—" Katy's voice broke off. "What if it's too late!"

"Don't think such things." Bailey grasped her hands and lifted her eyes to meet Katy's. "We can't move forward in our efforts if we despair."

"She's right." Amelia reached out her hands on either side of her. "We've all done it privately. Let's join our efforts together, shall we?" She took Bailey's and Kelsey's hands on either side of her and Katy completed the circle. Amelia bowed her head. "Dear Father..."

16

TRUE
CONFESSIONS

Although her disclosure had cast a pall over the household, Bailey felt relieved that at the very least the women knew of the junta's plans to replace her. If necessary, she could make inquiries both in London and in Williamsburg by letter and take the necessary measures to make her departure ensue as swiftly as was humanly possible in the event that Johnston tried to remove her from the school. But if she did leave the school, she had promised Katy and Amelia that it would be an issue of force and not a resignation. To give in to Macarthur's junta would be the same as giving in to the devil.

Bailey had opened the windows to her room to invite in the fresh air and sunshine. She had brought out each frock for examination and found a few in need of repair. Before the last rays of sun escaped from her windowsill, she set about quickly to make the repairs. She scrutinized her handiwork on a pale blue silk Empire gown—a decollete gown with a high waistline. The color was so pale she would have thought the fabric to be white had it not been for the ice-blue folds in the cloth. She had tightened a loose stitch around the sleeve. Lifting off her cotton dress over her head, she donned the pale blue one, feeling the cool silk glide over her hips and legs in a soft caress. She was pleased with this French design and had so tired of bustles and petticoats, although she doubted that women would ever be entirely free of them.

She had just turned away from the mirror when she heard a soft rap at her door. A maid brought a message that someone had come to call on Bailey—an officer named Evans. Surprised that Evans would appear after all these months, Bailey hesitated. She sighed, unsure of her own feelings. Not wanting to appear impolite, she opened the door to the servant girl. "Pardon me, but did you say Evans?"

"Yes, miss." The girl stood with arms akimbo, awaiting her reply.

She responded in the manner expected, but her thoughts went astray. "Would you please inform the lieutenant that I'll be down to see him in a moment?"

The girl nodded and disappeared down the hallway.

Bailey checked herself once again in the mirror, although she truly cared little about how she looked for the lieutenant. Slipping her feet into a pair of leather slippers trimmed with a blue rosette and black silk ribbon, she mentally prepared herself for whatever the man had to say. She yet harbored a remnant of guilt in regard to how she had broken off their relationship. She had seen Jonathan at church but acknowledged him in the same manner as she would any other acquaintance. Perhaps she had mishandled the entire affair, and he wished to bring them to a more conciliatory arrangement. She decided to hear him out either way. And she prayed that she would listen more closely to God in matters regarding others' hearts. Thus far, she had been a complete failure, leaving a trail of pain in the wake.

Bailey descended the carpeted staircase. When she reached the bottom, the young servant informed her that the lieutenant had been invited by Mrs. Farrell to wait in the parlor. Bailey turned too quickly and, her apprehension evident, had nearly collided with the male servant who bustled past. "Pardon me." She smoothed her dress and quickly invited the servant to continue on his way but felt her cheeks redden. "For heaven's sake," she muttered to herself. She had no intention of allowing Jonathan Evans to behold her in such a state. He might interpret her anxiety in a way in which she had no intention of conveying to the man. She poised herself once again and entered the parlor with a calm surety, a pleasant smile spread across her face.

Evans, seated on Amelia's mahogany settee, stood at once, a strange, somber expression darkening his usually confident smile. "Hello, Bailey." He doffed his hat and held it in front of him.

"Jonathan." Bailey nodded politely but reservedly.

"I apologize for my abrupt appearance at your portals." Evans turned to pace in front of the fireplace. He placed his hands behind him, his fingers fidgeting with his hat.

"No need for apology." Seeing the man felt awkward, she said, "Please be seated."

Not looking up at her, Evans continued pacing, his words tinged with anxious tension. "No, thank you. What I have to say, I feel I should say at once, lest I allow myself to lie of my intention and therefore never speak the words I should have spoken to you long ago."

Pursing her lips together, it was now Bailey who could not lay her eyes on him. "Jonathan, if this is about us, then I must tell you, my handling of the entire affair—"

Evans turned about, his chin lifted deliberately. "You believe I've come to court you?"

Bailey started to shake her head. No assumptions of the sort had entered her head. But instead of answering straightaway, she wisely held her words and awaited his response.

"Well, you see that is the problem after all, isn't it?"

"I don't believe I understand." She seated herself, leaving him to stand.

"Allow me to explain." Evans positioned himself directly in front of Bailey, his eyes now riveted on hers. As he looked into her face, he could not disguise the tenderness or the affection that he held for her.

A strange pity for the man welled inside Bailey. But she could not mistake her feelings for anything other than pity, however hard she might wish otherwise.

"I felt certain of our courtship from the moment I saw you, Bailey. Your beauty lies deeper than your lovely face. You are a woman of purpose and of character. But at the time I also warned you that another man would be wooing you."

"Grant Hogan." Bailey had not uttered his name in such a long time that she felt surprised at the inward emotion she felt upon saying it. "He's gone, Jonathan. Why belabor the point?"

A look of contempt shot from Evans' eyes. He drew himself up and squared his shoulders. "He has had his pick of women in the colony, so it did not surprise me that he would set his sights upon you, as well as Emily Parkinson and any other unsuspecting female he wished to prey upon."

"You make him sound like a villain, Jonathan." Bailey looked away, uncomfortable with the subject.

"And of that fact, I am quite certain." His tone defensive, he continued pacing. "But of another truth, I am more certain."

Bailey could not help but sigh. "And what truth might that be?"

"That Captain Grant Hogan loves you."

Bailey shook her head, heaved a laborious sigh, and looked him squarely in the face. "This is all nonsense."

"Is it? What about the evening at the tavern and your private little walk along the shore?"

Her muscles tightened, but she maintained a casual tone. "I don't know what you're talking about." The lie stuck in her throat. She bit her lip and felt her face color. Speaking too quickly, the words had flown out like wild birds from a cage.

Evans chuckled, and his brow lifted cynically. "No? Miss Emily Parkinson has a dear friend who saw differently that night."

Bailey clasped her hands and brought her fingers to her lips. "Has she believed this story for long?" She kept her gaze toward the floor, believing he had read her thoughts.

"For the longest while she did not. Only recently did she catch wind of the gossip and demand that her young friend divulge the facts to her."

Now unable to lift her eyes to his, Bailey felt a wave of shame sweep through her. "I'm very embarrassed. She must think awful things of me." She clasped her hands in her lap. "Now it's all gotten so out of hand."

"Not entirely." Pushing aside his sword, Evans seated himself next to her. "She did not love Grant Hogan."

"How do you know such things?"

"Because I asked her, and she told me."

"I fail to see why such matters would interest you, Jonathan. You're obsessed with Captain Hogan. His exploits with females shouldn't be your concern."

"Oh, dear Miss Templeton, these matters are of grave concern to me. You see, Miss Emily Parkinson has consented to marry me."

Bailey almost choked on the words. "*You* are marrying Emily?"

The smug grin on Evans' face proved he was pleased with her

surprise. "I would like to believe you to be horribly disappointed, but I know differently."

Recovering, she said, "Of course I'm not disappointed, Jonathan." Bailey maintained her composure. The news had caught her off guard. But she could not disguise the surprise in her voice. "Congratulations to you. Miss Parkinson is a lovely young woman."

"Thank you. And I believe it providence that the events of the last year would bring our two lives together. But I have yet to be relieved of my obligation to you."

Now she tried to read his thoughts. She shook her head slightly and gave him a sidelong glance. "You've absolutely no obligation to me. None whatsoever."

"I have but one."

"And I swear that you don't." Bailey grew more insistent.

Reaching into his coat pocket, Evans pulled out a tattered letter. With gloved fingers, he opened the letter and gazed down at it. "I've lost a great deal of sleep over this letter. Not so much due to its contents but mostly because I failed to deliver it as promised."

"You've a letter for me?"

"From Captain Hogan. You see, when he received his abrupt transfer, I was the last familiar face that he saw at Sydney Cove. His fate, in essence, had been placed in my foolish hands."

"Grant asked you to deliver a letter to me, and you kept it?"

"Please understand, Miss Templeton, that you have two villains in your life, and one"—he swallowed hard, but forced himself to continue—"is me."

The stunning news flew at Bailey, and she struggled to quell her anger. "I don't understand why you would do such a thing!" Her voice shakier than she had intended, she lifted her face somberly, her eyes filled with questioning. "I don't understand."

"Don't you, Bailey?" Evans lifted his right hand and cupped it beneath her chin. "Even the best of us can fall into obsession."

Bailey pulled her face away, shocked at his candor. "Don't!"

"I swear to you, I never will again." He held up his gloved hands in surrender, the letter still in his grasp. "I am cured—thanks to Emily." He stood once again and donned his hat. "But know this— you gave up the best man for the worst."

"I disagree." Bailey had tired of his disapproval of Grant Hogan but wished to direct the conversation elsewhere. "I've given up nothing, and I've gained nothing in return. Within weeks, Sydney

Cove may be nothing to me but a vague memory. Major Johnston, I've discovered, has made other plans for the school, and they don't include me." She walked Evans toward the front door. "So you see, you don't know everything as you suppose."

"Of that fact, I am most certain. But the burden of the letter has been lifted from me—that is my greatest relief. All else will take care of itself. I've never known Bailey Templeton to lose a war." Evans gently grasped Bailey's forearm. "And I would be grateful to know that you do not despise me." Lifting her hand, he tucked Grant's letter into her palm.

Bailey beheld a glint of guileless apology in his eyes. She smiled, no longer in need of guarding her emotions. Grasping the letter, she chose to read it in a more private setting. "I don't hate you. And I'm happy for you, Jonathan." She kissed the side of his face. "Emily Parkinson is a lucky woman."

"And you aren't the least bit jealous?" He held her out at arm's length, giving her a sidelong glance.

Bailey's amusement was evidenced by her smile as she opened the door. Her face brimming with honest forthrightness, she said simply, "I'm jealous of your happiness."

"You're more deserving of it than I, Bailey. The good Lord hasn't forgotten about you, I'm sure of it."

"I know He hasn't," she answered in a gentle tone. "But it's the refining that hurts sometimes." She bid farewell, allowed Evans to depart, and remembered that she still wore the Empire gown. She needed to change into a more practical dress for dinner. Striding toward the staircase, she heard Katy call out to her.

"Well, Miss Templeton, I see you had a gentleman caller."

A strange melancholy welled from inside Bailey, although she could not determine exactly why. "Hello, Katy. Yes, he had good news. Lieutenant Evans wished to announce his engagement."

Katy met her at the foot of the stairs, her eyes welling with sympathy. "Dear Bailey, I am sorry. Does this news distress you?"

"No. Nothing like that. I'm happy for him." Bailey still held the unread letter from Grant Hogan in her hand. "Actually, Katy, I'm relieved. I knew that I didn't love him. It's much better this way."

Holding her hand to her breast, Katy's face softened with relief. "I'm so glad to hear you say that. He's a wonderful man, but I suspected as much about you." She walked beside Bailey, and together they made their way upstairs. "So who is the lieutenant's lucky young woman?"

Almost fearing her response, Bailey hesitated. "It isn't someone that you would guess right away."

Katy bit her bottom lip, her eyes gleaming with curiosity. "Tell me now before I burst."

"Miss Emily Parkinson." Before Katy could speak, Bailey quickly interjected, "I know this all sounds so abrupt. But they're in love, Katy. I could see it in Jonathan's eyes."

Katy looked straight ahead as though she studied the matter. "Yes, of course. It does make sense, doesn't it? And can't we always see it in the men's eyes first. We women are so clever at hiding our feelings." She followed Bailey into the guest room. "But the men— they can never fool us."

"I don't think that's true of everyone." Bailey took the letter and slid it under a pair of gloves on the dressing table. She enjoyed Katy's company, but curiosity as to the letter's contents rose inside of her like a brush fire.

"Let us take my cousin for example. You know, Grant Hogan?"

Gathering up the skirt with her hands, Bailey lifted it up to her waist. She did not wish to respond to Katy, apprehensive that her own emotions would betray her. "Can you help me with my dress?"

Katy grasped the silk hem and lifted it over Bailey's head. "This gown is stunning. I've nothing like it." She turned the dress back out and shook out the long, silky skirt. "As I was saying, though, I could always tell that Grant really cared nothing for Miss Parkinson. Theirs was merely a friendship—nothing more."

Pulling the other dress over her head, Bailey mumbled, turning her lips inward so as not to smudge the fabric. "What makes you think so?"

"It wasn't so much in the way he looked at her"—she assisted Bailey with the small buttons at her bodice—"but rather in the manner which Grant . . ."

Hearing the hesitation in Katy's voice, Bailey's lashes flew up. "Go on," she said casually.

"It was the manner in which Grant looked at you."

Turning away, Bailey did not wish for Katy to see the red spots appear on her cheeks. "Dinner should be ready soon, eh?" She desperately wanted to change the subject. But when Katy gave no reply, she whirled around, her face feeling flushed.

"Would you look at that!" Katy folded her arms across her chest, a glib expression lighting her countenance. "I knew it all along, Bailey Templeton. I just knew it!"

"You're certain you can't join us, Gabriel?" Grant had hoped to coax Robert Gabriel into joining himself and Lawson in the search for Donovan Farrell.

The three of them had gathered in the tavern for a final farewell. "No, lads. I must take my leave at once, for England beckons. It does sadden me to leave without a proper farewell to the Farrells, but it is much better this way. You will write me, Captain Hogan, and tell me of your search for Katy's boy?"

"I shall write. I swear it. And I will be ever indebted to you for coming for me and Lawson." Hogan determined to make good on his promise to the captain.

"Aye, Gabriel, I'd grown weary of Hobart." William Lawson lifted his wide-brimmed hat and raked his fingers through his dark hair. He was a tall, sinewy man with sun-toughened skin due to his explorations in New South Wales. He had befriended Robert Gabriel five years hence and was glad to be of service to Gabriel's friends. "I'll be even more gratified to you if I can assist in findin' this Farrell lad." He ordered up an ale for himself, his small, deep-set eyes full of sympathy.

"No need to thank me. Just send me tidings of your success, and I'll live out my days in peace," Gabriel assured them.

"So, Gabriel, tell me of this widow in England. Is she a pretty thing?" Lawson bantered with the captain.

"She's a good woman with a rather plain face but hair as gold as flax. She's meek and polite and a good mother to her children." Gabriel accepted a pannikin from a tavern girl who passed around a tray to them.

"How many children?" Hogan asked with a hint of humor in his tone.

"She has four children. She lives with her sister and brother-in-law, and they see well to her. But she's grown lonely of late and has written me twice."

Lawson took a long draw on his pipe and downed his ale. "I've never known Robert Gabriel to leave behind the sea for long. Will your lady friend want to keep you near her hearth?"

"You don't know all about Robert Gabriel, I vow. I have grown weary of the voyage and look ahead to purchase a farm in the countryside." Gabriel defended his plan with good humor.

"Gabriel grows soft in the head." Lawson drew a finger to his forehead and winked at Grant.

"Hah!" Setting his mug atop the table, Gabriel leaned back against the chairback and chuckled in a low tone. "I've not grown soft, just wiser."

"My congratulations to you, my good man." Hogan offered his best wishes. "You've made a decision that I'm certain will bring you great happiness."

"Thank you, sir!" Folding his muscular arms across his chest, Gabriel cocked his head back and gazed upward. "I've taken my blows in life. It's high time Robert Gabriel got his reward, I vow."

"And you're certain you don't wish to visit Rose Hill one last time?" Hogan persisted amiably. He knew that Jared had grown fond of the sea captain and his wild tales. But in his loyalty to the family, he also knew of the strange tension between his cousin Katy and her spouse.

Gabriel shook his head. "More than certain, Hogan. The Farrells don't need me underfoot. What they need is peace in their world. I pray the good Lord will grant it."

"Here, here." Lawson nodded in sober agreement.

"Let us take our leave, then, good Mr. Lawson." Hogan pushed himself from the table. "Give us Godspeed, Gabriel, and we shall be on our way."

"Godspeed, Captain Hogan, and to you as well, Mr. Lawson."

The men shook hands and stepped out into the early twilight. "If we make fast our departure, Mr. Lawson, we should reach Rose Hill by midnight. Pray Katy will be so glad to see me, she'll not lynch me for the odd hour of night." Hogan chuckled.

"Hogan? Is it you?"

The sudden voice behind him caused Hogan to turn about in surprise. He called out a quick salutation and then beheld who had spoken to him. "Dwight Farrell? I'll be—it is you, old man!"

Dwight threw his arms about him and shook him vigorously. "You've returned! Katy will be overjoyed!"

"Not as happy as I am to be home, I'll grant you that." Hogan spoke buoyantly.

"What brought you home?" Lifting a heavy pack from his shoulder, Dwight hefted it to another man who assisted him at once. "Amelia's cooking?"

"That would do it, but . . ." Hogan hesitated, realizing the pain that Dwight must feel. "Robert Gabriel came for me. Dwight, we've come to search for Donovan—myself and William Lawson—if you'll allow."

Dwight's face reflected his serious consideration of his words. "I'll be forever indebted." Heaving a sigh of resignation, he said finally, "You're a good man, and I always knew it, Grant Hogan. Of course I'll allow." Glancing around, Dwight finally asked, "And where is—Robert Gabriel?"

Stepping out from the tavern doorway, Robert approached Dwight slowly. Extending his hand, he tipped his cap to him, his eyes full of earnest sincerity. "I am here, Mr. Farrell."

His face betraying his brokenness, Dwight returned Robert's handshake. "I'm indebted to you, Captain Gabriel." His words sounded somewhat wooden, but his eyes softened and his tone took on new meaning. "You've brought ol' Hogan back to us and perhaps the means to find my son."

"Glad to help. You're a good husband and father. This settlement would flounder without men like you. It's a privilege to serve such an honorable man." Gabriel clasped his other stout hand atop Dwight's.

The two men stood like tall, dark silhouettes against eventide's curtain of still blue twilight. Their hands locked in an amicable gesture, they gazed wordlessly, and the night fell silently while old wounds began their steady healing.

"They could be listenin'. Keep your voice low." John Macarthur leaned against the cold iron cage of his captivity. He faced the man who held the key to his escape. "Johnston, are the men rallied and ready to oust Bligh?" His clipped Scottish brogue rumbled in a low tone, although sparked with emotion.

"They're with us, sir." George Johnston's voice quavered, his eyes wide. "Do you think we can pull it off? Depose Bligh, I mean?"

"Don't be a coward, Johnston. Bligh's a fool and everyone knows it. I ran this colony with the full support of all until England sent us their refuse. He'll not soon forget John Macarthur."

"How do you think England will respond?" The fear crept back in Johnston's eyes.

"Slowly." Macarthur drew out the word, bathing it with assurance. "By the time they hear of it, we'll be shippin' them back the profits. As long as they're getting their cut, they'll hail us as heroes."

"We can have the men rallied in a blink, sir."

"Give it a fortnight, but wait for my word. Then capture Bligh first. They will not turn guns on their own. The rest will be a matter o' dischargin' the dissenters. Any man not willin' to join the Corps is not fit to serve New South Wales."

"Aye, sir." Major Johnston gave a knowing glance to his co-conspirator. It was now time to play out their masquerade before the guard. He cleared his throat and, using his most convincing histrionics, said loudly, "You'll be confined for months, Macarthur. Our governor won't stand for officer interference, so take your medicine with dignity, and your lesson will not soon be forgotten."

"Please extend to our governor my deepest apologies," Macarthur retorted, his dark eyes flashing conspiratorially.

"Guard!" Johnston called out with authority.

The guard did not appear at once but showed his face in the barred pass-through when Johnston called out a second time.

"Comin', sir. Must o' nodded off, I did."

"Do that again and I'll have you flogged, man!" Woodenly, Johnston faced Macarthur, nodded his approval of the new guard, and departed without ceremony.

Walking as she had so many sunlit afternoons in Katy's English garden, Bailey sipped warm cider and put as much distance between herself and the main house as possible. She seated herself on the ivy-colored bench behind the rose arbor, then untied the sash from her bonnet and fanned her neck with the as-yet-unopened letter. Having donned her favorite walking dress, she took care not to crimp the polonaise of green foulard. She glanced around, hearing distant conversations from the house servants. Grateful at finding herself alone, she quickly opened the captain's mysterious letter. The paper was now somewhat worn and the ink slightly faded, so she smoothed it carefully with her slender fingers. Inhaling deeply, she glanced up at the sky as though awaiting heaven's approval before she gingerly opened the letter. With great anticipation, she began to read the penned words that so long had been kept from her eyes:

My dearest Bailey,

You will not understand my abrupt departure from Sydney Cove to Hobart, and so I must trust that you will hear the words of my heart from the faceless page before you. Hobart is without medical aid. Although I question the motives of those who have so abruptly shipped me away, I shall remain dutiful in my responsibility, however much it grieves me to leave behind such a fine lady as yourself. Had I known that our lives would so rudely be torn asunder, I most assuredly would have informed you of the news the same night that you stole my heart. Our time on the shore meant more to me than one brief instant of bliss—although its memory lives within me like a fire. But I can neither be at your door on this night nor any other. If I perchance can ready a new man in Hobart to aid with the current needs of this settlement, I will return at once to beg your forgiveness and begin anew what was so abruptly interrupted . . .

Finishing his polite salutation, Bailey read and reread the letter, seeking out some grain of news informing her of his impending return. But such tidings were not found and so diminished any hope she held for their worlds being reunited in the near future. She glanced once more at the letter—*our time on the shore.* The words summoned the memory to her mind, flooding her heart with the pain of separation. But at the same time, her emotions were filled with relief in knowing that their separation was as painful for him as it had been for her. Although consoled that he had not purposefully abandoned her as she had first mistakenly assumed, Bailey saw that he offered little hope of a speedy return. She shook her head, filled with the pain she had never allowed herself to contemplate until now. The small part of her that wished their paths had never crossed now gave way to a small flame of hope. Another part of her longed to lay eyes once again upon his hale countenance—*but not for only one brief moment.* "I must see you again, Grant Hogan," she whispered. "But when?" Closing up his letter, she laid it aside and sat alone in the garden until just before candlelight.

17

THE REFINING POT

Christmas passed swiftly at Rose Hill. Katy's depression had deepened. But Amelia, determined to honor the Lord's birth honorably for the sake of her grandchildren, had seen to the handmade gifts as well as a proper feast. Bailey had assisted in adding to the gaity, although she battled her own cloud of worry. With December behind her, she had cautiously laid out her plans for her pupils in spite of her shaky futre.

But without warning, she found her well-intended plans dashed upon the rocks of corrupt politics.

Bailey stormed through the government building, her court train of deep red faille rustling against the wooden floor. She gripped a letter in her hand and occasionally glanced down at it, her face taut with frustration. The letter had been delivered by messenger yesterday, January tenth. In no mood to observe protocol, she marched briskly past the private who was seated behind a desk at the entrance. The hallway, long and hollow, echoed her approach. The six o'clock hour sounding the end of the workday had emptied the building of patrons, which gave her only small relief in knowing she would stand a greater chance of being granted an audience with Major George Johnston. She felt dread well up inside her as she mentally formulated her words. She knew that to speak from the raw pit of her emotions would only reduce her to a mewling female in this man's sight. She paused outside of Johnston's door and listened. The sound of shuffling paper could be heard faintly through the door. She straightened her bodice of strawberry satin and then repositioned her ostrich-plumed bonnet. With firm assurance, she reread the letter, took a deep breath, and rapped firmly on the door. The sound of a chair leg scraping the floor confirmed an occupant. She knocked once more but did not wish to identify herself right away.

"Smith?" Johnston's voice rose loudly and gruffly from the silent office.

Bailey bit her lip and closed her eyes but offered no reply.

"Coming!" Impatience now emanated from the major's tone, and she could hear him muttering. Another shuffling sound ensued, followed by the hard pounding of heels against wood.

Taking a deep, controlled breath, Bailey stood erect as the door opened slowly before her. She fixed her eyes instantly on his, dismayed to see his gaze turn ice cold upon seeing her. "Major Johnston, I believe you've been expecting me."

"Miss Templeton." The major tempered his words, although agitation clearly rose from his eyes. "No, I wasn't expecting you. Actually, I've sent for my carriage to take my leave for the afternoon. I'm certain we can meet at a later time. Private Smith can arrange—"

"I can assure you, Major, that this matter will not keep for later." Bailey placed her slender gloved hand against the door, preventing the man from closing it in her face. "You can surely guess the meaning of my visit, can you not?" She stepped into his office without invitation but maintained an air of gentility.

Exasperated, Johnston stepped back, allowing her to pass. "Won't you come in?" Sarcasm tinged the resignation in both his speech and manner, and his brows lifted with surprise. Turning up the wick on a lantern, he positioned it on a bookshelf near his massive desk. "Let's not dally, Miss Templeton. I presume you received our correspondence?"

Bailey held up the letter near her face. "You certainly don't mince words." She snapped open the letter and read aloud, *"We have documented our proof that the ills brought into our colony are too heavy a burden for any lady to bear."* The paper crumpled in her grasp. "What proof, Major? On what grounds can you dismiss me without notice?"

"You know of the complaints lodged against you by the Dobbins family?"

"Blaine Dobbins is a frustrated man attempting to rear his son alone and without any restraint or discipline. You have other proof, I assume?"

Johnston hesitated and a cold, calculated stare arose from him. No longer bridled with diplomacy, a more fierce nature ensued. "Very well, Miss Templeton, if you demand to hear the naked truth, so be it." Lifting a brass key from his desktop, he walked deliberately to a glass-paned cabinet and unlocked the smoothly finished door.

Bailey shifted uneasily. He pulled out a small stack of letters and laid them directly in front of her.

"Read them all—go on. You wish to know everything," he said smugly.

A sickening feeling swirled inside of Bailey. She knew instinctively that the colonists would never raise complaints against her. But rather, if she asked, she could easily double or triple the families willing to write letters on her behalf. "You've attempted every vicious avenue in your quest to run me out of Sydney Cove, Major Johnston. You've coerced me. I've suffered physical assault. Now you attack my character? How do you sleep at night?"

"Very well, thank you." He fingered one of the letters, positioning it squarely in front of her. "But as for a physical attack or some campaign to run you off, as you say, I am innocent. I only have the school's best interest in mind. The families of Sydney Cove are my chief concern."

"Yes, don't I know of your compassion, Major Johnston?" Bailey slid the letter in front of her. She read silently, forcefully retaining what shred of composure she could. The first letter, penned by a mother of one of her students, stunned her. The spiteful accusations flew at her like hurled stones, shaking her sensibilities. She read the poorly scrawled handwriting of the emancipist parent. "This isn't even true—" she whispered mostly to herself, for it did her little good to argue with him. Her lashes flew up. "This is a lie, Major Johnston!" She brushed aside the letter, no longer fearing his rigid intimidation. "Has it come to this—that you would be forced to pay a starving family for trumped up lies? Have I caused you so little grief that you would feel compelled to fabricate evidence against me?" She stood, not wanting to wait for his reply. "I considered for a brief moment the possibility of leaving Sydney Cove to seek a teaching position elsewhere. But you blackguards have left me little recourse. I'll fight you, mister! Until the bitter end!"

She marched from his office, incensed by his vicious game. As much as she wanted to relieve the Farrells of the burden of her risky presence as well as leave behind the woes of Sydney Cove, she could not allow herself to be stripped of her dignity. *Governor Bligh must know about this treachery right away. He'll stop them! I'm sure of it!*

"Must we leave at once, Dwight?" Grant tightened the leather girth on his mount's saddle. In need of supplies for the long trek into the wilderness, the men had stayed overnight in an inn near the government stores. Hogan had stayed with them, reluctant to complain in lieu of Dwight's worry. He would have to put aside his own personal agenda and rally his energies for Donovan's sake. Loaded down with supplies and rested for the journey, they had all risen at dawn and gathered for last-minute instructions. Lawson had mapped out a search strategy that would canvas the land from Parrametta to the base of the Blue Mountains. A thought struck Hogan's mind. "Katy doesn't even know I've arrived back in town."

"All's the better, eh, Hogan?" Dwight studied Lawson's maps. "The less Katy Farrell knows, the better. She's out of her mind with worry. It's better this way."

Hogan feigned agreement with a nod of his head. As much as he had missed his own family and the Farrells and the Prentices, he ached to lay eyes once more on Bailey. He was sure he would be able to ascertain at a glance whether or not she hated him. *At least I could find peace, if I only knew for certain.* He attempted a different avenue with Dwight. "So you say that the schoolteacher now resides at Rose Hill?"

"Yes, we feared for Miss Templeton's safety. We had to insist— she's a stubborn one."

Dwight appeared distracted by thoughts of the journey ahead and did not appear to notice the tension in Hogan's face. Hogan continued, his tone casual. "Yes, I do remember her stubborn streak. But why fear for her safety? I left her with a proper escort and instructions for her protection." Rolling up his oilskin, he tied it to the rear of his saddle. "Were my orders not followed?"

Without looking up from his packing, Dwight sighed, apparently reluctant to answer.

"I say, Dwight, has Miss Templeton been endangered?"

Tying the final knot in his pack, Dwight faced Hogan, his face somber. "Bailey Templeton was shot—"

"What!" Hogan's face flushed, a rage kindled in his eyes. "I'll kill the—"

"But she survived it." Dwight, fast to interject, glanced obliquely at his wife's bullish cousin. "Had we known of your concern, we would have told you of the incident in our letters to you." Folding his sinewy arms across his chest, Dwight spat at the ground. His brow furrowed and skepticism sparked his gaze. "For some reason, Katy felt your interests lay in hearing of Emily Parkinson."

"Well, I can't help but feel responsible for Miss Templeton. After all, I so foolishly brought her here."

"You and I sound as though we're speaking of two different women. You speak of a helpless type. I'm referring to Bailey Templeton—a tower of strength. She'd have to be to accomplish so much with our sons. Even young Jared is beginning to enjoy his studies. And during our grief over Donovan's disappearance, she's been a bastion of support for Katy."

"How glad I am to hear of it." Grant tempered his words with an even amount of sympathy. But with his thoughts now fraught with guilt, he felt even more driven to see her. "We should ride past the schoolhouse then. I'll offer my apologies to Miss Templeton for all her troubles."

Lawson mounted a gray stallion. "It's too far from our journey, I'm afraid. Won't the matter keep until we return? I fear for the lad now." Dwight nodded behind him.

"Of course, Mr. Lawson." Hogan made swift his apology. Lifting his boot into the stirrup, he felt a swell of anxiety mingled with self-reproach. He had toiled too long in Hobart, and in the meanwhile, those who needed him most had suffered. "Our most urgent need is to find our dear Donovan safe and sound." A cloud of mixed emotions followed him throughout the day. The farther behind they left Sydney Cove and Parrametta, the more anxious he became to find some shred of hope to lead them to Katy and Dwight's son. And then as swiftly, to return home.

They followed a cattle trail all day until Lawson signaled them all for a rest beneath a stand of trees. "We can water our horses in the stream bed back here. We've only an hour's worth o' daylight left, so may as well make our camp now."

"If we've another hour's light, then why not journey on?" Dwight brought his steed up next to Lawson's.

Hogan wiped the sweat from the back of his neck. "If you've the energy, I'll stay with you, Dwight. Lawson?"

"We can rise an hour earlier, and it won't make any difference," Lawson countered. "Mr. Farrell, don't drive yourself into the ground, or there'll be nothing left o' you when we reach your boy."

"If we waste one hour, it could be an hour of peril for Donovan. I've a feeling we should move on. Please, men." Pleading, Dwight swung his leg over the saddle horn and leaped to the ground. Adjusting his pack, he kept his eyes on Lawson.

Hogan felt too guilt-ridden to agree with Lawson's sensible proposition. He saw the pain in Dwight's eyes and watched the resignation fall across Lawson's leathery countenance.

"We'll go on, Mr. Farrell, if you prefer. But the horses 'ave to be rested for a bit." Lawson dismounted and didn't look back again at either of them as he walked his horse to the stream.

With the troubles at Hobart far behind, the weight of the Farrells' plight now loomed over Hogan. He knew Dwight was not at all himself. At least not his reasonable self. He reached for the reins on Dwight's black mare. "Why don't you rest under that tree, Dwight? I'll water your horse for you." He could easily see the fatigue taking its toll on the man. "As a matter of fact, I insist."

"If I sit down, I fear I'll never rise again."

"You will. I'll see to it." Drawing out his flask, Hogan tipped the remainder of warm water into his parched mouth. "I'll replenish our water supply as well." He joined Lawson on the shady banks.

The air cooled as the sun diminished on the far horizon. Hogan could feel drowsiness overtaking him. "I'd best check on Dwight. If he falls asleep, he'll blame me for it."

Leaving Lawson and Dwight's field hand to see to the horses, he shook off the strong desire to curl up next to his saddle and succumb to sleep. As he suspected, Dwight had propped himself against a mossy tree trunk and tipped his wide-brimmed hat over his face. "Farrell!" Lifting his muscular leg, he jostled Dwight with the toe of his boot. When Dwight did not stir, he chuckled to himself. "It would serve you right just to leave you to sleep until morning." Just as he lifted Dwight's hat from his face, Hogan saw another rider approaching them.

The rider waved his gloved hand in a friendly gesture. Hogan could see the man was dressed in farmer's attire. He knew most of the settlers, but as the rider drew near, he realized the man to be a stranger. "Hello, sir!" he called out and returned the salutation. He heard Dwight's faint moan of drowsy protest but chose to ignore him.

"Needin' to water me 'orse, Officer." The older gentleman justified his presence, a necessity in the wild when approaching an unknown party.

"Join us, then." Hogan stood and tipped his hat in a gentlemanly fashion. He reached for the man's bridle and steadied his horse while he dismounted.

"Thank ye, sir."

Extending his hand, Hogan offered, "Name's Grant Hogan, Captain Hogan of the Royal Navy."

Heaving out a restless sigh, Dwight sat up, his annoyance evident. He blinked and stared up at the rider and frowned.

"Here now, you needed the rest, old man." Hogan helped him to his feet.

The farmer had already started walking his horse to the stream. He had only ambled a few yards when Dwight shouted, "You there! Halt!"

Seeing evidence of Dwight's anger, Hogan whirled around to calm him. "Here, now, Dwight. He's only a farmer come to water his horse. Wake yourself, now." He reached out to grasp Dwight's shoulder in an amicable gesture, but Dwight lurched forward, bolting headlong toward the farmer, his eyes blazing with a strange vengeance.

Hogan tore after him, worried about the farmer's bewildered assessment of them both. "Stop, Dwight! Do you hear!" His annoyance turned to anger.

"*Thief!*" Throwing himself at the old man, Dwight knocked him to the ground beneath the horse's withers.

The steed stomped and whinnied around them, and Hogan feared they would both be trampled. "Dwight! You lunatic!"

From the woods, Lawson came running toward them, gripping his musket. "What goes on?"

Realizing he must act quickly, Hogan grabbed Dwight's head

in an armlock. With a powerful thrust, he yanked him free from the old man and threw him to the ground. The three of them lay sprawled across the ground, gasping for breath.

Allowing his weapon to rest at his side, Lawson's gaze traveled from Dwight to Hogan. "Somebody want to explain?"

Still panting and furious, Dwight yanked his arm free from Hogan's iron grip. "It's Donovan's. Look, can't you all see?"

"Donovan's *what*, Dwight?" Hogan looked all around, hoping to humor him.

"It's his horse. The old man is riding me boy's horse." Dwight stood and lifted his hand to stroke the stallion's jaw. His eyes misted, and a deep, guttural sob racked his body. *"Donovan!"*

"He's right!" Hogan helped the old farmer to his feet but cast a chary eye his way. "It's Donovan's steed!"

Bailey ran through her bedroom doorway, tossed her reticule onto the bed, and seated herself quickly at the small table and chair. *I must send a letter to Bligh at once!* She lifted the pen from the well and pulled out a sheath of writing paper. Her hands trembled, and any prior worries had now become full-blown anxiety in the pit of her stomach. *They dismissed me without reason! How can I explain this to my family? Dear Lord, please—*

The door opened slightly, and a slender hand rapped upon the doorframe. "Bailey?"

In no mood for visitors, Bailey composed herself as best she could. "I'm here," she answered quietly, although her voice held a tremor.

"It's me, Kelsey." The young Irish woman peered inside. "I saw you running up the stairs. Are you all right?" Her brows pinched together worriedly, she curled her fingers around the edge of the painted door and opened it the remainder of the way.

"I'm fine, Kelsey. Not to worry." Bailey felt a twinge of guilt for the falsehood. She laid the pen aside and pulled a comb from the drawer. Lifting the bonnet from her head, she placed it on the tabletop. Her dark hair hung in glistening strands around her face. She combed the loose hair upward and tucked it back into her coifed braid. Lifting her eyes, she saw Kelsey watching her.

"Bailey Templeton, I know you well enough to know when you've a problem!"

"Kelsey, I— " Bailey felt her words choke in her throat. To continue, she knew, would ensure the spilling over of her emotions. She rested her face in her hands and heaved an inward sigh.

"Tell me, girl. Don't be holdin' it in only to make it worse for yourself. You've no need to carry such a thing alone." Kelsey pulled up a chair and seated herself next to Bailey.

"It's bad news." Bailey felt the weight of the last few months come crashing in on her. "Johnston discharged me from the school." Feeling the gentle embrace of Kelsey's arm around her shoulder, she succumbed to the urge to cry, all the while chastening herself for losing control. Kelsey pulled her close, and the two of them cried together.

Bailey heard Katy's voice at the door. Katy ran to Bailey to offer her comfort also, and the two women sat at her side while she wept. Johnston's words echoed in her mind, and she remembered the stinging letters used against her. "I've failed all of you," she finally muttered.

"Don't you say such things," Katy said gently. "Johnston is Macarthur's wicked crony. Neither of them care who they destroy as long as their little kingdom prospers. You stood up to them, and it made them look weak."

"If only you could've seen the letters from the emancipists, Katy. I should've left long ago. I feel I've been so blind." Bailey dried her face with a handkerchief handed to her by Kelsey.

Katy spoke with a firm confidence. "It couldn't have been more than two or three, now—truthfully, Bailey."

"Three that I saw in addition to the Dobbins boy's father. And how many didn't send letters who felt as they did?"

"Do you know how many emancipists have been paid off by Macarthur's corps? With so many of them starving, what is the price of a letter when offered a crate of rum and a few shillings?"

"In my mind, I suspected as much and told him of my doubts. But in my heart I can't help but feel that I never should have come to Sydney Cove."

Kelsey summoned a maid and asked her to bring up some tea for all of them. "Does Bligh know any of these circumstances?"

"I doubt it, Kelsey. I'm about to send him a letter just now." Crestfallen, Bailey tilted her head back and closed her eyes. "But another part of me wants to simply pack up my bags and shake the dust from my feet."

"Please, Bailey, at least send the letter to the governor. Make one last attempt, and then leave it in God's hands. If Bligh can't help, then we're all doomed anyway." Katy met the maid at the door and took the tray from her. "I realize that there are times when God sends us in new directions. But not every situation that seems a defeat is truly that. 'The refining pot is for silver, and the furnace for gold: but the Lord trieth the hearts.' We have days when we're supposed to stand against the tumult and be strengthened by it."

"And I've stood, haven't I? Haven't we all?" Bailey asked and received a knowing nod from both women. "But when am I supposed to accept defeat? I've been dismissed, Katy. When am I supposed to accept the fact that God must surely be finished with me now at Sydney Cove?"

Katy's face paled, and she cupped her hand to her mouth. Without looking up she implored, "Please don't leave, Bailey. Stay at Rose Hill."

Glancing somberly first at one and then the other, Bailey shrugged. "Why?"

"Because we love you." Looking up from the tea service, a faint smile curved Katy's face.

Kelsey nodded in kind.

"It's insanity!" Beholding their liquid eyes, Bailey heaved a heavy sigh, centered the paper in front of her, and dipped the pen into the well. "I can't believe I've agreed to such a thing." She scrawled out the address to Bligh's office, her eyesight still blurred from the tears. "Where can I find a messenger?"

18

BLIGH
FOREWARNED

Hogan steadied his mount. Surveying the thickly wooded terrain before him, he could not help but feel overwhelmed at the expanse of mountains they prepared to penetrate. Ahead of him, William Lawson trekked silently on foot, looking for freshly disturbed foliage or earth. For two days they had circled much of the mountain's eastern bounds, believing they had hit upon their first scent of evidence in finding Donovan Farrell. A feeling kin to despair, accompanied by the fatigue of travel, nipped at his senses. As Lawson neared him, he asked quietly, "Do you believe the old farmer, Lawson?"

Lawson held a bit of tattered fabric in his grasp. His piercing blue eyes told of his hope in the matter. "I do, Captain. The farmer bought the horse from one he described as a traveling vagabond. It did not sit well with me that the man had not questioned the vagabond regarding how he acquired such a fine specimen of horseflesh."

"Nor I."

"But the farmer paid the man for the horse. He had a bill of sale."

"That he did, Lawson." Hogan remembered the honesty in the man's face and his fear upon realizing the horse belonged to a missing boy. The farmer had pointed them in the direction of the man's journey and said he joined two other men who were also without mounts. But Dwight, mistrustful of the man, had also begun to question Lawson's leadership. The farther they traveled, the more Dwight was on edge. "What's that in your hand?" Hogan noticed the torn piece of cloth.

"It's from a heavy fabric and is worn. Looks like it's from a man's trousers."

"What is it?" Dwight approached on horseback and noticed the men gathered in a circle.

"Lawson found it." Hogan hoped to sound encouraged to the despondent Dwight.

"Where'd you find it?" Dwight's tone snappy, he held out his gloved hand anxiously.

Hogan noticed the tension between the two instantly. He sighed and his brows pulled together in a show of displeasure.

"On a bush. Could be anyone's." Lawson tossed the swatch into Dwight's outstretched hand.

Dwight quickly smoothed out the cloth, examining all sides. "I just can't remember if Donovan had anything made of this type of material." The frustration rose in his voice, and a bead of sweat trickled down his temple.

Hogan heard the inflection in his tone, saw the guilty gaze, and knew at once that Dwight was punishing himself. "I don't recall Donovan wearing anything like that. Easy now, ol' chap. It could belong to one of the men who stole his horse."

"It could be anyone's," Lawson said, detached. "But it's the only thing we have to go on. I studied the terrain. It hasn't rained in a week. I found footprints headed up the mountain, and I also scratched around a disturbed bit of earth. Found a campfire underneath the dirt that looks pretty recent. Most men living out of doors will smother the fire, but they won't try to hide the whole thing."

"But did you see any smaller footprints?" The persistence in Dwight's tone only served to further exasperate Lawson.

Lawson studied Dwight's face. But instead of anger, a pity emanated from his face. "Let me show you the footprints, Mr. Farrell."

Dwight dismounted, slapped the dust from his pants, and followed along behind the explorer.

Securing the horses, Hogan left the ranch hand to keep post near the animals. Instead of following the others, he decided to climb up a short distance to survey the trail ahead. Reaching up, he found a solid handhold from where he stood at the mountain's base. Securing his boot against a large imbedded rock, he scaled the easily accessible terrain. Finding first one good landing and then another, he eventually found himself looking down upon the party of men. He glanced around, hopeful of discovering a better perspective on the lay of the land. Waving at the others, he cupped his hands to his mouth and shouted, "I'm going farther up! Wait for me."

The wind picked up and Hogan pulled his coat more tightly about himself. Ascending twenty or thirty more feet would enable him to catch a greater view of the path ahead of them. His foot secured and his body snugged tight against the bluff, he prepared to pull himself onto the crag just above his head. Knowing that Dwight Farrell would soon grow impatient, he planned to descend after one last look off the side of the mountain's foothills. He grabbed the edge of the ledge and heaved his body upward. His footing slipped and he froze, hearing rock skittering beneath him to the ground below. Steadying his weight, he groaned and with one last physical thrust, he dragged himself onto the flat ledge. Rolling onto the limited expanse, he lay still for a brief moment to catch his breath. A smattering of clouds promenaded over the blue mountain peaks in a pure white parade. Reading them as clearly as a book, Hogan saw no evidence of rain. Grateful for the sign, he closed his eyes and asked God for a little more time before watering the earth. Although a good tumult would increase the chances for visible muddy tracks farther ahead, it might also sweep away the few human tracks in their path at the present. *Lead us to Donovan, Father. And keep him well and safe until we find him.*

Hogan stood and surveyed the territory ahead. More thickly wooded than he had realized, the trail wound around the mountain, forking off in two directions. Slapping the dust from his gloves, he prepared his descent. Soon he joined the others and found Dwight arguing again with a disgruntled Lawson.

"If we travel a few more hours, we could gain time on these men." Dwight's tone suggested that he wished to usurp Lawson's leadership. He had already made full use of his authority over the hands that accompanied them, and now he appeared fully prepared to take the lead of the search party. "I'm taking my men farther, Lawson. I know these hills as fully as any man."

Hogan, feeling the hair tingle at the back of his neck, reached out and grasped Dwight's arm. He could no longer hold back his worries. "May I have a word with you, Mr. Farrell?"

Resistive, Dwight threw back his shoulders and tried to pull away. "Hogan, don't interfere!"

"If you will excuse us, Lawson," Hogan persisted. He watched as Lawson shook his head and walked away from them both.

With tightened jaw, Dwight grabbed at Hogan's iron grip on his arm. "Turn me loose, or I'll clout ye, mister!"

Hogan heard his threatening tone, but instead of letting him go, he reached and grabbed the other arm. "Listen to me!" His face taut, he eyed Dwight with some alarm. "You've not been yourself this entire journey. We've all excused your actions, but you're pushing Mr. Lawson beyond any man's limits. He's a commissioned explorer, Dwight. He knows the terrain better than anyone and can track these outlaws. But we can't go farther with his leadership threatened." Dwight relaxed under his grip, and he let him go. "Do you want Lawson's help, or don't you?"

His eyes full of frustration, Dwight shrugged and turned away.

Bailey sat at the dining table, the early sun just lightening the room in a pale yellow aura. Bligh had sent a messenger to respond to her correspondence. She read his letter with keen interest, for he expressed a strong desire to see her at once. She spooned some hot meal into her mouth, never taking her eyes from the letter.

"What does he say?" Katy could no longer bear the wait.

Her mouth moving silently for a moment, Bailey finally lifted her eyes, and a relief-filled smile dimpled her cheeks. "Bligh requests a meeting with me. He wants a full report from me in person."

"Does he say how soon?"

"This afternoon," Bailey answered quietly, her gaze reflecting her deep thought on the matter. "I may as well go. I'm not allowed even so much as to step foot near the school."

"They've no right!" Katy muttered while she spooned a loose

tea leaf from her cup. "It is Macarthur's way, though."

"Macarthur's in jail, Katy. We've all believed him to be the culprit behind having me forced out all along. But how could he?"

"Because of who he is." Katy held her cup to her mouth but did not sip.

"Perhaps Major Johnston fully believes that I'm incapable. I've had nothing but disturbances for the last few months. I can see his concern now. Before I couldn't."

"Is that what you're going to say to Bligh?" Katy set down the rose-painted cup and drummed both hands in front of her. "Because if you do, you may as well wave a flag of surrender."

"No. But how can I accuse a man in jail of orchestrating my unfriendly exodus? I don't know how to fight them." Bailey knew when she spoke the words that she had ignited Katy's ire. "You said yourself that you've tried to fight the corps. They'll trample you."

"We've never stopped fighting the corps, Bailey. And we've lost many a battle. But one day, men like Macarthur will see their last victims, and their power will be broken. If not by our hand, then by God's."

"I pray for the sake of New South Wales that what you say is true. And will you please pray for me that I will never sound defeat unless forced to do so?" Bailey pushed aside her bowl, and a servant cleared it away at once. "I must go and dress now. It will take several hours to arrive at Bligh's office. I shan't be late."

"I shall have a driver for you, then. Would you wish for me to go with you?" Katy's arms crossed in front of her, she glanced obliquely at Bailey, a hopeful glint in her eyes.

"No." Bailey chuckled and stood to make her exit. "I swear to you that I'll be strong and do all in my power to see that the children's best interest are given priority."

"Do you want to stay, Bailey? Please tell me that you do."

"I do. You know that I do. But I don't think it's best to try to air my feelings right now. I'm too out of sorts." She walked toward the dining room doors, then turned and offered Katy one last smile, her yellow gown brightening her countenance in the early dawn of day. "But if God wills that I must leave, my heart will ache for all of you. You've become my second family. For that I'm grateful." Seeing Katy's eyes grow misty, she turned, quickly gathered her things upstairs, and departed in the carriage that Katy had requested for her.

On the journey into Sydney, she read and reread the letter from

Bligh, wanting to be certain that she did not read hopeful meaning into its contents. But Bligh's writing, crisp and concise, carried a weighty concern about her dismissal from the school. More than anything else, she felt relieved that the governor had not had a hand in the matter. In spite of the controversy with his military subordinates, he had been a good friend to her. She felt an odd hopefulness well inside her as she approached the government building.

Bligh tucked a pinch of tobacco into his cheek, signed the last document that had been laid in front of him on this January eighteenth morning, and then sorted the papers into neat, well-organized stacks. "I hear all you say, Lieutenant. But if I may allay your fears, we have a full guard on Macarthur's jail cell. He is going nowhere until I so order. His power, as you so adeptly name it, has been thwarted."

The young lieutenant paced in front of Bligh's mahogany desk, his eyes on the carpet, his face clouded with worry. Making another attempt to persuade Bligh of a potential coup, he stopped and faced the governor directly. "The ranks, sir—"

"Are under my full command," Bligh assured, his face bland and carrying no shade of concern. "Your loyalty to my office and to the Crown are fully acknowledged, but your worries are all imagined." Bligh filled his pannikin with spirits.

"But I know these men. Their loyalties are divided. Many of them have acquired much land and wealth because of John Macarthur. He is, to some, their monarch."

"I know of Macarthur's abuses of authority. That is exactly why he rots behind bars! Do you question my authority among the ranks, Lieutenant?" Bligh downed the liquor with a flick of his stout wrist, his ruffled sleeve waving like a flag.

"Not I, sir. But some of the men—the Corpsmen—they have but one loyalty."

Bligh rubbed his heavy jowl with his hand, heaved a heavy sigh, and centered his gaze on the officer. "Nonsense!"

"Sir, you know of my respect for you and your office, but does not my persistence and my detailed reporting in this urgent matter suggest my awareness and my competence among the ranks? I know what I speak of and am fully convinced that John Macarthur is planning a full-scaled overthrow of your office!"

Bligh weighed the officer's words, studied the report that he had placed in front of him, and smiled with full confidence. "Nonsense!"

Upon hearing a rap at the large oak door, the lieutenant pulled on his gloves, saluted respectfully, and said quietly, "I offer my deepest apologies, Governor, for disturbing your work today."

"Not at all. And please do not hesitate to share your concerns at any time. The office of governor of New South Wales shall henceforth offer an open ear to all concerns of the military. You are the backbone of this colony."

His face offering a bleak, tight-lipped smile, the lieutenant departed without further ceremony. Stepping in at once, a private announced, "The schoolmistress 'as arrived, Gov'ner, upon your honorable request, sir."

"See her in, please, Private." Bligh stood and poised an emotionless smile upon his face.

Bailey bustled in without hesitation. "Greetings to you, sir." She curtsied and awaited his reply.

"Please be seated, Miss Templeton." He offered her a tapestried chair. "I wish to express my deepest apologies on behalf of the government of New South Wales. It appears that you've fallen prey to some minor impropriety in our ever expanding system. As you were made fully aware when you arrived in our harbor, we are growing this young colony far from England's shores." He poured himself a cup of tea and offered a cup to her. "From time to time an error may ensue, and the problems to follow unfortunately will affect an individual's livelihood—in this case, your own."

"No tea for me, thank you." Bailey took her seat politely and prepared to listen fully to anything the official had to say.

"For the present, I appreciate your patience in the matter as a full investigation is launched."

The word *investigation* troubled Bailey, but she did not show it in her expression.

"I've invited you to the government building today, hoping that you will offer as much detail as possible so that we may better expedite your cause." Straightening his cravat with some ceremony, Bligh took his seat slowly, keeping his gaze on Bailey.

"Thank you. And I'm most happy to oblige, Governor, but to be honest, I'm quite weary of the entire matter. Proving oneself in this colony has become a greater chore than the one I was hired to do."

"Understood." Bligh folded his hands across his stomach. "Private," he called out, "please, I've need of your assistance." He made immediate request that his man witness and take a written account of all that the schoolmistress had to say. The uniformed man complied by taking a place behind Bailey.

Feeling their eyes on her, Bailey licked her lips and began her story. She explained as she had earlier at the governor's estate of the personal attacks on her home. She reiterated the fear that the Corps had initiated her being shot and wounded that day on her journey from the minister's home, although Bligh already knew fully of those details. She also relayed her discussions with Major George Johnston, being careful to add nothing to their exchange of words over the past few months. She realized that by naming Johnston, she would most likely be asked to repeat her words in his presence, and she wanted to be certain of the validity of her complaint. She also described in detail the letters of grievance lodged against her.

"Do you need Miss Templeton to repeat any of her story, Private?"

The soldier shook his head.

"Although I believe in delegating full decision-making authority to our subordinates, I must question Major Johnston's motives in having your replacement primed and awaiting your dismissal—and the man having been shipped over from England, no less, without my full knowledge."

"My feelings exactly, Governor Bligh. And I hope to reiterate that it is not my wish to question Major Johnston's abilities as a military commander or his loyalties to you. But rather, I ask that the investigation be focused solely on the merit of my interest in seeing that Sydney Cove's schoolchildren will always have the best education that can be offered them. If indeed this Mr. Atkins is proven to be a better replacement, my passage from here will be as swift as his arrival."

Pleased with her words, Bligh smiled. "Your integrity shines like the stars, Miss Templeton. So be it."

Snugging her black gloves against her fingertips, Bailey quietly excused herself from the governor's presence. She felt grateful for the audience she had gained with him, but she also felt a sense of skepticism, fearing that the investigation would soon be lost in a churning sea of corrupt bureaucracy. Bligh, known for his rigid organizational skills, had yet to unearth any proof about the sniper or any clandestine efforts on the part of any junta member to oust her from the school. In regard to his daily abilities, his reputation waxed impeccable. But under fire or duress, he had earned a less than perfect record. At one time Katy's brother, Caleb, had recounted a ship's mutiny against Bligh. The investigation had cast Bligh's leadership in a doubtful light. The mutineers had escaped to an island, and to this day they inhabited it, untouched by England's long judicial arm. Bligh, she realized, was no savior of herself or even perhaps of the colony.

As hopeful as she had been about her meeting with Bligh, she now knew without a doubt that she could trust no man to smooth her troubled road. *I trust only in you, Christ Jesus. You control the sun, the moon, and the rain. My times are in thy hand.*

19

THE RUM
REBELLION

JANUARY 26, 1808

Hogan shifted in his saddle and watched uneasily as Dwight Farrell and his field hand disappeared up a stone-encrusted ridge. Sure of himself, Dwight had scouted around the area where the footprints had been discovered. Once Lawson had identified the direction in which he was sure the tracks were going, Dwight had announced his change in plans. Certain that by taking an uncharted pass through a mountain ridge he could head off Donovan's abductors, Dwight split off from the other men and determined to map his own search. Hogan could be neither angry nor in agreement with Dwight's abrupt decision. Had he been forced to walk in the despondent father's shoes, he was not altogether certain that he would be of sound mind himself. Departing with his older hand, a bare bones of a man in Hogan's estimation, Dwight headed into unknown Australian wilderness.

"I am sorry, Mr. Hogan," Lawson apologized for the second time.

"Lawson, don't blame yourself. I've known Dwight Farrell for many years now, and I can vow to you that he's not himself right now. All we can do is move forward and try to find the lad—that is, if you're still willing?" Hogan studied the man with a degree of uncertainty.

"Of course we'll go ahead, man. What do you think? That I would abandon a boy to the wilds on account of a petty disagreement?" Cinching up the saddle, Lawson checked his water supply and put away his hand-drawn maps. "Besides, I've nothing but pity for Mr. Farrell. It's his son he's thinking of, and he's not apt to trust the search to anyone but himself." He secured the extra ammunition in his leather pouch.

Hogan mounted and soon he, Lawson, and the one ranch hand left behind by Dwight journeyed into the wilderness grove at the rise of the Blue Mountains. The journey passed for many hours without incident. The men swapped stories, and Hogan began to appreciate Lawson's livelihood. Commissioned by the Crown to survey the unexplored regions of New South Wales, he lived his days with a lean-to for his roof and the unforgiving ground for his bed. His experience in the wilderness proved invaluable to the road-weary band. They usually had fresh meat or fish for dinner and a ready supply of tales. It mattered not how exaggerated the accounts had become, for the telling of them helped to relieve the anxious moments of the search.

"These men, if we've found the culprits, must be escaped convicts. They grow more and more careless as they go along." Lawson lifted his hand to a broken limb on a bush. "Someone's passed through here in the last day and a half. They were fools to venture into this terrain without a mount. We're catching up to them, Hogan!" Lawson sounded encouraged.

Hogan inspected the damaged foliage. Seeing the core of the shoot still green, he nodded his agreement, but Lawson's comment troubled him. "Why would convicts burden their escape with the likes of a boy?"

"That I don't know, nor do we know that we've found Donovan's captors." He tempered his words but could not mask the gravity of the situation. "We've yet to discover a shred of the boy's garments or his tracks. It all worries me, I tell you." Lawson's voice trailed off, his eyes surveying a clearing ahead with uneasy futility. "God help that poor lost lad."

"Shall we journey on, then?" Hogan awaited Lawson's expertise.

"Forward on." Lawson, his jaw set, brought his whip to flank. His gaze was somberly aloof as he marked a distant point with his eyes and headed into the clearing.

The private stationed at the government building's entrance sighed, his lethargy giving way to drowsiness. Folding his arms across his chest, he allowed his head to drop. He never saw the entrance doors slowly open nor the armed soldiers who skulked past his station.

Led by Major George Johnston, the band of British soldiers split into two units, each party posting themselves outside the officers' doors, weapons at the ready. Seizing the moment, Johnston instigated the strike on the government building exactly as he had been instructed by John Macarthur. He stood with his back against the wall while his Rum Corps soldiers crept past. Assessing the silence, his face tightened. His voice a hoarse whisper, he ordered, "On my command prepare to seize the building. Arrest all of Bligh's officers as instructed." He lifted his gloved hand. A bead of sweat trickled down his forehead. "Now!" His arm swung downward, and the men bolted through the closed doorways.

The surprise attack on the officers worked well. Preparing for the end of their workday, they never suspected that an uprising smoldered among their own ranks. The mutinous soldiers charged the offices, three men to a room, wielding their pistols on Bligh's unsuspecting subordinates. With fierce rapidity, the coerced officers stumbled out into the dimly lit halls, followed by their captors.

"You'll hang, McComb! They'll be standin' you on a swingin' shelf in the blink of an eye!" an officer barked to his insubordinate aggressor.

The private whirled his rifle around and drove the butt between the officer's shoulders. "Shut up, you, 'fore I use the other end on you!" Staggering forward, the man winced and slammed against a doorpost.

Johnston nervously eyed the incident. "Watch it, now!" He directed his words at the officer. "Don't give us reason to use our weapons!" He glared threateningly at the officers who filed before him. "Take them out front, men! Line them up good and straight along the wall. Bind them with leggings and irons."

The private who had sat sentry on the entrance saw all eyes on the battered officer who struggled to his feet. Slipping quietly behind his stunned peers, he passed unnoticed through a side door. He had almost escaped without incident when the door's hinge gave out a rusted squeal. Without turning to see who chased hotly after him, he bolted for the bunkhouses. Bligh, he knew, had been out with several of the officers on a grounds inspection. The governor must be warned!

"Please have some of the blankets replaced, Lieutenant Fields." Governor Bligh noted the moth-eaten bedding with a degree of distaste. "The floors should be swabbed every day with sulfur to ward off contagion."

"Aye, sir." Fields made note of every detail.

"Next week, have the men take brooms to the ceilings. Cobwebs are everywhere."

Gazing upward, the lieutenant nodded, although a hint of confusion marked his gaze. "Cobwebs, sir?"

"Yes. These barracks could turn into a haunt for disease if not properly maintained. Running a white-gloved finger along a windowsill, he held it up, rubbed the dust from his fingers, and impatiently sighed.

"Governor! Governor Bligh!"

Whirling around, Bligh beheld the red-faced private stumbling against the doorway as he gasped for air. "What is it, man?" he bellowed.

"Insurrection in the ranks, sir! It's the Corps. They've stormed the government building. They're arresting officers—"

A rage building inside of him, Bligh stiffened his back. "Who would dare?"

"Major George Johnston, Governor! He's lining up the officers now and having them put in chains."

"Johnston? What a fool! England will hang him! And so will I!"

The private's countenance now drained of any color, he stepped away from the door and shouted, "They're coming, sir, headed straight this way!" Slamming the door closed, he disappeared from view.

The sound of musket fire thundered outside the barracks. The door was kicked open with a force, and ten Rum Corps soldiers burst through the splintered doorpost with muskets aimed. A sulfured stench of gunpowder wafted into the barracks, preceding the entrance of Major Johnston. His men leading the way in fierce sentry fashion, he slowly stepped around the cots of empty barracks.

"I got one over here!" a lieutenant shouted.

Crouched behind an empty ammunitions' crate that had been turned up on its side for storage, Fields slowly stood, his hands raised. "What do you want, Johnston? What is your aim, pray tell?" He held a subtle tone of reasoning in his voice.

"Where's Bligh?"

"I don't know!" Fields snapped.

"He's lyin'!" The young lieutenant drew back his rifle butt and took aim at the man's head.

"Halt!" Johnston ordered gruffly. "Our dear lieutenant is a reasonable man. True?" He turned his gaze on the shaken lieutenant. "We've taken back rightful control of the government building, Lieutenant Fields. It's only a matter of time until Bligh is found and sentenced for treason against the Royal Navy. If you stand with him, you fall with him." His eyes narrowed, and the mark of newly seized power rose in his face. "Macarthur will be freed within the hour. You can stand with us now while there is yet the time." One brow lifted along with the question that sparked his gaze. "What will it be, Lieutenant?"

Fields gazed down the hard, cold barrel of his fellow officer's musket. "This is madness!"

"Well and good, then." Impatience darkened his gaze. "You'll be stripped of your duties at once. Take him away." Pushing back his tricorn hat with the splayed tip of his duck's foot pistol, Johnston once more surveyed the room. Resolving to garner a search party to find and arrest Bligh, he prepared to follow behind his bloodthirsty entourage when a slight movement in the far corner of the barracks caught his roving eye. Silently, he made a motion with one hand and signaled for several of his men to follow. He planted himself at the foot of a military cot, nodded knowingly to his men, and directed their gazes to the rickety bed. Two of the men seized the bed and dumped it on its side while the other made ready his weapon.

Crouched facedown with his hands clasped atop the back of his head, Bligh stiffened upon realizing his hideaway had been found. Slowly he rose while the soldiers chuckled quietly.

"Governor William Bligh, we hereby arrest you in the name of the Crown! You will go peacefully and await your trial and sentencing." Johnston spoke in a monotone, although his eyes filled with the drunkenness of power.

"You're insane, Johnston! On what charges?" Bligh demanded to know.

"Treason against the military government of New South Wales," Johnston answered coolly.

Standing stiffly while his limbs were wrapped with chains, Bligh asked with controlled fervor, "And by whose lunatic authority do you carry out such orders?"

"John Macarthur's command. He is the legal authority recognized by our military in this colony."

"Bah! He's in jail!" Bligh was shoved forward by Johnston's men and led against his will toward the stone jailhouse.

Across the compound, a guard posted in front of a row of jailhouses shouted at three soldiers who rushed toward him. "Halt, I say, or I'll shoot!" He lifted his musket threateningly. Suddenly, he felt a cold, hard pressure against his temple. His knees locked and he glanced sideways, his mouth agape. "Who goes there?" he asked in a strained voice but dared not turn his face.

"Don't move!" a harsh voice ordered, and the jailer's keys were yanked from his coat pocket.

"Wot are you doin', pray tell?" The jailer found himself surrounded at once by the other soldiers.

The man holding his weapon against the jailer's head did not answer him but instead barked out his orders to the others. "Get 'im out!" He tossed the keys to an anxious private. The men set about trying out the keys until they found one that tumbled the lock open. Then throwing back the iron-barred door, the men ran inside, carrying a lantern to light the dim, cramped cell.

Soon they emerged, led by the jailer's commanding captive, John Macarthur. He blinked in the full sunlight. Stretching out his limbs, Macarthur yelled, "Throw in the jailer and lock him up. I'll deal with him and all the others later."

The soldiers complied nervously, their emotions piqued by their risky endeavor.

"Where's Bligh?" Macarthur surveyed the activity that had erupted at his command. He allowed one of the men to assist him with disposing of the prison garb, then in full sight he donned his military uniform. "I want to see him in chains."

"They're bringin' him in now," his attendant answered in a low tone.

Macarthur espied the approaching party. Seeing Bligh surrounded by armed Corpsmen, he allowed a faint smile to crease his cheeks. Swiftly, he buttoned his collar and slid his sword into its sheath while the naval underling helped him slide on his boots. Facing the moblike brigade, he stood strong as a boulder awaiting their approach.

The squadron stopped and shoved Bligh out to face Macarthur. Without emotion, the two British leaders locked gazes. An irreverent silence passed between them. After a time, Macarthur took a deep breath and spoke with a deliberateness. "Have you anything to say, Captain Bligh?"

Refusing to qualify his query, Bligh stiffened his back and looked away.

"You'll answer me now or answer me later at your trial."

Still no answer.

His ire raised, Macarthur's lips whitened and his face grew taut. "Take him away—out of my sight!"

The troop of soldiers ushered their governor into a stone hold, and still no cry emanated from the deposed leader's lips. The only sounds heard were the rattle of chains and the echo of the slammed jailhouse doors.

❖

"Won't we be happy when the men return?" Wearily, Katy knelt to the side of a foaling mare. She and Bailey had acted as attendants to the animal for the entire afternoon and now well into the night.

"Caleb should return tomorrow from the pastures," Bailey assured her. "And hopefully we'll see the return of Dwight and his search party from the mountains at any moment." She brushed particles of hay from her apron. "Besides, we can help this mare as good as can any man. I've aided my father in many a foaling."

A farmhand scattered fresh straw behind the mare's flanks.

"It's beginning." Bailey crept cautiously forward toward the skittish animal.

The mare whinnied as the foal's head and right front limb appeared. Appearing wet and black as onyx, the foal awkwardly lifted its one free limb. Bailey reached and grasped the other slowly emerging hoof and firmly began helping it out into the world. Katy joined her in the effort, pulling the animal out and back toward its mother. They watched in awe as the little black beast attempted to stand with its wobbly front limbs. After a time, the birth was complete, and the mare sat up to nuzzle its newest arrival.

Katy called in more hands to clean up the stall and to watch the animals for a short time. She joined Bailey at the barn's entrance. "I'm exhausted," she said, pushing her hands against her back and arching to stretch out her aching muscles.

"But it's a good sort of exhaustion, don't you think?" Bailey rinsed her hands in a fresh bucket of well water. "Rose Hill has a new colt," she said with quiet satisfaction.

Katy cleaned her hands as well, scrubbing lye soap beneath her nails. "Nothing will feel in order until my family returns home. I ache for Donovan more now than I did at first."

Bailey had grown accustomed to seeing Katy red-eyed and emotion-drained.

"I think not knowing anything at all is worse than knowing some evil has befallen him." Katy dried her hands on a cloth and folded her arms about her waist.

"I believe that's true," Bailey agreed. "Although there are some things in life I would be all the better for not knowing."

Katy studied her with some scrutiny. "Such as?"

Bailey strode toward the house, turning momentarily to allow Katy to join her. "I wish that Laurie had never written to me about Gavin. And I wish that I had never read the letters of complaint from the emancipists."

"But what if you returned home years later only to find Laurie and Gavin married. Would not that be the more difficult medicine to swallow?"

Bailey saw the questioning in Katy's face as well as the pale shadows under her eyes, cast partly by fatigue and partly by the twilight. She hesitated. The matter had long been dismissed from her thoughts. Resurrecting the pain of the past had never been an easy chore for her. She sighed inwardly and agreed. "It would."

"I am sorry. I shouldn't have asked you such a question. Here I am so full of self-pity that I must examine every conviction that doesn't line up with my own." She looped her arm through Bailey's. "I can never leave well enough alone. Just ask my mum," she said with deep resignation.

"No. Don't apologize. I want to grow up, Katy. I want to accept whatever perils come my way with courage and with God's assurance that He will see me through." She stopped and adjusted her shawl. "And I don't want to hide from life's realities. But I disappoint myself quite often on this account."

"You and I both," Katy agreed with the same sadness that had dominated her spirit now for months. "I sometimes wonder if I shall ever stop disappointing myself." She drew closer to Bailey and lowered her voice as though revealing a deep secret. "Tell me, Bailey, do you ever compare yourself to others?"

Bailey smiled faintly. "All the time."

"Good." Her brows pinched together with frustration. "At least I'm not alone in my imperfection."

"Far from it, my friend."

A rider approached, his silhouette outlined by the moon's glow, and the women could see that he headed straight for them.

"It's one of Caleb's hands." Bailey recognized the man.

"I pray all is well with Caleb." Katy's voice tensed.

"Mrs. Farrell!" the man called out. "Is Mrs. Prentice about?"

"Amelia or Kelsey?" Katy poised herself.

The man pulled up his horse abruptly and dismounted in one motion. "It's Mrs. Kelsey Prentice whom I seek."

"She is most likely gone abed after putting down her wee ones," Katy answered forthrightly. "Is there a message I can deliver for you? Is Mr. Prentice well?"

"Oh yes, Mrs. Farrell. And sorry to alarm you at such an hour. But Mr. Prentice is delayed a day in the fields and sent me for supplies and to relate the news to his dear wife so as not to worry her."

Bailey and Katy breathed out a grateful sigh. "Thank goodness!" Bailey exclaimed.

With anxiety punctuating his words, the horseman wound the

reins around his hand. "But Mr. Prentice knows nothin' of the trouble in the borough, and I feel it me duty to warn you ladies of the matter."

"Go on, then." Concern etched Katy's face.

"The Corps—Macarthur's Corps has deposed our governor and seized the government building."

"Tell me it isn't true!" Katy's eyes closed in disbelief.

"I wish that I could say as much, dear Mrs. Farrell, but the truth o' the matter is that the Rum Corps has seized control of the government o' New South Wales."

"How do you know this?" Katy persisted.

"I went into the borough to buy supplies. The government stores has been taken over by Macarthur's men, and the best goods taken out for their own use. What was left behind was priced so high that I knew Mr. Prentice would not wish for me to pay it."

"This is outrageous!" Bailey's face hardened with contempt.

"Most o' the shopkeepers is stayin' the night in their shops to guard from looters. The town square is in a miserable state, wot with all the governor's officers bein' dismissed. Some o' them 'ave been locked away in the jails."

"Where is Bligh? Does anyone know?" Bailey questioned him further with grave concern.

"No one that I asked knew about 'im, miss. But if I know ol' Bligh, he'll have Macarthur's men tied and quartered before sunrise."

"If they haven't done away with him already." Katy spoke with light bitterness.

"Governor Bligh surely wouldn't allow such a thing," Bailey interjected. "He's a willful man, for certain, and not one to be crossed." She remembered her short encounters with the man. "He'll surely have the matter corrected before Macarthur can breathe his next breath." Recalling his promises to investigate the corruption in the school matters, she felt anxiety rise from the pit of her stomach. "I pray God's intervention in the matter."

Bailey could not sleep and tossed all night in her bed. She watched the dawn rise on the land and prayed that New South Wales would enter the day with a victory for its inhabitants and a promise of hope for its future. But in spite of the brilliant light peeking beyond the treetops, she somehow knew in her heart that a new nemesis had manipulated its way into their world. She fell to her knees and prayed and wept for Sydney Cove and for its children.

20

A BUCKLER TO ALL WHO TRUST

Night had fallen, and Grant Hogan and William Lawson were ready to settle down for another discouraging evening in the chilly reptile-infested mountains. But venturing onto the next rise, Hogan caught sight of a distant campfire, and following Lawson's warning, they took their party back down the mountain a few yards to set up their own camp for the night. They all agreed that to start a cooking fire too high up the mountain might attract unwanted attention or spook their human quarry, so they settled for tasteless smoked meat and stale bread.

"You men stay and watch our belongings," Lawson instructed the hands. "Hogan and I will scout ahead to see if we've come upon Donovan's captors. This could be the stroke of luck we've all hoped for." He stuffed a pinch of tobacco into his cheek and rolled it back and forth with his tongue. "Then again, maybe not."

Hogan bit down upon the tough, sinewy beef, and his jaw popped. He had grown tired of the wilderness fare but until now had refused to raise a note of complaint. "This stuff's inedible, mates." He shook his head, yanked off a small piece with his teeth, and began the laborious process of chewing it. He wondered if starving to death might not be the better option. Pushing the leathery bite to the front of his mouth, he drew in his cheeks and spat out the jerky with a degree of contempt. "Not fit for dogs!"

"It's sustenance, Hogan," Lawson said chuckling. "I've stayed alive on much less."

"We just passed a stream," a hand reminded them. "I'll catch us some fish in the mornin' for breakfast."

Lawson rolled up his maps and tied them with string. "Well, Hogan, I've some new ideas from some inroads into these mountains. Remember that first day? Too laborious, that route. The land beyond the eastern pass is easier to traverse. We'll take the southeast route on the way home, and I'll wager we'll gain better than a day's journey."

Hogan helped the explorer put away the maps in his knapsack. "You've been invaluable to us, Lawson. I only wish that Dwight had stayed with our search party." He folded his arms for warmth and snugged his deerskin gloves ever tighter. "I pray he uses wisdom out here in the wilds." He remembered Dwight Farrell's troubled gaze before he parted their company and especially his imploring green eyes. Questioning and troubled, his eyes had swept over him, all but pleading for his intervention. Hogan could not decipher the depth of Dwight's silent plea and hated himself for it. But men were always like that with each other, he realized. Women could read one another's thoughts and respond to their feelings, an enviable trait. But men kept their thoughts inside the caves of their souls, unexplored and unmined.

"A father's love can make him take irrational risks." Lawson turned to gaze toward the distant fire once more. Quietly, so the others could not hear, he remarked, "I, for one, should know. I had a boy once. A lad about the age of Donovan Farrell—when he died, that is."

The news surprised Hogan, but he could sense the pain in the man's words, so he held his tongue.

"His mother had died when he was born, and her sister helped me in bringing him up. When he began to come of age, he begged to follow me into the timberlands. That lad always loved the out-of-doors." A detached smile flickered around the corners of his mouth. "I'd been hired to locate suitable timber for a shipyard."

"This was in England?" Hogan asked.

Lawson nodded. "We'd found a forest of hardwood, prime for cutting. Being a fortnight from any signs of civilization, we killed some game and prepared for a hot meal and a restful night. But my son, Thomas, fell ill. The fever was so slight at first that he neglected to tell me of his condition. By the time I noticed the change in him, the fever had progressed beyond any help I could offer."

"I'm sorry," Hogan said sympathetically. "What did you do?"

"I panicked. Traveled with him throughout the night, foregoing any sleep. I drove my horse all night like a madman. By the time the dawn began to catch up with us, the beast was frothing at the bit and nearing madness itself. Then the weather grew worse, and the cold winds caused Thomas' condition to grow worse. He died two days later in my arms."

The silence between them spoke louder than words. Hogan lifted his pouch from the ground. "But now you're aiding another desperate father." He poured as much encouragement into his voice as possible.

"I could never resurrect my dearest Thomas. But perhaps if Donovan lives—" His voice broke off.

"Mr. Lawson?" The hand had walked up beside them, but the darkness had now so overtaken them that they could scarcely make out one another's presence. "If I may suggest, sir, I could take the horses down farther, down the backside and build a fire. What with those men so far down the other side, they would never see our fire. The wind blows eastward down here, away from the other camp."

"Good idea. Go ahead." The weariness in Lawson's tone yet made room for courtesy.

"Why don't you take a rest, Lawson?" Hogan sensed the explorer's need for a little slumber.

"No. I didn't come this far to make you a hero, Hogan. We'll both go. If we find the Farrell boy alive and well—" he stopped to draw on his thoughts—"I can always catch up on a bit of shut-eye tomorrow."

Hogan detected a smile in Lawson's inflection. "Let's go then, mate. It's a healthy boy I'm intent on finding tonight!"

The women gathered around the small table in the kitchen. Bailey sliced bread and laid it out on a plate. With a large spoon she scooped out hot chicken and broth and ladled it beside the bread. Handing it to Kelsey, she lifted another plate and repeated the process for the hungry hands while the cook and maids scurried to put all the valuables under lock and key. "The Smithfields, settlers who live a few miles away, had some looting last night. They sent a rider to warn all the neighboring farmers." Bailey hoped to offer some grain of motivation to the news-hungry hands. She studied their sun-toughened faces, their dirt-encrusted brogans, but most of all, their worried faces. They had all been accustomed, she realized, to following the orders of Dwight Farrell and Caleb Prentice. Most likely, they would not desire a dictating woman at their helm, let alone an American. She and Katy would need to find a captain among them, a leader who could garner their respect as well as keep the men on guard against the mindless looters.

"Dwight and Caleb have yet to return to Rose Hill," Katy expounded further. "We've gathered all of you here today to alert you to our dilemma."

Holding his hat in his hands, the oldest hand, Weaver, spoke up. "The men is nervous, Mrs. Farrell. The junta has power beyond England's reach."

"How well I know." Katy stood with her arms folded across her waist. "We'll do well to keep body and soul together through all this, I vow."

"Have we much ammunition?" Bailey asked Weaver with a degree of caution. She widened her eyes, and her brows lifted with an uncharacteristic look of defenselessness.

"We've some. All of us have some. Mr. Farrell keeps his weaponry locked up here in the house, most likely." Weaver munched on the steaming chicken and fumbled to wipe his prickly mustache, as though a cloth napkin had never touched his lips. "This is good eats, miss."

Bailey affirmed his compliment with a nod, hoping that a mutual trust had begun to form between them. "The stores have escalated their cost of food and ammunition. Because of the panic among the settlers, a lot of the supplies are being depleted."

"Better to buy it now," Weaver cautioned, "than to wait for the prices to drop and it all be gone."

Katy tossed aside her apron and pushed a curl from her face. "What do you think, Bailey?"

"Perhaps we should count out our ammunition. We would have a much better idea of where we stand." She relaxed her tone and made it a point to address Weaver. "But what do you think, Mr. Weaver?"

The sheepherder shrugged, swallowed down the remains from his plate, and then nodded. "We could bring all our arms together here to the house and take a count." He looked around uneasily, as though awaiting his comrades approval.

Without hesitation, Bailey ladled another generous serving onto Weaver's plate. "That sounds like a wise decision." She did not look up but kept her eyes on his plate.

The other hands nodded, and Weaver, seeing they agreed with him, announced his decision. "We'll protect your land, Mrs. Farrell. We can post men along the trails and around the houses and barn. We'll collect all the ammunition we can muster. We can store it in the food cellar."

"Did you say it's Macarthur wots taken over the government building?" another emancipist laborer asked, but the timidity had dissipated from his voice.

Katy nodded. "Yes. And there's no trace of Governor Bligh."

"That lout Macarthur—he cheated me out o' wages once." The laborer sopped his bread around the center of his plate.

"The dickens, you say?" Weaver devoured the second plate of food. Swallowing hard, his pale blue eyes glinted with a fire. "That's wot Macarthur's always been about—collectin' others' dues."

"An' you can bet England's none the wiser." The laborer shook his head but kept a civil tone as though resigned to the matter.

Bailey glanced at Katy, a faint flicker of encouragement turning up the corners of her mouth.

"Mr. Weaver, we are indebted to you for your courage and to all the rest of you men," Katy said.

Sensing the growing camaraderie, Bailey agreed and announced, "Rose Hill can be a refuge to other settlers who are in need of help."

"Indeed." Katy instructed two maids to gather up their plates. "Is there anything we can do to help, Mr. Weaver?"

The old hand shook his head. "Please promise you'll not take it in your head to travel alone, and if you need anythin' at all, you'll tell ol' Weaver." His grave face reflected an honest sincerity.

"You've our solemn vow, Mr. Weaver." Katy's face relaxed. "We've our little ones to consider."

"Let's go and gather all our ammunition and bring it back

here." Weaver corralled the other hands through the rear kitchen entrance.

Awaiting their departure, Bailey rested her hands upon a chairback and breathed out a relief-filled sigh. "We did it," she said quietly. "We've secured their aid."

"You were right about the hot chicken and bread, Bailey." A faint laugh followed Katy's smug response.

Pursing her lips, Bailey wiped her hands with a towel. "I didn't intend on exploiting them, Katy. But we had to rally them, didn't we?"

"That we did."

Bailey turned a brief, quizzical glance over her shoulder. "Won't Dwight and Caleb be surprised?"

"Hopefully we'll know soon on that account. Dwight's been gone longer than even he anticipated. And we never heard word from Captain Gabriel and his explorer friend." Katy set the unused plates inside the dish cabinet while the maids cleared away the dirtied ones.

Without looking up, Bailey gathered the fine linen napkins onto a wooden tray and said quietly, "Nor have you heard word from your cousin."

"My cousin?"

"Captain Hogan." Bailey could have kicked herself for stumbling over the words. So she moved away, hoping Katy would not detect the flush across her cheeks. But her hopes were dashed when she heard an affectionate chuckle spill from Katy's lips. She pretended not to hear and opened the door to the laundry closet to deposit the soiled napkins.

"Your interest in my cousin has certainly grown of late. You once would go days without mentioning his name. Now you can't seem to wait even a few hours."

"Nonsense!" Bailey was already prepared to defend herself. "I've not mentioned his name at all today." Returning with the empty tray, she saw Katy's knowing gaze, and her shoulders raised with indignation. Then the truth rushed at her like an enraged bull. "Or have I?" Resignation muted the force of her words.

Katy looped her arm through Bailey's. "Shall we adjourn to the parlor, Miss Templeton"—her right brow arched and her lips were pursed like an old spinster's—"where we can chat?" With a nod toward the kitchen maids, she acknowledged their departure and led Bailey into the parlor.

Bailey instinctively knew the prodding that was forthcoming. She sighed and allowed herself to be dragged schoolgirl style into the private chamber for the inevitable interrogation. Katy patted a tufted chair, inviting her to take the seat, and then drew herself up another one right next to Bailey's.

Before Katy could utter a single inquisitive word, Bailey toyed nervously with a broken fingernail and said, "I know what you must think."

"It's not what I think, Bailey." Katy showed no mercy. "It's what I know."

Bailey's lashes flew up, and her liquid brown eyes widened. "What you know?"

"What everyone in this household must know by now."

Closing her eyes, Bailey implored in a whispered breath, "Please don't say it, Katy."

"What? That you're in love with my cousin?"

Bailey lowered her face and rested her head in her hands. She sat silently as a curious smile played around the corners of Katy's mouth. Lifting her face, she clasped her hands in front of her almost in a prayerful gesture.

Katy muttered to herself, "I'm sure of it now!"

21

A MOMENT OF
WEAKNESS

Hogan listened intently, the sound of the cicadas rising from the thicket. He crept slowly in the darkness, knowing that to silence them with his human presence might alert the four convicts scattered around the campfire. Lawson, leaving his side to circle around, had asked him to wait for a signal. He would pick out one of the men seated cross-legged next to Donovan Farrell and grab him from behind. That was Hogan's signal to surprise the three men from the flank. He watched the slovenly bunch parlaying their lurid stories back and forth and worried that Donovan had seen and heard too much for a boy his age.

He breathed a silent prayer and hoped any arms they bore lay in the bedrolls and not close by.

Peeling away a large, leafy branch that blocked his view, he kept careful watch of Donovan. He seethed when the lad asked them for food and they ignored him, continuing with their raucous laughter and feeling smug and secure in their folly. The boy's face had a pale cast in the firelight, a weary, wrung-out expression that caused Hogan to ache for him. Soon, Hogan vowed, Donovan would be home with Dwight and Katy again, and this night would be long forgotten. He had to convince himself, no, promise himself, that no more harm would come to the lad save that which he had already experienced.

The thought of returning home enlivened his own senses. He would be elated to see his family as well as his cousin. But he would not allow himself the luxury of bringing to mind the other longing that dogged his mind, hitting his senses like a hammer against an anvil. And it was not so much the memory of her hair blowing in his face, or the enchanting curves of her feminine frame when he had held her close. But he now determined it was the lingering scent of flowers that haunted his memory. *You've been gone far too long in the wilderness, Hogan.* He knew nothing of perfumes or other female frills, so he had never asked her what she wore. But as he had retired that night, her fragrance had permeated his room, and he had fought his own will, a weakening refusal to ride back to her and steal her for his own selfish keeping. And the only restraint that had lashed him to his lonely bed had been the knowing of her strong character and her morality, because his own had waned. For that, he had hated himself. But he knew that to make such a rash move would dishonor her, this noble, delicate creature who drove him to madness.

He peered once more into the convict's camp. If Lawson had made it to the other side, he had managed to do so invisibly, for the men were none the wiser. Hogan listened intently to their conversation.

". . . And it's not likely to blow over soon, fer the Corps is settin' things right fer all our good," commented a disheveled man with a gash beside his eye. He appeared to be the leader.

"Or fer their own bloomin' good," said the man seated next to him with a degree of contempt. "And you two are sure no one followed you up here?"

The two men acting as Donovan Farrell's abductors shook their heads hungrily while gnawing a bone.

"They all think the boy up an' ran off, that's wot," the largest man commented casually.

"We made the waif brush away his tracks behind him with a leafy branch. It looked like two men on foot," the other kidnapper continued. "Henry an' me, we made no mistakes, you can bet on it."

Donovan kept his eyes to the ground but repeated what he had said aloud a few moments earlier. "I said, I'm hungry."

The large kidnapper picked some meat off the bone and handed it to the boy. "Take this and leave us be or you'll get clouted."

"Or eaten yourself." The third convict glowered at Donovan Farrell.

Donovan pretended not to hear the threat but instead ate ravenously.

"I hear tell of some mates in the bush who eat human flesh." The convict continued his grisly tale. "They'd like a tender young boy like you for their supper."

"No, they wouldn't!" Donovan snapped back without fear. "I'd eat them first!"

The escaped prisoners howled with laughter.

Hogan lifted his pistol and poised himself for the assault.

A piercing voice, harsh and tinged with a violent air, split the air from behind Hogan. "Halt where you stand, mate!" The cold tip of a rifle pressed hard against the back of Hogan's head. Surprised by the ambush and rebuking himself for being caught off guard, he tensed and closed his eyes, ready for the inevitable. *Stay where you are, Lawson. Please stay where you are!*

Gunfire sounded distantly in Bailey's dreams. She did not awaken, but instead the sound of the midnight barrage became a part of her slumber, invading her peaceful dream. A nightmare ensued with dark images shooting at her from every direction while she ran with the schoolchildren like a hen gathering her chicks. She could not think reasonably, and so without scheme or plan she ran and ran throughout this dark netherworld, prodding the children to race ahead while the junta rapidly gained ground behind.

Her eyelids fluttered, and Bailey came awake. The realization that she slumbered in the Farrells' upstairs guest room gave her comfort, but the horrifying reality of the nightmare lingered in her senses. She could hear her heart beating in her ears, and her gown clung to her clammy skin. She listened intently to the silence. Then a shock reverberated through her as the sound of musket fire rang through the sleepy dales of Rose Hill. The gunfire had not been a dream as she had imagined.

Tossing aside her bedcovers, she quickly pulled on her night jacket and crouched in front of the window. A musket sounded once more, and she saw the glow of lanterns moving, undulating like fireflies from all corners of the farm. The Farrells' barn was surrounded by men with torches, and the hands, anticipating the attack, converged on them from all directions.

Without rising, Bailey stayed low and ran out of the room. She was met in the hall by Katy, who carried three-year-old Corbin. "They've come, Katy!" Bailey whispered hoarsely.

"Will you help me?" Katy asked shakily.

"I'll awaken Jared." Bailey read her mind. "Where shall we meet? In the parlor?"

Katy nodded and fled downstairs with her daughter "I'll fetch Mum and Kelsey. They're all sleeping in the same room tonight with her children."

Throwing open Jared's door, Bailey gently shook the boy to waken him and helped him to his feet. "Come quickly, Jared," she whispered, wrapping his sheet around his shoulders. Half asleep, he mumbled nonsensical gibberish while she led him down the stairs. "It's all right, Jared, but we must keep quiet," she said soothingly. "We've got to keep our voices down for our game."

He muttered again, but this time his lids opened partly. "What game, Miss Templeton?" he asked sleepily.

"We're pretending that the parlor is our hideaway from the outlaws." She steadied him against her until they reached the foot of the stairs.

"All right." Jared nodded, pulled the sheet tight around his half-clad bony frame, and followed her into the parlor. Gunfire punctuated the still night air once more, and the sound of horseshoes beating the ground grew closer. "Hurry, Jared!" Bailey found Katy sitting in a rocker, the lantern dimly lit on the table next to her. Huddled in a corner, Amelia's face held an ashen cast as she held Kelsey's infant close to her bosom. Kelsey sat stilly, not wanting to awaken her other child who slumbered on a blanket on the floor.

"I'll lock us in." Bailey acted swiftly. "No windows to worry with in here."

"Something's wrong! Mum?" Jared beheld his mother's frightened countenance. He walked around Bailey and gazed up at her. "We're not really playing a game?"

"No. I'm sorry, Jared. You're such a big boy now—I . . . I should-d've told you." Bailey apologized to him, lightly stroking the cowlick at his temple.

"The settlement's being looted, son." Katy held out one arm, and he ran to her. "That means that some bad men are trying to steal from others, but we won't let them, will we?"

"I'll get Papa's gun!" Jared ran for Dwight's gun cabinet.

Bailey stood in front of the locked cabinet doors. "Your father's men are going to protect us, Jared. And God will keep us safe." She hated the disappointed way he looked at her. When he whirled around to run back to Katy's side, her eye fell on the brass key that lay atop a small oak stand. She clasped it between her fingers, slid it into the gun cabinet, and the lock clicked. Most of the muskets had been gathered into the hands' sleeping quarters, under Weaver's watchful eye. But a single musket had been left behind in the event that Dwight or Caleb would return.

"What are you thinking, Bailey?" Katy asked nervously.

"Just to be safe." Bailey lifted the weapon into her hands and examined the chamber. "I hunted with my father more than once."

"We're in need of no hunters." Katy smiled faintly, cutting her eyes askance.

"Let's hope not." She kept the weapon at her side and pulled a chair close to Katy.

⋘◇⋙

"Look wot I found, boys—a spy!"

Hogan held up both hands and stumbled along while the ruffian held him by his hair. His hopes were dashed when he saw the other three bolt for their weapons. The man behind him being shorter than he caused him to stand with his neck turned sideways.

"You've disarmed me, mate." He attempted to reason. "Mightn't you let go my hair?"

The man finally let go but shoved him forward into plain sight of all.

Seeing Donovan's eyes widen, he knew that to reveal his identity would lessen his chances for getting out alive. So he stiffened and cast a guarded glance the boy's way. "I'm sorry to intrude on your camp. I suppose you felt that I was aiming to rob you or the like."

Donovan must have sensed his ploy, for he crouched back down and looked the other way.

"Why *are* you prowlin' around our camp?" the scar-eyed convict queried suspiciously.

"I lost my horse right at sundown. A snake caused him to bolt while I watered him. I've been wandering around the dark for hours now. When I saw your fire I hoped to bed down, but if you prefer to send me on my way—"

"He's lyin'!" The youngest of the men spoke anxiously. "He's here to—"

"Shut up!" the leader ordered. In an almost apologetic tone, he excused the man's anxious tone. "Young Flynn over here's worried that you've escaped from the convict camp in Sydney. They do run up into these mountains. A miserable thievin' lot, they is."

Agreeing at once, Hogan nodded. "One does have to be careful. I can assure you, however, that that is not the case with me." He pondered quickly. "You see, I am"—he straightened with a degree of ceremony—"William Lawson, an explorer sent by England to map out the new land. That's why I simply must find my horse. It has all of my charts, my maps—I'm in a dreadful fix." He remembered his uniform, but fortunately he had buttoned up his oilskin. They appeared none the wiser that he was a naval officer. Glancing obliquely, he saw the corners of Donovan's mouth turn up and hoped the men did not detect the exchange of humor between them. He was enjoying the ruse, adding a bit of flamboyance to flavor his role.

Flynn lifted his weapon and scanned the surrounding bush with his small, dark eyes. "No one's with you? You're a commissioned explorer, and you've come out here without a man to aid you?"

Realizing his credibility was slipping, Hogan folded his arms astutely across his broad chest. "No . . ." He hesitated, seeing the alarm in their eyes. "My assistant who travels with me journeyed in one direction and I the other in hopes of rounding up my steed. I was also in hopes that he, too, would be drawn by your fire." Assessing their gazes, he could only guess that they had found his story believable, so he asked with grave concern, "So, no traveler has come your way on this night?"

The scar-eyed one shrugged, dropped his pistol at his side, and answered, "No one but you. Flynn, give the man a blanket."

"He can have mine," Donovan offered before Flynn could raise a note of protest.

"Dim the lamp, please, Katy!" Bailey whispered. The sound of splintering wood sent an unnerving wave of fear through them. The farm's large dogs could be heard yelping and howling. Katy trimmed the lamp, and Bailey took a step toward the parlor entrance. Listening to the murmuring voices that stilled their silent peace, she knew at once that they were no longer safe and alone in the house. "They've broken in!" She grasped Katy's arm and felt every fiber of her tense with anxiety. Her stomach knotted and her throat went dry. She surveyed the only entrance to the room. A shadow flickered beneath the door. Hearing a whimper, Bailey put her arms around Jared. "Hush now." Placing her lips against his ear, she whispered quietly, "They'll hear us. Be brave like your papa." In the dark, she could feel Jared throw his arms tightly about her, and spasms of fear caused his breathing to quicken. "You're so brave." Bailey continued to keep her mouth pressed against the boy's ear. She held him tighter. "So brave." Her forehead pressed against the side of his head, she placed a gentle, assuring kiss upon the crown of his head.

The sound of boots pounding up the stairs unnerved the lad once more. "Sweet Jesus, keep us safe. Make us invisible to our enemies," Bailey prayed fervently, hoping the words would somehow speak comfort to Jared. "Protect Dwight and Caleb," she continued her prayer.

Jared's small voice said in a tremulous whisper, "Yes, God, and please take care of our Donovan."

Shattering glass exploded from upstairs, and Bailey heard Kelsey's infant cry out. Kelsey frantically tried to calm the baby girl, the squeak of the rocker adding to the danger.

"I'll nurse her." Her voice trembled, but she spoke with a determination. The infant responded, settling against her mother, and soon a few quiet coos were all that could be detected.

Jared relaxed his grip, and Bailey could sense that his courage had increased. "We're going to be fine, Jared, just fine," she assured again. Jared gave no reply, but Bailey knew instinctively that he had grown more calm.

An hour passed and soon the house grew silent. Bailey had seated herself on a settee with Jared and pulled his sheet about them both. "I think they're gone," she whispered to the lad. The boy did not stir.

A faint smile creased Bailey's cheeks. "Katy?" She raised her voice slightly but maintained a degree of caution. "You want to turn up the lantern?"

When Katy gave no reply, she stood, laid the slumbering boy on the floor, and crossed the blackened room toward where she thought Katy had been. "Amelia? Kelsey?"

"I'm here," Kelsey whispered. "I believe they've all fallen asleep."

Bailey lost her bearing and stumbled against some furniture but eventually found the table with the lantern. She turned up the wick, and the parlor became illuminated with yellow light. On the floor, sleeping peacefully were Katy and Corbin curled up next to Amelia. Her eyes misted and she felt an overwhelming sense of well-being. *They're sound asleep. You did it, heavenly Father. You made us invisible to our enemies, and you gave peace enough to sleep.* Lifting a quilted throw from the chair where Katy had previously been seated, she laid it gently across the mother and child. *I prayed out of my doubt, but you were faithful.*

Retrieving the weapon, she garnered her courage and went to the door. Before turning the lock, she stooped and peered beneath it. She could see broken debris scattered around but heard no threatening sounds. Breathlessly, she unlocked the door and squeezed it open. She peeked out guardedly, ready to close and bolt the door again in a moment's notice. The home had been ransacked. Furniture lay overturned, and a vase of fresh flowers that graced the entrance had been dashed to the floor. Hearing a voice from behind her, she whirled around. Her throat tightened, and before she could think, she shot out, "Who's there?"

The servants' door beneath the stairwell squeaked open and three maids peeked out, their eyes wide with fright. "It's only us, miss," one said in a soft, trembling tone.

Bailey ran to them. "Are you all right? Did they hurt you?"

Straightening her cap, she answered, "No, Miss Templeton. We're unharmed. Mary, Velda, and me. We 'id in the root cellar. The men—they must 'ave thought the 'ouse to be vacant." She shook her head in wonder. "It's a mystery why they didn't come lookin' for us. But where's our mistress a-and her wee ones?"

"Asleep on the parlor floor. We're all safe here, but I'm not so certain about the men. We should check the grounds—"

"Oh no, miss! Don't step a foot out until we 'ear from Mr. Weaver. Please—"

Bailey heard the sound of men's voices again and loud stamping against the planks on the front porch. Her mind froze, and she could not think. Numbly shouldering the musket, she planted her feet squarely and took a bead on the entrance. The maid gasped and scurried for cover. "Run, miss!" she shouted over her shoulder. "There's too many o' them!"

But with no time to flee, Bailey felt her will weaken, and the room seemed to spin. She could no more explain her actions than she could recall her own name. Her mind shouted, *Run and hide!* but her feet were immovable. Her eyes blurred and she could not see. The door flew open, and she felt her head tilt back with icy fear.

"Bailey!"

Bailey was seized with a stronger trepidation upon hearing Katy's voice. She shouted hoarsely, "Run, Katy! Back in the parlor and lock the door!" She did not look back but rather kept her aim on the entrance.

"Hold it, missy!" a familiar voice shouted from the entrance. "Don't shoot us!"

Bailey felt her arms go limp. Her stomach churned sickeningly, and the musket fell at her side. "Mr. Weaver!" She could scarcely speak. She staggered forward and braced herself against a table. The maids poured out into the room, and Katy ran to her side. A groggy Amelia peered out from the parlor.

"Mercy sakes!" the maid shrieked, her fingertips pressed against her colorless cheeks. "Wot would you have done, Miss Templeton? Taken on the entire Corps, if ye 'ad to?"

"I don't know," Bailey spoke almost inaudibly, her head pounding like an incessant drum. "I didn't have a plan, I just—"

"You're a little mad, that's what! You nearly scared me to death, Bailey Templeton!" Katy wrapped her arms around Bailey's shoulders.

Weaver half dragged a wounded hand into the room. Behind the sheepherder filed his weary band of volunteers. "We need some medical attention, ladies!" He assisted the staggering laborer to a tapestried sofa. "Bandages, some ointment, too, but lots of bandages. This man's been shot. A couple o' others, they took a blow as well."

"Right away, Mr. Weaver." Katy launched into action. "Mary, see to my children, will you? They're asleep in the parlor."

"Right away, miss! I'll get them upstairs and in their own beds."

"Wait!" Katy cautioned. "Mr. Weaver, please have one of your men escort Mary upstairs to inspect the damage."

Weaver picked out two able-bodied laborers, and they ran up the stairwell, muskets readied.

"Velda, why don't you two begin to clean up some of this mess?"

The maids curtsied, relieved to resume their chores.

Bailey seated herself, still shaken, and accepted a glass of water from one of the maids. "Mr. Weaver, do you know for certain— have all the looters gone?"

"We subdued them, but a few slipped away and made fast for the house. They wore sacks on their heads, but we shot one." Weaver's thick brows shadowed his eyes. "Don't know the man— he's dead. Could be military or could be convict. Don't know. Some o' the louts, they did some damage, but we 'eaded them off."

"Some of them broke into the house." Bailey surveyed the damage. "We hid from them in the parlor."

Weaver eyed the musket still in Bailey's grasp and shook his head. "I apologize for that. Two of 'em slipped past and broke open the front door. Three of my men saw the beggars and chased them, but a few of your pretties—" He hesitated, his eyes full of apology. "I'm sorry, Mrs. Farrell."

"You saved us, Mr. Weaver." Katy offered a somber word of encouragement. "You should all be commended. We can replace a few pretties." She laughed quietly, her eyes meeting his with grateful approval.

Outside, the dogs barked out another warning. Weaver's men whirled about, their weapons lifted.

A voice called from outside, riddled with distress. "Hello! Anyone about?"

Bailey stood and tried to see over the tops of the men's heads who had gathered curiously about the door. She could scarcely make out the men in the dark. But it appeared that two men carried one onto the porch. "Make way!" Weaver ordered, and the laborers parted.

Pulling back her skirts, Bailey glanced down and was horrified to realize that she stood in the presence of all these men in her bedclothes. Her cheeks blushed a bright rose, but to her relief, the outside activity had drawn all of their attention. She started to turn to Katy and excuse herself, but the sound of a familiar voice caught her ear.

"Is Mrs. Farrell about?"

Bailey and Katy exchanged glances. Stepping forward, Katy answered, "I'm here."

"Katy!" The stout man lifted his head, his eyes full of sorrow. "It's your dear husband I've brought home. I'm afraid—" He glanced down at Dwight Farrell's lifeless body.

"Captain Gabriel?" Bailey silently mouthed. She saw the flicker of apprehension in his eyes. Walking slowly, he and Dwight's best hand carried in Dwight Farrell.

Drawing her slender fingers to her lips, Katy shook her head, beholding her husband. Her eyes widened and her voice was choked with emotion. "Dwight? What has happened, Robert? Tell me, please!"

"Your hand said that Dwight separated from Donovan's search party."

Katy ran and knelt beside her husband. Brushing his matted hair from his face, she could not hold back her emotions. With a broken sob, she spoke his name once more. "Dwight?"

Bailey glanced around, hopeful of seeing the lost boy returned, but her eyes disappointed her.

"He's been snake bitten, ma'am. I brought him back as fast as I could, wot with carryin' a wounded man on my horse an' all." The old hand doffed his hat and held it in his hands. "I couldn't even tell you what kind o' snake, Mrs. Farrell. It was just too bloomin' dark. I apologize, ma'am, if I acted wrongly."

"You did the proper thing," Gabriel assured him and then offered an explanation to Katy. "Unable to travel swiftly, he found a man who acted as his runner. The man found two of us on the road, and we traveled by wagon to retrieve Dwight. Your man here had treated the bite with a sharp blade and whiskey until we could arrive." He laid a sympathetic hand atop Katy's and said quietly, "We brought him here as fast as we could manage."

Katy placed her ear against Dwight's chest. "Is he—alive?"

Gabriel nodded, but his face was etched with gravity. "Yes, but his heartbeat is weakening."

A frantic maid ran in with blankets. "Put these on him, Mrs. Farrell! You should keep him warm."

Gabriel stood. "If you will excuse me, I'm going to wait out on your front landing—" He hesitated awkwardly, his eyes appearing to absorb Katy's pain. Turning, he addressed the men. "Why don't we all move out of here and allow in the medical help?" The laborers each offered encouragement to their overseer's distraught wife and filed past Captain Gabriel and out the front doorway.

Bailey knelt beside Katy. "Dwight will make it, Katy." She gripped Katy's shoulders but cast her eyes away, not wanting to reveal the despair she felt. Dwight's face had turned ashen and his wrist, when she had held it, felt clammy. He'd been bitten on his forearm, which had swollen and appeared dangerously discolored.

Katy glanced up at the departing entourage of men. "Thank you all," she said brokenly. Rising to her knees, she stood with poise, trying to maintain her fragile control. "Thank you, Robert, for all you've done."

Robert bowed with a gentlemanly flourish and offered a smile, though Bailey felt certain she saw his bottom lip tremble.

Waiting for the room to clear, Bailey helped Katy to her feet. "Let's let him rest a bit here before we move him upstairs."

Katy nodded, her eyes distant. Her shoulders trembled as she struggled to speak. "First I lose my Donovan . . . now Dwight . . ."

Bailey held her dear friend close and allowed her to cry without reproof. She could think of nothing to say and so held her words for a better time. Katy Farrell had been strong enough for ten women in her lifetime. She was long overdue for a moment of weakness.

22

HOMECOMING

The hours had passed slowly that night in the upstairs room where Dwight and Katy Farrell once peacefully slept. The laborers had tarried for a bit but then returned to their quarters for a much-needed rest.

The Whitleys had arrived shortly thereafter. Rachel ministered over the patient, bathing his face and limbs to reduce the fever, and then ordered Dwight moved to the comfort of his bedroom. Heath gathered everyone together and prayed for Dwight, for the missing Donovan, and for the entire household. Katy found comfort and renewed strength from Heath's prayers.

Captain Robert Gabriel had bid his *adieus* and regretfully informed Katy that he could detain his ship no longer. He would set sail for England in two days. With the colony facing unrest, both the crisis and the Corps had prevented Robert's initial departure. But now Macarthur was burdened with Bligh's colony—a stolen responsibility that garnered him no loyalty. Gabriel would seize his shipment while the junta licked their wounds. And he would personally take the colony complaints to Parliament.

Katy passed the night checking Dwight's fever and feeling for his pulse just as Rachel Whitley had instructed. The venom had weakened his heart, and to worsen matters, exposure to the elements had left him with a disturbing rattle in his chest. Surgeon White had appeared an hour after the Whitleys had departed and performed a bloodletting, assuring Katy that Dwight must have the poison drained from his body. Dutifully, she tended to the dishes beneath his wrists, emptying them religiously, but Dwight had not stirred nor had he responded to any of the medical treatments.

Bailey peered anxiously into the room as she had done all night, but now her mission had taken on a newer meaning. She saw that Katy had seated herself once again next to her husband's bedside and had repeated her ritual of dampening a cloth to cool his brow. Seeing her worried countenance stirred Bailey, but she knew that she had reason enough to intrude. "Katy?" She could not contain the smile of elation or the tears that coursed her cheeks.

Her face wan from the night's vigil, Katy glanced up with no air of certainty. "Bailey, please, you should rest yourself now. There's nothing more that can be done." She stole a second glance at her friend, her eyes narrowing speculatively.

"But you've a visitor. I thought you might like to receive an important guest—"

"At this hour?" Agitation rose in Katy's tone, but she did not direct it at Bailey. Wearily she asked, "Who in their right mind—"

Bailey, no longer able to withstand the pure joy of the moment, flung open the door. Behind her stood one who had lost all patience with Bailey's mischievous game. "Mother!" Donovan shouted.

Katy fell back against the chair, reacting as though she beheld a ghost. Her voice trembled and she gripped the chair, lacking the strength to stand.

Gratified at having revealed her secret, Bailey stood back to allow the joyous reunion to unfold. She recalled how earlier she had crept downstairs, unable to sleep and feeling certain that another pot of water should be boiled and some more tea made ready in the event that Dwight should awaken or that Katy would desire another round of black brew to keep her awake. She had almost ignored the rap at the door, thinking that her mind played tricks on her. But the knocking persisted, so she approached the massive portal, keeping her caution for the undesired return of unwanted guests. Calling out, she had suspected a dirty trick in the works when she heard a male voice reply strongly, "Open the door and allow in your lost lambs!"

Unbarring the door with all the strength afforded her at such an hour, she held her breath and peered out into the night. Rushing to throw his arms around her waist was a disheveled but elated Donovan Farrell, flanked by the grinning pair of Hogan and a man he called Lawson.

"Captain Hogan?" She was astonished—no, shocked—that he would return with the boy. When Dwight had returned without his son, she thought all was lost. "How. . . ? I don't understand."

Grant Hogan looked weary beyond measure, and she felt pity for him as well as another unbidden emotion. "Captain Gabriel came for us, and with the family crisis impending, I managed a transfer back to Sydney Cove. We hooked up with Dwight and his search party, but he separated from us. We found Donovan in a convict encampment—bushrangers, most of them, but one army private. They had taken him away. They were hired men—"

"Hired? By whom?"

"Major Johnston, your old friend."

"But why? Because of me?" Guilt pricked at Bailey's senses.

"The Prentices and the Farrells have grown too influential in the colony. The Corps felt that a little diversion would tip the scales their way as they staged their little coup."

"How did you get past them?"

"Ingenuity and a little help from my explorer friend, Lawson." He nodded appreciatively at Lawson. "We waited for them to fall asleep, and then—"

"We ambushed them, Miss Templeton!" Donovan said with vengeful fervor. "And gave them back to their prison keepers."

"Not a cunning lot, those men." Grant could not contain his mirth. "We met a small naval detachment on their way into the convict colony. They gratefully took them off our hands."

"England won't stand for this, Grant." Anger seethed in her eyes, but she also felt a tinge of worry. "Will they?"

"Time will tell. What has happened to our Governor Bligh?"

"Rumors say that Macarthur and Johnston have deported him. But he could be dead, Grant. No one knows for certain." Bailey slid her hand around Donovan's, but then addressed Grant. "You say that Captain Gabriel took you to Dwight?"

"Yes, but Dwight did not stay with us. He was so anxious—" He paused, his gaze distant, then continued, "so concerned about his dear son. I fear for him, Bailey. I must return to the bush and find him." He gave Donovan an assuring pat on the shoulder. "And we will! But first, I must go and tell Katy." Frustration rose like a specter in his eyes.

Grasping his forearm, Bailey interjected, "No, Grant. Dwight's come home. But—"

"Dwight's home?" He read the meaning in her eyes. "Something's wrong. Tell me."

Seeing the worry in his face and the fear in Donovan's young eyes, she kept the details short and precise. Explaining the events of the evening, including the attack on Rose Hill and Captain Gabriel's rescue of Dwight, she added, "I'm glad you've come home, too, Grant—that is, I'm certain Katy will be glad to see you. But first . . ." She stroked Donovan's matted locks with kind affection. "First, I believe we should surprise your mother, young man."

The boy, so weary he could barely speak, forced out, "Is my papa—is he going to live?"

"Let's go up and see him, shall we?" Like a coward, she had avoided his direct question about his papa's condition. "But keep your caution. Your mother may faint at the sight of you." Before escorting him to his mother, she had gazed again upon the man once called Conquering Hogan. But now she saw him through new eyes. *You truly are a conqueror, Grant Hogan. But they were wrong about you, and so was I.* But she could not bring herself to relay her thoughts. This was not the time. All her attention, she realized, had to be directed upon the boy and on escorting him quickly to his mother and to his father's bedside. Politely she had invited Grant and Mr. Lawson to take their liberties in the larder and the pie pantry, and then had offered them a gentle smile as she and Donovan made their way to the stairway.

Now watching Donovan and Katy reunited, Bailey pulled her thoughts to the present and smiled, wiping her eyes with the sleeve of her gown. "Welcome home, Donovan."

"How did he come home, Bailey?" Katy kissed his soiled and tear-streaked face once again. "Donovan, what happened to you?"

"Some men—some bad men took me, Mum." He broke into a sob. "But your cousin Grant—he came for me, he did—" His voice waned. He could not continue and fell into her arms, exhausted.

Dismayed upon hearing the news, Katy lifted her brows inquiringly.

"Katy, it's as he says. Grant and another man have returned Donovan to you tonight, and they're downstairs in the kitchen. Shall I bring them up?" Bailey offered.

"Please." Katy nodded, unable to contain her emotions, and as yet unable to release her hold on her son. "I love you, son—"

Bailey could hear Katy's tearful affirmations repeated as she walked barefoot down the hallway. Stopping at the top of the staircase, she hesitated before descending. The emotion of the night had begun to weigh heavily. Something uncontrollable welled up inside of her, and she leaned against the banister for support. She heard a sob emanate from her throat, although she would have sworn that it came from another, thinking herself soberly under control. Too weary to fight the mixture of pain and elation she bore on behalf of her friends and too confused to deal with her own uncertain world, she succumbed to the desire to weep and collapsed in a heap on the floor. She hated herself for crying and prayed that Katy would not hear her. Her body heaved with uncontrollable sobbing, so much so that she scarcely noticed the rapid tramping of boots upon the carpeted staircase.

Before she could look up, she felt strong hands lift her, and she could do nothing but fall limply, helplessly against the source, her wrists crossed against her chest.

"Bailey!" Grant held her close against him while she continued to cry. "Bailey, I'm here!" He ran with her down the stairs while Lawson looked on in bewilderment as they darted past. He continued speaking in gentle tones, and she continued crying, although she could not lay the blame on any one source. She attempted to apologize, but the utterances were inaudible, and the only words she could intelligibly form were, "I'm sorry, so sorry."

Grant carefully propped her up on the sofa. Brushing back her tousled hair with one hand, he stroked her cheek with the other. "*You're* sorry? I'm the one who should be—"

"Please don't!" She bent over, holding her face with her hands. "I can't think clearly right now. We must behave responsibly." She raked her fingers through her long locks and pulled her hair from her face.

Grant glanced up and saw that Lawson yet stood staring in astonishment at them both. Lifting one brow, he signaled with a head gesture and waited as the explorer snapped around and marched back into the kitchen. A smile creasing his cheeks, he answered her gently, as he wished that he had done on countless other occasions. "Behave responsibly?"

"Yes." Struggling to regain her composure and feeling ashamed at her outburst, Bailey mustered an ounce of self-will and said, "We should all get a good night's rest. Tomorrow we can discuss matters as adults, when we're—when I'm in a more stable frame of mind." She hoped to assure herself as much as him.

"Bailey Templeton, I am not one of your pupils," he said with a smile.

Bailey glanced up at him and saw the humor in his gaze. Suddenly feeling as awkward as one of the youths in her schoolroom, she stuttered out her reply, "I . . . I'm sorry. I didn't mean—"

"I don't want you to be in your right mind. I want you to be as insane tonight as I've been on so many sleepless nights." He turned about, drawing himself up on his knees and facing her.

With his face now close to hers, Bailey could think of no reply at all. Her mind a total blank, she relaxed in his presence, feeling as though her soul had been wandering in a desert and had finally come home. She allowed her eyes to gaze upon each facet of his face, and meeting his eyes with her own, she searched their depths. He tenderly brushed a tear from her cheek. Nothing she thought or desired made sense, but she reveled in the folly. She drew closer, and before she realized it, her tear-salted lips were gently brushed by his. Her lashes flew up in surprise, and then he caressed her cheek with his own and held her out as though he desired nothing more than to look at her.

"I've rehearsed this moment many times, Bailey Templeton," he said with quiet surety. "I want—"

"Bailey!" Katy called out from the top of the stairs. "Grant! Come quickly!"

Standing at once, Grant took Bailey's hand and helped her to her feet. Drawing her unexpectedly close, he held his lips to her ear and said, "You will not escape me this time, Miss Templeton."

Bailey stood still momentarily, refusing to admit how much she enjoyed his attention. But she knew that eventually she would be forced to tell him the truth about her situation. Turning her face soberly, she called up to Katy, "We're on our way at once!" Lifting herself onto her toes, she felt herself drawn to him like a magnet. Slowly, deliberately, she pressed a kiss against his cheek and tried to rush away, but she felt him grip her forearm and whirl her about. She shook her head, her eyes wide and guileless. "Katy's waiting, Grant."

261

"And we must go to her." His brow arched, and he pulled her against his chest. "But not until I make you hear the words I've— Bailey, I've hated myself for not telling you."

A mélange of emotions swirled through her, but she knew that Katy needed them both at her side.

"There's much to discuss, but we need more time," she said weakly, knowing in her heart that he would persist.

"I want to tell you—"

She attempted to be strong but felt herself succumb to his strong embrace. Placing her hands against his chest, she pushed herself away. She had to face the inevitable and so would he. "Grant, I feel I should tell you that I've been dismissed from the school." She studied his gaze and continued. "It's all Johnston's doing. There's no one to stop him." Her words hung in the air like the silence between them.

Grant ran his broad hands up her back to the soft curve of her shoulders. Then gripping her slender arms, he said in tender tones, "You don't have to leave."

She forced out the words, yet unsure of his answer. "Why don't I?"

"Bailey? Where are you?" Katy's voice sounded more agitated, and several servants scurried up the stairs with anxious faces.

A gasp caught in Bailey's throat, and she gazed pleadingly at Grant.

His merciful, magnificent green eyes said more than words. Bending toward her, he reciprocated with a kiss upon her forehead and then turned her about to face the stairs. "We'd better go."

Quickly ascending to the second floor, Bailey and Grant approached the Farrells' bedroom door, where they saw Katy bustle inside. The servants were gathered out in the hallway, muttering in anxious tones among themselves. Not wanting to parade her fears, Bailey poised her countenance and made her way through the throng. "Pardon us, please." She stepped into the room, now brightly lit by two lanterns. Drawing her hand to her mouth, she beheld Donovan stretched across his father's chest, weeping. Katy stood behind him, fully dressed and stroking her son's head. On the other side of the bed stood Kelsey and Amelia, their faces bearing the weight of the moment.

"Katy? Is Dwight—"

Dwight's eyelids fluttered partly open. "Not yet," he whispered, then coughed hoarsely.

Katy smiled broadly. "He's awake."

"Well, old man!" Grant strode quickly to the opposite side of the four-poster bed. "You're a hard man to keep down, don't I always say?" He folded his arms across his chest, his elation evident. "Welcome back to the land of the living."

Dwight nodded, his pale face struggling to form a faint smile.

Bailey slid her arm around Katy's waist. "What a happy morning this will be!"

A frown darkened Katy's gaze, but she offered no immediate reply. Bailey, sensing her discomfiture, pressed her lips together and whispered, "Something's wrong?"

Katy nodded, but she did not need to offer a response. Bailey could see it in the transparency of her gaze and in the depths of her blue eyes. She looked once more at Dwight and saw the shadow of death upon his face.

Dwight struggled to speak, and it became evident he wished to address his son.

"Donovan, please look at your father," Katy said quietly.

The lad lifted his head and turned his red-eyed gaze upon his dying father. "Yes, Papa, I'm listening." The silence hung heavily between them. "I love you, Papa."

Bailey could see that the boy struggled to maintain a manly courage, but in the face of such pain his young heart battled helplessly.

Dwight spoke haltingly, stopping to cough and to struggle for another breath. "I . . . lay for a long time in the bush . . . thought . . . knew I would die alone out there. But God . . . He heard my prayers. I asked to see you once more, Donovan, and to see my precious Katy and our children."

Tears spilled over the rims of Katy's eyes, and she gripped her husband's trembling hand. Calling out to her servants, she directed them with a quiet surety. "Hurry, please! Awaken our other two children and bring them to their father."

"But here you are, son. Hear me now . . . you live life as though each day is your last. You're my little miracle . . . my answered prayer, and I give you back to my heavenly Father."

"No, Papa, please don't leave me!" Donovan pleaded.

"It isn't long until we meet again. Somehow . . . I know that's true now. And I'll be waiting. There's a golden portal adorned with a pearl, and just inside, son, I'll wait for you there. Don't disappoint me—you come through that gate, now, mate." He glanced around at each family member who encircled his bed with their loving support. "I'll be waiting for all of you. Do you understand my meaning?"

Bailey felt herself nodding along with all the others. Her entire being quaked from the struggle to hold back the tears. She saw the years of struggle etched on Katy's face. She and Dwight had seen both the worst of times and the best, yet in the midst of it all burned their fierce love for each other. Katy doted over him like a new bride. More than once she had kissed her dear husband, fearing that each would be her last.

"My husband should rest now," Katy wisely suggested, detecting the mental exhaustion of all present.

One by one, all the servants disappeared down the hallway except one. Katy had asked Mary if she would assist her road-weary son with washing up and then put him to bed. Allowing Dwight to kiss a very sleepy Jared and Corbin, she also had them returned to their beds. But she refused to leave Dwight's side, determined to stand her vigil until morning.

Bailey and an emotionally drained Hogan parted with a solemn promise to speak more in the morning. She returned to her quarters and slept for a few hours, but suddenly she bolted awake and saw that her room had begun to lighten. Throwing on her bed coat, she pulled on her slippers and crept down the hall again to the Farrells' room. The door stood open only a few inches, and she could see Katy standing and staring out the large window with the curtains open full. The sunlight peeped into the room, illuminating Katy's face with the golden splendor of early morning. Quietly, Bailey joined her at her side. Sensing her presence, Katy faced her, and Bailey saw a single tear glisten upon her cheek.

"He's gone, Bailey." She inhaled a ragged breath and then began to weep aloud, slowly rocking back and forth.

Seeing Dwight's face had been covered with the crisp white sheets, Bailey nodded and embraced her compassionately. She stood silently while tears coursed her own cheeks. "I'm so sorry, Katy." She hesitated. "When did it happen?"

"Just as the sun broke. He went out with the dawn." She smothered another sob. "He fought death courageously, though. Just as he did the struggles in life and in this dreadful colony. He was a good man, Bailey. There was no better, loyal man than my dear, sweet Dwight."

Bailey nodded her agreement, knowing that all Katy said was

right. She stood with her while she continued to weep. Dwight Farrell had gone home on a Sunday. She did not know how long they both stood gazing into the dawn, but she did know that she had been privileged to know a father whose love for his family knew no bounds—he would willingly give his life for his family. How fitting that he now stood in the presence of the One who did the same for him.

23

FOR THE SAKE
OF THE COLONY

Hogan stood outside the government building waiting for an officer, any officer, to emerge. The last few months had been more painful than any he had encountered at Hobart. Not only had he been forced to deal with the remorse of returning to find the colony in a state of anarchy, but Dwight Farrell's death had delivered a blow to his senses from which he struggled to recover. He had blamed himself most of all for allowing Farrell to separate from the search party. Although Lawson had repeatedly reminded him of Dwight's stubborn persistence—"He wouldn't listen to reason, Hogan. You know that's true."—the guilt wound around his heart like a loose fence wire.

Even more condemning was the anger he felt toward God. He had watched many good men die in Hobart, some saints and some sinners. Although at times he had felt a minute part of himself die with each human loss, he also had found that with time, an unexplainable peace would replace the sorrow. But to see Katy weeping morning and night over her husband's death was more than he could bear. He felt helpless and useless, and offering comfort seemed in vain. Watching her grieve had created an inner turmoil that had thrust its venomous hooks into his very soul. Dwight Farrell had not been just another emancipist. His life had epitomized perseverance and hope where others had wallowed in drunken despair. He was a father and husband, loved dearly by his wife and children. He had taken a floundering sheep operation and made it succeed in a wilderness where most had failed. *How will Katy ever make it without him, Lord? And what of Donovan, a mere boy who blames himself more than any other?* But in spite of the cloud over Rose Hill, he knew that he would have to pull his mind out of the doldrums and forge ahead for the sake of the colony. But his letters and requests for an audience with the new Macarthur regime had gone unanswered. After futile attempts to see either Major Johnston or John Macarthur himself, he resolved to wait outside their offices until sunset. Sooner or later one of them would emerge from their unscrupulous little vulture's nest, and he would be there waiting for them.

"Captain Hogan?"

The voice startled him from his troubled stupor. He whirled around to find Lieutenant Evans gazing from red eyes, the dark circles that sagged beneath his eyes foretelling his plight. "Evans? The dickens, soldier! What evil's befallen you?"

Evans glanced nervously around the compound as though he feared an informant might overhear his tremulous story. Only the good Lord knew how many spies lurked about. "I was dismissed, Captain." He clasped his fingers inwardly, his knuckles white. "And me with a new bride."

The news only further ignited his ire. "Dismissed by what scoundrel?" Keeping his voice low for Evans' sake, he ventured a sure guess. "Macarthur, I presume?"

"It was Johnston, but they're one and the same, if you ask me. I was asked about my allegiance, and I swore that my loyalties lay with the Crown and with our dear Governor Bligh. That answer, I fear, was my undoing. All of the men have been called in for questioning. If you haven't, they'll question you next, I vow."

"Not the case so far, I'm afraid. I've attempted an audience with both Johnston and Macarthur. I've been largely ignored and informed that I would have to wait weeks for a meeting." Hogan kept his attention focused upon the entrance. "It has now been months."

"Perhaps they fear you, then. But men of higher rank than you have been dismissed. Macarthur will allow none to stand in the way of his Corps."

"But he cannot maintain his grip without cooperation. The settlers are demanding answers. They plan a meeting, and if Macarthur refuses to appear, he could have a worse mutiny on his hands than even Bligh ever imagined."

Evans did not respond at once but pressed his lips together as if his words might weigh too heavily. "Are you—have you been asked to speak on behalf of the settlers?"

Seeing the worry of his gaze, Hogan replied mutedly, "That troubles you, I presume?"

Evans nodded with a glint of caution in his eyes. "You'll be axed for certain. They'll accuse you of inciting an insurrection or something like. I'd never tell a captain what his business was, but if I were you, I'd turn and leave now with my rank intact. Let the settlers handle their own matters."

"Too many people feel that way, Evans. That's why Sydney Cove's in the state it's in now."

"As God is my witness, sir, you know I've never cowered. That's why I was discharged. But this Rum Corps, as some call it, is too big, and none can beat it. We're too far from England, I fear."

"Not bigger than God, I trust, Evans?" Hogan waited, hoping to look Evans square in the eye.

Evans' face flew up, and his pale cheeks reddened.

Hogan read the silence between them. "I'm sorry. I know you're in a quandary. I know you're frightened, man. Who isn't? But if we give up, then everyone in New South Wales loses."

"Sir, I have a wife to tend to. My family has some means of their own, but I never would have taken Emily for my wife had I known that I would be without my personal wages. When her family hears of it, they'll be demanding answers, and my loyalty to the governor will mean little to them."

"What do you intend to do?"

"That's why I've returned today. If our new government demands allegiance, then I'm not going to be the lonely soul to stand against it—"

"Evans, you cannot call Macarthur's puppet regime a government! Once England receives the news that they've deposed Bligh, they'll all hang—Macarthur, Johnston, and the whole lot. Anyone who stands with them will fall with them." In spite of Evans' personal plight, Hogan could in no way find common ground with him. "It's only a matter of time."

"I hope that all you say is true." Evans' eyes narrowed stubbornly. "But the truth of the matter is that Bligh has been deported, and he's not coming back. Macarthur is a respected leader and will have more than enough support here to back up his story. He'll paint Bligh as an incompetent despot, and they'll believe him. Macarthur has been planning his overthrow for a long time." Evans' eyes widened with anxiety. "If you can't see it now, you will soon enough. Macarthur has finally won."

Hogan was well acquainted with Bligh's reputation. He had suffered an infamous mutiny upon his ship, *The Bounty*, but in spite of that blemish on his record, he had been restored in England's sight and hailed as a reputable and capable leader. Evans was reacting out of fear. "As long as we believe that we're defeated, it will be true." Hogan cast his gaze beyond the lieutenant's disconcerted mien. The front door opened, and he patted Evans' shoulder with a degree of diplomacy. "There's a meeting tonight at Rose Hill, Evans. Why not bring your new bride and hear what the colonists have to say. Perhaps you'll find that Macarthur is without a country after all."

"It isn't possible, Captain. How will I live without—"

Hogan could hesitate no longer. His awaited moment of truth had arrived, and he could tarry no more. Brushing past the lieutenant, he excused himself. "Pardon me for interrupting, but I've a meeting I cannot miss. See you tonight." He spoke confidently, fully believing that Evans would see the light.

Evans followed Hogan with his eyes and then cautiously took two steps back. Walking out onto the front landing of the government building was none other than John Macarthur. He watched as Captain Hogan strode toward him with the determination of a starving grizzly. Stepping behind a tree, Evans hid himself, not wanting Macarthur to believe that he was fraternizing with Hogan. Most of the dismissed military men had secured a ship's passage to England to take up their case with Parliament. Evans hated himself for his cowardice, but with so much at stake personally, he could not leave and had no margin in his life for politics. He would return tomorrow and pledge his loyalty to the new government of Sydney Cove. Hogan was a good man but foolish. He would learn eventually what everyone else had come to know—nothing or no one could withstand the power of the junta. No power on earth or in heaven. He breathed a useless prayer on behalf of the captain and slipped away to join his distressed bride around his father's table.

Bailey pressed Laurie's letters into a neat stack and tied them together with a ribbon. In spite of the pain she had suffered by reading them, her love for her sister far outweighed her mixed feelings about the marriage. And in the last year, she had begun to feel a healing taking place in her life. She truly believed that she could now look both Laurie and Gavin full in the face and bless their happy union. That was why she struggled with a decision to return to America. Realizing that she needed to face her past straight on, she also wanted to remove any guilt that might tarnish Laurie's marriage. But worst of all, Atkins still held firm as the new headmaster, and Johnston would grant her no audience at all. She could not remain in Sydney Cove indefinitely without a position. Her income had rapidly dwindled.

But before making a decision, Bailey realized, she must confess her worries of this stalemate to Grant Hogan. As strong as her feelings were for him, she refused to rely on him as the answer to her problems. After Dwight's death, he had been a bastion of strength for Katy and her children. She had stood with him in that regard. And in consideration of her, he had courted her in as gentlemanly a fashion as had ever been done. But unable to make any headway in regard to the school, he had grown more frustrated by the day in knowing that she could not give up her desire to teach and that he could do nothing to bring about the needed change on her behalf. She wondered if it was providence that they had been separated for so long. If God did not bring them together, then she would be forced to accept the fact that she might once again be facing the pain of separation. *If it's by your hand, Lord, and none other, then so be it*, she thought with dread. Tonight, after the settlers' meeting, she would make her announcement first to Grant and then to her friends. Miserable resignation pricked at her senses. But the harsh reality was that she could not remain without a teaching position for much longer. Her life had become a bitter struggle.

"Packing already?" Katy peered through the doorway. "Not in a hurry, are we?"

Bent over the bed, Bailey continued sorting her personals but glanced up with a nod of affection. "Not packing in the truest sense, although I've decided to store some of my warmer clothing in my trunk. I'm trying to organize all of my belongings a little better this go-round. I can't believe I've accumulated so much in the short time I've been here."

A look kin to melancholy darkened Katy's gaze. "It has been a short time—too short." Her face said more than her words, as did the skirt of the black mourning dress that bustled around her feet.

Bailey stood erect, her arms akimbo. "If you start with the fare-wells now, I'll surely be a bundle of emotions I haven't made up my mind entirely, you know." She smiled, but her eyes yet reflected an inward pain. Katy was the only soul she had dared to share her fears with. "You know I want to stay, but the government here has made the decision for me." She hoped her face reflected an air of diplomacy and not the anguish with which she struggled.

Looking upward, Katy closed her eyes and stroked her throat, her entire mien suggesting an air of apprehension. Her tone hinged on exasperation. "But we could find other work for you. That teacher—Orville Atkins—whoever he is, can't last long. You can wait him out. You could outlast the man. I know you could."

"It's a temptation. But waiting in the wings is not my idea of living, Katy. And it seems I've spent my entire existence in Sydney Cove doing just that. . . ." Her voice trailed off. Then she felt Katy's eyes upon her. She shook out a blouse purposefully and directed her attention back to the task at hand. "It seems I'm always wait-ing." Since Dwight's death, she and Grant had agreed to approach their relationship slowly in order to devote more time to Katy in her time of grief, although they had not divulged to her their de-cision. And now with the realization that she may be forced to leave, she saw the wisdom of their decision. For Bailey Templeton, waiting had been the order of the day.

"I see that look of yours, Bailey. And I know another who has done his share of waiting as well. But you aren't allowing the man enough time. Please understand, when Hogan returned from the mountains with Donovan, our world was rocked. Dwight's death threw all of us out of balance." She looked down, her fingers grip-ping the ever present handkerchief.

"I swear to you that I understand all of that and more. Please don't think me insensitive. I haven't judged Grant nor do I feel he's neglected me. He's been wonderful. But can't you see God's hand in all of this? Perhaps this is the Lord's way of protecting me or him—both of us. Your cousin is a complicated man. He certainly doesn't need the likes of me muddling up the works."

"Posh! Bailey Templeton, you know very well that you would make Hogan a wonderful wife. He's mad about you." Katy strode around the bed and seated herself atop the cotton coverlet. "In addition, you'd become a member of our family."

"Wife? Grant Hogan and I never made it to that stage." Holding up a skirt, she popped out the wrinkles.

Katy picked up a stack of her blouses and held them against her. "You underestimate yourself, Bailey. Mark my words, if you announce to him tonight that you're leaving, I fully expect the poor soul to fall through the floor."

"Not likely." A serene gaze lit Bailey's face. "Our Captain Hogan is not the sort of fellow to allow the likes of me to send him through the floor."

Standing, Katy walked across the room and began rearranging Bailey's clothes and neatly placing them back inside her bureau drawer. "We'll see, won't we?" Her tone now took on a maternal quality.

Bailey's brows knit together. "Katy, those things go in the trunk."

Continuing on as though she did not hear her, Katy placed the last blouse in the drawer. "If I know my cousin as well as I think, he'll be furious with you." She turned on her heels and faced Bailey fully. "You'd best sneak out of town if you want to make it safely."

Folding her arms at her waist, Bailey shook her head. "Are you listening to anything that I'm saying?"

Katy nodded in an animated fashion but did not offer a smile. "Mm-hmm."

"Then why did you put all of those things back in the bureau?" She laughed quietly. "Now I'll have to bring them all out again."

Katy gathered up several winter dresses and began hanging them back inside the chiffonnier.

Bailey's right brow lifted. "You're deliberately ignoring me?"

"I'm saving you the trouble of packing. You're not going anywhere."

Bailey sat down where Katy had been sitting and watched her stubborn friend. Her eyes sparked with amusement. She yawned sleepily and stretched out across the bed in an act of surrender.

Katy would tire of her theatrics soon enough, and she would re-sume the tedious task of organizing her belongings for the pos-sible long journey ahead. Katy's opinions had proven accurate on many occasions, but now her heart stood in the way of her own intellect. Of this fact, Bailey was certain. To believe that Grant Ho-gan would sweep her off her feet and stand in the way of her de-cision was nothing more than childish fantasy. *Men like Captain Hogan don't succumb to the whims of capricious young women.* For this reason, she assured herself, she felt great relief. She respected a man who could in no way fall prey to manipulation. He had been level-headed when all others had lost control. She so admired him and would always remember their chance moment upon the wild shores, but she had slowly come to realize their worlds could never merge beyond that stolen moment. But as with Gavin, she would go on and be all the stronger for it. A wave of misery swept through her again.

A slight tap at the door caused them both to glance question-ingly toward the entry. "Yes, Mary?" Seeing the maid standing at the ready, Katy acknowledged the servant girl but did not pause in her self-appointed duties.

"Dinner is served, Mrs. Farrell. What with your meetin' an' all at the school, Mrs. Prentice felt we should dine a bit earlier."

"Thank you," Katy answered kindly as Bailey sat up and smoothed her skirt. "We'll be right down." Katy strode deter-minedly to the bed, scooped up two pairs of white gloves and, with an air of certainty, stuffed them into the top drawer of the bureau. "There we go. All done now."

Bailey could not help but smile at her air of triumph. She walked to the mirror to check her hair, then slipped her feet into her cloth shoes. "That's right." She nodded patronizingly. "All done"—her eyes softened with resignation—"for now." Clasping her hands in front of her, she looked down and then back up at Katy. "I would miss you the most, you know. You're the strongest woman I've ever met—you and your mother both." But her words fell on deaf ears. Folding her arms at her waist, she watched as Katy snapped her empty trunk closed. Then she walked to the door and held it open for Bailey.

"Shall we go down for dinner?" Katy asked confidently, but her eyes misted at the rims.

Bailey nodded, strode toward her, and with sweet gentility, she placed a kiss upon her cheek. Walking quickly past, she thought her ear detected a slight choke. But she did not look back, keeping her eyes straight ahead. She had witnessed too many tears over the last few weeks. Her heart could not bear the load of any more.

"The meetin' is called to order o' the settlers' o' Sydney Cove and of Parrametta!" A gavel pounded against a weathered podium, and a middle-aged colonist brought the crowded group of colonists to order.

A murmur ripped throughout the filled-to-capacity schoolroom. Many citizens had remained at home, choosing not to become involved in the government's pitiful state of affairs. But a large number had turned out for the assembly, if for nothing else than to satisfy their curiosity and be a witness to the latest controversy. Chattering women laughed aloud, sometimes sitting, sometimes standing. Recognizing a neighbor lady or the butcher's wife from down in the borough, they called to one another while wrestling with their unruly offspring. Men gathered in clusters, muttering about the escalated price of goods and the need for order among the rum-hungry inhabitants.

But an imposing figure strode through their midst to the front, smartly attired in the Royal Navy's proud dress uniform. Grant Hogan doffed his hat and bowed slightly while a respectful hush fell over the room. "Good evening. I am Captain Hogan of His Majesty's Royal Navy."

Bailey stood next to Katy, with Donovan and Jared on either side of them. Caleb and Kelsey stood close behind, each holding a child tightly against them. Amelia chose to sit outside in the carriage with Katy's young daughter. The throng pressed against the couples, so they moved slightly forward to create a small space between themselves and the crowd. Soon they were joined by Reverend Heath Whitley and his wife, Rachel. They conversed quietly with one another, their concerns evident on their faces. Bailey clasped her gloved fingers and attempted a faint smile when she thought Grant had cast a glance her way. But with his duties before him so paramount, she determined to draw as little attention to herself as possible.

Katy flapped a fan at her neck. "If they don't open a few windows, I will surely faint dead." She loosened her black bonnet.

Hogan began. "Citizens of New South Wales, we are gathered

here at candlelight and have little time left between now and the hour of our waking." He spoke with calm authority, as though above him dangled England's Crown. "At this time of evening we begin to put the weight of the day's problems behind us and begin to think that tomorrow will dawn, and we will be handed the responsibility of a new day."

Bailey cut her eyes askance, trying to read the thoughts of the curious onlookers.

"We have watched the birth of a new land, sometimes with dismay as it floundered like an unwanted orphan, seemingly cast aside by parent England."

Bailey and Katy drew near each other as the mutterings among Sydney's emerging gentry grew louder. With dignity, Bailey kept her attention upon the speaker.

Luring the crowd's attention back to himself, Hogan continued confidently. "And we will know soon if indeed we have been abandoned. But let us take heed, dear ladies and gentlemen of the land, to the matters at hand. Our own Governor Bligh, appointed by the Crown of England, has been deposed, banished from our midst, and forced into illegal exile in Van Diemen's Land. And those blackguards who plotted against our government—did they to ask us if they could speak on our behalf?"

Shaking a grungy fist in the air, an emancipist shouted, "No! They did not!" Others standing around the man countered with their own protests.

Nodding methodically and with a surety, Hogan responded, "No, they did not. And when they seized our newly emerging government—and, might I add, with the lightning-quick response of a viper—"

The crowd stirred more intently, but Bailey felt a peace swell inside of her. Hogan held them spellbound. *Just as you've done so many times with me, dear Captain.*

"—what was the result of their having commandeered our people, our land, our livelihoods into their greedy possession?" He waited, garnering their silent attention. "Lower-priced goods? Stronger government? Increased wages?"

A shout went up from the crowd. "No!" Tempers flared, and the shouting echoed the angry sentiments that swarmed throughout the room.

"Bring us Macarthur!"

"Hang the blackguards!"

"Gentlemen!" Seeing their hostile mood, Hogan lifted his hands in the air to quiet them. "We now find ourselves facing the candlelight years of this land. The darkness falls, but do we despair?" He offered a solemn pause. "No. We do not! Is all lost? Must we fold our hands and close our eyes and allow anarchy to be the curtain of night upon our land? No! We shall not. For tomorrow is a new day, and with the passing of night comes dawn's light! As no man can withhold the sun, no criminal can withhold the justice that will surely come."

Bailey found herself hanging on his every word. *He is so eloquent*, she thought but dared not voice her opinion. Making their way through the throng was Lieutenant Evans and his new wife, Emily. Bailey acknowledged them with a polite smile and then focused her eyes to the front once more.

"Hang Macarthur! Flog Johnston!" chanted the crowd.

"Please believe me when I say that I hear your cries." He nodded once more to acknowledge their demands. "It was my intent to ask our *self-appointed* leaders to come and speak to us, to offer them the opportunity to voice their intent. But I could neither request nor coerce either John Macarthur or Major George Johnston into honoring us with their presence, for during our meeting yesterday, they foolishly attempted to release me from duty—"

Jeers floated around the anxious mob.

"—a task at which they failed. For I, Captain Grant Hogan of His Majesty's Navy, do not recognize the authority of illegal anarchists—"

Cheers rocked the schoolhouse. Bailey looked down, pressing her lips together to hide her smile. Placing her lips to Katy's ear, she said, "I do believe our kind Captain Hogan is fomenting a revolt."

"Upon my attempt to try to once again create a bridge between myself and The Great Perpetrator John Macarthur, I was told after dawn on this day that John Macarthur has left our shores"—the cheering throng nearly drowned out his final words—"without a trace."

Bailey pulled Jared close to her. The deafening, gleeful roar caused the lad to place his hands to his ears. Men tossed their hats in the air, while the ladies embraced one another. Bailey glanced at Katy, and the two shook their heads in wonder. Making one final attempt to quiet the excited citizenry, Hogan added, "Abruptly departing as well was his most worthy associate, Major George Johnston. After being strongly convinced of their dwindling support, many of their most loyal followers have also fled. We trust their journey will—" Hogan, forced once again by the cheering throng to halt his eloquent speech, threw back his head and began to laugh.

Bailey felt Katy squeeze her hand but dared not look her way, already feeling her knowing glance.

Settlers and emancipists alike began directing questions at the podium. With the news of Macarthur's departure enlivening their interests, the fear of a dismantled government loomed strong. Hogan acknowledged their concerns.

"We will organize our military to provide protection as always. I will assure you of that fact. And our request to England for a new governor, well, that is forthcoming, we believe. Can we survive as civilized beings until our government is restored? That answer lies in your hands, the citizens of New South Wales."

"Wot about the government stores? An' the school?" The questions kept coming.

"We will continue to operate the stores just as we will continue to receive supplies from England. But at the prices, of course, to which you are accustomed." Clasping his hands behind him, Hogan glanced out across the crowd, examining their pleased expressions.

Bailey prayed he would not draw her into the discussion in regard to the school. But his eyes locked with hers, and he smiled with the same assurance, maintaining the confident bearing he had asserted all evening.

"In regard to our school, we have a serious deficiency. Our judge advocate, Mr. Richard Atkins, and his brother have also fled the country, leaving us without a schoolteacher at the present."

Bailey could no longer ignore the eyes of her friends upon her. She felt tears well as the corners of her mouth turned up in elation. Katy kissed her face on her right while Rachel kissed the other side.

A rumble arose and one woman waved her hand wildly, hoping to be recognized. "Wot about the American, Miss Templeton? The one that vicious lot run off!"

Bailey saw a woman eyeing her and then bowed her head when the woman shouted, "She's standin' right here! Miss Templeton is here!"

If it had not been for the pressing throng, Bailey would have turned and slipped quietly away. But those around her continued to draw attention to her whereabouts. With a heavy sigh, she glanced reluctantly up at Hogan.

"Yes. I see she is here." Hogan made a sweeping gesture, motioning her to come to the podium. "If you do not mind, Miss Templeton, you may be more easily addressed if you join me here. I have two questions to ask of you, and then we will detain you no longer."

Shaking her head was of no use, for Katy stood behind her, urging her to go forward. The people ahead of her parted, smiling as she passed. She nodded at each one but could not prevent the bright pink flush upon her cheeks. Approaching Hogan, she turned her face away from the onlookers and said quietly so only he could hear, "I've something to tell you."

But he would not allow their conversation to be a private matter and said aloud, "Yes, we want to hear all you have to say to our citizenry, Miss Templeton."

Bailey turned her head sideways, her eyes wide with disbelief. She placed her fingers upon the podium, cleared her throat, and looked out at the anticipating faces. The room grew uncomfortably quiet before she could form the words. Finally, she began. "I want you all to know that I have no ill feelings toward you or toward the government of New South Wales. Captain Hogan, when I arrived in your harbor, it was my full intent to make Sydney Cove my home. I made it my home. I made all of you my friends." She glanced at Katy and the boys and then at the Whitleys. "Some of you are like family to me now. Although it was not my decision to leave the school, I believe that it was for the best. After all, I am an American." She saw the bewilderment in some of their faces but determined to make fast her explanation and then dismiss herself from their midst. "I can't even make a cup of your British tea."

Seeing her comment sparked humor in their midst, Hogan interjected, "Alas, she speaks the truth—she cannot." His brows lifted with droll amusement.

"You taught me boy to read, Miss Templeton. And you gave him higher ways o' thinkin'," an emancipist mother said loudly over the mutterings of the crowd. Others nodded around her. "You taught him the ways o' the Good Book, too."

"Your children are all precious to me as they are precious to God. I hope I've taught them to read, but more than that, I hope I've taught them to go beyond the daily tasks that I set before them within the confines of the schoolroom. It is my desire to see them use the tools I've passed on to them. Captain Hogan spoke to you about the responsibility handed to us with each new day. The future of that responsibility lies in your hands and in those of your children. I trust you will not take that obligation lightly." Having said all of that, she suddenly felt at a loss for words. Opening her mouth to speak, she paused and glanced obliquely at Grant. "Was there—Captain Hogan, you said that you had two questions you wished for me to address. True?" She hoped he would rescue her from floundering in the full sight of all.

Hogan nodded and stepped forward. "Yes. I trust we will all take to heart Miss Templeton's words. May they be engraved indelibly on our minds from henceforth. But let me not digress." He faced her at once, somberness his driving force. "My first question has most likely been answered, but I will ask it, standing hopeful of the answer."

Seeing that he waited upon her response, Bailey merely nodded, but her eyes questioned his intent.

"We are at a crossroads as a colony, Miss Templeton. And we are at the mercy of England, being hopeful she will act swiftly on our behalf. But we do not want our children at the mercy of chance"—he looked out for the approval of others—"not if we can take a strong measure to improve their circumstances." Receiving the necessary nods of agreement, he continued. "For the sake of the colony, Miss Templeton, and for the sake of the children of New South Wales, will you reconsider your decision to return to America? We need you here. Our children need you."

"Please stay, Miss Templeton!" Ellen Simons, the woman who had been Bligh's housemaid while Bailey had been a guest in his home, proclaimed aloud what all others were thinking. Her response sent a wave of approval through the crowd.

Dade, her once personal guard, smiled up at her and winked.

Bailey glanced out and saw the faces of those whose children she had been privileged to teach. Even those she would have sworn were against her were now speaking out on her behalf.

"I don't know what to—that is—" Her eyes locked with a ruddy-faced boy who smiled his approval. *Cole Dobbins?*

Hogan lifted a gloved hand and placed it beneath her delicate chin. His eyes sparked with intrigue. "We *all* need you, Miss Templeton. *I* need you."

Glancing to the side, she saw Katy beaming through a tear-streaked face.

"I need you, too," she whispered. She felt foolish crying in the midst of so much celebration. Katy ran to her and threw her arms around her neck. They held each other and cried even more. It seemed like a dream to Bailey. *A wonderful dream!* "Yes! I will stay."

Donovan and Jared wrapped themselves around her skirts, and she could not help but laugh and cry all at the same time. As she kissed them each, Hogan declared the meeting soon to end.

Then Katy shouted above the tumult, "Captain Hogan, I believe you had two questions for Miss Templeton. You've asked one already. Have you another?"

Bailey wiped her eyes and composed herself. "I'm sorry. Yes, Captain Hogan. One more question, and then I believe we should allow these good people to travel to their homes."

"Of course," Hogan continued. "Thank you for your patience. You may all expect that by daybreak tomorrow our military will resume their duties in the government stores." He faced Bailey again. "But for the sake of all, Miss Templeton, I felt many would wish to know the answer to my final question."

His voice sounded grave, and understanding his strong ways, Bailey prepared to answer whatever question he posed as forthrightly as she knew. "Yes, Captain, go on."

He drew himself up, clasped her slender hands inside his own large ones, and asked, "Miss Templeton, for the sake of the colony—will you be my wedded wife?"

Bailey had never been one to faint and refused to succumb to such a desire now. But looking up into his emerald eyes so full of anticipation, she hesitated, wanting her answer to be the right one. Without taking her eyes off his, she took a deep breath and silently prayed.

24
SUNRISE

JANUARY 1, 1810

As the harbor sky lightened just beyond the peak of the Government House, carriages and buckboards rattled into the crowded borough. Many folks had donned their best, although their best might be others' worst. Men helped ladies alight from their carriages and then faded into the current of spectators who streamed in from all points of the compass to join together in the government square. The assemblage had begun to gather much earlier than the colony officials had expected. The eager citizens stood in the dusty square like chess pieces in the blue-gray shadows of early dawn.

Grouped to the side of the Government House, a fife and drum regiment clustered in a casual aggregate, conversing in low tones. A few public officials, wearing military dress and bearing parchments, busily meandered in and out of the building. Draped with colorful silk and flanked by flags, a massive table became the central focus of the assembly. A stout passenger ship captain milled through the spectators. He had a vested interest in the coming ceremony, for he had personally conveyed the guest of honor into the sparkling Sydney Cove harbor. Buttoning his coat, he straightened his tricorn hat and anxiously surveyed the crowd. Believing he recognized a familiar face, he addressed an officer who stood with his young wife. "Excuse me, sir. But have I made your acquaintance?"

The lieutenant, a tall fellow with a passive countenance, smiled cordially and studied the captain's rugged countenance. "Yes, I believe we have met." He turned to his wife. "Emily, dear?"

The young woman, halted in the process of retying her bonnet, lifted her long lashes and smiled brightly. "Why, you're a friend of Katy's, aren't you? Katy Farrell?"

"Yes," the captain answered quietly. "So sorry to hear of her grief."

"We all are, sir," the lieutenant said soberly. He extended his hand. "I am Lieutenant Jonathan Evans, and this is my lovely wife, Emily."

"I remember now." The captain nodded at the couple. "I'm Captain Robert Gabriel."

"I've heard all about you," Emily said. "It was your ship that brought us Lachlan Macquarie." Her eyes shot forward when a murmur went through the crowd. "There he comes now—our new governor."

The crowded square buzzed as the recently appointed governor of New South Wales mounted the platform. They had awaited his arrival for two years, since the fall of their prior governor.

Robert Gabriel, holding his hat in his hands, blew out a sigh. Shifting first on one leg and then onto the other, he bit his lip and then asked the lieutenant, "How fares she?"

Absorbed with the commencement of the ceremony, Evans did not respond right away. But seeing the captain awaiting his answer, he asked, "I beg your pardon? What was that?"

Pursing his lips together, Gabriel took on an awkward tone. "I asked you how she fares. Do you know how the widow is getting along?"

Glancing first at his wife and then at Gabriel, Lieutenant Evans drew his finger to his lip, a quizzical gaze drawing his brows together. "Pardon me once more, Captain. But I don't follow you."

Casting his eyes downward, Gabriel rotated his cap nervously in his grasp. "My apologies. I speak of Mrs. Katy Farrell. I simply asked if she is doing well now."

"Oh, I see." Evans turned his face slightly, and his eyes narrowed dubiously. "Dwight Farrell left his widow well taken care of, and she has her family around her. I believe she has recovered as much as can be expected. But she loved her husband very much, and I am certain that her grief still lingers to some degree."

"She still wears her mourning frocks, I've noticed." Emily looped her arm through her husband's. Lifting her chin, she said, "Look, dear, they're starting the ceremony now."

"So they are, and it's certainly been slow in the making." Evans gave a polite nod to Gabriel. "If I see Mrs. Farrell, I will tell her that you asked about her and that you extend your most sincere condolences."

Gabriel waved his palm. "Oh, that won't be necessary, Lieutenant. I spoke with Mrs. Farrell on the morning of her dear late husband's interment. She knows of my condolences. I only meant to inquire of her current state of affairs. I made promise to her mother that I would inquire when at all possible to be certain of her situation. It has been two years now since Mr. Farrell passed on, and I wish to always make good on my promises."

"Then be at peace in knowing that their estate has doubled in size and that she and her brother have managed their holdings as her husband would have wished it done. Even beyond his hopes, I might add."

Seeing the officer's attentions drawn to the platform, Gabriel politely excused himself. "I find comfort in what you say, sir. Thank you." He turned and prepared to return to his ship.

"Captain Gabriel?" Emily called out.

He glanced back. "Yes, Mrs. Evans?"

"I'm not supposed to know, but I can tell you where to find her this morning."

Not wishing to reveal any personal sentiments in the matter, Gabriel threw back his shoulders and lifted one brow with an air of no great consequence. "Then I shall leave that matter for you to decide, Mrs. Evans."

The lieutenant shook his head impatiently as his wife brushed past, a mischievous smile lighting her gaze. "I will tell you, then. . . ."

The first beams of sunlight warmed the rocky, moss-coated

ledge overlooking Rose Hill. The ledge had been specially selected for its view of both the land and the sunrise on this eucalyptus-scented morning. Flower petals strewn along the trail leading up to the ledge rolled gently around the feet of those who trod the path up to the lookout. The elegantly dressed women chatted and laughed quietly with one another, their dresses billowing softly in the pristine breeze of dawn.

Amelia Prentice walked slowly, holding to the pudgy hand of one of her grandsons. She chatted to her widowed daughter and remarked how pleased she was to see Katy finally don something less dreary than a black dress.

"It has been difficult, Mum, these past two years without him. But I've tired of the black dresses as well. Will some of the women think poorly of me if I wear something a little brighter?" Katy held out the gold taffeta folds of her brocaded gown.

"When has Katy Prentice Farrell ever cared what the women in the borough think?" Amelia chuckled.

"I know. But this is a different matter. I wish to honor my late husband as long as is necessary."

"You've always been regarded as honorable, Katy. But it's high time you joined the ranks o' the living."

"My mind agrees, but it is my heart that chains me to the grave. I do believe I've come a long way, Mum. But does it ever stop hurting?"

Amelia shook her head. "No."

"That's comforting," Katy mused, with a hint of sarcasm.

"It becomes manageable, though. All pain inevitably leads one back to God."

"That I *do* know." Taking their place a few feet from the ledge, the two chided the children who ran giddily around them like flighty goslings.

Caleb and Kelsey, attired in their finest Sunday garments, walked arm in arm up the path, smiling broadly. Katy and Amelia greeted them.

"They said to meet here at sunrise. Here we all are. Where are they?" Katy strained to glance around the large monolith of rock and shrubbery that blocked the view of the curving trail. Her countenance brightened when Rachel Whitley appeared from out of the bush.

Attired in an olive green box-pleated gown of moiré taffeta, Rachel stopped to adjust her dainty hat, plumed with ostrich feathers. "Heath and I had to leave the carriage down the hill a bit. I'm out of breath." Rachel tucked the red strands of hair back into her coif.

"We are all out of breath!" Katy exclaimed. "Bailey Templeton is such a romantic sort."

"Is she here yet?" Rachel asked.

"Yes." Amelia patted Jared. "Stand next to your mother, please. I'll see what's keeping them."

Donovan came running up the path, his arms out to the sides, holding a violin in one hand and a bow in the other. "I'm coming, Grandmother!"

"We're waiting," Amelia called out to him. "What's keeping them?"

"Dr. Hogan is coming. I don't know what happened to Miss Templeton. I can't find her."

Dressed smartly in a black waistcoat with tails, Grant stepped sheepishly up the pathway. "So sorry to detain you all, Amelia. Bailey is one for detail."

Standing with arms crossed, Amelia shook her head. "Grant, where is Bailey?"

"She doesn't want me to see her. I'm to take my place on the ledge."

Amelia laughed out loud. "Trainin' you early, I see. Very well. We'll all assume that the bride will show up when she's good an' ready." Amelia nodded at the dashing young man who trailed behind Grant. He was new to her acquaintance, but she had heard a great deal about him from Bailey. "Hello, sir," she called politely.

Fast behind Grant came Reverend Heath Whitley. "Let us all gather, shall we?" He took the lead. With his book of vows cradled underneath his arm, he stood Katy to the side with her daughter in front of her. The little girl squatted at once and began playing with the scattered petals. Rachel stood beside Amelia and began a futile attempt to seat all of the children onto the soft, mossy grass. Behind them stood Caleb and Kelsey.

Nodding at Donovan, Reverend Whitley opened the book and smiled at all of them while Donovan began playing a melodious tune on the violin. The tune drifted down the ledge, making harmony with the birds, the softly swaying myrtle trees, and the nodding eucalyptus.

Bailey lifted her face when she heard the violin's strains. Hiding behind Amelia's carriage, she had put the finishing touches on her attire with the help of her doting attendant. Carefully, the two of them adjusted the petticoats and straightened her wreath of flowers upon the crown of her head. "Thank you for coming, Laurie." Bailey kissed her sister on the side of her face.

"I've been so worried about you, Bailey. Mother will be so pleased to hear how well you're faring in this dreadful colony." Laurie checked the buttons on the front of her own dress. "You look stunning!" She beamed proudly. "And your groom is equally stunning—a surgeon, at that."

"Grant has worked hard in his studies. And the colony is in desperate need of a good doctor."

"I'm glad you will keep working at the school," Laurie affirmed quietly.

"So am I. Sydney Cove needs us, Laurie."

"Well, the good Dr. Hogan has waited patiently for two years. Perhaps we should detain him no longer." Laurie held her nosegay in front of her.

"After you." Bailey smiled. The day was perfect, the sunrise perched just behind them as she had hoped. And now her sister would be at her side, if but for a short time.

The wedding party gathered on the grassy cliffs above the fertile soil of Rose Hill. Dr. Grant Hogan and Bailey Templeton had deliberately selected this sunrise ceremony as a symbol of their hope for the rising of a new day in their fledgling colony.

Katy wiped her eyes as the young couple pledged their eternal love. She felt peace rise inside of her, welling up as the swelling tide along Sydney's wild shores. She gazed out at the land, the grazing flocks, and the road that led to her first real home. She saw a horse and rider traveling down that trail and riding in their direction. He had a stout carriage and appeared to be in a hurry. Curiously, she glanced at her mother, Amelia. She knew of no other guests, for Grant and Bailey had requested a private ceremony. She let out a sigh and then drew her attention back to the happy couple.

Bailey and Grant completed their vows and sealed their words with a kiss. They bowed and prayed for their own future, for the future of New South Wales, and for the new governor whom they would honor in the coming days with a celebration and a feast of hope.

The women showered the couple with petals, and the children squealed in delight. Bailey wiped tears from Laurie's eyes and then allowed her brother-in-law, Gavin, to kiss her gently on her cheek. She had found a new world for herself in Sydney Cove, a world that her family would never understand, but one they had graciously accepted out of love for her. The Lord had answered her prayers in granting her a heart of forgiveness. He had also taught her patience and long-suffering. She had found that the latter prayers were answered more often than not. And in exercising patience, her joy was now made complete in joining her life with that of Captain Grant Hogan's. No matter what the future of New South Wales, she could face any uncertainty as long as she could be at his loving side. She felt her princely groom clasp his strong hand around hers. Following him down the flower-strewn path, she felt the sunrise on her shoulders and knew that as long as the sun would rise and set on Sydney Cove harbor, God held New South Wales in the hollow of His hands. She prayed as much for her beloved America.